"Worth the read."

"A wonder . . . highly recommended."

"The #1 fan, the devoted housekeeper, and the hired ghostwriter provide real chemistry and often funny scenes throughout the book. And by the time you reach the last chapter, you may find yourself rooting for the good guys, booing the bad guys, and mourning the loss of a great voice in opera."

"A funny literary caper, Lockwood moves around, writing the book as fast as he can. The reader is treated to a look at world of writing for a living, the glamour world of real stars, and the possibility of romance if one has the courage to grasp it. This one is a winner!"

"Gorgeously written . . . poignant."

"A fascinating look inside the world of opera and the acclaim that comes with being a diva. Bravo!"

THE
WONDER SINGER

THE
WONDER SINGER

GEORGE RABASA

UNBRIDLED BOOKS

Unbridled Books
Denver, Colorado

First paperback edition, 2009
Unbridled Books trade paperback ISBN 978-1-932961-69-0

The Library of Congress has cataloged the hardcover edition as follows:

Rabasa, George.
The wonder singer / by George Rabasa.
p. cm.
ISBN 978-1-932961-56-0 (hardcover)
ISBN 978-1-932961-69-0 (paperback)
I. Title.
PS3568.A213W66 2008
813'.54—dc22

2008017194

1   3   5   7   9   10   8   6   4   2

Book Design by SH • CV
First Printing

For Juanita, always

THE
WONDER SINGER

OH, THE SECRETS SHE TOOK WITH HER.

There are moments when the order of life collapses in midbreath, when a missed heartbeat brings on an earthquake. At such a moment, this story takes an unexpected turn.

Perla, the day nurse, calls out from the Señora's bath, "*Oye*, Lockwood!" Her shout, cracking with anxiety, cuts through the morning stillness.

Mark Lockwood sets down a mug hard on the kitchen counter, wincing as hot coffee splashes the back of his hand.

"Lockwood!"

He hurries across the living room to Señora Casals' bedroom. Perla stands at the bathroom door, her easy familiarity with him turning grave, as if at the click of a switch.

A moment later the nurse and the writer are staring down into the sunken marble tub where Mercè Casals, the legendary soprano, floats motionless. She is a sight, so fleshy and pale, blubberous and opalescent, buoyant in her fragrant bath, green eyes open and staring up out of the water as if at a precise point on the ceiling. A question seizes Lockwood's mind: What did she think the moment before dying that would cause her to open her eyes in wonder and turn the corners of her mouth in what is distinctly, even as her features are settling into death, a smile?

He reaches reflexively for the notebook tucked into the hip pocket of his khakis. For months he has been writing down the insights and telling details that will help his task as ghostwriter of the Señora's autobiography. "She loved a long bath. It was the perfect way to start her day." He scribbles down the thought as he speaks.

In the dim light, in the steamy warm air, in the scent of the orchids and the ferns and the snaking tendrils of ivy and clematis and jasmine, Lockwood hears himself think: *My diva is dead.*

Perla was usually in the bathroom only long enough to help the Señora out of the water and into a plush robe. Now, past any options that would have resolved a medical crisis, she sits on a brass chair, ready in her crisp white uniform to take on her professional role. "I always envied the Señora's bathing in such a lovely space. And now, an appropriately sensuous end to her life."

Lockwood gazes down at the tub where Mercè Casals lies undisturbed. Her thin dyed-red hair, undulating in the slight motion of the water, is a halo around her head. "Somehow it's not as bad a sight as I imagined."

Perla looks at him curiously. "You've never seen a dead body before. A *muertito?*"

"How can you tell?"

"Everybody has the same impression. 'My, she looks peaceful, like she's sleeping.'"

Lockwood agrees. "Serene, I would say."

"I've seen maybe a hundred dead people," Perla says. "I've seen them when they're going, I've seen them when they've gone, and I've seen them when they're just a collection of parts. But this is the first time I've seen the Señora naked. She wouldn't have liked that, the two of us gawking."

"You're her nurse. It's a professional thing."

"You're her writer. Is that professional?"

"It won't be easy to find another famous lady in need of an autobiography." He sighs unhappily. "What now?"

"We look for work."

"No, I mean after someone dies, and they're found, what happens next?"

"I call her doctor. There's paperwork. Approximate time of death. Probably between seven and eight. Tuesday, October 14, 1999. Too bad. She had been looking forward to celebrating the turn of the millennium. It meant a lot to her to live to the year 2000."

"She had a sense of her place in history."

"You will go on with the book, right?"

Lockwood shrugs. "I'll call her agent," he says. "He's also my agent. Kill two birds."

"Dumb choice of words, for a writer."

Lockwood tries not to stare at the submerged body. "She wouldn't want us to send her away yet. I feel her spirit needs the company."

"She died in her favorite room."

The bathroom is a jeweled grotto, with only a faint glow from lights recessed into the ceiling, so that the tiles gleam like gems and reflect each other in mirrors and polished gold fixtures and black marble bases under the basin and the tub, where air jets and a spigot sculpted into a brass dolphin are aimed to whirl and spray and burble on all the right places from aching vertebrae to the elusive hot button. Sconces on brass pedestals burn sage and myrrh. To drive away devils. To attract male angels with golden curls, pearly teeth, fleshy earlobes, small penises. From hidden speakers would come the voice of Mercè Casals as Floria Tosca, as

Norma, as Violetta, always the Señora listening to herself. The remembered songs took her breath away and made her heart pound.

Lockwood can hear her still: *Ah!* she might have exclaimed to herself. *How I held that B-flat in "Vissi d'arte." It was as if God was breathing through me and the note would resound for all eternity.*

Did I die of natural causes? Lockwood thinks she might ask at the end of her memoir. He asks Perla.

"Whatever makes you die is a natural cause," Perla says briskly.

He dips his fingers into the still tepid water and brushes a stray wisp from the Señora's forehead. "I think she died of her years weighing heavily, each like a stone upon her chest, as she tried to feel a little lighter by floating in her tub."

"Nobody dies of things like that." Perla is suddenly authoritative. "Too much bacon fat clogging the veins and causing a heart stoppage. As natural as death by Nembutal or Absolut or China White."

Lockwood shrugs; hard science is not about to cancel imagination. "Oh, the secrets she took with her. Just look at her expression."

Perla glances toward the Señora's face. "Cardiac arrests often bring on what looks like a smile. But it isn't one, not really."

He loves it that she can turn, in a heartbeat, from playfully seductive to coolly rational.

After nearly one hundred visits, past countless confidences and evasions, Lockwood had not wanted to go to the Señora's condominium the morning she died. Vague apprehension had tightened into a knot. Locked into the thick of traffic, with little choice but to continue grinding down I-5 toward La Jolla, he listened to her legendary "Sempre libera" of thirty years ago, turning the volume high—above road whir, traffic hum, engine whine, wind flap. Louder. The melody uncoiled dangerously, the consummate soprano slicing through the tape hiss in his cheap player, buzzing the speakers and sending a vibration all the way up his chest to the metallic frames of his sunglasses. Brushing anxiety aside, he drove on; a day without Mercè Casals' meandering talk would be like the silent yawn of an empty house.

Still, diminishing returns had set in; week by week, their ongoing conversation added up to less and less. Lockwood could handle being the Señora's hired scribbler, "Marcos Loco": also tapeworm, father confessor, unpaid shrink, reliable yes-man, royal hack, and bad-dream exterminator. She was, after all, a client; he'd had worse, and none of them famous.

At forty, Mark Lockwood felt on the verge of his first big book. Only modestly successful in his home-based business—Mark My Words, Inc., freelance writing of just about anything—he'd been promised a big share of the advance and a cut of the book-club deal, foreign rights, perhaps a miniseries. With his anticipated success, he had also become prone to moments of unexpected anxiety. Along with the disturbing evidence of his braking metabolism—softening flesh, thinning hair, dying brain cells—had come a heightened awareness that his recent good fortune could unravel in an eyeblink.

He already had on tape five hundred hours of reminiscences, confessions, gossip, and the occasional rant; they were bound up in a Gordian tangle. "You can busy yourself with the unraveling after I'm done speaking into your little box," the Señora had promised. "But first the story has to come out. In whatever way it chooses. Ask and listen. Leave the arias to me." He had gone along with her. There would be time to follow the thread that wound through the singer's triumphs and disasters, her loves and betrayals.

Lockwood wedged his tennis shoe of a car into a tight slot inside a garage studded with Benzes, Range Rovers, and Jaguars in Vortex Black, Eternity Blue, Gunmetal Gray. He reached into the backseat for his cassette recorder, blank tapes, extra Uniball pens, notepad with curling pages, and a brown paper bag containing two mangoes that had been ripening for three days, their scent now jammy and promisingly sweet. He felt a rush of anticipation because he was bringing them to Perla as a special gift.

By the time he reached Shore Tower, he was resigned to whatever approaching turmoil his stomach was signaling. He tucked the tails of his white shirt into his khakis, slipped the tie knot to the collar, and checked his hair in the lobby mirror; the Señora was critical of his appearance. Preston, jovial behind the concierge desk, let him into the lobby.

"A glorious day," Preston offered, because it was not in his nature to be less than radiantly optimistic. "Will be nice and bright once the fog lifts."

They chatted about the traffic on I-5; Preston wanted a full report so he could relay the information to Tower residents venturing out to San Diego or LA, out for an early start on hair and nails, Neiman's or Saks, and always the doctors, legions of them, the cardio man, the knee jerk, the chemo gal, the diet director.

The guard's affable reception lifted Lockwood's spirits. The elevator carried him up to floor twenty-eight, where he expected to sit one more day, listening to Mercè Casals, his thumb poised over the *pause* button of a cassette recorder, a $29 antique from Radio Shack that produces tapes to play in his car and office boom box,

Perla, here since seven, greeted him at the door. "Señora is still in her bath," she said. "I'll check on her soon." The Señora was usually dressed by the time Lockwood arrived.

He hovered in the kitchen and drank the coffee Perla offered him. He persuaded himself that every one of her gestures of goodwill was evidence of some erotic current flowing between them. He found her exotic:

a big-city girl from the DF, the Mexican capital. After considering the variations on olive and cinnamon used to describe Latino skin, he decided hers was nutmeg. Lustrous black hair, cut short and combed into a boyish part, gave her a bold, somewhat dismissive look. Her brisk Spanish accent was by turns amusing and provocative.

This morning he tried to please Perla with a mango. He took it out of the wrinkled brown bag and held out to her the plump yellow fruit.

She showed him how Mexicans eat them, stabbing a fork through the mango's rump to the seed, then peeling down strips with a paring knife to reveal the golden pulp awaiting the first bite of her perfect teeth.

"I'm having a hard time keeping this under control." She laughed, the back of her hand wiping the juice that ran from her mouth.

"Few acts are as sensual as a woman biting into a mango," he observed.

"You're pushing your luck, Lockwood."

"I've made an impression on you at last."

"Not necessarily a good one."

"Perla, what a heartbreaker you are."

"*Tontito*. You don't think adolescent behavior comes with risks?"

He sighed unhappily. "It's nice of you to worry."

"I'm a nurse."

"Do you have any professional advice?"

"Yes. Back off a little."

"You're not telling me to go away, though."

Perla only shrugged.

"It could lead to something interesting?"

"Don't count on it, Lockwood."

He liked Perla to call him Lockwood. He found the mixture of familiarity and distance wonderfully unsettling. Sometimes she called him

"Mark-in-Time Lockwood." Or "Top-of-the-Mark" when she wanted to flatter him. It beat being called Marcos Loco, as Mercè Casals had done when she'd first met him.

"Señora is taking a long time with her bath." Perla nodded toward the closed door beyond the living room.

"Let her," he said, clinging to her presence. This moment alone was a gift, possibly planned by the Señora, prolonging her bath so her scribbler and her nurse could be alone. She was like that in her sense of fun, her meddling. "Will you know when she's ready to come out?"

"She'll ring her bell, and I'll hold up a big towel in front of my eyes." She added seriously, "I'd better check on her." Disappointed, Lockwood watched her march toward the bedroom. Even as medical fashion tended to pastels, the Señora liked Perla in white because it was the professional color for a nurse. Lockwood was both attracted and frustrated by her crinkly whites, the panels of starched fabric boxing and masking the roundness of womanly shapes, boat-like shoes and opaque hosiery inhibiting his imagination.

When the job of day nurse to Señora Mercè Casals had been posted, Perla had called immediately. Señora Casals explained the position. "I want you to wear a uniform at all times. No, I'm not sick, and beyond handing me my pills at the appointed times and informing my personal physician, Dr. Velasco, when my blood pressure reads high, you will hardly need to do anything medical at all. But wearing your nurse's uniform will keep our relationship serious. It's too easy for two women spending day after day together to become too chummy. I need you to remain a professional. We will become friends, of course. I like you already."

"*Gracias*, Señora."

"But it's even more important that you like me." The Señora had sighed, as if she were already despairing of the young applicant's rising to such a challenge. "I will be able to tell, you know, no matter how cheerful and efficient you are. If you are covering up negative emotions, your hands will give you away. I will ask you to rub my neck when I feel a headache coming, massage my feet when they swell, spread lotion on my back when my skin is thirsty. I cannot bear to be touched by someone who holds back. It's a special, rare gift to be able to touch another person and let her feel the goodness of your heart by the weight of your hands and the movement of your fingers. Timing is all. If you withdraw your hands too soon, I will sense reluctance; if you prolong touch past a certain point, it will be cloying and insincere. You will also bring my morning coffee and afternoon tea. And you will tell me the story of your life and your dreams and fears because we will have much time to get to know one another. But mostly, you will spend a lot of time by yourself staring at the wall. That's the most difficult part of the job."

Perla smiled. "I have some reading to catch up on. There's TV. I can write or call my family in Mexico."

"Unfortunately, no, not when you're on duty," her new employer said firmly. "I wouldn't want to feel I'm interrupting a greater pleasure when I call you. You can knit or crochet. You will be happy to answer my call."

o⊶─┤ IT WILL BE YOUR WORDS.

After years of dealing with corporate clients and their concrete objectives, Lockwood had felt out of his depth for the job interview. Six months ago, he'd waited in the gloom of Mercè Casals' shuttered condo and tried deep breaths that came up short on oxygen and long on the blended scents of cut flowers and dishes of potpourri.

Standing before wall-to-wall windows, he parted the heavy brocade curtains. From twenty-eight stories above the ocean, he imagined he could see south to Cabo San Lucas, north to Santa Barbara.

The Señora wore rhinestone sunglasses with lenses so dark she would haltingly feel her way from a wall to a lamp to her chair. Her world was fragile: chalky bones in the hips, knees, shoulders. Around her, glass cats and goldfish and frogs by Lalique. Chinese vases and Murano bowls. Tiny Limoges boxes in fanciful porcelain shapes—trunks, clocks, purses, pianos, pea pods and dogs, clown hats, and party shoes—all down to the details of the enameled latch and the interior glaze, with the signature that said they were a higher class of knickknack.

On that first afternoon, the Señora's aspiring writer waited on a velvet couch that drew him into its pillowy depths, a silk-and-feather quick-sand that rose all around him, giving way under his butt and elbows and spine, so that he felt his knees rising and the whole of him curling up.

Lockwood reached down to the end table beside the couch and plunged his fingers into a candy dish. He grabbed a couple of chocolates wrapped in heavy gold foil and put them in his pocket as Mercè Casals emerged out of the shadows into the living room. She went to him, ex-tending her hand and smiling warmly. Lockwood started to rise, but he had sat so low that his knees had lost their leverage and his character its will. His hand let go of the softening chocolates.

"I see you've been admiring the goodies," she smiled. It took long moments before he realized she was speaking of the figurines on the shelves.

"I'm a bit of a collector myself." He exhaled with relief. "You know—books. Good books, old books, unread books. It's a writer's obsession."

She smiled benignly from her wingback chair, as if waiting for him to go on and explain why he was here. "You are not at all what I expected," she said, trying to be diplomatic. "My agent, our agent, Mr. Holloway, assured me you were a real writer. That you have earned your living writ ing for twenty-five years and that therefore you would certainly look the part. Silly me, I was expecting horn-rimmed glasses and a pipe, and a jacket with leather patches on the elbows."

"I have a corduroy jacket somewhere." He heard the strained light-ness in his voice and feared his eagerness was too obvious.

"Has lovely Perla offered you something to drink?"

Lockwood wasn't thirsty, but the possibility of getting another look at the nurse prompted a request.

"Anything diet would be fine," he said. "Diet Pepsi is the elixir of po-ets." Then he added, as if needing to explain himself again, "Especially of the overweight ones."

"But you're not a poet," she said. "You are the exterminator." She explained: "Someone hired to flush the rats from my past."

"I wish you wouldn't look at it that way."

"Oh, let's move on, shall we?" she said. "I already have a first impression of you."

"A bad one?"

"Heavens, no," she laughed. "I'll just have to reconsider my idea of what a writer should look like. Rumpled khakis and a baggy shirt with pockets for notebooks and pencils might yet fit in with my idea of a real author. But a tie might indicate a professional attitude."

He was glad for the respite as Perla brought Pepsi and ice in a tall glass. He tried to catch her eye and smile in gratitude, but she resolutely avoided his gaze. *"Gracias,"* he said.

"What makes you think you're suitable to write my story?" He could feel the Señora's gaze behind the sunglasses.

"Experience." Lockwood found himself at a loss for words.

"As a music expert?" She smiled.

"Well, no. I write about everything."

"Everything?"

"Sex, drugs, teenagers, farm machinery, weather patterns, horses, computers, retirement plans, insurance policies, shopping malls, sleep apnea, mobile-home bank loans, periodontal disease, gardening, cooking, digesting—"

"Please. Stop, for the love of God."

"I've written about those also."

"What?"

"Love. God. They're part of my *How to Talk to Your Teen* series."

"Have you written about music?"

"Sure, here and there. A few notes." He tried to signal his joke with a smile.

"I seem to have made you tense. I'm sorry. I have a right to ask, if I'm to consider you for the job."

"Of course, Señora." Lockwood felt that there was little he could do to rescue the interview. "You have my résumé. Writing samples," he said lamely.

"I'm an artist. But you will tell me if I sound like an insufferable egotist?"

"A bit of ego won't hurt, Señora. Readers will expect this of you."

"The whole of my life story, since I first sang publicly at age four, seems like one long, uninterrupted performance. Not just the great roles as Lucia and Gilda and Norma and Violetta. The way I slurp soup in a restaurant has been observed by someone. A moment of whispered conversation raises speculation. The dash of a pen when I sign my name, the ornate M, the bold C. Everything I do is considered a deliberate artistic act, measured by someone somewhere. It has been a cumbersome way to live, you understand."

"I can only imagine, Señora."

"Good. I need your imagination, your empathy. I'm afraid to trust my life to a hack."

He cleared his throat defensively. "There's something to be said for hacks. They get the job done."

"Well, I certainly need you for that. I'm eighty . . . something; my memory is erratic, and I've already been paid an advance for my memoirs."

"I'm your man."

"Of the first five writers I've talked to, you are the only one who isn't a bigger prima donna than I."

"It will be your words that matter, Señora."

"Understand this, Mr. Lockwood: Singing is a spiritual act for me. Not one of those churchy things with men in taffeta and triangle hats.

When I sing, there are aspects of the universe that take on a sharp and luminous clarity. I am like Einstein—without the mathematics."

"I'm eager to hear your story."

She nodded as if already taking his cooperation for granted. She pushed herself off the chair and walked to a cabinet at the end of the living room. After some consideration, she selected a disc from the rows of tightly packed CDs.

"Take *Tosca* home. I sing Floria. It may give you a headache the first time you hear it. Keep playing it until it doesn't hurt. Don't sleep, read, eat, or talk through it. You can glance at the libretto. But only at the Italian. It doesn't matter if you don't understand every word. Just sit and listen. Then call Mr. Holloway, if you still want to do this."

By early afternoon the tying-up of the Señora's affairs is in full progress. Earlier, Perla made phone calls, wrote a report, filled in her last time sheets. Lockwood collected his notes and then went through the stuffed file wallets the Señora had always kept at her side to search when his questioning made her want to reach beyond her memory into the interviews, letters, photos, reviews she had saved through the years. On impulse, he hastily stuffed the folders into his leather satchel. It had taken only moments for the now unmoored Lockwood to reach a decision: He would finish the project they had started together.

Perla came up behind him as he buckled the satchel. *"Ladronzuelo,"* she teased. Little thief.

"I've still got her book to write," he explained.

"I won't tell." She pressed a finger to her lips.

Dr. Velasco and Hank Holloway arrived at the same time to take care of the two sides of the Señora, the body and the legend. The two men studied each other discreetly in the elevator, one in a smoky-gray suit and starched shirt, armed with a leather medical bag, the other in lime-green pants, black linen jacket, carrying an alligator attaché case. They finally acknowledged each other, one through Ray-Bans, the other through tortoiseshell bifocals.

"Quite a tragedy," they murmured when they realized they were both going up to the twenty-eighth floor. "Yes, indeed."

"The passing of an era," said Holloway, also known as Hollywood Hank. "A wonder for the ages."

"Death by drowning," the doctor decided ahead of his examination. "According to the ancient Mexicans, it's the passport to the happiest of all heavens. To the realm of Tlaloc with no detours or side trips. It's the only happy place in the afterlife, where the Señora will become like a child again to sing and dance and chase butterflies in a rain as soft as mist. I can see her, you know, truly happy for the first time."

"Are you some kind of writer?"

"No, you can trust me. I'm her doctor."

"I knew her well, too. I'm her agent."

They shared parallel objectives. Dr. Velasco would deal with a police report, sign the death certificate, and let the nurse go. Hollywood Hank would do his best to get rid of the writer amicably. Settling accounts with the nurse of a dead patient presented no ambiguities. The matter of the book-in-progress would be awkward.

As soon as he'd heard of the Señora's accident, Hollywood Hank had placed a call to Alonzo Baylor with an offer to do the life story of the famous diva. The celebrated author had shown, with his highly intrusive Salvador Dalí and Martha Graham biographies, that he was good with the passions of art and flesh, the longing of the old and the regrets of the famous. Alonzo Baylor might not know anything about opera, but then,

Hollywood Hank was sure he hadn't known a whole lot about modern art either, before he'd taken on the great Dalí.

Dr. Velasco was in the business of life—as opposed to death. He held the Señora's wrist, his fingers feeling for her pulse even though anyone could see that it was too late for such ceremonies. Gazing down on her face in the water, as accustomed as he was to the placid expression of death, Dr. Velasco was nevertheless moved to observe, "Ah, those are pearls that were her eyes!"

Standing before the naked floating Señora, Hollywood Hank could only muster a solemn nod or two, a requisite sigh. Waiting beside him was the writer he had sent to Mercè Casals to help her pour her heart out. At the time, Lockwood had been what was needed, a proficient wordsmith who knew how to crank out the prose and deliver a manuscript on deadline with a minimum of fuss. After sending his client five other writers, this was the one that Mercè Casals had decided she liked, and trusted. "He's a listener," she had said.

The agent took Lockwood by the arm and gently, almost seductively, pulled him away from the bathroom and into the parlor, as if the tenor of the conversation that would follow might disturb the dead Casals.

Things were different now. Hollywood Hank envisioned royalties for all eternity and special commemorative editions and tributes to the fallen star. La Casals was a gift for the ages, her book in the hands of someone more marketable than Lockwood would sell for as long as her voice was on CDs. The agent tried to be reasonable: A ghostwriter was no longer required. What was needed was a famous author, a name comparable to the dead queen's. It was a dog-eat-dog publishing jungle and only a major Big-Game Book Gun would do.

But *I've* got the recordings," Lockwood explained patiently. "Five hundred hours' worth. I will tell her life in her words. It will be her final aria."

"Listen to me, Lockwood. I want a brand-name writer to tell her story. A real wonder boy for the wonder singer." Holloway raised his hand to signal there was nothing else to discuss. "You'll receive a generous kill fee. For the time you've spent on the project."

"This is not about time," Lockwood protested, weakly because Hollywood Hank had already made a grab for the project, and he didn't know how to stop him. "It's all about the story. Don't you see? This a really great story I'm telling."

"Give me directions so I can send someone to schlep your files."

Lockwood bristled. "'Schlep'? Is that agent talk for scooping up, grabbing, stealing, and surrendering?"

"Where can I pick up the interviews?" Hollywood Hank repeated in a steely tone.

"I'll mail them to you," Lockwood evaded.

"I'll send a courier to your house in Anaheim."

"I need to listen to them. Do some editing."

"I'll take care of the editing."

"Some of the stuff is personal. Strictly between the Señora and me."

"Your secrets are safe."

The two men faced each other from opposite sides of the parlor, Lockwood standing, the agent sitting back on the red velvet couch, his arm extended along the back, his fingertips lightly caressing the upholstery. Hollywood Hank dangled one boot over the other; his foot twitched nervously. He masked his increasing frustration by breathing out a long sigh. "Do you really think Alonzo Baylor gives a shit about *your* secrets?"

"It's not my privacy that is at stake here. I was entrusted by Mercè Casals with her life. Her life became my life. It was going to be her book, in her own voice. I made promises. Nothing would go into it that she did not choose to reveal. Alonzo Baylor, the Hemingway throwback, ham-fisted, bare-knuckled, coulda-been-a-contender, monosyllabic, semicolon-impaired, cliché-rich *typist* would like nothing better than to be able to pick over her lifeless bones." Lockwood paused to catch his breath.

Across the glass table, Hollywood Hank slouched into the folds of the plush sofa. He looked wiry and small in his black-and-green Armani ensemble, his feet sweating inside the Tony Lamas, a blue amoeba expanding under the leaking Mont Blanc in his shirt pocket, his face reddening as if he were resisting a dark impulse to spring out like a snake. "We'll need to talk again," Holloway sighed. "Stay in touch."

⊶—╫ I SAW WHAT YOU DID.

Days after Mercè Casals' death, Lockwood has nowhere to go. He rises later than usual, for a moment disoriented that he's not, as on other mornings, already barreling south on I-5. While he slept, his wife, Claire, has rushed off to vague appointments and meetings. He realizes help-lessly that she has been putting together a life in which he has no part. She's evasive: a job interview, a long lunch with a friend, real estate class. He feels entitled to details, but hasn't found the right moment to ask. She is not entirely oblivious of him—there is half a melon on the kitchen counter, coffee in a thermos—but he's too impatient to eat breakfast. The Señora awaits.

Lockwood remembers to take a blue blazer to wear over his t-shirt and khakis. He will look presentable for the visitation at the Rossini Fratelli funeral home in San Clemente. Carlo and Frigo Rossini are two strutting crows in their black suits, white-on-white ties, patent-leather hair. They walk with a slight stoop, ready to bend into a bow, all the while rubbing their hands with fluid enthusiasm.

Everything is perfect for *la diva divina*, Mercè Casals. The open casket, brass overlays on silky black mahogany, the inside tufted in gray satin and lace, and the Señora herself dolled to perfection, hair coiffed to a fluffy red toque, fresh new features painted on her face. Her imposing bosom seems about to release the breathless floating *Vieni!*—Lady Macbeth's time-stopping command holding a packed house captive in deep, anxious silence before the tragedy pushes on.

Carlo and Frigo maintain order in the line that winds around the corner outside the visitation room. Fans from all over the country have gathered to view the Señora. The brothers admit ten visitors at a time along a path of red carpeting past a velvet rope on brass stanchions to the front door. For a respectful moment the mourner gazes into the casket, then moves to the back to sign the book, perhaps to write a pithy goodbye, *addio, adeu, adiós, adieu,* to God.

The Rossinis relish the attention. Their arched wrought-iron entrance has been on the evening news coast to coast: Rossini Fratelli Mortuary, embalmers and morticians to celebrities. In all cases, from oak to steel, undertakers who understand, the cream of cremators. What they say, they mean: "Every death is premature. Every death diminishes us all." They went to UCLA and got MBAs in mourning. Grieving is an art. There is much to think about: calming music appropriate for different faiths, the flowers, the guest book, the smelling salts for the faint. There are memorial cards, gilt-edged and engraved, the prayer, the psalm, even the pithy message for the nonreligious. ("Men fear death, as children fear the dark"—Francis Bacon.)

"It's a madhouse out there," says Frigo cheerfully. He distributes coffee and cookies from a tray. Mercè Casals used to do this on cold mornings for the fans queuing up outside the Met. She would walk down the line and clasp hands, kiss an occasional youth on the cheek, and personally thank everyone for braving the elements on her account. *"Gràcies, molt agraïda, amics meus,"* she would say in her native Catalan. "Tonight I will sing principally for you."

It was fitting that the tradition be continued for her last appearance. To that end she left in her will a generous amount to cover refreshments for those waiting to pay their respects. Notable guests would enjoy a lavish buffet with platters of smoked salmon, roast beef, and pâté, a cheese board with runny Camembert, fragrant Roquefort, and soft chevre, plus a bread basket and a tray of petits fours. There was a choice of good rioja and a sparkling cava from Catalonia.

Lockwood puts a handful of cookies in his pocket and holds the steaming cup by the rim. He pulls one of the Rossinis by the sleeve, discreetly murmurs a request: "Do you have a special entrance for associates and personal friends?"

"Of course," says Carlo. "My brother has the list. If your name is on the list, then you go in through the side door." He puts on reading glasses and takes the papers from his brother. "Give me the list, Frigo." He flips noisily through the pages on a clipboard. "You said your name was?"

"Lockwood."

Carlo runs his index finger down the names, hopeful at first, then simply shaking his head. Frigo looks over his shoulder. "That's Lockwood, with an L?"

"How would *you* spell it?"

"Nothing under the Ls," Carlo says, attempting to look crestfallen. "Perhaps under Wood-lock? No, nothing. Perhaps under your first name?"

"Mark."

"Afraid not, sir." The two brothers gaze at him; their eyes, as they travel from the soles of his running shoes to his tousled graying hair, darken with suspicion.

"I might be listed as Scribbler," he ventures. "I was her writer, you know."

"Mr. Scribbler?" Frigo and Carlo exchange looks. "Ah! There is definitely some confusion." The undertaker cannot stop frowning quizzically at the potential for an error at his carefully orchestrated event. "The truth of the matter is that another writer has already come to pay his respects. A Mr. Furman Taylor is here at this moment. Perhaps you are acquainted with him, a colleague?"

"Never heard of him. You didn't make him stand in line?"

"Oh, no, the Signora Casals' personal manager, Mr. Hank Holloway, put his name on the list. See?" Frigo points to the name under the T column.

"Are you sure it's not Alonzo Baylor? He's famous."

"Writers are a mystery to me," Frigo shrugs.

Hollywood Hank has begun to push him off the project, smuggling in the famous writer under an alias. Lockwood doesn't know what Holloway has told Alonzo Baylor about giving him access to the Señora's sources, opening her life up for him. But without the tapes and the memorabilia, Baylor has nothing. Scouring the Internet, pumping her friends and colleagues, a few visits to her husband, Nolan Keefe, will not provide what Lockwood has collected in six months of listening to the Señora.

The *fratelli* Rossini offer him one last cookie from the tray and move on down the line consoling the mourners, promising that their wait will be rewarded with a private moment of remembrance.

It's a varied group. There are the obligatory music students, violin cases in hand, music sheets sticking out of their backpacks. Others, loyal old fans, rely on memories still lively with the sounds of their favorite Aida, their most endearing Liu, their most pitiable Mimi.

He sees a few who knew her: Preston, the doorman, considered her the premier resident in the building. Serena, the hairstylist, alone knew how to conjure up her recognizable red hair out of a secret formula of henna, L'Oreal no. 47, and reduced beet broth. Romualda, the Filipina shoe clerk at Neiman Marcus, kept a lookout for the new arrivals from Choo and Manolo and knew the Señora's arches, toes, and bunions as well as her own.

Mercè Casals had not performed in public in nearly twenty years. By noon, there is an air of celebration, as if the Señora had consented to come out of retirement for one more aria, a parting gift for those who have loved her throughout the years. Some of her fans are oblivious to the world as they wait in line with eyes shut, lips in a dreamy smile, ears wired to their iPods. Everywhere hints of "Casta Diva" intermingle improbably with a crackling *"Ridente la calma"* and snatches of *"Vissi d'arte."*

And then, as if out of some stage production gone curiously awry, appears a six-foot-four Violetta in a white, lacy gown of five concentric flounces, a corsage of fading camellias pinned to an enormous foam bosom. He's got the details right. It's an exact replica of the costume for the DiStenza Covent Garden production of 1963. He has pancaked his ruddy face to a deathly pallor heightened by cherry-red lips, inky mascara, and a perfectly placed mole on the chin. A cluster of rhinestones protrudes out of a pinkie ring from a hand that touches his breast as if to still a galloping heart. *"Sempre libera . . ."* He lip-synchs the soaring soprano to the boom box at his feet. The crowd applauds happily. Violetta takes a bow at the end of the aria, then marches off under the escort of a nervous Rossini brother.

As the public line shuffles toward the casket, the VIP guests hover by the buffet table behind a purple velvet rope, out of the reach of the not-so-famous. Once Lockwood stands in the Rossinis' inner sanctum he realizes that not everyone is here to help provide for the Señora's final send-off. Even as he is being squeezed inside the stuffy parlor, his movements inhibited by the rope that keeps the mourners in line, Lockwood recognizes Alonzo Baylor from the back of his head as he bends over the table, building himself a thick sandwich with slabs of bloody roast beef, slathered with mustard and mayo and horseradish, capped with a thick slice of raw onion. Possibly feeling Lockwood's eyes on him, Alonzo Baylor turns around, meat juice running down his hand. He faces dozens of eyes fixed on him as he opens his mouth to bite into the wondrous construct.

Lockwood's eyes meet Baylor's and there is a flicker of recognition. The thick neck, the wiry gray hair, and the pugilistic nose are unmistakable, and intimidating. Baylor makes literature look easy, as one terse sentence inevitably builds on another. He has time to write books *and* to pal around with film stars, prizefighters, beach bunnies, and ex-convicts. He pisses off academics and feminists with his pronouncements. And his books weigh a ton, packed as they are with gristly prose and squat paragraphs as compact as fire hydrants.

A mere ten feet away, Lockwood stands with head bowed, hands clasped, his gaze apparently on the Señora's feet squeezed into pink satin pumps. His attention, however, is fixed on Alonzo Baylor, who hovers at the head of the casket, sandwich in hand.

The world-famous author dabs the corners of his mouth with a napkin, wiping away a smear of mustard. He looks in both directions, then places the half-eaten sandwich on a stanchion and leans into the coffin to gaze at the Señora's placid face. He appears (or pretends, thinks Lockwood) to be too involved in his grief to notice the steady shuffle of the crowd as it files past him. A man so absorbed should not be disturbed. Even when he is recognized, and whispers flutter about him, he is able to ignore the nervous shiver that his presence elicits. His name is handed down the line until, as in a game of telephone tag, Alonzo Baylor becomes Shoreman Sailor becomes Roman Taylor becomes Norman Mailer and Alonzo Baylor again, here to pay tribute and mourn Mercè Casals out of an old friendship, perhaps a secret passion.

Baylor has the moves of a thief. His sneaky fingers creep along the outside of the casket until the right hand is poised just above the Señora's head. The fingers, casually dangling over the edge, descend until they ever so lightly brush the side of her face. With his left hand firmly supporting his brow, Baylor glances darkly around, and in a moment's sleight, the right index curls itself around a few of the Señora's fine red hairs and yanks them out swiftly. Her head barely nods. Lockwood winces. He expects the diva to cry out.

Thinking he has escaped notice, Baylor is emboldened. He slips the hairs inside a white envelope. Next, he places the envelope on Mercè Casals' famous mouth and obtains a lipsticked imprint of her lips. Baylor hangs over the edge of the casket, his shoulders convulsed in theatrical sobs, as he pockets the envelope. Lockwood imagines him gaining some insight or other into his biographical subject by taking the samples for DNA analysis. Maybe something occult, like a reading of tea leaves or a channeling of the newly departed spirit.

This time Lockwood looks directly at Baylor and stares at him with a look that says, *I saw what you did!*

Baylor meets his gaze. The message is clear: *I know you saw what you saw. Why would I give a damn?*

⚬———⊣| ONE, 900, DR. PHONE.

When Lockwood returns to Anaheim at the end of the day, the Señora's absence continues to absorb him. He decides that grief and shock feel like the flu; the day's events bring on a dull ache in his chest. A scattering of unopened mail and unread newspapers lies by the door, but he goes directly to his office upstairs. He sits at a heavy oak desk; to one side his Mac workhorse; on the other a printer and two metal filing cabinets stacked like a fortress. He is surrounded by fiberboard bookcases, their slats swaying under the weight of handy references: dictionaries and a thesaurus, Bartlett's quotations, *Books in Print,* volumes with maps and holy books of all creeds, *America's Most Beloved Poems from Auden to Whitman, The Unabridged How Things Work, Trees and Plants of North America,* Audubon's bird books, insect books, fish books, and *1001 Jokes, Insults, and Toasts for Every Occasion.*

The gooseneck lamp on his desk sheds scant light on the rest of the room, where Claire, half in shadows, is a vaguely reproachful presence. "You're here," she says.

"Yes, I'm here." He starts. Then he turns from the pile of tapes and papers cluttering his desk.

"You could've said hello."

"If I don't organize the interviews as soon as I get home, I'll end up with a mess. I didn't want to disturb you."

"I was making dinner. What's there to disturb? It'd be nice to see you once in a while, Mark. You left this morning without making a sound."

"You need your sleep."

"I get enough sleep."

"Why are we having this conversation?" Lockwood shakes his head in exasperation.

Claire leaves and closes the door behind her.

He could ask the same question about all the conversations he has been having. He is in fact surrounded by conversations in which he has no role but to listen. Radio banter wakes him up in the morning. TV banter puts him to sleep.

Lockwood suspects that writers wear out their souls in the same way that prostitutes or spies or beggars do. When put on the spot—to write a brochure inviting retired union members to invest in waste-management start-ups or a fund-raising letter for the evangelization of Guatemala, to name two recent examples—it is not his role to question but to rent out his craft.

The voice that calls Lockwood belongs to a lesser Muse—the deadline, the mortgage, the fear of failure. A hundred typing chimps might, with the help of a decent editor, write *Hamlet* in a thousand years. Point a gun at Lockwood's head and he could do it in a month. The world, however, doesn't want another *Hamlet* so much as it does a reassuring *How to Prepare for Your Colonoscopy*.

His résumé lists several accomplishments, including the six-page fund-raising letter for Amnesty International ("Sincere emotion, honest indignation, principled righteousness!") which won the Direct Mail Association's Gold Award in its category and pulled an unheard-of 6.7% response, and the booklet *How to Talk to Your Teen About God* (part of his series for the Troubled Teen Press covering Drugs, STDs, Safe Driving, Money, War, Divorce, and Sexual Orientation), which has been recommended by hundreds of ministers across the country, mostly Unitarian but also a few of the more easygoing Presbyterians, Episcopalians, Congregationalists, and such.

The myth that hack work is effortless, a notch above typing, was fostered by writers who have never been called to produce three thousand words on "Accident and Disability Insurance Exclusions." Once you're over the limitations of subject matter and intended audience, the good old mot juste is discovered just as joyfully while explaining to a teenager how to put on a condom as while narrating the death of Emma Bovary.

A younger Lockwood wrote his debut collection of short fiction—*Two Loaves of Bread and Other Tales of Fame and Famine*—with the fervor of a stone carver chiseling the words into eternity. It earned him an MFA from the Writer's Workshop at twenty-three and sold 875 copies, mostly to libraries, some to friends and to his mother, who bought a carton to distribute on birthdays, weddings, and graduations.

The unsold books remain packed in a dozen boxes. Occasionally he offers a copy to a client. He gave one to his dentist and to his favorite mechanic at the Saab shop. He also made a dent in the inventory by abandoning copies in busy places—airport gate areas, bus seats, phone booths, coffeehouse tables, taxis, shelves in small-town libraries. For years he took books wherever he went. He signed his name on the title page and underneath wrote his phone number—312-693-3126. He still fantasizes a stranger picking up the book and being moved enough by its contents to call him: "Yes, I read your stories. I cried at 'The Onion Peeler' and laughed at the end of 'The Perfect Uncle.'"

Over the years there have been a couple such calls. One woman wanted to know his address so she could return the book to him. Surely he had left it by mistake at a Northwest gate in the Minneapolis–St. Paul airport. He asked her if she had read any of the stories. Oh, she was not much of a reader. She had started a couple, but had not gotten very far with them.

Another caller said he was a psychiatrist. He had found the book on a bench in Central Park, had read the stories with great interest and claimed to have detected the writer's morbid fascination with his own body fluids. All those references, he observed, to urine and tears and saliva and semen and sweat. Not natural, not healthy. "What a sad loser you are!" he sighed. "I think I can help you."

Lockwood stared at the receiver and hung up. When the phone rang again a minute later, he grumbled a tentative "Hello?"

"Hang up on me again, and I'm done with you."

"What do you want?"

"I didn't pay for the book. But I am interested in your career. Which is not going anywhere, unless you get professional help."

"That would be you?"

"Yes. Take down my number. Just in case you feel like exploring some ideas."

"Shoot."

"One, 900, Dr. Phone."

"A 900 number?"

"Yes. 24/7, $3.99 a minute."

"That's $240 an hour."

"I do charge more than a regular psychiatrist on account of the convenience. You don't have to schedule your dreams, your phobia attacks, your crises to correspond to Tuesday–Thursday appointment days. I'm here for you, day or night, help at hand. And you don't have to pay for a fifty-minute hour. The moment a crisis hits, dial 1-900-Dr Phone."

"Sure, maybe sometime."

"You need help now, you idiot."

"Why do you keep calling me names?"

"My active therapeutic style is suited to your passivity."

Lockwood sighed unhappily. "Fine, don't call me. I'll call you."

"Remember, I believe in you," the voice was saying seductively as Lockwood disconnected.

He kept writing through the years. The thin notebook in his shirt pocket was full of tantalizing beginnings and provocative themes. He rose at four in the morning and sat at his desk until it was time to go to work as a copywriter at the Freidl and Perez advertising agency.

In the dark misty mornings, the fog from the sea crawled inland. It softened the silhouette of the hills and seemed to carry the sounds of the waves crashing on the rocks. Lockwood thought of it as the dreamer's time, the moment for poetry, the space of the imagination. After a cup of strong French roast and a slice of baguette spread with Bonne Maman strawberry jam, he would open the small window beside his table and let in a rush of air, imagining he could smell the tide's deposits of weeds and mollusks and rotting driftwood.

Brimming over with the warm well-being that came to him for doing the virtuous thing, for getting up in the morning, for doing the important work of his life first, Lockwood would prepare to write: three deep breaths. Ten fingers wriggle above the keyboard like hungry baby snakes. The back is straight for attack. The gift that goes unused will atrophy. He writes in order to write. Write first, think later. Appease the unseen reader. Hands up! Your words or your life. If the Muse betrays you, shoot the bitch. He considers the possibility that the 72,349 words of *Two Loaves* may be all he was born with—the cool sparks from two happy planets rubbing against each other during a cosmic nanosecond back there at the Workshop in the middle of the corny prairie, in his very own Year of Great Promise. He buries the thought. Somewhere there are reserves that can still be tapped, like the last precious organ cells that keep an anorexic alive.

"Who are you talking to, anyway?" Claire calls up again. "Your dinner's getting cold."

He waits until he is seated at the table. The steam from a bowl of pea soup clouds his glasses. "She's dead, Claire. I can't get over the reality that she's gone."

DARLING, DON'T GET PUSHY.

The regal one was a sight. She had wrapped herself in a black-and-gold lamé caftan, punctuated by her tomato-red hair, her strands of amber and pearls and gold coins, fingers ringed with diamonds and rubies and emeralds, her small feet bunched up into silk pumps with three-inch heels. And all the time she sat, smug and queenly, and stared at her ghostwriter with a mix of suspicion and amusement.

"When was the last time you sang, Señora?"

"Just last week. A little of the Brahms 'Lullaby' for my neighbor's grand-daughter. Her name is Esther. She is ten months old but already quite discriminating. I sang very, very softly, so that only she could hear me."

"In public, Señora. The last time you sang before an audience."

"Darling, don't get pushy."

"It's just that there are certain things your book must talk about. We can't go on and on about trivia for five hundred pages. People will expect to get something of substance for their $29.95. Actual events in your career."

"That story has been told a hundred times."

"I haven't heard it."

"Every performance has been documented, reviewed, analyzed, praised, or lambasted in the world press. Get thee to a library."

"We use the web now, Señora. But that's not the point."

"And what would the point be?"

"That this book is your own story. In your words."

"We are talking in circles."

"Only because you don't want to go forward."

"I do, Mark. It's you who wants me to look at the past. Let's talk about the future. I may not be up to a full production of *Tosca*, but even now I'm making plans for a series of recitals. I have contracts and proposals on my desk. They want me for master classes at Juilliard. The Japanese need me to inaugurate their new concert hall in Hokkaido. There is a recording of Catalan folk songs being planned."

"Your first *Tosca* at La Scala. You were twenty-two."

"I was so scared, my stomach kept churning. Imagine that, a Floria with belly rumblings. Are you going to put that in? I truly hope not. I'm telling you just for your understanding."

"You were cheered."

"I was hissed. I was replacing Callas of all people."

"You won them over. From *'Vissi d'arte,'* the hisses had turned to bravos."

"It's a grim play, isn't it?"

"You sang it beautifully."

"How would you know?"

"All the papers said so."

"There. That proves my point. I don't need to talk about all this. You can go to your computer and get the facts."

"I need your words," he insisted.

"Turn that thing off. And please, please go home now. I need to think."

"Writing is not about thinking, Señora. If it gets thought but not written, it's as if it never happened. The hired gun is the purest kind of writer; he places another's head over his own, lets another's heart beat within his chest."

"You give yourself too much importance," she said.

"But look," Lockwood might say now, if Mercè Casals were still alive. "Read this sentence, this passage. It's about you. It sounds like you. I am speaking in your voice."

○━┤ . . . ENDURING RICHES.

The Señora was anxious about how she and Lockwood would work. She wanted to set rules, limits, options. There would be confidences he would have to respect, words and thoughts that must be left out of the published version.

"Fair enough," Lockwood said amiably. "And you will tell me things you have never told another soul in your life."

She sighed and shook her head almost imperceptibly. Clearly, this fellow would turn out to be more difficult than she had anticipated; she was not getting through to him, and they hadn't even begun.

"Are you going to be stubborn?" she asked.

"You won't know until we start."

"Ask away. I'll let you know if you wake up any rats." She sighed again. "You can be the exterminator."

He would have to probe gently, wary of what he might find behind the facade of the famous and spoiled diva. He would be a therapist, then.

"We'll scare the rats away," he allowed. "Then you'll be free."

He clicked on the small cassette recorder he had placed on the table between them. "We can start at the beginning and travel in time." She would soon forget about the machine as their voices triggered it to start and stop automatically. "Were you happy as a child?"

"I don't think I've been happy since age nine." She paused as if waiting for Lockwood to cue her. Instead of saying anything, he pushed the cassette recorder closer to her.

She took a deep breath and continued, "My mother died at childbirth. I loved my father, even though he kept passing me off, first to one aunt, then to another, but having to take me back when times were lean for the relatives. By the time I was nine, in 1929, he pretty much took care of me by himself.

"We lived in a three-room apartment in the center of Sabadell in the northern Spanish province of Catalonia. The street below, Carrer Brutau, was a narrow, potholed route that echoed day and night with the crunch and clatter of delivery carts and sputtering trucks loaded with fabric bolts from the textile mills. During the time of the grape harvest in late summer and early fall, it was a treat to get away from the sooty little town and travel with my father throughout the festivals in the villages.

"He liked taking me on his sales calls, teaching me about business for when he would have enough capital to open a shop in the Passeig de Gràcia; father and daughter would proudly stand behind the counter and wait on customers. Meanwhile, I would learn all about the fine hand of quality woolens and the sheen of Egyptian cotton and the brilliance of silk from China.

"In the meantime, in one village after another, the tailors, seamstresses, and milliners who were my father's customers doted on me. I was a serious, quiet girl, and I had proper manners in the company of adults. I sat with good posture and pulled the hem of my simple cotton dress down so that it covered my knees. When the summer heat was most intense, I gave up my knee-high socks and leather shoes and wore cool espadrilles.

"During the day, I sat beside Father and watched him take orders for his lines of fabrics, sewing threads, knitting yarns, and buttons. I would wait quite still, growing sleepy with boredom during one visit after another, happy eventually to perform a song for the customer. Then Father would celebrate the day's business with a few brandies at the nearest café.

"One night I remember taking Father's hand, or rather wrapping mine around two of his sausage-like fingers, and steering his drunken weaving away from the bumps and potholes that seemed to wait in ambush for him. I was relieved that the road led to the Hostal de l'Hort. It was a two-story white stuccoed farmhouse topped by pots of geraniums in a row along the roofline. A door of heavy bolted planks opened onto a main room with two long, rough-hewn tables lined by slat-backed chairs with seats of woven straw. The inn was packed with fairgoers. Like Father, they were mostly peddlers from Barcelona and Valencia, and even from as far as Marseilles, but also petty delinquents, engaging in gambling and thievery.

"We had stayed up late at the hostal, which offered the traveler cramped rooms but hearty boiled dinners, or thick omelets of potatoes and onion, and always large servings of blood sausage and cured ham. That night, a group of travelers had gathered at the inn to eat and drink and prey on one another over card games.

"Father was having a successful trip. Closing a sale made him feel loved and respected. Whenever Father gambled and won, he was certain it was the result of the secret pacts he made with higher powers: *Let me win tonight, and I will feed three beggars tomorrow.*

"That night, however, he was losing to a glum, dark man at the opposite end of the table. The gambler's name was Pep Saval. He had arrived at the inn late and had taken a solitary seat in front of a reheated bowl of *escudella*, slurping spoonfuls of the oily broth brimming with potatoes and carrots and gristly chunks of beef.

"From the moment Pep Saval joined the game, he drew the best hands. But even while winning, his face, weathered to a dark shiny bronze and topped with slicked-back hair, was without expression. Poised massively between his shoulders, his head seemed out of proportion to his torso. His large pink ears wore, like some fleshy pendant, fat lobes tufted with spikes of black hair. He wrapped his hands around the cards and held them close to his mouth as if to conjure the winning suits with every moist breath.

"Father had ordered another pitcher of wine. Other players had dropped out but had kept their places to watch with ill-disguised fascination my father's plunge into insolvency. It was past midnight and I had long since fallen asleep on a bench close to the kitchen. The innkeeper kept whispering in Father's ear that he should settle the price of the room and the night's refreshments.

"I was jarred by Father's shouting. 'Not yet, *mesonero*. We must give luck a chance to turn.'

"'That is the truth,' the other man agreed. 'Here is a usually fortunate man going through a brief eclipse of his star. No matter how much he loses, my friend here has been blessed with enduring riches.'

"'I have?' Father lifted his bloodshot gaze.

"'In the human realm, if not the material,' the stranger clarified.

"'Yes, yes, *naturalmente*,' he stammered.

"The stranger slapped his winning cards down on the table. Father looked wan with disbelief. He started to shove the pile of coins toward the winner when he felt the other's hand pushing the money back.

"'It's over for me.' Father forced a sickly smile.

"'To leave while you're behind seems an imprudent thing. In the course of a game one will both win and lose. You owe it to yourself to continue playing. Then, when you are in a winning position, leave the table and take your money to bed.'

"'I have no money left.'

"'Perhaps, my friend, there is a way to settle this wager with a currency sweeter than mere pesetas.' Pep Saval nodded toward me. 'It is said that your girl has an extraordinary voice.'

" '*Ven aquí, nena,*' Father called me.

"I looked up from under a wool blanket. *'Sí, papá?'*

He pulled me to the table and laid the blanket over my shoulders.

"'And what is your name?' Pep Saval asked.

"'Mercè Casals.' I did the small curtsy that so charmed strangers.

"'This gentleman would like to hear you sing,' said Father.

"I was accustomed to performing on the spur of the moment. That night, I sang "El Noi de la Mare." Pep Saval closed his eyes; the beginnings of a smile danced at the corners of his mouth. After the scattered applause had died down, he slapped several coins on the table. 'There must be twenty pesetas there. I will gladly bet them against one more song from your girl.' He scribbled some numbers on a scrap of paper and pushed it along with the pencil toward my father, who read it with series of unhappy nods, signed his name under the column of figures, and placed the paper over the coins at the center of the table."

The Señora was quiet for several moments. After the initial rush of memories, she seemed to have grown suddenly shy. Lockwood broke the silence. "Ah! Your name on an IOU. Your first professional contract, Señora."

"Poor Father. He was so drunk that night." She shook her head sadly.

"You realized what was going on, of course."

"Nothing was going on as far as I could see. Father often had me sing for people."

"In the middle of the night?"

"It scared me to go to bed alone in a strange room. I was jealous of missing out on the excitement."

"Daddy's little girl."

"I was nine. Whose little girl was I supposed to be?"

"Certainly not Pep Saval's."

"Not yet, Scribbler."

"Not that night? Not the next day?"

"I mean that I'm not talking about Pep Saval yet. Ask me about him some other time."

In the afternoons the Señora tired. She would lean her head against the back of her chair and allow her eyelids to drop. She seemed to be gazing inward, as if a film were rolling past, bearing with it the images of those years. An occasional sigh signaled her gradual retreat from the moment. Her eyes closed at last, the lids quivering now and then as if in reaction to a voice or face that had triggered some memory, quick and sudden like the prick of a needle, over before she realized it.

Perla was left holding the plate of cottage cheese and apple slices that were her afternoon snack. "You've let her fall asleep," she quietly accused Lockwood.

"I didn't think it was up to me to stop her."

"She's supposed to eat first, nap second."

"Who says?"

"Stick to the writing, will you?"

This was the first time Perla had been irritable with him. It was not what the Señora hoped for; she had ventured the theory that they would fall in love.

"She has lovely skin, Perla does," the Señora had pointed out to Lockwood. "I think she is repressed. She used to have a boyfriend, a certain Haskell or something, a plumbing contractor. When they broke up eight months ago, she got his red pickup truck. There hasn't been anyone since. Now she works for me all the time, six days a week, twelve hours a day. She must ache to be touched. We women crave another's touch. Sometimes after she has given me my massage, I ask Perla to get under the sheet and lie with me. I don't look at her or let her see me. It's nothing sexual, you understand. We lie side by side, pressing against one another, the whole length of her slender legs touching mine. She does it for me. But I know she needs it, too."

"We're getting off the subject."

"The hunger in my skin is the subject. You'll find a way to put it all in my words when the time comes, won't you?"

"What shall we talk about this morning?" the Señora asked two days later.

"We should pick up on the story about your father's card game with Pep Saval." Lockwood clicked the recorder on and settled back in his chair. "That way we can go into your childhood more or less chronologically."

"I haven't been able go past my childhood in eighty years," she said. "You're welcome to try."

"We don't have to talk about anything that causes you distress. We'll ease into things."

"We can leave the big rats for another time, Señor Exterminador?"

"Sure," he said amiably. "But it might be better to drive them away now."

"You are heartless."

"Did you anticipate that first night how your life would be affected by Pep Saval?"

"I watched my father stare at the half-dozen slips with my name scribbled on them, at the coins that had piled up in the middle of the table, finally glancing up at the stranger's face, now flushed with the success of his winnings. Pep Saval noted that there were enough songs there to last a year. 'Do you know who I am?' he finally asked.

"Father rubbed his eyes and held a match to the burned-out stub of his cigar. He stared through clouds of smoke at the man opposite him.

"'I am Pep Saval.'

"'Ah, Saval, the *empresario*.' Father stared at him suspiciously. 'The famous Pep Saval should be in Barcelona or Paris or Milan. Not in a humble inn in some out-of-the-way village, *un poble de mala mort*.'

"'There are not so many gifted artists for me anymore.' And then with a long sigh he added, 'Your child is very much a talent. If she would sing again, well, that would be the brightest light yet at the end of this long night.'

"'*Nena!*' my father called. 'You must keep your father from the poorhouse.'

"'What is your pleasure, sir?' I asked with grudging humility.

"'Anything you choose. Something appropriate for ushering in the dawn.'

"Father tilted his head toward me as I whispered. 'She would like to sing for you "El Cant dels Ocells,"' he announced.

"'Ah, yes, "The Song of the Birds."'

"I met his gaze directly for the first time, but didn't return his smile. I was about to begin when he held up his hand. 'Come closer,' he said. 'I want to hear every note.'

"He placed two fingers on my throat. I didn't move away. I began to sing."

"You didn't think all this was very strange on his part?"

"At his touch I felt a tingling right at the place inside me where I knew my voice resided.

"Nobody had ever listened to me like that. I imagined my voice resonating inside his own throat so that he would know exactly what I felt as the song poured out. I fancied that my low notes settled in his chest. My highest range could make his hair stand on end. My saddest songs make his eyes smart."

"You made his eyes see pesetas."

"There was more to it than that. Pep Saval withdrew his fingers as if feeling heat from my throat. He sat erect on the chair, both feet firmly planted on the ground, his fists like stones on the table. When I finished the song he sent me to where the innkeeper's wife waited with a bowl of hot milk flavored with coffee and a slice of yesterday's bread, buttered and sprinkled with sugar.

"Pep Saval waited until I had gone back to my place near the kitchen, out of hearing range. He flipped through the slips with Father's signature as if he were shuffling cards and selected one. He slid it across the table. 'There. Now you only owe me twelve songs.'

"'I don't force my daughter to sing. Mercè sings because she loves to.'

"'She sings stupidly,' the man corrected. 'She pushes her upper register. A singer has only so many high notes in the bank. She shouldn't spend them all while she's still a child. In six or seven years we will know if she has a voice.'

"'I don't understand what you're saying,' he snapped. 'Her charm is that she is spontaneous.'

"Pep Saval sighed. 'She needs a teacher.'

"'We can't afford one.'

"'I could give her advice. Teach her to care for her voice. You could leave the girl here until you return tonight from visiting clients.'

"'I'm to hand over my daughter to you?' Father's eyes narrowed.

"Pep Saval nodded as if he had reached a conclusion after giving serious thought to a grave matter. 'A man would not take such a task casually. This would not be for my benefit.'

"'For mine, then?'

"'It would give me much satisfaction to help such a gifted child.' He shrugged as if the merit of his idea were self-evident. 'And you would be released from some of the debts incurred at this table.'

"A pallor washed over Father's face. He stood up unsteadily and bounded up the stairs without a glance back.

"Sometime in the morning, wearing a clean shirt, his face glowing from a recent shave, his breath masked with clove, he clattered down the steep wooden stairs and emerged into the room, armed with his sample case.

"He led me by the hand. '*Nena,* I feel you didn't sleep well last night. I want you to stay here today. These good people will take care of you until I return.' He leaned down to kiss my forehead.

"I stared at Father with disbelief. 'When will you come back, *papá?*

"'In the evening.' He called over his shoulder to Pep Saval, 'You can give her advice with her singing if she lets you.'"

THE ABANDONED CHILD.

Lockwood didn't trust his memory. The shadowy area between remembering and imagining was a trap. He would have liked to believe that Mercè Casals was an object of his own creation. That he was the one calling the tune—could say, "Señora, do this, stand there, say that, sing." A realm where she could be any age he wanted her to be, as beautiful as he could imagine her, as passionate as he could feel her, as unhappy as he could bear her to be.

And yet Mercè Casals was the author of her own life. He was not to think of her as the voice in his head but as the voice on the tape. The cassettes were multiplying. He kept them in chronological order, in stacks of ten, neatly labeled, rewound, and cued up. In time he would listen to all of them. At home in the evenings he sat on his creaking leather chair and cleared a space on the glass-ringed desktop, buffed by years of slow, anxious writing. He rewound the day's cassettes, stuck a label on the box, and wrote the date of the interview along with the subject of the conversation:

1) The snakes at La Scala (a hired claque hissing from the gallery)

2) Fucking the Prince (not language that La Señora would like, but she need never know)

3) Drowning in Florence (the Arno flooding)

4) Favorite foods (Camembert, artichokes, *crema catalana*)

5) Her first Lucia (How she loved going mad!)

6) Singing for Franco, J. Paul Getty, Nancy and Ron Reagan, Mao, and Nixon (he could hardly hear a thing for the thickets of hair sprouting out of his ears!)

7) Trying to sing flamenco with gypsies in the caves above Granada.

8) Great lovers with small penises (as they say in Barcelona, *el pot petit té bon confit*)

He listens to a cassette labeled *The abandoned child*. He remembers the moment clearly because the Señora never spoke of her father again. Sitting at the Mac, he types in the latest working title, and the bold 16-point Times Roman makes everything official: *The Wonder Singer: My Story*, by Mercè Casals as told to Mark Lockwood.

Now, as her words flutter all around him, he listens to her voice from deep inside him. Facing the silently scolding blink of the cursor, he waits for the courage to inhabit his subject:

Looking back, I can see that the story of my life is punctuated by men. Men as heroes and men as villains. I was abandoned by men. I was owned by men. Men taught me, manipulated me, stifled me, adored me, exploited me. And finally, I gave up the last man in my life in much the same way one gives up smoking or exercise. Painful at first, but ultimately liberating.

The last time I saw my father was in 1929, in the ripeness of summer long before the war between brothers and sisters brought its horrors to Catalonia. When night fell and he hadn't returned, Pep Saval didn't know what to say to me. He told me I had the most beautiful voice he had ever heard in a girl my age. When I did not acknowledge the comment he went on to explain to me that he had been a manager of singers, that he could help me take care of my gift, learn how to sing without strain. I didn't know what he was talking about.

By evening I had retreated to a corner of the main room wrapped in a borrowed blanket. My mood from earlier in the day had not changed. I had awakened knowing that my father would not return. Children are like that, anticipating abandonment even in routine absences. I had started grieving from the moment he had left without me. Pep Saval did not know what to do with an unhappy child. I returned his quizzical smiles with empty looks.

That first night after my father disappeared, I didn't want to sing. I turned down the innkeeper's wife, who offered supper in return for a few songs. I resisted the entreaties from some of the inn's guests who had heard me the night before. Then when a cook brought out a bowl of broth with a chicken wing, I looked up to Pep Saval and he encouraged me with a nod. Instead of expecting me to sing for my supper, he placed a coin on the table. I ate with relish, ignoring everyone around me, and held my dish out for a second helping.

The next day, waking up to the knowledge that Father was not coming back, I couldn't stop weeping.

To cheer me up, Pep Saval argued that there were towns we could travel to, where fairs were being held and where my father might still be found, if his health was sound and his mind had not suffered some derangement. I didn't know what to believe.

Perla confided to Lockwood that sometimes, especially toward the end of the week, after six twelve-hour days taking care of the Señora, she felt she could hardly breathe. The thermostat, in response to the mild fluctuations of the weather, was set either too cold or too warm. The air inside the apartment grew close and heavy.

Occasionally the Señora complained that smells of burning beans and ripening garbage and soiled clothes were seeping in from neighboring apartments. She guessed that the source blowing in through the air conditioning was most likely the wealthy young couple with babies in 1409 or the incontinent old German in 1807 who tried to court her. At such times she ordered the vent flaps to be shut and the air conditioning turned off. She attempted to mask smells that only she was aware of with essential oils combined in therapeutic aromas and simmering in a little electric diffuser.

Nothing was allowed to express its own smell. Linens were laundered in "fresh-scented" Cheer, the kitchen counters had to be wiped daily with lemon Fantastik, the bathroom fixtures with Formula 409, a special carpet deodorizer was sprinkled after vacuuming, containers of round blue pellets hung inside toilet bowls.

Other times the Señora feared that she might be the one exuding a not very pleasant body odor. So she soaked in hot, scented baths and squirted on Giorgio or Givenchy or Joy. These gave Perla headaches and made her nose itch.

"God, I need a breath of air," Perla exclaimed when the Señora seemed to have dozed off. She actually craved a cigarette. Lockwood did not tease her about her brand of fresh air because he had been trying to ingratiate himself with her for weeks.

She left Lockwood in charge and went for a walk along the beach. He would have offered to accompany her, but the Señora would be upset to awaken and not find either of them at their posts.

Lockwood listened for signs that the Señora was awaking from her chair by the window. It was only two in the afternoon, and their schedule called for him to be working on the autobiography through a six-hour day, plus evenings at home sorting out his thoughts and reviewing the recordings. The material was richest when she groped for the significant event and brought up instead a small telling moment.

The Señora's pleasures were simple. She took long baths, she listened to recordings of her past performances spinning out endlessly, sometimes loudly, at other times faintly in the background. At four P.M. chatting stopped so she could watch her favorite Mexican soap opera—*María la del Barrio*—about a domestic worker who was employed by a rich family and ended up marrying the young heir to the ancestral fortune.

"These are wonderful stories of poor girls blessed by the fates, against all odds, to gain true love and unimaginable wealth," she said to him. "Do you know that Mexican *telenovelas* are watched in Russia, in Turkey, in many other countries around the world? These stories hold a moral lesson."

Lockwood laughed. "Even if you are sunk in poverty, you can still be saved by dumb luck."

"You're being obtuse. One is saved by goodness."

"It's not a fair world." Lockwood shrugged unhappily.

"Fairness is not the issue. Understanding is. If your understanding is warped, you suffer the consequences."

"People screw up all the time."

"Because they don't know any better. You're bored in your marriage, so you feel you're entitled to fun in your middle age and therefore you want Perla. It's not a question of morality. You figure you're entitled to the thrills that Perla might provide. The consequences will come regardless of what you feel your rights are. Perla will end up humiliating you. You will lose your wife's love. Your dog will snarl. And you will be so racked with guilt you'll never write a true word again."

"A raw nerve up for the hitting." Lockwood forced a smile.

The Señora fell silent, suddenly distracted. She gazed out the window at the massive gray clouds that were gathering. At intervals they blocked out the sun, and their shadow on the water gave the sea a metallic cast. She waited until the wind seemed to tear through the thinning edges of a slow-moving, bloated nimbus, splitting the light into brilliant spikes.

She turned toward him with a sparkle of optimism. "On the other hand, you and Perla will perhaps find great pleasure in each other. Maybe you will conduct yourselves with dignity. You and your wife will separate amicably, which is something you should have done years ago. Your dog will continue to sleep at your feet. And you will be so liberated that every word you write from then on will be true and wonderful and beautiful. Because you will once again have a story to tell."

"You're playing with my head, Señora. That's a side of you I had not yet seen."

"Where is Perla, anyway?" she said impatiently. "It's time she made tea."

"She went out for a walk while you were napping."

"For a cigarette."

"Yes, that, too."

"What are you going to say to her when she comes back?"

"Nothing," he said after a long pause, certain that, for now, coming on to Perla was something best enjoyed as an unrealized idea.

"Nothing is not an option, silly." She laughed, apparently delighting in the turmoil she had sown in his mind. "You'll have to say something to her. Eventually."

He added weakly, "I love my wife."

"Good for you!"

"We need to get back to your story."

"Where was I?"

"Start anywhere."

Months after that conversation, Lockwood is poised at the keyboard; he listens to the recording and lets the Señora speak through him. He types the title page, stark, pristine, full of promise. The title, her name, his name. He begins to write.

THE WONDER SINGER: MY STORY

BY MERCÈ CASALS AS TOLD TO MARK LOCKWOOD

The Girl in the Trees

Every hour that my father did not return to the inn was spent in a fog. I would be awake for hours, eager for the sound of his voice, his heavy steps on the stairs. During the day, I would avoid the other guests by sleeping. I dared not face what was happening. I didn't like the pitying looks people gave me. However, I was cared for. There was hot food for me, and a cot in a quiet corner, even though I had to give up the room my father was no longer paying for.

By the third day, I was aware of impatient looks, muttered questions: Did I have any relatives I could go to? Clearly the innkeeper was not looking to adopt an orphan. While I was having my *café con leche* and bread for breakfast, the innkeeper's wife packed my clothes and placed my suitcase by the front door. I realized I was leaving, though I did not know where I would go, or with whom. By midmorning, Pep Saval was leading me out the door and onto the road. Not understanding what was happening, I dragged my feet and kept falling behind.

"Are you scared of me?" He stopped several meters away from the inn and challenged me in a tone more gruff than I believe he intended.

"Do you know why my father has gone?" I asked at last.

"No, my sweet. Disappearing is the last thing I expected from him."

"He owed you money."

"It was only a game to pass the time. I wasn't going to drive your father into poverty."

"So you won me instead."

"Only a few songs."

"You've been cheated. My voice does not belong to my father." I paused a moment. "Are you angry at me for saying that?"

"No, it makes me glad."

Moving down the road, following the contour of the dusty, wilting vineyards toward the open country, Pep Saval kept trying to persuade me that I was to feel safe in his company. I finally mumbled assent to stop him from going on and on.

We walked for the better part of the day. We established a contest of wills; he would not tell me where we were going. I wouldn't ask. As long as he was willing to carry both our bags, I was content to follow. We walked through an occasional village, but rested only briefly to drink at the town well.

He finally suggested we stop to eat under the shadowy foliage of an oak. I sat on a flat rock and watched while he cut a tomato in half and rubbed its pulp onto the crusty bread with a generous drizzle of olive oil. *Pa amb tomàquet.*

"It needs salt," I complained after taking a tentative nibble.

"Really?" He frowned, trying not to act pleased. "I think the bread is salty enough. Too much salt hides the taste of this perfect tomato, sublime if you compare it to its flavor yesterday and how it would have tasted tomorrow. We must eat it at this very hour, at the peak of its existence."

"Didn't you bring any salt?" I insisted.

Pep Saval sighed. Of course he carried salt. He opened a packet and took some grains to sprinkle over the bread.

After eating, Pep Saval leaned against the tree trunk, pulled his beret down over his eyes and, lacing his fingers over his belly with a long, happy groan, drifted off to sleep. I was free to leave, but he knew I had nowhere to go.

When he awoke after half an hour, he realized that I was no longer sitting under the oak. He walked around the tree as if circling a reluctant dancing partner. He uttered a simple prayer, his eyes gazing toward the sky, then sighed with relief when his prayer was answered: I couldn't prevent the creaking of the branches when I shifted my weight, followed by my stifled laugh.

"Come down," he called up. There was a slight stirring as I found a high perch in the V formed by two limbs.

"I'm right by a nest!" I called back.

"If you disturb the eggs you'll get pecked by the mother bird."

"I'm just looking at them."

"I could tell you about the time I saved three baby robins," he boasted. "Only I'm tired of shouting and not seeing your face."

"Start the story," I pressed. "If I like it, I'll come down."

"*Nena,* come down," he pleaded. "It's not the kind of story one tells by shouting."

"If you keep calling me 'child,' I will never again do anything you want me to do."

"If you don't stop acting like a child, I'll never ask you to do anything. I won't tell you to eat or sleep or bathe. You'll be free to be the little savage you obviously enjoy being. A monkey that enjoys hanging from trees."

I scrambled down to a lower limb, but remained concealed by the thick foliage. "You don't have to shout now."

Taking a deep breath, he leaned back against the tree's wide trunk and began softly, "When I was a boy, just outside the town of Sant Quirze the woods were thick with oak. There was one tree that was the king of all the trees. It was older and taller and its gnarled branches spread out wider than any of the others in the forest. We called it Old Father Tree. When we wanted the highest vantage point in the region, that was the tree we climbed."

"Can't you speak louder?"

"I used to spend the hot summer afternoons within the shade of Old Father Tree. It was the place where I felt the safest."

"I thought you were going to tell the story of the robins." I had climbed down to a branch just above his head.

"This love of heights was true of the birds, too. Since the children of the village loved to hunt them down with sling shots, it was only in the depths of Old Father Tree that a bird was safe."

"Is that where you discovered the nest with the robins' eggs?"

"I looked down on the nest that was secured just below the branch where I was sitting. The eggs were like jewels," he said, hardly above a whisper. "The most elusive color of blue. Blue like lilacs at the time of their blooming, blue like some girls' eyes when the light strikes them just right, or blue like a certain star that appears sometimes in the midwinter sky. I hardly dared breathe for fear of disturbing them. And they were so lonely. I thought I had scared their mother away. By six o' clock a wind that smelled of rain started to blow, and fat, cool drops were falling down on us. At first it was dry within the foliage, but as the leaves began to drip, the nest got wet.

"I laid my felt cap over the eggs to protect them and went home. I thought about those eggs all through the storm. In my thoughts I kept blowing my breath on them and hoping the mother robin would return finally and lift the edge of the cap like a blanket to reveal her eggs await-ing safe and cozy."

"Did she?"

"When I returned the next morning, the cap, soaked now from the rain, remained undisturbed over the eggs. I was happy to see that the wool had kept the eggs dry and warm through the night."

"Then what happened?"

"The mother bird never returned. I figured she lost track of her nest because it was hidden by my cap."

"That is so sad."

"The story has a happy ending."

"Then tell me," I demanded.

"I will, at my own pace. After all, not everything took place at once. There was first one thing, then the other and the other and so forth."

"What. Happened. Next!"

Pep Saval laughed out loud. "I put my sweater over the eggs to keep them warm. I wanted to be there when the chicks were born."

"What, for days?" I asked in disbelief.

"For a few hours, as it turned out. Sometime around two in the after-noon, when the heat of the day was crowding in through the still air, I sensed a stirring under the sweater. I lifted up a corner to peek at the eggs. Imagine my surprise when I saw that from one of them, a tiny brown beak was breaking through the shell. Then some chipping started on the other one and finally, by the time the last egg was starting to break, a hole had opened up in the shell of the first one and the head of a wet chick was poking through. It was a scrawny thing that began chirp-ing crazily as soon as it was able to climb out of the egg. A minute later, the bird was joined in the chirping by his two siblings. I can see them still, their eyes closed and filmed over with viscous tears. Their feathers all sticky and matted down. Their beaks opening and closing like tiny pincers as if trying to bite some sustenance out of thin air. Birds are born hungry just like humans. Fortunately I had a jar with a few worms that I'd dug out of the garden that morning."

"You didn't say you had worms with you," I was quick to point out.

"I can't tell you everything at once," he argued. "I am telling you now, that when I went up to check on the eggs, I had an inkling that they could be born anytime, and that if their mother was not around to feed them, I would have to provide worms."

"You are telling me now because you hadn't thought of it sooner."

He threw his arms up. "I will not continue the story."

"Go on, but I won't believe it."

"Why would you want hear a story that you don't believe?"

"Because I want to know how it ends."

"Come now," he called up. "It's getting late."

"Where are you going?" I asked, suddenly worried I would be left behind.

"I want us to get to Planell before dark."

"But the story is not over yet."

"You'll get the rest of it as we walk."

↦ THERE IS SUCH A WEIGHT TO WEDNESDAY . . .

After Dr. Velasco had signed the death certificate—cardiac arrest causing drowning in bathtub—and Mercè Casals' body had been turned over to two beach-bum-blond fellows from the Rossini Fratelli Mortuary, Perla gave in to a sudden rush of tears. After eighteen months of service to the Señora, her charge was being lifted from her hands and carried off to be dressed and made up for her final appearance.

She had changed out of her white uniform into her street clothes— black jeans, a black halter top, and a black biker jacket, all steel studs and shiny zippers on buttery-soft leather. Lockwood, in his rumpled khakis and pocket t-shirt, felt he was in the presence of a dark angel angling for nurse duty in the afterlife.

She sat at the Señora's writing table, filling out her time sheets. This last bureaucratic chore took on the weight of ritual. Lockwood feared the moment when Perla would disappear, their paths never to cross again.

There were a few things left to settle with Dr. Velasco besides the last accounting of her billable hours; she would have to write a statement of how and when the body had been discovered and compile a list of people who had to be informed of the Señora's passing.

Heading the list would be the husband, Nolan Keefe, who at this time tomorrow afternoon would be sitting in the parlor at the Villa Age d'Or with tea service for two. At the end of the hour he would know something was wrong, that the love of his life would not visit him the following Wednesday either.

He had to be given the news gently. Perla would do it with all the kindness that Mercè Casals' most special friend and husband was entitled to. Lockwood would go along since it was part of his research and he had not yet met Nolan Keefe; this chapter in the Señora's life, the visits with her husband, which she had not wanted to discuss, were an important part of her story.

Lockwood got Wednesday afternoons off. At first there had been no explanation for the Señora's suddenly ending their conversation on that day each week. He just assumed she had a regular medical appointment. It was Perla who piqued his curiosity. She teased him by asking what kind of a researcher he was when this small but significant quirk was going uninvestigated. "Ask her, Mr. Escritor."

He did. "Where are you going this afternoon, Señora?"

She acted startled by the question, although she must've been expecting it. "There is such a weight to Wednesday," she began. "It's a day which, from the moment I get up and Perla brings me my tea and fruit, presses on my heart like lead. Of course, Wednesdays are another of my secrets, Mr. Lockwood. I will tell you something about it, building slowly to the truth, but no names. Not yet. You will learn about the woman, not the diva, not the Señora, not the ex-Princess of Montefino. And you will learn something about Nolan Keefe. He's an old man now, even by my ridiculous standards. A silly, cranky *viejo* who is more of an adolescent than a man. He frightens me, Mr. Lockwood, but I must sit in the musty parlor of the Villa Age d'Or and take my tea and nibble on their Danish butter cookies and wait out the endless gaps in our conversation. He brushes off the cookie crumbs that fall on his coat. They glimmer like flecks of gold under the window that catches the sun. I time my visits in this way, you see, to catch that precious sliver of light that comes in through that dusty glass.

"Often he does not touch his tea at all. It grows cold even as the last afternoon light wanes and we are left in the twilight of the parlor, waiting always until the last minute before turning on the lamp. There is no need for conversation when two old souls can sit side by side. We respond to each other like the tines of a tuning fork. When we speak it's about nothing in particular. The weather. The pattern on the tea service. Butter cookies instead of pecan sandies. Anyone overhearing us would get the impression of two married dullards, filling the emptiness of their lives with the motions of a relationship. Well, Nolan doesn't talk much because he thinks we have said everything to each other that is worth saying. If he reacts with a shudder to a chill in the air, he is commenting on much more than the temperature. It is a private language he speaks, and no amount of translating could convey the full meaning.

"I talk enough for the two of us: 'The new nurse's name is Millicent; I don't believe I have ever known a Millicent before. What does her name mean? A thousand scents? Well, she smells of Pine-Sol, and not much else. Nine hundred and ninety-nine scents to go—musk and basil and lilacs and the sea.' We could go on, my love and I. Once we started a list of scents we remembered, and every Wednesday we would add them to a yellow pad, and every new scent would lead us down a new path, would bring us face to face with a different place, a different hour, a different face.

"Every recollection was a delight, a gift of memory. We gave up on the list right after 'freshly pitched hay,' no more than thirty items or so. My Nolan grew tired of the game on the afternoon we were to reach fifty, a milestone day indeed—absinthe, Armagnac, aquavit, and fourteen to go. He tilted his head back and let out a big yawn such as cats do to mask their aggression. I nudged him, not because I didn't sympathize with his boredom, I was pretty bored myself, but because he looked so undignified sitting there being rude. Heads turned toward us as he let out a melodramatic groan. There were other people in the parlor, the Wednesday regulars, we called them. They have rules about proper behavior at the Villa Age d'Or. You must make reservations for tea. Far from being onerous, their rules give me a feeling of security, to know that as long as my husband is there, as long as I show up for our appointed time on Wednesdays, every effort is made to keep our lives on track.

"After all, this is a privileged table, the one that catches the light between five and five-forty, and there are many Wednesday regulars in this room who would kill for it. I lean toward him as if to whisper a bit of gossip in his ear and my fingers curl around his arm and tighten until I feel him jerk it away. He stares at me in surprise and snaps his mouth shut.

"Am I annoying you?" he asks when his eyes meet mine.

"Of course not, my darling," I reassure him. "But if I bore you, I will no longer visit you."

Now Lockwood and Perla would get together one more time. The anticipation of the meeting gave the moment a sense of adventure tinged with the hopelessness of their relationship. The possibilities quickened his pulse and made his ears ring. They would have lunch together at a quiet fish place in Del Mar, something easy to digest, light on the garlic, with a crisp sauvignon blanc. They'd take their time. Savor the briny sea air. Put a final flourish on the meal with a mighty espresso. And then, with a shared sense of the sentimental value of their mission, go hand in hand to comfort old Nolan Keefe.

✎—╫ ABSORBED IN THE OBJECT.

At night the dark house in Anaheim echoes with whispers. Lockwood turns the recorder down to a murmur, but the voices curl under the door, around the corners, up the stairs. They slide on the hardwood floor and crawl along the carpeting and cling to the walls and drapes. First the low questioning tones, then the rise and fall of the lighter voice, musical even in the rapid cadence of argument and persuasion, of apology and derision.

In the past few weeks the sound of this voice has become as familiar as any in his life. He fears he has spent more hours within its range than hearing those of his closest friends, his mother, his wife—no other voice in his life has gone on so continuously, so relentlessly. Yet this is a voice without clear features. Sometimes she is a girl of twenty, plump and good-natured; at others she wears a garish mask, features distorted by a pain bigger than ordinary life; in a book of press clippings, her expression is often angry, afraid, humiliated. But rarely the face in repose, as Lockwood has seen it, softened and humbled by forgiveness and time.

Claire has asked Lockwood about Mercè Casals. There is no one answer, he says. She was like anybody's grandmother. She was like any bejeweled crone on Rodeo Drive. She was an old woman fading, fading away. Mostly, her features changed. Her face often surprised him. Her eyes were some days dry and dull with cataracts. Other times, when she remembered a particular moment, they glistened with tears.

The long drive from the beach always brought Lockwood home with his mind brimming with the possibilities of the life he has been handed, but frustrated and impatient with the elusiveness of his story. Like a new lover, the scribbler cannot pull the sum total of his beloved's tastes and scents and features into a stable image.

"I liked you better before," Claire blurts out one morning over breakfast. She has started sitting at the far end of the table to give him the increased room he has demanded for the biographies, the books on opera, and the files of magazine articles he continually pores over. "You were not so moody. You were content."

Lockwood looks up from a scattering of clippings while the eggs and toast grow cold. "Ah, but I'm *happy* now, sometimes, anyway. Content is just one step away from resigned. I was getting resigned to being a drudge."

"More coffee?" Claire reaches for the carafe. She pours even as he's shaking his head. "Hell, Mark, drink coffee. It will help the foul mood you woke up in."

He holds his cup toward her. "Thank you. I've been a jerk."

"No, just somewhat self-absorbed."

"Just absorbed in the object."

"Of your affections?"

"Of my obsessions," he corrects glumly.

"Not the same thing?"

"Jesus, Claire. Do you really think I was in love with this woman? At eighty-something?"

"Well?"

"Actually, I like her nurse. She's from Mexico City. Very pretty. Twenty-six."

"Why are you telling me this?" She frowns.

"She thinks I'm a loser, actually," he adds cheerfully, as if to set her mind at ease. "I've got to run." He pushes back from the table. "The Señora always visited her ex-husband on Wednesday afternoons."

"Will they let you see him when they're expecting his wife?"

"I'll find out." He gathers the files and envelopes into a leather satchel.

⊶—⊦| I SHOULD HAVE DIED YEARS AGO.

Sometimes after talking for an hour or two, Mercè Casals would lean back in her favorite chair and turn up the volume of her singing, which had been gently flowing for hours. She would close her eyes and wait for the sound of her voice to spark a memory. Her singing soared on the wings of an aria, a lyrical Mozart or a powerful Verdi; her voice filled the room, animating the space with her overwhelming presence, a reckless C bringing out a glint of light here, a reflection there.

Just when he thought her concentration was drifting, her body would shudder with a sudden inhalation, her eyes would open, her lips smile at the recognition of a particularly poignant moment in the song, and she'd pick up the thread.

"Pep Saval bought me a Chinese doll. I kept it for years until it disappeared during one of my moves."

"He got it in China?"

"No, Casa Ribas, a very fine store in Sabadell. Her body was soft cotton and she was dressed in brocade with red-and-blue silk and golden threads woven throughout. Her head was made of porcelain—white as alabaster with all the details of her features rendered in the finest ink strokes. The delicate line of the eyebrows, the rosebud mouth, a perfect mole on her cheekbone. She had tiny pointy feet. Later I found out that the costume of the doll identified her as a prostitute. No, not as bad as that, a courtesan really, a concubine. Pep knew. It was like a statement from him."

"A doll, for Pep's little girl."

"Pep Saval became my first manager—as well as my chaperone, school teacher, voice coach, protector."

"How old did you say you were?"

"Eleven. It was all practically platonic. I was such a beautiful child that people couldn't help touching me. They reached out constantly to stroke my hair, rub my back, pinch my cheeks. Neither men nor women could keep away from me. Pep Saval would step in and gently remove me from their grip. Then at night, because I was a child and children need to be held, he would take me into his bed and pull me close.

"His skin in the muggy summer night glistened like copper. His chest was strong and the hair on it was springy. He smelled of dark tobacco and brandy, and later of a gypsy dancer's perfume. In the dark, when he smiled, two gold teeth gleamed. He would hold me until he thought I was asleep. Then he would slip out and spend the rest of the night with the dancer in the room next door. I could tell he was with her because I would hear his voice and her laugh and the jingle of bell bracelets. My hope was to make him feel as good lying with me. Then he wouldn't need to change beds in the middle of the night."

"You laugh, Señora?"

"Why are you surprised? I knew what to do for his good. The gypsy had left a husband and a child in Seville because her tips were better when she appeared to be available. I don't understand much about money, but I understood this much. She would trade the company of her family for money—how could she be anything but a gold digger to Pep Saval?

"By then I had figured out a thing or two about men. They just want to be touched, you know. Men don't want to do the work. At first, maybe, when they are young and a woman is new to them. But after a while, they want to lie back and be touched. I learned about touching men from Pep Saval. After a few nights, he stopped going to her."

"How long?"

"Turn that thing off. There are things I will not have on tape. You'll have to trust your memory."

"It's good material, Señora. You can edit afterward."

"Darling . . . I never call anyone darling unless I am angry at them. So do be on guard, you and your tape machine. If I say to you, 'That is enough for today, darling,' or 'Shut the machine off, darling, do it.'"

"Are we done, then?"

"No, but let's change the subject. Anything except men."

"Any fears, Señora?"

"To be old and weak and generally burdensome. To look like Jell-O with my clothes off. And like an overdressed blimp with them on. To have a brain that forgets and eyes that blur and a voice that cracks."

"Aging is unavoidable."

"I should have died years ago. At forty-seven, to be exact. I sang in *Madama Butterfly*, so petite, so happy-happy and sad-sad, so delicate and vulnerable and pitiful. I looked like Cio-Cio-San's mother in a kimono the size of a circus tent. I died on stage. I died in the reviews. I should have died in my hotel room."

"There were other more suitable parts where you triumphed still."

"How old are you, Mr. Lockwood?"

"Forty."

"Learn to sail. Read *Don Quixote*. Bathe in the Ganges. Finish this book. Live dangerously, but not past fifty-seven."

"I'll need years to accomplish those things."

"They won't get any easier. Finish up with your life before you go on too long, like me."

"You don't seem to be contemplating death. You are very much alive, Señora."

"Well, I do have a book deal."

"Yes, so do I. We should get back to work."

The Language of Hands

During those first years, I thought of Father every day. I searched for his face in the market crowds and in hostels, listening for his voice amid the lodgers bent over their cards. Along the road, I watched for the distinctive cadence of his walk, the rocking of his body, the puzzled frown of his expression as he ate, unable to enjoy the food until he had discerned its freshness and precise seasoning. I rehearsed what I would say to him: I would pummel his chest and kick his shins and demand to know why he had left me.

"Your father must be dead," Pep Saval tried to persuade me. "When he stepped out of the inn that day, he left you in my care with every intention to return in the evening after his customer visits."

"Don't say that."

"How else does someone disappear?" he said as if the answer were absurdly self-evident. "Señor Casals loved you and he wanted the best for you. That night, while on his way to see how our first lesson had gone, bandits came upon him on the road and killed him to steal the money he had collected from his sales."

I stared at him boldly.

"It would do you good to cry for your father," he said to me.

I remained sullen and dry-eyed, even after he scolded me for having a cold heart. He told me I would never become an artist if I was unable to shed tears.

We had been living in Vals, a town located along the fair circuit where Pep Saval found a ready harvest of easy winnings. We settled into two rooms in a dank, noisy building.

In the larger of the two rooms Pep Saval hung a sheet to divide the main brass bed where he slept from my narrow cot, on which rested a variety of dolls and plush animals. He had bought them for me as we went from town to town whenever I required quick relief from melancholy.

"We will respect each other's privacy," he declared. "This curtain is a sacred barrier. May I be damned to hell if I ever violate it." He crossed himself when he said this, even though I had never known him to acknowledge the existence of God or Joseph, Mary, and Jesus or the Saints. Except for the occasional scatological blasphemy, *Em cago en Déu*, when things did not go as expected, Pep Saval was happily godless.

The other room contained Pep's armchair, a table and two stools, a washbasin, a makeshift kitchen organized around a charcoal brazier where a pot of soup continually simmered. The Eternal Soup, Pep called it. I never saw him wash out the pot. When it ran low, he would add water, a couple of carrots, an onion, a potato. There was never meat or chicken in the soup because Pep claimed that animal fats coated the vocal cords and made the voice thick. With the soup there was always *pa amb tomàquet* made with stale rolls and soft ripe tomatoes.

I shuffled about the rooms in my stocking feet, shoulders slouched, eyes unfocused, red hair stringy and hanging over my face. Every morning while I stood at the small stove heating the milk for morning coffee, Pep Saval greeted me cheerfully: "*Bon dia,* Senyoreta Mercè." Then he'd lead me through the basic exercises. I went along grudgingly.

There surely was a hidden reason why this unruly child had landed in his care. Pep's life had been simple and unencumbered until he'd beaten my father at cards. The result of Father's bad luck had been Pep's losing his freedom to enjoy the rewards of a solitary life: to drink and fornicate and curse as exuberantly as only a single man can. I was a curious, skulking waif who had become the censor of his every movement.

Eventually, thoughts of Father receded, and I concentrated on the tasks that Pep Saval set for me. I drilled the pronunciation of German, English, French, and especially Italian by reading libretti. He assigned me deep breathing to increase lung capacity, and posture exercises that he promised would add centimeters to my height just from stretching the spine. "How can you be a queen if you slouch like an urchin?" he would scold.

Because I was still a child, he forbade me to sing to the fullness of my range. Still, if I sang recklessly, he would be caught in the experience when my voice would float on a high C-sharp. He sensed what it was like to be me at that particular moment listening to my own voice pour out as if with a will of its own, and the notes so pure and clear, a warm honey that flooded my mouth with a shocking sweetness.

Meanwhile, Pep Saval's vague intuition had grown into a conviction that his life would be dedicated to serving my gift. He would teach me, by example, to be a slave to my own talent. But even the most devoted servant needs a regular night out. Pep Saval found a game of *set i mig* at the nearby Café Jardí where he would earn enough from traveling innocents to pay the rent and keep the soup pot full.

As for me, when Pep Saval left in the evening, I felt as if a weight were lifted. I loved being free of his bullying, his smells of bay rum and cigar smoke, his vigilant gaze. With him away, I was free to brush the tangles out of my hair, comb it back and gather it at the nape with a silver clasp. I would open the score of Bellini's *Norma*, at the point where she confronts her lover Pollione and sings, *"Trema per te, fellon, pei figli tuoi, trema per me, fellon, ah per me!"* (Tremble for yourself, villain, and for your sons, tremble for me, villain, ah, for me!)

I would first declaim the words, standing erect in front of the mirror as befits the posture of the head priestess of the Druids defying the Roman invader and then, following the music, lift my voice into those mysterious forbidden registers. I loved to sing loudly, to open my chest and let my breath push the C out of my throat with so much pain and anger and shock all miraculously compressed into a single note. I was the priestess performing a secret ritual instead of the loneliest girl in the world living in two rooms and not attending school, with not a person in the world to care.

At night I stood in front of the window taking in the cool air, tinged with the smoke of charcoal burners and stoves. Pep Saval would have me shut the window to keep the haze out of my throat. But I was indestructible. I would sing out the window and let the world know who I was.

Vals was not the world. It was a mean little town with unpaved streets that were muddy from spring rains or dusty in the summer or rutted with ice and snow in the winter. The town boasted two spinning and weaving mills and one finishing plant that poured into the river a greenish-brown soup. In summer, families took the train ten kilometers upriver to the town of Oliva, which had no factories except for the press that collected the olives from the surrounding groves for the golden oil that was famous all over Catalonia.

For me, too, a Sunday outing to Oliva was the highlight of the week. On the esplanade outside the church, drummers and pipers would start the impromptu *sardanas*. Old women and married couples and girls would gather, seemingly out of nowhere, to form the circles. I would find a place in the innermost ring where the expert dancers raised their linked hands and set the count. Pep Saval, an awkward dancer, shuffled along the sidelines.

During the August festival to celebrate the year's pressing, there was an invasion of jugglers, acrobats, magicians, clowns. Musicians came all the way from Barcelona and Paris. A gypsy encampment settled outside Oliva within a cluster of wagons with flapping canopies and wooden wheels mired in the muddy clearing. Andalusian women with gold bracelets and necklaces jangling with their every move read palms at rough tables covered in threadbare velvet or dirty lace. Pep Saval brushed them away when they tried to sell him charms and amulets. Their hands would be all over him, picking bits of imaginary lint off his coat, smoothing out the wrinkles in his shirt, tugging at his belt, and sneaking into his pockets for loose change. He would triumphantly clutch one by the wrist until she surrendered the stray peseta. He laughed when they stared at his palm, affecting alarm or delight at what it revealed. Whatever he could anticipate happening the day after tomorrow was all the foretelling he needed.

However, the *señorita* in his charge had a whole life ahead of her, and a hand that had never been read. Here was the real mystery, not the fortunes of a man in the autumn of a battered life, but the fate of a girl with many years to come.

The gypsy held my palm up to her cloudy eyes and began a thin, keening wail. Suddenly she threw off my hand as if it were burning her fingers. I curled it into a fist. After that, there was no getting it to open for a second look. The gypsy's cries subsided. She shook her head as if she had just gazed into the most dire of fortunes. I curled my hand against the dry, wiry fingers that kept digging under my knuckles trying to pry it open. I kept my hand closed for days.

And for days, I was distracted, lost in an angry turmoil. When my hand did open to grasp something, the palm was red and marked with four deep wedges from my nails. Throughout my life, my marked palms would remind me of the door that had opened a crack and then slammed shut to reveal no more than a sudden glimpse of a black, fat-bellied spider clinging to the inside of my throat. It was all in the open hand, the line of life, the mound of love, the unformed M of death, the crossed paths of lust and loneliness. "Wait," the gypsy had called after me. "There is more."

Pep Saval kept trying to set me at ease. The gypsies were meddlesome women who fed off people's fear and greed and loneliness. "The more you fear your life, the more you will pay for the best possible fortune they can tell. Here are some pesetas. Go back. Tell the old busybody that I insist you be rich and famous and live to a fine old age and die a happy death in the midst of luxury in a foreign land. America will do fine. Ever thought of going to America? That is the place to die. Under big open skies, surrounded by grazing buffalo and the cries of eagles overhead. Don't die in Spain, all shriveled up on a wooden table surrounded by wailing old women, hovering about like crows, scheming to plunder whatever you'll leave behind. Believe me, you will be different. The rest of us, your father, the man you will marry, your friends and teachers and colleagues, will all die like lost dogs on strange roads. You, however, will die a queen. Go to the fortune-teller again. Show her your hand. That's what she will tell you."

WHAT'S A GHOST WITHOUT A CONFESSION?

Long after he'd given up waiting for a novel to unfold, and money was rolling in for words on toothpaste, insurance, and adolescent skin afflictions, Lockwood found himself caught up in someone else's story. He had been interviewing Mercè Casals for weeks when they reached an impasse. One moment she was wide awake and spinning a thread of her experience and the next with a nod she was out.

Lockwood waited for her to resume her narrative. He coughed lightly, clicked the pause and record buttons on his recorder, played back the last few words.

She woke up irritable after a few minutes. Staring at him across the room, her eyes seemed to question his presence. A frown creased her brow as if she were trying to recall who he was and why he was sitting in her living room. She picked up the notebook on her lap where she kept a list of the topics under discussion and read through the last few notes she had made.

"I think this is all a waste of time," she murmured. "There is no way I'm going to be able to tell you the whole story of my life. Too many details are lost. And one of these days, I'll fall asleep like this and you will think I'm about to wake up any minute, but I will die before the story is done, just to spite you."

"That would be tragic, Señora."

"Of course. What's a ghost without a confession?"

"I was not thinking of myself."

"*Mentiroso.*"

"The history of opera will not be complete without your story."

"Go on," she said with a pout.

"The great diva must sing the aria of her life."

"I hate that word 'diva.' Don't use it about me. It smacks of temper tantrums and petulance and petty cruelty. Callas and Tebaldi and Caballé and Ponselle and Moffo are divas."

"I've been listening. Just like you said. I took the tape of *Traviata* you gave me. I listen to it in the car. The more I drink of your Violetta, the thirstier I get."

Her lips formed a wistful smile. She toyed nervously with a large ring on her right index finger, two pearls laced together by a thread of tiny diamonds. Then her fingers traveled to the top buttons of her silk blouse. She undid one, then another, as if she were growing warm under the waning afternoon light that poured through the open windows of the terrace. Fine blue veins coursed under the skin. Lockwood looked away.

"What's the matter? Did I say something to make you nervous?"

"Nothing, Señora. I was admiring how the sunset was reddening the sky."

"And this made you blush? My, what a poet you are!"

"I wasn't aware that I was blushing."

She met his gaze and looked down at her chest. "Ah, my breasts embarrass you! I will be glad to cover up for your benefit."

"Please, Señora, don't mind me. I've spent too much time in the suburbs. I don't see many women who dress like you."

"How sweet of you. To play the part of the naive young man to my sophisticated woman of the world."

"Shall we get back to music?"

"Of course, we've got work to do, don't we?" She assumed an erect posture and briskly buttoned her blouse. "I'm glad you liked *Traviata*. There is more than one role that I'm famous for, you know. Tonight I will give you *Norma*."

"I look forward to hearing you."

"What the world must understand, Mr. Lockwood, is that my voice has had a life of its own. Naturally I take care of my throat and strengthen my breathing and learn every note and analyze every syllable in the phrasing. In the end the voice does what it wants. It's never hungry or thirsty, cold or hot, never sad or angry, guilty or innocent. It doesn't shop or gossip or tingle to another's touch. It just is what it wants to be. All I can do is open my mouth. If the voice wants to sink on the same notes where yesterday it soared, so be it. The voice rules. I am a bellows to make wind, vocal cords to make a vibration, a brain to remember words and notes."

"You are an artist."

She coughed lightly as if to clear her throat. "You must have gotten good advice when you were hired. Hollywood Hank probably said, 'Feed her ego. She'll spill her guts.' Is that what he said? That is his style."

"No. What he said to me was, 'You are nothing without Mercè Casals. She's the wonder. You are little more than a tape recorder that knows grammar and punctuation.' That's what he said, in so many words."

"You're more than that," Mercè said. "You listen."

Seeing the Voice

"Singing takes strength," Pep Saval would say. "You're an athlete lifting the world with the tiniest muscles in your body." It was all drills and exercises and breathing and stretching. I would learn to pronounce gracefully and precisely. Each day of the week was devoted to a different language. He would have me sing nonsense syllables, *perico-palote* and *cling-clang*, endlessly up and down.

"Faster," he would shout.

"Perico-palote-pica-piedra." I would glide up and down the scale until I thought I would faint.

"Breathe."

"Mamá me mima, mamá me mima."

"Smoother."

Sundays were for Latin. "The church will be your most generous employer," he would remind me. "There are only twenty important opera houses in the whole world, but twenty thousand churches. Every day there are funerals and christenings and weddings. Rich people think it pleases God to have singing in their services. You can be the instrument of their salvation."

Pep Saval had me memorize the Latin mass. He took me to church and made me sit through three or four services, culminating in high mass at noon, where there would be a choir and soloists.

"Watch the priests," he would tell me. "The good ones move like royalty. Through their performance they're telling us they own heaven right here on earth."

On some Sundays, Pep Saval would rouse me from bed with a *café con leche*. He would lay an acolyte's red cassock and white lace surplice over my thin body. "You will feel what the priest feels. Only then will you understand the mass."

He placed a board over the backs of two chairs, and on it he laid out the other objects he had bought which would remain special and somehow sacred because they were only to be used for my instruction in the ritual—a pewter goblet, a leather-bound *Don Quixote* to represent the Bible, a tin of Belgian butter cookies, an ankle bracelet of linked bells. He gave me a missal and told me to start reading. Then as I read, he would place his hands on my shoulders and push me like a doll around the makeshift altar, indicating when I was supposed to ring the bells for prayer, when the Bible should be moved, when to pour the wine and break the wafers for communion.

Pep Saval insisted that I could experience music where there was none. To me the words of the mass were exotic sounds. *Gloria in excelsis Deo. Et in terra pax hominibus bonae voluntatis.*

"*Ho-mi-nibus,*" he corrected.

"*Hominibus,*" I repeated.

"*Ho-mi-nibus,*" he said again, and again, holding firm my head and my body so I listened.

"I don't understand what I am saying."

Pep Saval let out a sigh. "What could be so hard to understand in words that have been repeated for thousands of years?"

I threw the missal at him. The booklet struck his chest as he was trying to catch it, and loose pages scattered at his feet. "I must know what the words mean," I said. "Otherwise I'm just a parrot."

Pages firmly gathered, Pep Saval pulled a chair from the dining table and set it up in the middle of the floor, facing the makeshift altar as he would a stage. He busied himself putting the missal back in order.

"From the beginning," he said.

"Kyrie eleison," I answered.

"Slowly," he said.

"Christe eleison."

He forbade many of the songs my father was so proud to have me sing. "They're too demanding for a girl," he explained. "This is not superstition. There are occasional breaks in your voice, almost invisible, like hairline cracks on porcelain. If you keep singing this crazy way, these tiny cracks will widen and you will sound like a crow before you're thirty. Nothing in the body lasts forever. But unlike eyesight that you can prolong with glasses, and ears that you can enhance with a hearing trumpet, your voice will no longer serve you if we don't allow it to heal now. There will be time enough to push later, when it will need to escape the chorus and find its way to the last rows of the balcony. For now, stick with folk songs. Learn how to think with your throat, let the tissue just beneath the surface find the best place for the notes. The easiest, gentlest movement along the vocal cords will produce the sweetest sound. Find feeling in your nature, not in volume. Sing softly and the audience will quiet down in order to hear you; sing loudly and you will have to make yourself heard above their chatter. Let them come to you."

I have never liked being told what to do. This has sometimes been a problem with directors and husbands, on stage and in the bedroom. In

Pep's case, I said yes to everything, but when he wasn't around, I sang whatever I wanted to sing, at the top of my lungs if I felt like it.

"There is something I want you to see," Pep Saval said one day. He pulled his battered black suitcase from under the bed and extracted very carefully an object wrapped in velvet. It was a gleaming, vaguely medical-looking steel rod with two distinct finger grips to hold it steady. At one end it had a small round mirror and at the opposite end a larger oblong one positioned to catch the other's reflection. "This thing will let you see where your voice comes from."

I shrugged. I knew where my voice came from.

"It is a laryngoscope," he explained. "The famous singer and teacher Manuel García invented it to see what caused the breaks in his voice. He figured if he could see where the cracks came from, then he might be able to heal his throat. And the throats of others, too."

"There is nothing wrong with my throat."

"No, and there was nothing wrong with Señor García's either. But I want you to see how tender and fragile that particular place is, the one that makes your voice."

"What does it matter what I see?"

"You need to respect your body. The more you know about it, the more you will care for it. When you look into your throat, you see that the part of you that sings is as independent and unwilled as your heart beating and your lungs breathing and your stomach digesting. The whole of your body is involved. The vibrations of every cell and the light that floods your eyes and the rush of blood in your veins are all woven into the music. Now, you can't see any of these things happening, but thanks to the scientific genius of Señor García, you can peer deep inside. You will see, and feel wonder."

What I felt that day was a gagging, choking response to the cold steel invading my throat. Pep Saval had me drink two full glasses of wine and kept trying until I surrendered my throat to the spoon-like mirror at the end of the rod. "Open as fully as you can," he told me. "Relax your throat as if you were yawning. If you don't learn to surrender, you will continue to choke your voice. The throat must learn to yield. It's not something that comes naturally. It has to be learned. Open wide and yawn," he insisted.

I looked up at the larger oval mirror above Pep Saval's hand, where I saw reflected the slow descent down the blotchy pink shaft of my throat mottled in shades of red and pink. "Keep breathing, child. You are feeling sleepy and relaxed and your mouth is opening in a yawn."

A moment later the vertical cleft that is the glottis appeared in the mirror. "Now look, my singing princess. This is you." Pep Saval explained in a hoarse whisper that the folds at either side were the vocal cords. "But they are cords only in that they vibrate when you sing, as sounds can be directed up and down a guitar string. It is the cords that govern volume, pitch, and intensity of your voice. This is where the voice is born. And when the cords are healthy and elastic, they have a mind of their own and let sound take over the whole throat so that you feel there is no throat at all, just voice, and the music that is its reason for being."

I was sitting on the chair that Pep Saval had tilted against the wall so that my open mouth and throat formed a single line and my eyes were looking straight up at the mirror. My heart quickened and with its increased pulse the folds around the glottis throbbed as if caught by a rush of excitement. I found it hard to believe that this strange gaping thing, all mucusy and wet and raw, was part of me. I felt I was looking at some dangerous slippery creature that had found its way inside my throat, and which common sense dictated must be expelled at once. I gagged at the thought, and the sudden constriction of my throat made me choke on the long instrument. I flailed for breath and pushed up blindly against Pep Saval's hand. I felt the burn of a slap, first one then another and another. As I cried out in shock, my throat suddenly relaxed and Pep swiftly withdrew the rod.

For the rest of my life I would remember the sudden cold pain and the panicked choking and that last glimpse of the wet, throbbing thing with all the substance of an oyster. As hard as I tried to cough it out, it was forever ensconced inside my throat. This was the Voice, *"La Veu,"* like that in capitals.

Years later, I realized that the praise was not really for me but for the organism I had seen inside me. If I earned a lot of money it was so I could take care of the moist, willful beast that lived like a prisoner in the cave of my throat. I was barely the prisoner's keeper. Together, this odd pair could hardly aspire to a normal life—the one that could be seen was not the one that could be heard, and the one that could be heard was never to be seen. It was the keeper's secret. This gaping, shy mollusk had its own secrets as well, but they were so well-guarded the keeper never knew them.

⊶—┨ I'M ATTRACTED TO WOMEN WHO DIED SAD.

Lockwood sleeps in Anaheim and dreams he's in Barcelona. In his house it's 1999; in the dream it's 1937. Beside him lies his wife; when he reaches out he touches Mercè Casals. He is Nolan Keefe, twenty years old, a Lincoln Brigade volunteer on leave from his regiment. He and Mercè Casals lie quietly on a mattress pushed into one corner. He speaks Spanish haltingly, and the only English she knows is memorized out of Handel's Messiah. They don't yet know how deep their love will be. They cling to each other seeking safety from the surrounding chaos. Her body fits into his compliantly, her hips press against his groin. In the dream Nolan makes himself think of other things rather than let his lust frighten the girl away. He thinks of baseball. DiMaggio and Gehrig. The Yankees beat the Dodgers. The white sphere flies over the expanse of pure green. It's the perfect example of the unpredictability of the universe. Prepare to meet the ball at any moment, be vigilant, expectant, because you never know when it will fall toward you. The sparse geometry of the game stills his passion. He falls asleep with his body spooning Mercè's. Lockwood knows that is what Nolan Keefe must have done.

He awakens to insistent electronic beeping. Claire hands him the phone. "It's for you." She says it like it's his fault that the call has blasted both of them out of their slumber.

"I'm asleep," he says hoarsely.

She places the phone on the pillow next to his face. "I told him you'd call back. He wants to talk to you now, not later."

"Who?" He hopes it's not who he fears.

"He said he was a friend of Mercè Casals. He wasn't clear." She adds with a shrug, as if signaling that some human behavior is beyond her understanding, "I think it's Hank."

"Claire," he groans, "please tell him to leave a message."

Claire nods. A high-pitched voice is heard squawking in her hand. "I think he heard you." She picks up the phone and points it at him while the voice continues to buzz like a bug caught in a jar. "He's asking what time he can send for the tapes."

"Tell him I'll drop the recordings by his office this afternoon. That I'll need a receipt." He adds this last point because he thinks it makes the promise of delivery credible.

Claire repeats the message. She hangs up and looks at Lockwood with a helpless shrug. "He says thanks very much, that he'll come by for the stuff at noon."

"He doesn't believe me."

Lockwood gets up, rushes into his study, and sweeps the pile of cassettes, hundreds of them, a thousand spoken arias, the words of a lifetime, into his satchel, along with the files from Mercè's apartment. He lugs the bag to his car and slips it underneath the driver's seat. Back inside, he pulls jeans and two shirts from the closet, grabs socks and underwear out of his dresser, then gathers toothpaste, brushes, comb, razor and crams everything into a gym bag.

Claire stands at the bedroom door, not quite blocking his exit but forcing him either to talk to her or brush past without a word. "So, what is happening now?"

He stops in the middle of zipping the bag, his fingers frozen in mid-motion, his head still down. His eyes rise to meet hers. "Claire, darling, I know." He makes a pacifying gesture with the palm of his hand. "I owe you an explanation," he says.

"Good. That would be wonderful."

"But not now. I'll call you." He looks down to finish closing the bag with a quick snap of the zipper. When he looks up, Claire has disappeared. The way is clear. When Hollywood Hank shows up he'll plead and argue that it's for everyone's good that he get the interviews. Lockwood will receive payment for services rendered as soon as the matter comes to an amicable conclusion. A kill fee in the hand, Hank will whisper, is worth two deals on the run.

Lockwood keeps glancing at the rearview mirror, searching through the traffic bunching up behind him. He's got at least four hours on Hollywood Hank, plenty of time before he has to worry about the snub-nosed, yellow-eyed black Porsche 944 gaining on him. Time enough to find Perla.

Her apartment building is one of many two-tiered, motel-like structures situated around the hospital complex. The layout seems open and vulnerable; an intruder such as himself is free to roam up and down the halls.

He stands before her door and tightens his grip on the satchel. He feels like a salesman. "You're just the woman I was looking for," he offers earnestly when Perla opens the door after the third knock.

She is looking very much like a nurse, in green scrubs, brisk on her way out. "Why doesn't that make me happy?" she asks.

"Can we talk for a minute?"

"I'm due at the hospital. I'm taking care of a terminal, a wheezer, a fighter, a spitter, a difficult case."

"You've got to help me," he blurts. "I have the Señora's tapes," he adds when she looks at him uncertainly. He raises the satchel and gives it a loud slap. "Hollywood Hank and Alonzo Baylor would kill for this."

"I'm done working for the Señora," she says with a shrug. "Her body is at the Rossini funeral home. Go see her. She looks beautiful."

"I was there yesterday morning. Those Rossinis do a nice job." He pauses and searches for the right words. "The Señora may be gone, but I still have her life to save. I need to hide the files."

"In my apartment?" She looks at him with disbelief.

"For a day or two until I figure out what to do."

This is intimacy beyond his expectations. Perla's bedroom is fragrant with the clean smell of her hair, of her skin. She slides the case under her mattress. With the help of a couple of books and a fat terrycloth robe strewn on the blue quilt, the bag's presence, barely evidenced by a bump at the center of the bed, is well disguised.

It takes Mark a moment to take in the things on her walls—posters of the unfortunate Ophelia and Juliet and Desdemona, Posada's La Catrina baring a toothy grin under the brim of her flowery hat, photos of Janis Joplin, Mama Cass, Maria Callas, Sylvia Plath, Anne Sexton, plus Frida Kahlo with a monkey.

"I'm attracted to women who died sad," she says in response to his look.

"Do you think the Señora was unhappy when she died?"

"Actually not. I have an image of her reaching an orgasm under the Jacuzzi's jets, just floating along, letting the happy stream bubble up between her thighs, like a thousand little tongues nudging and kissing and tickling her to one orgasm after another. She was a multi, you know."

He shrugs skeptically. "It's not in the interviews."

"Oh, I think she would have gotten to it. She really did want to reveal everything to you. By the time she died she was just a memory away from floating above the earth."

"Actually," he says with renewed authority, "there are memories that would keep her tethered to earth forever."

"You're talking about the war. It happened so long ago, she must've gotten over that in time."

Lockwood takes a deep breath. "I keep listening to her stories. You can't separate the Señora from the Spanish Civil War."

Touched by Fire

If you've ever lived through a war, you know you don't come out of the enmity among friends and brothers and neighbors without some shame. There was a shortage of food. If I sang for butter and coffee, I felt shame. If I flirted so I could get a permit to see a friend in the hospital in Lleyda, I felt shame. If I vomited when I had to break his bones in order to dress him after he died, I felt shame.

I was fifteen when Pep Saval took me to Barcelona and enrolled me to study with the famed Anjelica Brullet. I would live at the Casa de Dispesa, a rooming house that served as a safe harbor for girls whom the war had dislocated from their families. Lugging my scuffed suitcase, its lid bound shut by a leather belt, I moved into the *pensión*. The complex honeycomb of sunless rooms with makeshift partitions and dark hallways leading to a couple of cramped bathrooms chilled my spirit. Pep Saval had begun to disappear from my life.

It was July 1937. Barcelona had been quaking with the force of the militias' growing strength against the army. Bands of young men and women in fashionably proletarian overalls, denim caps, and red kerchiefs were rising into a new workers' elite. Random groups would gather spontaneously and tramp up and down the boulevards, unfurling banners outside factory gates, chanting in front of the banks, the newspapers, the cathedral. *Strip the bankers. Hang the factory owners. Burn the priests.*

Barcelona had gone red. Scarlet handkerchiefs and banners and ribbons fluttered from trees and light poles and rooftops. Flags denoting various political affiliations in varying patterns of red and black hung from balconies, flapped from the backs of trucks, and waved at the heads of the impromptu parades that turned up around every corner. There were the diagonals of the republican left, the hammer and sickle, the muscular typefaces of the various political parties, the POUM Marxists and the FAI anarchists.

For the first time in Spain, women were involved in politics; they joined in the marches, striking with the men in the spinning mills, the bakeries, and the ironworks. Civil war had erupted in confusion amid a strafing of shouted slogans and flying leaflets. There had been a *pronunciamiento:* General Franco had declared the Republic in shambles, had said that the president and the congress had lost control of orderly life. The speech played on the radio, over and over throughout the night, as if to be made true through repetition. The next day the young socialists and anarchists and communists poured into the streets and declared the uprising a failure. They portrayed the cocky little general as a strutting, lisping windbag whose pronouncement had energized them to rise in renewed democratic fervor.

Out in the street, I felt self-conscious in my modest cotton skirt and white blouse with lace collar and cuffs, which I had sewn myself. I was tall and large-boned; I wore my copper hair in a single braid; I carried myself with grace and presence as a result of Pep Saval's coaching. ("Nobody will want to recognize your singing at first. You must learn to claim dramatic space with every step, every look, every breath.")

When I was not studying under la Brullet, I was to attend sewing classes with my friend María del Mar. The streets were much too interesting for us to close ourselves in with our squinting classmates and the teachers of the sewing academy. That afternoon the Rambla was particularly festive, the flower stands and bird sellers and news kiosks teeming with the latest issues of *Vogue* and *Elle* and *Harper's Bazaar* direct from America.

We sat at a sidewalk café table and sipped lemon seltzers. The cost of a drink served at one of the outdoor marble-topped tables was more than when served at the bar. Still, it was worth the extra money to be seen by the young fellows marching down the Rambla singing "Els Segadors" at the top of their lungs.

Toward evening, the hot summer afternoon shook off its languor and awoke to frenzied chirping from the bird sellers' cages. The crowd along the Rambla abandoned its leisurely strolling for a restless pace. Swarms of students and union workers could be heard chanting as they tramped up from the Columbus obelisk and down from Plaza Catalunya to converge at Carrer Garcés. Like some coherent organism, the marchers coiled purposefully around the corner toward Iglesia de la Enseñanza. A cool overgrown garden shielded the graceful Gothic church and convent where Sacred Heart nuns watched over girls' early schooling.

The crowd of union members had swelled with housewives doing the marketing and children fresh out of school and men who had left their posts in the offices and shops near the center of the city. I started out walking along the margins of the throng, but I was soon drawn into the rhythm of the march. Something terrible and strange was happening just ahead, beyond view.

The nuns are coming! The nuns are back from the dead!

I squeezed through the crowd to the plaza in front of the church.

A moment before, militias had stormed the crypt where the ancient fathers and mothers of the church, along with several town notables, had been laid to rest. Niches had been pried open and the dead exhumed. Just ahead, a dozen mummified nuns leaned against the church walls, poised stiffly outside the church, like sentries ready to brave the pressing crowd. Some were stripped naked, revealing leathery bodies, folds of skin and flesh hanging from protruding bones. Others wore their habits, thin and ragged from decay, their remains flaking in the summer sun, limbs not quite attached to joints, heads lolling off shoulders, hands and arms disconnected from sockets. The tissue and fabric that crumbled from the bodies became dust under the hot winds that swirled dead leaves and ashes and shreds of political leaflets.

Three nuns had been positioned as if in conversation, heads tilted toward one another to hear better, one's arms crossed, the others' hands joined or lifted palm to palm in a piety at odds with their gaping grins. Standing in front of the entrance, as if to welcome the faithful, was the mother superior herself, a rosary coiled around her yellowed hand, her bald skull emerging from the rich folds of the bishop's new gold-and-rose vestments in which she had been dressed. I recognized, hanging from her thumb, the drooping balloon which Pep Saval had claimed was one of the great moral advances of the civilized world.

Some of the older women and men in the crowd pressed back, covering their mouths with handkerchiefs dipped in cologne, as if afraid that some germ could be resurrected and infect them with this new madness.

The church was washed by the waning light, its bells long silent; an uneasy yawn seemed to emanate from its stillness. Suddenly a scattering of shouts sounded from the sacristy door. Hoarse male voices echoed in the square. The crowd recoiled a few stumbling steps to clear a path.

"Here he comes!" a man shouted. "Make way for the scoundrel!"

An old priest clutched the hem of his black soutane above his thin white shins and ran frantically out the door. Mercè recognized Father

Anselmo. He'd been a reliable fixture at mass, an abrasive nag who frequently warned the faithful against the evil in Marx and his godless cohorts, his bony Adam's apple quivering as he harangued with a voice that rubbed like sandpaper, sentencing automatic excommunication for joining the Party.

He paused uncertainly. Then, his eyes searching the crowd for help, he started to run again. Three men, proud in their workers' overalls, chased after him, teasing him with their red kerchiefs, blocking his escape in one direction, then in another. They yelled, *"Toro! Toro!"* as if performing tricks at a bullfight.

When they finally caught him, two held him by the arms while the other showered gasoline on his head and down onto his robe. The priest was panting, trying to breathe fresh air through the fumes. "I baptize you Francisco Franco, in the name of the father, the son, and the whore of a mother that delivered you," the man yelled to the crowd.

A white-haired official in a blue double-breasted coat buttoned tightly over a starched white shirt and tie waddled self-importantly to the group. Holding a burning taper, he approached the priest, who stared at him through bulging eyes. Lowering the candle like a wand, almost delicately, the man touched the flame to the priest's soutane. The men released the priest and jumped back.

A column of yellow smoky fire engulfed Father Anselmo as he ran blindly around the plaza, lurching and then turning in place like a dervish. He clawed at his face, tearing out layers of burning skin that clung in shreds to his fingers and sent new flames dancing up his arms. The space around him was darkened by oily plumes that smarted my eyes and burned the back of my throat. The cloying smell of charred flesh was both new and strangely familiar. I felt the heat on my cheeks. I couldn't help thinking of the tiny lamb chops that Pep Saval occasionally grilled over red coals. I wanted to vomit.

There were some initial faint cheers from a few in the crowd. Then, as if the frenzy of the moment were contagious, the excitement spread and everyone was laughing and yelling as the flames surged. The priest ran in a spiral, desperately plunging into the crowd, which opened up and then closed behind him and reformed the circle a prudent distance away. A boy of about twelve used a broom handle to push the priest away, sending him in a different direction. The priest ran back and forth until his bandy legs would carry him no farther and he fell to the ground, his body folding protectively into a fetal curl. Someone came upon him and, almost charitably, as if to end his misery, added more gasoline to the blackened body. Flames and oily billows erupted again. No one dared move until there remained only a smoldering heap in the middle of the plaza.

The violence was happening all over the city. In many cities. Even in smaller towns. It was a madness. I had to look away, as we now look away from AIDS and gangs and meth dealers in the schools. There was a war going on. Awful things were being done by everybody. I was too busy trying to be a normal seventeen-year-old. I was free for the first time in my life since my father had left me with Pep Saval. All of a sudden, I was on my own and the feeling was tinged with danger and excitement and anticipation. All kinds of things were suddenly possible for me, and I wasn't about to let a war ruin my life.

WHERE ARE THE TAPES?

The wrong people keep trying to get hold of Lockwood these days. They beep his pager and his cell phone, leave messages on his voice mail and on Perla's answering machine. Suddenly, he has a passel of writing assignments. No time, he says. I'm writing the story of my life.

Most insistently, Hollywood Hank wants to know why nobody was home when the courier showed up to pick up the tapes. "Where the hell are you? Where are the tapes?" he keeps asking, merely irritable at first, but later his voice straining with frustration. "I paid for those tapes. I paid for Mercè Casals' story. And I paid for you." Lockwood sees him red-faced, bug-eyed, and skew-haired, jerking his blue silk tie loose, sweat circles dampening his Irish linen shirt.

The phone rings from extensions all over Lockwood's house: beeps in the kitchen, bells in the basement, buzzes in his study, and chimes in the bedroom. He cannot get away from the phone. He holds Claire by the arm, raises a finger to his lips as the answering machine goes through its clicking paces after five rings.

"This is Hank Holloway. Please, Mrs. Lockwood," he says. "I want you to think of me as your friend. I don't know what you have discussed with Mark. But trust me, your husband is way out of his league here. All I'm saying at this point is that you and I have things to talk about. Not true for Lockwood and myself; communication has broken down between us. A shame, too, because at one point I said to myself, 'There is real rapport with this guy; he's not an egocentric jerk, but a fellow one can reason with, a true professional who knows the value of a client, and a check.' Boy, was I ever wrong about him. He's turned out to be a two-faced, double-crossing snake in the grass. I don't envy you, being married to him. Anyway, I'm sure you are by far the superior human being of the couple, a person of sense and sensibility, a rational, balanced woman of the new age. I know your type. You work out, you have a juicer, you subscribe to Oprah's *O* magazine and to *Vanity Fair*. You're the babe-with-brains type. I ask you, from one rational being to another: Please pick up or I'll just keep on talking until I run out of time. I don't care if neither of you wants to hear what I have to say. The truth of the matter is that Lockwood is way, way out of his depth on this issue. It's an important point that bears repeating. The league I have in mind includes names that I'm not at this point able to reveal because of strict confidentiality agreements. And because the principals involved are afraid your husband may take violent action against them. These are names that you would recognize if I spelled them out for you. But I will give you a few hints. The author of *The Authorized Biography of Mercè Casals*, currently in progress, is no mere scribbler. We are talking a heavyweight household name here. A muscle writer. There is buzz of a million-dollar advance. Which is not at all unusual for this particular writer, whose name rhymes with Gonzo Taylor. There is talk of a bidding war among three publishers whose names I'm not at liberty to disclose. These are the giants of the publishing world, the editors of which would not give your husband the time of day even at the height of his glory days as a star MFA at some writing school. You want to know what publishers I'm talking about? I know you do. I can't tell you, but I'm sure you can guess. Think big. You won't be far wrong. Think of a flightless bird with webbed wings and feet who inhabits Antarctica. Think of the company that gave you Woody Woodpecker. Think of Bill Sorrow, whose editor is not called 'the sphinx' for nothing. Need I say more? These are major deals your husband is gumming up by hanging on to those tapes. It is futile of him to do so. Nobody will get behind a book by a nobody, even if he did have hours of one-on-one chitchat with the dead fat-lady subject of our collective concerns. That material in itself is worth nothing. It was her name on the book your husband was going to write, which I understand he had not even started when his subject came to her untimely end. That name would have sold books. But now with our heroine's final breath, we've gone from a big publication to a posthumous work by an unknown ghost. And make no mistake about this: Even without those tapes my guy can still write a Big Book. This man is a power writer, a sausage-fingered, ham-fisted keyboard banger. Once he gets his money and he's off the blocks, he can deliver six hundred pages, three hundred thousand words, ten pounds of manuscript, a couple of gigabytes in about four months. Give or take a few weeks for fact-checking and copyedit and our book will be on the best-seller lists before your hubby is done listening to those tapes. Nevertheless, I am willing to propose a settlement, amicable and productive for all parties concerned. I know that my book-deal makers will come to terms quicker if there is no question that our pugilistic keyboard jabber, the aforementioned Jones-o Smiler, has the wonder singer's own words to work from. We need to talk, of course. But all your hubby has to do is hand over those tapes and sign a letter saying he has no intention of writing any book, fiction or otherwise, based on

Mercè Casals or Nolan Keefe or Prince Liviu Gregoriu or (what the hell, we've got an investment to protect here!) even opera in general. After five years, of course, he can write about anything he wants. Lockwood does the letter, I do the check. He gets the most money he's ever gotten, without having to write a word. Nothing could be simpler. Nothing could be sweeter than instant cash without the brain bash. So, dear Mrs. L., if your lamebrained, cheese-flinging, hack-hearted scribbler is around and listening to this, tell him not to be a principled loser. He had a nice ride chatting up Mercè Casals, *and* her nurse, as you may well know by now, but the time has come to collect his chips and go on to his next game. He can keep the memories, he can keep the nurse, but he just can't keep the tapes. He even gets to keep some money, a kill fee as it were, out of which I'm willing to make an exception and not collect my usual fifteen percent. It's all net between him and the IRS. *How* much, we still need to discuss, but we're thinking five figures would be adequate. Really, middle five figures. I'm truly sorry to be carrying on like this, but if your scribble-happy husband likes to listen to tapes, then he's going to get an earful on this one. My voice is not going away; every time you click the play messages I'll be filling in the gaps, dangling non sequiturs, trailing off into the distance. And it's not all good news, either. I mean, it's good news if he deals with us. If he doesn't, we can still get those tapes. Make no mistake. The lead players in this town always get what we want. Please do not construe this as a threat, but we have ways to relieve him of what he doesn't own. I can slam down court orders on the knuckles of all ten of his typing fingers. I can send professional persuaders—lawyers, locksmiths, lien servers. I can sue him for the indentured servitude of your unborn children, his mother's memory, a pound of his flesh—what else have you got? I can get that, too: home, car, your womb for hire. Clearly for him to risk all for the dubious possibility of turning the musings of a crazy old lady into a work of cultural elitism that won't sell five thousand copies is idiocy bordering on tomfoolery. I'm being too harsh, you might say? Not by half, little lady. In the end those tapes mean nothing in your husband's hands and are gold in ours. I take it I am explaining myself to your satisfaction? Feel free to ask questions if there are any doubts in your mind. The number to call, toll-free, day or night, is 1-800-MY-AGENT. Ask for your friend Hank Holloway. Seven days a week, twenty . . ."

His voice is abruptly cut off and the red message light keeps blinking frantically, saying in luminous code, *Listen! Listen! Urgent shit for playback!* Neither Lockwood nor his wife wants to touch the machine for fear that Hollywood Hank's endless spiel will play again. Yet the blinking red light is a constant reminder that threatening powers lie in wait just outside the door, at the other end of the phone line, down the road.

"I'd better go," he says as he embraces his wife.

"Where will you be?"

"The race is on. I'll be holed up somewhere doing ten solid pages a day until this thing is finished."

"Will you call?"

"They can tap a phone."

"I need to know where you are," she pleads.

"It's better that you don't know."

"Great. Pull out my fingernails. There's nothing I can say that will stop the pain."

"I'll check in from pay phones. We'll have a code. Don't answer the phone unless it rings three times in succession, one ring each time. Then you'll know it's me."

"I can't believe we're talking like this."

"I know. The house could be bugged."

"No, what I'm saying is that this is nuts."

"Meanwhile, don't open the door to anyone."

"Fine." She nods glumly, as if she is already too tired to resist the melodrama brewing in Lockwood's mind.

"The Señora trusted me with her life. I cannot abandon it to some hack," he says, his eyes darting about him. "Her life is now my life."

The novelty of his agent chasing *him* has worn thin. Lockwood calls Holloway's office at two in the morning from a pay phone; caller ID will show him to be about a hundred miles from anywhere. "Hey, Hank? This is Mark Lockwood returning your call. Sorry I didn't find you. I'll be in and out myself through the rest of this lifetime. But maybe we can meet up in the hereafter."

Lockwood has decided the safest place for the satchel is with him at all times. It makes him look and feel like a man with a purpose, rather than an unemployed guy killing time at a café. He cradles the bag like a baby while he sleeps. He squeezes it between his legs while he eats. It rests beside him while he drives. Occasionally, he will pull out a cassette and play a random segment from the life of Mercè Casals. As he listens, he grows increasingly possessive of the grand story he has been entrusted with.

He stops by Perla's apartment and talks her into a walk down Ocean Boulevard. He is exultant, feeling that they are more than friends—they are accomplices and partners and potential lovers. The touch of her fingers is so exciting it almost makes him forget the bag in his other hand. He spies his reflection in shop windows, happy beside Perla, and can hardly believe the couple that rises out of the sidewalk and bounces back at him. At any moment he expects her image to vanish, and all he will be holding will be the satchel. To have both the Señora's story and the girl is the height of good fortune.

Lockwood leads her to a bench on the edge of the beach. Ahead, the rhythmic crash of the surf against big gray rocks masks the silence that occasionally yawns between them. He rests his arm on the satchel between them as if it were a child they were protecting. The scene has a distinct flavoring of domesticity, a shared understanding beyond the need for words.

"We should be paying attention, shouldn't we?" he asks. "I want to remember this day with special clarity when we are no longer together."

She shakes her head emphatically. "No, *querido*. I don't think we should consider this a memorable moment as such."

"More of an inadvertent moment of awkwardness?" he ventures apologetically.

"Less than that, a casual break."

He can feel Perla retreating from him. "We could get together tomorrow when we go visit Nolan Keefe again. This time we will definitely have a glass of wine by the ocean."

"Poor Nolan Keefe. We're using him in all kinds of ways, aren't we? I think you're much too married to come out with your sexual intentions directly. The idea of screwing around is enough to make you hyperventilate. In any case," she pulls her hand away, "holding hands seems so adolescent."

They have kicked their shoes off and dug their toes in the sand around the bench and watched the moon, a big silvery disk with all its wrinkles, craters, and pocks thrown into distinct relief against the clear black sky. Lockwood turns to Perla suddenly, as if unable to contain the thoughts that crowd his mind. "I know what you are thinking."

"What am I thinking?"

"My intentions."

"I should know what they are?"

"They're to have sex with you."

"Why don't you just come out and say it?"

"I think I just did."

"You think."

"I didn't?"

"Only you know for sure."

"I suppose I could grab you and throw you on the beach." He takes a breath to still the tremor in his voice.

She dismisses the whole idea with a shrug. "You have one hand in a death grip around the case handle."

"I could start with one small but potentially significant gesture," he says. "I could use this hand to brush the hair off your face and then feel your skin on my fingertips."

"Yes, you could do that," she agrees seriously. "There would not be much commitment in such a gesture. It would be easy to withdraw your hand and then go on as if nothing had happened. As if you hadn't touched me at all."

"Such a small gesture. Hardly the stuff of adultery."

"A natural response to this moment, to the silence under the surf and the lateness of the hour."

"To the moon."

"Explain that to your wife."

"Let's not bring her in."

"Shall we make believe she doesn't exist? Fine, touch me. And don't for a moment think of your wife. I won't think of her either."

She turns toward him boldly. In the moonlight, her eyes are more violet than blue, the details of the black pupils and the striations of her irises as sharp as crystal.

HELLO, I'M THE SEÑORA'S NUMBER-ONE FAN.

Lockwood left his house a week ago. He has rented, under the assumed name Sherman Sailer, the apartment next to Perla's, which he has furnished from the Salvation Army store with a futon, a vintage La-Z-Boy, a steel office desk, and a filing cabinet. The surface of the desk is scarred with glass rings and ink stains and a dozen notches evenly spaced along the edge. The tubular chair with a flowery plastic cushion he borrowed from Perla's dinette set. Glossy fan-club pictures and press clippings of Mercè Casals are tacked to the walls. By calling it his garret he endows the shabbiness of the place with a bohemian dignity.

Lockwood keeps the satchel open when he's writing. A boom box on the desk spins out Mercè Casals' voice. The words drone on whether he's paying attention or not. Occasionally, he will be tapping away on his laptop, and a thought unrelated to the subject at hand will push him in a different direction with hardly a pause in his often disjointed re-creation of the Señora's life.

At other times the flow turns to sludge. He pushes the chair back and rests his feet on the desk and listens to the Señora's voice. Eventually she says something that will get him writing again.

Lockwood keeps the blinds of the apartment shut and, except for a black gooseneck shining dimly over the desk, the lights off. A battle is raging outside and his only coherent strategy is to duck out of the fray. He hears steps in the hallway, pounding on Perla's door, muffled curses. Lights are snapped shut, the cassette player is clicked off. They are out there: Baylor's research hacks and Hollywood Hank's lawyers.

Today a glimpse between the drapes reveals a tall man in a leather coat. A tangle of blond curls crowns a vaguely familiar face with an aquiline nose, pale skin, and a square jaw. He has been waiting outside Perla's door for the past hour, occasionally buzzing her doorbell as if sheer insistence might cause her to materialize. Lockwood knows that Perla is at the hospital working long hours with another terminal. He expected the man to go away after getting no response to his rings. Instead, the stranger leans back on the hallway railing, lights cigarettes, and stares vacantly in the direction of the parking lot. From the back, the smoke rising above his head makes it look as if his bushy hair is smoldering. His eyes sweep the nearly empty length of asphalt looking for Perla's truck. Lockwood guesses he is paid by the day. By early evening, a drizzle begins to fall. Lockwood loses sight of the man as he leans against the wall, away from the rain. Not being able to see him increases the aura of the man's menace.

A few minutes after six, Perla's red pickup swings into the parking lot. Finally, she has turned over to another nurse the oxygen tubes and feeding tubes and Demerol tubes of a real Hell's Angel who had the misfortune to be sideswiped by a semi. "Hang in, there, Mr. Roswell," she cheered him. "I'll be back *mañana*."

Lockwood watches her pull her leather jacket over her head and run in the rain, skipping around puddles, nearly slipping on the slick pavement, finally crossing the parking lot and climbing the stairs to the second story. Even as he worries about her, he finds delight in the long, even strides of her running, easy like a barefoot child's race across a meadow. He wants to rush out to the railing and call out a warning: *Ambush. Bad guy on the horizon. Thug in the shadows.* But, it's Lockwood they are after. He expects the man will lose interest in her once she assures him that she hasn't seen Lockwood lately, doesn't know what tapes they are talking about, has never heard of Hollywood Hank. She will do this with great aplomb.

From the hallway just outside his door there's a rumor of conversation, not angry or excited as he might have expected, just greetings, comments on the weather, and then Perla's soft laugh. Her door closes and there is silence. Lockwood presses his ear against the wall that divides the two apartments. He tries to make sense of the murmurs from the other side.

He extracts the cassette that has been playing and replaces it in its box, which in turn goes inside the satchel that he buckles up and locks and sticks behind the garbage can under the sink.

After about twenty minutes he wonders why Hollywood Hank's henchman has not left Perla's apartment. He puts on a raincoat and walks down to the parking lot to stand in the rain a few moments, then climbs the stairs back to the second-story hallway; he doesn't want to look like the guy next door. He takes a deep breath and raps bravely on her door.

Inside, the voices stop. "Oh, hi," he says tentatively when Perla opens the door. He peers around her shoulder and sees the man sitting on the rug, legs stretched out, his back against the front of the couch. "I didn't realize you had company," Lockwood murmurs, taken aback by the visitor's familiarity.

"You're in time for wine," Perla says brightly.

The man eagerly pushes himself off the floor and reaches to shake Lockwood's hand. "I'm in luck," he says. "You're the writer!"

"And you are . . . ?" Lockwood takes in the green velvet pants, the gaucho boots, the black silk shirt. He clasps the other's hand.

"Hello, I'm the Señora's number-one fan," he announces. "Orson La Prima. I was at the visitation. But you probably don't recognize me. I looked somewhat different."

Lockwood tries to remember the day, and the image of the six-foot Violetta, lip-synching to a boom box, takes shape in his mind. "Right. You do look different."

"I'm not a full-time drag artist. It's a hobby."

"Sit, sit," Perla invites, cheerfully patting the couch. "We were just talking about you."

"Well, not really about *him*," Orson corrects.

"No, about our Señora. But wishing you were here."

"If only we could wish her back to life," Orson says. "I'd give up all my wishes for that single one."

Lockwood finally takes a deep breath. "You're not a lawyer or a summons server." He shrugs off the wet raincoat and drapes it over a stool in the kitchen. Perla pours him a glass of wine. "Why were you waiting out there for over an hour?"

The three fall suddenly quiet. Perla stands in the middle of the room. "Orson is the Señora's greatest fan," she announces.

Orson nods emphatically. "*Número uno.* Ever since I saw her for the first time, at the Met. I was eleven." He adds, "I've seen the Señora on stage twenty-three times. I own about a hundred recordings, covering recitals, compilations, full operas. *Quel horreur!* I've spent a fortune. You two are the closest I've been to her."

"It's a pleasure to meet one of the true believers," Lockwood says.

"That's me. I get into bar fights with Tebaldi twits and Moffo mafiosi too stuck in the past to recognize that La Señora was greater."

"How do you compare them, anyway?" Lockwood is thinking like a writer again.

"Divas come in flavors." Orson glances under arched eyebrows from Lockwood to Perla. "Distant unrealizables, present unreachables, legendary unknowables. We will never hear another Jenny Lind or Nellie Melba. One can admire them and at the same time worship the dearly departed Casals."

"To La Señora." Lockwood raises his glass. He takes a long drink of wine and gratefully feels a warmth settle at the center of his chest. He is in love. With Perla. With Orson La Prima. And with the memory of Mercè Casals.

A Wartime Romance

The first time I heard Nolan Keefe sing was in 1937. He had a brilliant, effortless tenor that rose over the din of the marching crowds and the clatter of trucks mobilizing for the front. He was one of the many artists, sympathizers of the Spanish Republic, who had traveled from the U.S. and various European countries to support the loyalist struggle. Some led the singing of revolutionary songs, "The Internationale" and "Els Segadors"; others, the writers and actors, read poems and put on skits ridiculing Franco.

Nolan was a dandy. He had his suits made out of the nicest fabrics (he loved a subdued herringbone!) with the pants tight around his butt and the jacket cut short and fitted to his waist. His hair was pomaded down flat and shiny like patent leather. A pencil-thin mustache gave him an Adolphe Menjou look. Girls were crazy about Menjou.

This boy's awkward attempts at courtship were a novelty. All the other men I had met, starting with Pep Saval and then some of the *milicianos*, felt they were heroes and that young women should fall at their feet. No-lan, on the other hand, seemed grateful for my every smile.

We began to see each other. Walks down the Rambla, arm in arm, licking custard or the sweet filling inside a cream puff. I began to miss him when he was away. He would perform for the loyalist garrisons around the country, but always at the end of the month return to Barcelona for a few days. I wanted to travel with him, but he insisted I stay and continue studying with Anjelica Brullet.

There was such a desperate need for men at the front that Nolan was tricked from entertaining into fighting. He assumed that the slow, swaying train to Manresa was taking him to sing for the battle-weary recruits. Upon his arrival in the scarred industrial town late that night, he was greeted by a glum committee of three loyalists, union organizers from a sausage factory, now sitting at the same table in front of three mounds of dun-green uniforms, roughly divided into jackets, trousers, and overcoats.

There would be no concert. His accompanist had been arrested as a suspected fascist, the piano had been splintered by erratic gunfire, and Señor Keefe was already scheduled to stand the midnight-to-three-A.M. watch with a Springfield rifle at his shoulder.

He was told to hand over, for safekeeping, his U.S. passport and the Spanish Republic's identity document, a typewritten sheet splitting at the creases from repeated inspections. In its place he was given a crisp new letter of appointment as an international volunteer, subject to all the rules and obligations of military discipline, mainly that desertion or cowardice under fire were firing-squad offenses. Even though he had been assigned to sentry duty, there was no ammunition in his rifle; some was promised for the following day.

Nolan loved to tell the story of his one military stint. He stood under a winter drizzle for three hours with a soaked greatcoat around his shoulders and on his head a felt cap, fragrant with the previous owner's hair oil. He spent the night mostly awake, in a cold ruin of a building that had once been occupied by the Guardia Civil until it had been set on fire by the townspeople and a militia company had moved in. Much of the roof was gone, and what was left leaked. The heavy door, charred and burned at the edges, could still be secured with a beam from the collapsing roof. Beds and tables were pushed close together while the persistent early-winter rains dripped down into the open sections of the barracks. The men took turns going out for sentry duty, returning to sleep under whatever was left of the roof over the building's main hall.

From the time his watch ended at three Nolan Keefe slept restlessly through the clinging stink of burned timber and soaked brick, the wet winds gusting through the exposed frame, the snores and groans and curses of the men lined up head to toe on a variety of improvised sleeping surfaces from mattresses to commissary tables.

He awoke with a sensation of dread. After shivering through his watch and then poking around to find room to curl up on a damp mattress, it took an hour before he was able to get warm under the steamy coat. Nolan Keefe was not suited for military activity; he disliked uniforms, he feared pain, and he was in love.

A churning in his guts finally drove him to his feet. He wrestled on the boots, the greatcoat, and the hat and stumbled out into the misty morning. A Sergeant Mateu pointed him in the direction of the place in the woods where the creek was most accessible. "Don't use dry leaves to wipe yourself with," he laughed.

"Thank you, Sergeant," Nolan acknowledged with a grin after he had mentally translated the advice from barely functional Catalan into French and then into English.

"And take your rifle with you," the soldier counseled. "The woods are teeming with fascists."

"But there are no bullets."

"The enemy does not know that," the man explained, accustomed to the gradual initiation of new recruits into the realities of an impecunious war effort. "The procedure is straightforward: One man points first, the other one runs. Running is not an option for a *miliciano*. Acts of cowardice mean the firing squad. So it's a matter of survival that you get your gun up before the other man."

Rifle on shoulder, his military coat buttoned to his chin, cap tilted at a rakish angle, Nolan marched into the woods in search of fascists and the creek, whichever came first.

After his first bowel movement as a soldier, Nolan Keefe calmly became a deserter. He turned his coat inside out to hide the military insignia. He buried the rifle and cap in a clump of bushes and started walking north, staying in the woods, intuitively following the road that led to Port Bou and across the French border to Perpignan. Along the way, he ripped up his military identification. It would be better to be questioned as a foreigner who had lost his passport than to show his militia identity while skulking around a hundred kilometers from his brigade.

Later, Nolan would recall the two days it took him to reach the border as a quiet, unhurried time. The rain stopped. The nights grew warmer. Nobody challenged his presence. He knocked at farmhouses in the middle of the day when he knew the men would be away. He flashed his boyish grin and women fed him leftovers and gave him worn clothes to replace the uniform. By dusk of the first day he had found the main road and was able to weave his way in and out of the forest whenever he heard vehicles approaching. In a blowsy tunic, old pants belted with a strip of cloth, and rope-soled espadrilles, he looked like a country youth on an errand. He spent the first night on the march, wrapped in a thin blanket under a starry sky.

The journey became complicated on the afternoon of the second day, just outside Carner, when he was questioned by a pair of adolescent *milicianos*, peasants from farms that had joined together in a collective.

One was pudgy and cross-eyed and kept squinting at Nolan with great suspicion. The other was smaller and younger-acting and obviously scared of the stranger approaching their sentry post in the shade of a large oak. They carried old shotguns that had been used for hunting partridges and rabbits before being converted into artillery.

The boys took turns asking his name and his village and accusing him of being a fascist or a priest in disguise. They said he had better not be a *miliciano* running away from his brigade because a deserter was as good as a traitor and therefore they would have to shoot him on the spot without further conversation.

Nolan stood impassively before the barrage of questions, suddenly too confused to come up with any story that would be plausible in his mangled Catalan. Then, in a burst of inspiration, he frowned and cupped his hand around his ear and uttered an improvised, unintelligible babble. He nodded enthusiastically and smiled amiably and replied to their questions with gibberish. The boys laughed and stuck out their tongues and rolled their eyes wildly. Nolan nodded cheerfully as if unaware of being the butt of their jokes. For the time being, he was content to be deaf, mute, and safe.

The boys grew bored and led him to the café in the center of the town. It was a simple place with a stone counter and a pair of rickety tables and chairs. They stood on either side of him and poured him a glass of wine and laid slices of smoked ham over *pa amb tomàquet*. He ate hungrily while the young *milicianos* tried to communicate with him. They asked him if he had a lover or a wife by rotating their hips suggestively. They asked him if he had children by cradling an imaginary baby. They suggested he was a fascist by marching up and down the bar and greeting each other with the extended arm salute. Nolan played along. He marched beside them, the three bearing down on their heels, goose-stepping like the Germans in newsreels, making a racket on the wooden floor. Sponsored by the two *milicianos*, he was able to rest in the comfort of the café as long as he stayed on guard and did not let on that he understood what was being said around him.

Warm at last, snuggled against sacks of potatoes, onions, garlic, he slept soundly for the first time after three wary nights.

When he awoke around four in the morning, he felt as if he were coming out of a dream where everything had been at peace, where he had only to hold the tremor in his breath to hear the distant singing of the lovely and singularly gifted girl he had fallen in love with. He felt in his heart such an ache that he marveled at the intensity of his love. Nolan claims my presence suffused the whole of his body, fitting like a second skin, spreading a warmth like a fluid more vital than blood.

In the cool larder redolent with the hearty fare of the Catalan countryside, Nolan helped himself, stuffing in a sack chunks of bread and a couple of eggs, tomatoes and a full head of garlic, olives, and a thick slice of ham. He waddled like a portly burgher through the dark café, silent except for the stirrings of a couple of guests who had stretched out on the table benches and fallen asleep under the weight of too much wine. He placed a few pesetas on the counter. In those first minutes he resolved to cross the Pyrenees and find work in Marseilles or Paris, and to send me enough money to leave Spain and join him. He estimated he was about a day's journey from Port Bou and about a month from the time when I would receive his letter.

I still have that letter, at the bottom of a trunk full of musty clippings and old programs and contracts. It's in a stained brown envelope. You can see the parts where the censors blotted out anything at all compromising. By the time it had been opened and read and reread by the postal inspectors and the censors and the government snoops, the whole town knew I had a suitor in France. That made me special. Somewhere along the line they decided it would be disloyal for an artist such as I to leave the country in the middle of its great crisis. Perhaps it was unsurprising for a foreigner to turn tail and leave us in the lurch, but I was essential to the cultural and spiritual health of the Republic. In fact, my very correspondence with such an erratic ally as Mr. Keefe was in itself questionable. And it was only through the generosity of the chief censor that the inspectors would continue to allow his letters to me and my brief notes to him to pass through.

I was measuring life from one letter to the next, holding my breath, skipping heartbeats between letters, the time between them slipping by as if in a restless dream. And the day a letter from Nolan arrived, well, that was like having the sun shine in the middle of the night.

But I was young, and people thought I was wasting my life. There were men available who were sick or wounded and mustered out of the service, and returning to their families. Or what was left of them, in the case of older brothers lost in another front or grandparents lost to old age and privations and younger siblings grown older and rebellious or marrying and leaving home. Life was hardly normal after those three or four years, and what the young men wanted most of all was to reenter life. That usually involved keeping company with a girl, because in war the only women they'd had time to get close to had been prostitutes during leave, or nurses if they had been wounded or come down with typhoid.

Some returning boys were music students who had heard me sing and were eager to meet me. If their families still had money, they bought me stockings or chocolates, and if they were poor they gave me flowers and asked me to stroll down the Rambla or go to the cinema. I resisted their invitations but often accepted their gifts. Even if I gave them nothing in return, it became harder to write Nolan. It seemed silly to refuse some boy who knew how to have a good time at a dance or a café in favor of Nolan's letters, full of vague hopes and the reckless promise to send me steamer passage so I could join him in New York.

Even if I should receive permission from the government to leave Spain, to marry a known leftist and unreliable American artist, I was afraid of venturing so far. The only English I knew had been memorized phonetically, with hardly a clue as to meaning: *For unto us a child is born.* I had no business going to America—not with Nolan exulting over the great singers there and how much I would love to hear Rosa Ponselle and Bessie Abbot.

The truth is that I was never thrilled by another woman's voice. And I didn't want to be dependent on Nolan Keefe for survival in America. I'd already done that with Pep Saval. I was not going to be someone's child again. Not at nineteen. New York was fine for him, not for us. And that was what I began telling him every time I wrote.

But in his letters Nolan went on and on as if he had not read mine. They were such beautiful letters. Even when he didn't have much money, he used the finest onionskin paper and a Parker pen with ink the color of lapis lazuli, and always his scent on the paper, the mixture of bay rum and the licorice drops he liked and the lemony tonic he used to slick back his wavy hair. He had delicate handwriting, like a girl's, everything nicely rounded, the capital M done with a flourish. Every time he wrote out my name he seemed to be celebrating it. I would read my name and see myself reflected in his consciousness. Sometimes he would write my name very small and I would sense he was saying it in a whisper, for my ears alone. Occasionally mercè would be spelled out in uppercase, and it sounded in my mind like he was shouting it from the rooftop of the tallest building in New York. Once he even wrote the letters like notes in a pentagram, so that I could hear him singing,

MER . . . CE . . . È

He wrote wonderful things, but in the three years that we corresponded without seeing each other, those lovely thoughts tended to blend one into the other: *I love you, and I can't wait to see you, and I want so much for us to be married, and I'm being true to you night and day.*

That last part, I eventually learned, was rubbish, one of those assertions that Nolan felt a lover was obligated to make. It became clear that the boy needed sex every day as some people require coffee or tobacco. A day without lovemaking plunged Nolan into a dark and cold malaise. The thing between his legs was a serpent that needed to be fed on a daily basis. A girl's unguarded laugh or the glimpse of bare legs under a summer dress or the scent of freshly washed hair came into its awareness, and the thing would stir.

He would hover about Bloomingdale's necktie and handkerchief department or at the chorus auditions or among the usher staff at the Met. He would turn on the charm, and maybe open up his wallet or whisper veiled promises of influence for a featured role. He did whatever it took to feed his beast. If the beast was not happy, Nolan couldn't sleep, eat, work, or even sing to his proper level.

And so he was often racked with guilt. One time, after I had caught him with a girl, he offered to cut his penis off; whatever it took, he pleaded, to make him chaste and me happy. He dropped his pants in the kitchen and took out a butcher knife from the drawer under the sink. At the first drop of blood, I screamed for him to stop. "Not until you forgive me," he demanded. Of course I forgave him. Men do what they do because they are what they are.

I've always been jealous of men's ability to have uncomplicated, organ-centered, functional sex. Don't let anyone fool you; most women who give the matter some thought end up with penis envy. It starts when they realize how efficient it is for peeing and masturbating and inserting into a variety of orifices. Always ready to spring into action. Doesn't every man love having one?

The letters from Nolan held me back from the normal fun that other girls my age were having. The words were often more frightening than seductive because I didn't quite understand the things he was telling me: I was his food, his drug, his air. The taste of me was on his lips. The sound of my name pulsed unspoken through his veins. My scent remained on the fingers that had caressed me years before. He was losing me with every postal delivery.

For over a year, I had answered each letter the night it arrived. The post was delivered in the afternoon. In the evening I would take a bath, put on a pretty robe, and sit in my room with a candle flickering on my writing table to answer the letter. If I had plans, I canceled them. Nolan's letters came first.

Eventually, inevitably, writing letters became a chore. I tried not answering Nolan's to see if they would stop. With censorship holding mail hostage, it took weeks before Nolan realized something was wrong. As his letters took on a nagging tone, it became harder to stay home to write him. I escaped to stroll along the Rambla on summer evenings, not fully relaxing, of course, always alert to the bombing raids that sent people scurrying for shelter with little warning. I had a regular group, girls who were students at the conservatory and boys stationed in Barcelona in easy jobs, organizing civil defense, coordinating supplies to the front, keeping the records of who was on leave and who was wounded and who was dead.

I was, even in the midst of war, optimistic about my destiny: I was promised to a famous American tenor without having to be with him all the time; I could flirt without committing myself. Like bad weather, the war occasionally interfered with the normal rhythm of life. Bombs fell, but I stayed out of their way; there were shortages of sugar and meat and flour, and I did without; boys I knew were taken away to the front and came back sick or wounded. It was something to be dealt with, like the occasional epidemics of typhoid and smallpox that would sweep through a neighborhood. None of it interfered with a girl's knack for enjoying herself.

In any case, I did not fear bombs as much as Nolan's letters. I got so I wouldn't read one for days, leaving it unopened on top of the bureau, the onionskin envelope screaming my name. There might be two or three letters, one on top of the other in the order in which they had arrived. Eventually, I would try to shake off my guilt by dashing off a single quick note in reply to all three. In my answers I reassured him that there was no other man in my life, that when the war ended I would leave Spain and join him in New York, that we would marry and live there happily.

Actually, until the day I sailed to America, I would have said there was only a remote possibility that it would happen. But in our letters to each other, we promised repeatedly that we would marry. When the time came, we went ahead and did it without giving the matter a second thought.

Nolan arranged a simple ceremony, and afterward a dinner with a dozen of his friends from the Met. Then, walking along 38th Street to the Fallows Hotel, which was then quite a gracious place, we passed in front of a Rexall drugstore. Nolan led me to the cosmetics counter. I had never seen such a variety of lipsticks and eyeliners and blush creams. He told me to buy anything I liked. Meanwhile, he went to the opposite end of the store, where a male clerk placed a variety of foil packets on the counter for him to choose from.

Because this was a special night, he told me as he demonstrated their use, he'd bought the condoms made with natural lambskin membrane.

They were the most expensive because they were guaranteed to feel the most natural. However, when I thought about the sheath made with real animal tissue, I wondered if I would feel like a ewe being penetrated by a goat. I wanted him to throw out the condoms because from the first time, I was hungry to have his child.

"People like us have been blessed by a higher gift," Nolan declared. "It's not in our destiny to have children."

I eventually became disillusioned with Nolan. No one could guess in a million attempts what finally turned me off him. Once a woman's heart cools, one small thing brings down the house of cards that is love.

It was his shirts. A man should change his shirt daily, especially if it's white. Men think they can get by with a second wearing as long as they use colognes and deodorants. Not so. I'd smell Nolan's second-day shirt, and his selfishness, his pathological womanizing, his vanity would come rushing into my awareness in one huge wave of unpleasant sensations and images.

○━┼ A SEMBLANCE OF DESIRE.

One night during his exile in the garret, Lockwood lurks outside his house like a thief. It's sometime after two, and he knows Claire is asleep. He could let himself in like any normal guy, home late after a night out: twist the key in the lock with such delicacy that it won't make a click or a snap, push the door firmly shut so that the hinges won't squeak, remove his shoes at the door, take his clothes off in the bathroom, and sneak into bed as if he's been just been up in the middle of the night to piss. If his wife wakes up and asks when he got in, he'll mutter, Hours ago.

Lockwood could do all that. But he doesn't have his house keys with him. After drinking three bottles of wine with Perla and Orson La Prima, he had been touched that they were so comfortable with each other, as if they'd been friends forever. The three were happy to be foolish and sappy together. But when he tried to put his arm around Perla, she pulled away from him because, she said, theirs was a professional relationship until such time when he resolved his family life. *Llama a tu esposa*, she challenged him. Tell her you're not coming back.

Orson realized that a sharp note had been struck. He put his glass down. "We have shared a moment here," he sighed. "Obviously, we are bound together by a really strong but really *subtle* connection, because you two," he nodded to Perla and Lockwood, "are the closest people to La Señora that I have ever met. Can we touch each other? Would it embarrass you if we stood up and just hugged, the three of us?"

They stood in the middle of the room and put their arms around each other's shoulders. They hugged so that their heads were close and they could smell each other's winey breath. Together they formed a three-headed, six-legged creature, moving across the room, reluctant to let go, stumbling over a chair, nearly tripping over the coffee table, squeezing out of the apartment and onto the outer walkway, where the rain continued to fall.

Lockwood tried to kiss Perla as he was leaving, but she pulled away again. He shrugged. He said he was going to his house to get clean clothes and have a talk with his wife. It was time, he said, that he pour out all the turmoil inside his head. Somebody had to listen to it, and Perla pleaded fatigue. He pulled the briefcase out from under the sink and ran out of the apartment. It was only as the door slammed behind him that he realized he had left his house keys inside, all hooked to one ring. But there was no way to get back inside the garret unless he was willing to wake up the building manager. He did, however, have his car key in his pocket. During the drive home he listened to a tape of Mercè Casals doing her signature Micaela. From the first phrases of her opening aria he fell into an unshakable sadness.

And now, hours later, standing in the rain at two A.M., he's locked out of his home. He circles the house, feeling his way in the dark, his fingers testing the secured windows and the locked doors, a stalker in his own neighborhood. He finally takes a deep breath and presses on the door-bell. He rings several times before lights go on.

His real story, he tells Claire when she comes to the door, is that he needs to come home for just a short while. She sends him to the couch in his study. "Sleep it off. We'll talk in the morning."

He wanders about the house for about an hour, restless in his under-wear. Eventually, he pulls a blanket over his head and goes to sleep. The satchel makes a hard pillow, and he wakes up with a neck so rigid it hurts to move his head. He moans so loudly that Claire comes to inquire about his pain. "Touch me there," he says to Claire. He takes her hand and places it on the stiff muscles enveloping his spine. His neck hurts when he turns or tilts it. He rotates his whole torso, twisting from his shoulders to face the sun that streams into the kitchen. It warms his face, sends purple blobs swimming against a void behind his eyelids. Claire pulls back her hand before he feels much relief. "Take aspirin," she says. He realizes that, given the circumstances of the past week, this is going to be the extent of her concern for the pains of his flesh and spirit.

Lockwood sits straight at the kitchen table and follows Claire with his eyes as she makes tea, pops in toast, standing with her back to him. He gazes at the blue enameled kettle, at the Sunbeam toaster, at the jewel-like preserves of cherry and orange and blueberry sparkling inside thick tumblers of hand-blown glass.

The things in Perla's apartment feel random, gathered hastily, spoons so light they bend against hard ice cream, mugs with radio-station logos, plastic place mats. But in Lockwood's home every object is imbued with meaning, a material code for the immaterial traces left behind by years of being looked at, touched, tasted. There are things here that he and Claire have used daily for almost twenty years, and which might never need to be replaced, inanimate objects that trail after them from city to city, from one neighborhood to another, apartment to house, and eventually to rest home and mausoleum. The idea of leaving even one of these things behind, perhaps the brown English pot with its permanent tea stain and the chip on the spout rubbed smooth and darkened by the years, fills him with regret.

When she goes to pour, Claire moves with a soft, buoyant grace, surprisingly light in spite of her sweet, fleshy form. Her expression says nothing. But as the moment grows he realizes that this nothing is indeed something; her refusal to meet his eyes or respond to his smile is a quiet hostility against the errant partner. Suddenly self-conscious of her looks after all these years, she brushes a wisp of blond hair that falls down her forehead. He reaches toward her as if to keep her hair in place, but her head jerks away. She hands him the cup to discourage further contact.

He sips slowly. It's the first tea he has had in a week. Perla tosses down black espressos. Tea offers a subtler kind of stimulus, not the kick that Perla brews to fuel his jittery twelve-hour writing push when his fingers fly, his mind leaps, and his ears pick up every creak and knock and voice that could herald the presence of Hollywood Hank or Alonzo Baylor. Anxiety and coffee fuel Lockwood's creative juices. Still, you don't get attached to a Krups espresso maker as you do to a P&K teapot. He sips the Ceylon, and its fragrance rises in waves of memory and emotion. He can hold back no longer. His whole body hurts with sadness and remorse. He breaks into a series of hard sobs. Fat tears pour out of his eyes and roll down his cheeks, falling into the corners of his mouth, dripping into the mug he holds. This is the first time he has cried in years.

"Can't we talk about things?" he asks.

"Of course," she says blandly. "What things?"

"There must be things you want to know. I won't tell you anything you don't want to know. But of the things that you do want to know, those I can tell you about." He takes a deep breath and steels himself to lie.

"Shit, Lockwood." She smiles kindly. "You think I want to know about your girlfriend. Why would I want to know that?"

"'Girlfriend' may be too conclusive. I don't think Perla would refer to herself as my girlfriend."

"Perhaps only a collaborator, right?"

"But a friend, too." He tries to explain, "We had this experience together, you know. The experience of knowing Mercè Casals. And being there when she died. We were both important to her, in different ways. We came together quite accidentally."

"'Serendipitous' is the way you writers would put it."

"Yes, a random collision."

"Do you have sex?"

"Not so much the act itself. But a semblance of sexual tension."

"A semblance of fucking?" Claire smiles resolutely through her use of the unaccustomed word.

"A semblance of desire."

"You make it all sound so vague."

"Some relationships are by nature undefined."

"Slippery."

"No, Claire. Not slippery. Not vague. Nothing like that."

"You moved in with her," she accuses.

"Hardly. I visit. We have coffee. I have a separate place for work. For hiding, if you must know."

Her voice turns sad. "I never imagined you could leave like this, Mark."

. . .

After hiding for a week, Lockwood feels free to be himself in a secret place, to carry inside his own life the not-quite-finished life of Mercè Casals. It's as if she has died before her time and left it up to him to deal with her unresolved business, her small guilts and fierce grudges. He looks at the satchel, the stitching on the leather handle imprinted on his palm. He can almost hear the Señora's voice. "Here, Scribbler. Here is my baggage. Run with it."

But there's no running anywhere with this bag. He can barely move from one room to the next without carrying the case along. It tugs at him while he's trying to write, eat, drive, make love to Claire. Which is how the breakfast showdown ends: with an escape to the bedroom, *their* bed still, of course, even though he'd been refused entry the night before. Lockwood's crying, his blubbering like a baby, finally softens Claire. She stands in front of him and pulls his head toward her full breasts. He breathes her scent and glories in her generosity. These are the comforts of the married, bodies eager to accommodate, knowledgeable of their appetites, expert in satisfying the familiar demands.

Perla's body, compared to Claire's, is an elusive organism, one moment pulling at him, the next slipping out of his grasp, a distant and stubborn thing. Somehow all the more ungenerous because of its imagined sparseness, the small, tight buttocks, the barely defined breasts, the flatness of its tummy, all conspiring to be denied, to retreat from his touch, to shrink into alien territory.

Claire's is the country where he belongs. He leans on his elbow and gazes down at the territory of his wife's topography. Milky dunes and waves and mounds rising and falling with the soft, contented breathing of her body at rest. A silky garden, a tender crevice, blunt protrusions. Faintly, under the delicate cell mosaic of skin, there's a lace of fine blue veins spawning capillaries, tributaries debouching onto the main rivers that in turn feed or return to the rush of the wellspring. Pressing his ear to her chest, he can hear the blood flowing, the even beat of her heart, the sough of a weary exhalation. His own body is calmed by the heat that rises from her. He closes his eyes, and senses her drifting away from him. Lockwood surrenders to thoughts of Mercè Casals. He embraces a shadowy unfamiliar body; her touch feels foreign and forbidden; the face is heavily made up, with deep purple shadows over the lids and oily mascara lining the eyes and sweat streaking the powdered skin and a red, open mouth swallowing his gaze down the throat as the end of a red moist tunnel to the red swollen flaps on either side of the glottis. There is a sound in his ears that no human could possibly make.

Claire's voice pulls him back. She says, "I'm not happy anymore, Mark."

⊶—⊦| IMAGINE, MEETING NOLAN KEEFE . . .

Lockwood has planned his first foray into adultery with all the wile of the habitual cheater. Ostensibly he and Perla will discuss their visit to Nolan Keefe at the Age d'Or, though, in truth, he has amassed several hundred dollars through various cash withdrawals to keep traces of his adventure off his credit-card statements. No matter that Perla has become accustomed to seeing him dressed in t-shirts and khakis, he has had his silk shirt dry cleaned and ironed his good slacks. His hair shows evidence of a $60 stylist. And he has made reservations at George's on the Cove in La Jolla. Nice touches await their meeting—a window table with an ocean view, a bottle of pinot grigio, an orchid from Fiorella's. He attributes the queasiness in his stomach to the guilt of the first-time philanderer. He'll get better with practice, he imagines.

His message to Perla is brief, but he hopes, provocative: "Ah, Perla, alone with you at last! George's, twelve-thirty."

Her message to him about an hour before the appointed time is equally succinct: "George's? *Por favor*, Lockwood, you're unemployed! See you at Benny's Taco Shack in Del Mar."

He gets to Benny's half an hour late because he has stopped to cancel the reservation at George's and pick up the orchid. Perla, sitting at a corner table with a bottle of Pacifico, is relieved to see him. "I was wondering if you hadn't gotten my message," she says. "I was about to call the restaurant and get them to kick you out."

Lockwood shrugs with embarrassment. "I thought you would like a special lunch."

"Because you think there's something special going on between us?"

"Hoping, anyway."

She finally acknowledges the gift in his hand. "Wow, an orchid!" She spoons the ice out of her water glass and puts the flower in it. "If I had to get a boyfriend, you are certainly the type I would want."

"So there is hope for me?"

"No. You are hopeless." But then she grins like she doesn't mean it, and he recovers his wavering self-confidence. She leaves him at the table and goes to the counter to pick up another two beers and a platter of fish tacos. "Here," she says, "the first round is on me."

He is still too nervous to eat, sobered that Perla is so carefree as she expertly takes a taco, the fresh tortilla still fragrant from the grill, spoons the hot salsa onto it, then holds it closed with the three middle fingers, using the pinky to keep the end up. She eats two more tacos before she speaks to him again. "These things are delicious!"

"I love a woman with a lustful appetite."

"I'm just hungry, Lockwood."

"Well, it's sexy anyway."

"Sure, if you think of yourself as a taco."

"I have the feeling you're not taking me seriously."

"Oh, Lockwood." She laughs. "You're a pathetic seducer. But I am here, as you can see."

"But not because of me."

"Not exclusively."

"Partially?"

"Sure."

"I have a book to finish."

"And I can't let go of the Señora. I was part of her story for three years. I want to know the rest of it."

"So buy the book when it's published."

"I'm thinking you need help, Lockwood." She smiles and pushes the taco platter toward him. "I knew her better than anyone. I saw her naked. She talked to me when she was not being recorded. She cared about me. I want you to do right by her."

"Lucky me, I get an editor before the manuscript is finished."

"You can start by not being sarcastic."

The guilt and apprehension of earlier in the day have vanished and Lockwood feels a kind of euphoria in the knowledge that they are both intertwined with the Señora's fortunes. He sips the last of his beer and now hungrily munches on the tacos—the best fish tacos, he could swear, that he has ever had.

"You got your appetite back," she smiles.

Lockwood feels that what has been returned to him is his sense of purpose. The Señora, with all her contradictions and whims, had the power to reawaken dormant qualities in people. Did she really translate *"Vissi d'arte, vissi d'amore"* for him? He had long ago given up on the idea that it was possible to live for art, for love. And if being the Señora's writer was not art of the highest order, it was work that lifted his spirit and challenged his craft.

"Finish your lunch, Lockwood," Perla says as she checks her watch again. "Imagine, meeting Nolan Keefe, the love of her life."

"A complicated love," he says.

"And a well-kept secret."

"She would not approve of our snooping." Lockwood smiles. "On the other hand, it's for a good cause."

Lockwood and Perla watch expectantly as Nolan Keefe is led into the parlor by a male nurse who steers him by the elbow around the other tables set up for afternoon tea, and pulls back a chair for him to take his seat at his customary corner table. Giving a final, critical look at his patient, the nurse straightens his tie with a tug. "You're looking good, Mr. Keefe. Two visitors today, one of them a babe." He turns toward the two visitors and says, "Call me if he misbehaves. We don't allow rudeness in the parlor."

Perla signals for the attendant to come near. She pulls his shirtsleeve with her thumb and index fingers to draw him a little closer still. Finally, she asks in a cool tone, barely above a whisper, "What's your name?"

"Hansen. But the ladies call me Handsome," he grins.

"Hansen," she continues tersely, "you're a *pendejo* to babble so disrespectfully in front of a patient." She waits as Hansen skulks away with a shrug, then she and Lockwood sit on either side of Nolan Keefe.

After a moment's uncertainty, Nolan looks curiously from one unfamiliar visitor to the other. "I imagine you will tell me, eventually, who you two are," he says quietly.

"Good afternoon, Mr. Keefe. I'm Perla. I've been taking care of Señora Casals. She has told me a lot about you."

The old man looks at her curiously. Then with a toss of his head in Lockwood's direction, he asks, "And what's he? Another doctor?"

"I'm Mark Lockwood, Mr. Keefe. A writer."

Nolan Keefe seems to give the answer a great deal of thought. "Are you a friend of Mercè's too?"

"I would like to think so. And I also worked with her."

"So you no longer work for Mercè," he observes. "I don't think anybody can stand her for very long, she's such a . . . Well, I'm not going to use that word. As you can see by my tea-time manners, therapy has been effective lately."

The old man takes a deep breath and surveys the tray with the imitation Limoges pot and delicate porcelain cups, the pewter pitcher with milk and the little silver bowl with sugar cubes. It pays to be a little fussy if one wants things to go smoothly. He looks up as if he has just noticed them for the first time.

"But you haven't explained why we are having tea together." He frowns, searching his own mind for possibilities.

"You have been told about Señora Casals, haven't you?" Lockwood asks.

"I imagine I've been told things. I'm not sure I know which ones are relevant to the question before us."

"There is something you should know, Mr. Keefe," Perla says.

"That Mercè has decided to stop coming to tea and opted to send the help instead?"

"It's not like she made an actual decision." Lockwood tries to ease into the subject at hand.

"No, she was always impulsive."

"We're not talking about a whim, Mr. Keefe," Perla finally says sadly. "The Señora will no longer come to visit you."

Nolan Keefe gasps as he strikes his forehead with the palm of his hand. "Oh, my God," he exclaims, and then quietly, "I see," he says. "This is terrible."

"We can come back another time if you'd rather be alone," Lockwood says.

"No, I'm fine." Nolan shakes his head. "It's to be expected at our age. I imagine I'll have a good cry later tonight."

"She didn't suffer. Her heart gave up while she was in her bath," Lockwood says.

"She's the nurse." Nolan points to Perla. "Therefore, you're her ghost scribbler."

"You remember, then."

"She said you were entrusted with her secrets. She wanted to know if I had any objections, being that some of her secrets were mine as well."

"And what did you say to her?" Lockwood asks.

"That I would sue her, and you, if I read anything about me that I considered in any way distasteful." He pauses for a moment to watch Lockwood's face redden. "That's the bad news," he adds. "The good news is that there is very little about my life that I'm embarrassed about. I mean, what is she going to tell you? That I begged her to leave Prince What's-His-Face and come back to me? Hell, I even begged the Prince to throw her back when I realized things were starting to unravel between them."

"It must've been a difficult time for you."

"Life has been a difficult time. I've lost my voice, my money, my wife."

"Is that in a kind of order?"

"Yes. From the catastrophic to the merely tragic."

"Do you mind if I tape our chat?" Lockwood reaches with feigned casualness into his briefcase for the cassette recorder.

"Yes, I do mind." Nolan slaps Lockwood's hand. "I will not say a word until you promise me you are not going to record any of this. This other fellow that showed up yesterday wanting to interview me also pulled out one of those gadgets."

"Alonzo Baylor," mutters Lockwood as he and Perla exchange glances.

"Yeah, he signed his biography of Salvador Dalí to me. Nice man."

It's a reality to be dealt with. With or without the tapes, Alonzo Baylor will cobble together a biography, hiring grad students to gather facts that he can then string out in a plodding linear rut. The whole thing, fleshed out with fan-club fluff, will read like an overblown eulogy. Measured innuendo and rumor will be added to create buzz.

"So, what did the two of you chat about?" Lockwood asks.

"Nothing, I don't receive visitors on Tuesdays. He said he'd be back, though."

"I'm sure he will." Perla reaches for the teapot and refills their cups.

"I like the way you serve tea," Nolan murmurs to Perla. Turning toward Lockwood, he adds cheerfully, "See how she holds the lid down with just the slightest pressure of two fingers and then so neatly pours into the center of the cup? Not a single drip."

There's a visible blush to Perla's cheeks.

"Yes, she pours with grace," says Lockwood.

"You know, I taught Mercè to drink tea," Nolan says softly, his eyes closing as if better to enjoy the cup he raises to his lips.

Perla nods. "One part Earl Gray, two parts English breakfast. She was particular."

"I was the particular one." He chuckles, and his expression brightens. "She used to drink instant coffee from a glass, mixing it under the hot-water tap in the hotel room. I don't think she had been in a kitchen in years. The sight of me engaged in the simple domestic act of brewing a pot of tea quite charmed her. I showed her my secret blend, taught her how to warm the pot beforehand, measure the loose tea, bring the kettle almost to a boil and pour the water in a rush. I taught her to wrap the pot in a knitted wool cozy that I'd gotten from my mother. I was serious about doing it right. Tea is that way, you know. The Japanese tea ceremony is not, after all, about rice."

With a quick, almost secret squeeze of his thumb, Lockwood reaches over and clicks on the recorder. "It would help me to record our conversation," he adds in response to Nolan's suspicious look.

"I'm told I have trouble remembering, too," the old man said after a moment. "They expect me to remember everything. Nobody remembers everything. I forget my vitamins, my keys, my dreams. I tell them my memory would improve if they would only serve beets more often. At any rate, I have more to remember than most people. Just the leading tenor roles in five different languages that I know by heart would keep me singing for seven days straight, night and day. I remember the very first words Mercè Casals spoke to me: 'You must be very stupid to give up singing in Nueva York to make war in Catalunya.' I remember the sweaty, garlicky smell of the dressing rooms at La Scala and the name of the wardrobe mistress at Covent Garden, Clotilde, and the feel on my fingertips of the glass-bead curtain at Bellas Artes. I remember the color of the famous Mexican movie star Amalia Camino's skivvies, purple."

"The Señora used to say that to remember is to live," Perla says.

"I won't sing again, you know. I sang for the last time in Mexico City at a free concert for a crowd of loyal fans congregating outside the Gran Hotel in the main plaza. Mercè thought I was going to leap off a twentieth-story balcony. An artist can aspire to no sweeter death than to go in the middle of his performance."

"I'm sure you've had a good rich life in the years since then, Mr. Keefe," Perla says kindly.

A thin edge of afternoon light comes in through the window and travels, minute by minute, along the dark burgundy carpet, setting the fibers aglow as it slices across the room. When the light reaches his slippered feet, Nolan stretches his toes under the new warmth and drains the last of his now cold tea. "Tea time is almost over," he says. "You'll hear the chimes." He tilts his head in the direction of the parlor's arched entrance. "I'll have to stop talking then."

"Why can't we go on chatting?" Perla asks.

"We need to make room for the next tea visitors."

"There's so much I want to ask you," Lockwood says.

"That's why Mercè finally died, don't you know? You got her jabbering until she was all talked out. How many hours a day? Six, eight? Not a healthy thing, as you can see."

"She wanted to tell her story. I only wish she had lived long enough to finish it."

"How do you know she didn't finish it?"

"Oh, there are a few gaps left," Lockwood says. "Material that I hope you will help us out with."

"I won't be quiet next Wednesday. You can come back then if you like. We'll have tea. I'm sure Mercè has held out on you. Did you ask her about Pep Saval during the Spanish war? And the one mistake she has never been able to fix." He winks at Perla. "You are so pretty," he sighs. "She is pretty, isn't she?" he says to Lockwood. "Is she your girl?"

"Ya quisiera." He wishes. Perla's mocking tone makes Lockwood wince.

"Yes, I'm sure he does," Nolan says kindly. He extends his hand toward his guests.

Lockwood takes it and marvels at the soft, dry texture of the palm, at the tiny bones just under the skin, so fragile, and nearly weightless, it's like holding a sparrow. He feels a surge of joy at having met Nolan Keefe. He is filled with love for the man, as if he could somehow identify with Mercè's most tender feeling for him at the height of their union.

THANK YOU, OH THANK YOU, GODS, ANGELS, PERLA.

Lockwood had stopped by his house to pick up clean clothes and do laundry. Now, close to three in the afternoon, he heads down the freeway toward the hospital where Perla is on duty. He's feeling suddenly care-free, as if all questions have been settled with Claire and now he has nothing to do but concentrate on writing—ten pages every day, one an hour for the next ninety days, with another month for covering up plot holes and weeding out verbiage. A couple of months of uninterrupted frenzy. There's no halting the momentum. He tightens the straps on the satchel containing the raw material of the Señora's life and places his hand on it as if to feel a pulse from inside.

He will maintain a state of vigilance until the book is in the hands of a publisher and a contract has been signed. It will be a way of life worthy of one of LeCarre's burned-out spooks, forever wary, constantly alert to lurkers and muggers and stalkers of various stripes. He takes the exit into downtown San Diego. He makes aimless rights and lefts, waiting to turn until the last instant before lights go red.

Once he's sure he's not being followed, he takes the coast highway south to the Scripps Hospital, where Perla sits in a private room and watches a real-estate mogul take his last breaths. Lockwood cruises the parking lot until he sees her red pickup. He drives into the empty space beside it and calls the ICU floor from his cell phone. It takes about ten minutes for an operator to find Perla. Lockwood feels like an idiot with the phone pressed to his ear while cheery on-hold music mixes improbably with one of the Casals interview tapes.

"I can't leave now, Lockwood," she says. "Come by tonight."

He turns down the sound of the Señora's voice. "Perla," he pleads, "I'm at loose ends here. I need to be with someone. You're the only friend I have."

"Why aren't you working?"

"I am, inside my head," he explains. "Just because you don't hear a keyboard clicking doesn't mean I'm not writing."

"Thinking paranoid thoughts is writing?"

"Jesus, Perla," he whines. "Just for a minute?"

"I'll come out for a cigarette in a while. Unless my friend here expires before."

"Great, I'm parked next to your truck."

"Just wait there. I might be an hour," she warns him.

He locks the car doors and leans his head back, closing his eyes, letting the rhythm of the tape's voices spin out. He's startled when forty minutes later she knocks on the window. She sits beside him with a sigh. "I got to quit early," she says. "I think the guy's wife gave him the pillow treatment while I was out talking to you. Just as well." She shrugs. She has changed out of her uniform into a black tank top and jeans, but a cloud of undefinable medical smells, a combination of acrid and clinical, hovers about her. It's covered up when she lights a cigarette. Lockwood rolls down windows on either side. He likes it that Claire doesn't smoke. He doesn't like it that Perla has to brush her teeth six times a day. Lately, he has been comparing the two women. Perla is unpredictable, unreliable, inconstant, infuriating, interesting. He doesn't wonder that he's in love with her. He does worry that he will end up with neither woman.

"So, are you free for the day?" he asks eagerly.

"All yours, Lockwood." She makes a fist and gives his shoulder a light jab. To let him know she's kidding? To foreshadow greater physical intimacy? He reaches down and covers her hand with his. It lies still. He feels like a dunce; Perla is not the kind of woman you hold hands with in a parked car. Still, she does not pull away. Her lack of response is ambiguous enough that she can be saying *Don't*, or *Not yet*, or *This is so boring I'm not going to bother to react*. He lets go of her hand and grips the steering wheel, preparing to drive off even as his mind searches for direction.

"Hey, want to go shopping?" Perla grins.

"Do you need to buy something?"

"All kinds of stuff. I'll drive ahead in my truck."

"Where are we going?"

"Just follow me, okay?" she says. Her mood is brighter now. "You will see, *querido*," she promises.

Lockwood feels a tightening in his chest as he follows Perla's truck at the exit from I-5 into La Jolla and on to the familiar building. He parks on the street, and runs the two blocks to catch up with her.

It's been two weeks since the Señora died, but still Preston greets them warmly. "Ah, the writer and the nurse gather once again. There's quite a crowd upstairs already."

"Come on, Lockwood." She pulls him by the sleeve. "All the nice stuff will be gone."

"No chance of that," Preston says. "The Señora had nothing but quality around her."

There's a sign on an easel outside her door announcing the estate sale, and within the apartment about thirty people shuffle about, weaving their way through the crowded spaces. Yellow tags signal prices on furniture, lamps, paintings, and her beloved treasures in porcelain and crystal; red dots identify what has been sold. A woman walks around with a clipboard, accepting checks and marking off items in an inventory many pages long. The crowd feels predatory, a flapping of crows picking over the bones of a life.

Lockwood recognizes some of the shoppers, neighbors in the building whom he's noticed in his months coming and going, possibly here only because the Señora's sanctum can now be breached. Serious buyers look around with a practiced eye, running their fingers along the upholstery, feeling the warmth of wood and the coolness of brass. Perla pulls him by the hand into the bedroom, where the Señora's clothes have been pulled out of closets and drawers and thrown in piles over the bed, the chaise longue, a couple of chairs. A tubular rack has been pulled in and packed with dresses and jackets on cheap wire hangers, robes and lingerie have been stuffed into cartons. The piles of clothing have released a strong scent of the Señora's favorite perfumes, blended into one unmistakable identity. Her spirit, more than in any other room, lingers most vividly here. He remembers how her voice would call out from the bedroom, "I'm almost ready for you, Marcos Loco. Make yourself comfortable."

Lockwood grows suddenly pale, unsteady on his feet. Perla rushes to his side. "*Qué pasa*, Lockwood?"

"The satchel," he says. "It's back in the car. Just sitting there in the passenger seat. Oh, Jesus, Jesus, what an idiot."

"Relax, man," she murmurs. "You're in a safe neighborhood. The car doors are locked."

"I don't know," he says almost in a whimper.

"You don't know what?"

"I don't always lock the car. There's never been anything inside it worth stealing." By then he has retreated from the bedroom; he quickly turns and crosses the living room in a series of long, anxious strides. Perla rushes behind him. As the elevator slowly takes them down the twenty-some stories to the lobby, Lockwood realizes that for the first time in his life, something might happen that would cause him to commit suicide. It's as stunning a realization as he's ever had. The thought of dying unful-filled stabs him with a sudden pang of sadness. In the three minutes it takes to dart out of the condo, startling Preston in the process, and sprint along Coast Boulevard to the parked car, Lockwood feels himself gripped with hopelessness. Surely Hollywood Hank's minions are hovering about the Señora's estate sale, maybe they've spotted his distinctive yellow Saab, have taken a look inside and grabbed the precious cassettes. From twenty feet away he can see the door pegs standing up unlocked. In a life plagued by near misses and blown opportunities, the unhappy end seems near and inevitable. How much despair can be crowded into three minutes? Still, a shred of hope keeps him sprinting until he collapses breathlessly on the Saab's hood, and through the windshield, as his eyes well up with relief, he sees that the precious leather bag lies inviolate and undisturbed on the passenger seat.

A moment later, the new fear that the cassettes have been removed and the bag left behind vanishes as he jerks at the door and flips open the flap. Nearly one hundred shiny plastic boxes glimmer under the faint dome light. Lockwood turns and, with a kind of desperation, hugs Perla, the nearest, substantial repository for the gratitude that fills his heart to overflowing.

"Thank you, oh thank you, gods, angels, Perla."

"Hey, I just came along in case I had to give you CPR." She smirks. "You almost died back there."

"I did die," he says. "And came back to life."

"*Qué dramático,*" she says.

"It's what six months listening to Mercè Casals will do for someone."

"You'd better not let go of that thing," Perla says as Lockwood takes out the case and slams the door shut. "I'll hang on to it when you need both hands. Am I a good secretary or what?"

"You're infinitely more than that. You're a certified angel."

"You're always jumping ahead," she says. "Okay, we continue our shopping."

The crowd inside Mercè Casals' apartment has grown as Perla pulls Lockwood by his free arm, edging back into the Señora's bedroom. He stands impassively as Perla runs her hands through a mountain of lingerie on the bed.

"You . . . two!" a voice sings right behind him.

"I should've guessed you wouldn't miss this," Perla says.

Lockwood turns to face Orson La Prima, who beams a wide grin, his arms laden with vinyl records. "It's all about claiming past glories," says Orson.

An hour later, the three are loading their purchases onto the bed of Perla's truck. Lockwood was able to buy the Señora's wingback chair with the poofy ottoman. At $900 it is a budget breaker, but he's hopeful Claire will like it. Besides, he'll claim it as tax deductible. Whenever he feels the

Señora's presence go dim, he will just sit in her favorite chair and get into her head, hear her words, speak with her voice.

The wingback sits like a throne on the pickup. Around it, Perla and Orson have stacked their treasures in cartons and shopping bags. Perla secures the whole thing with bungee cords.

"Oh, Perla is so clever," Orson enthuses. "Isn't she clever?"

"Very clever." Lockwood nods.

"Where to?" asks Perla.

"I don't know," Lockwood says. "I'm supposed to be handing over the tapes to Hollywood Hank. Except he doesn't know where I am. I'm surprised he didn't show up at the Señora's estate sale. It would have been the obvious thing to do."

"Oh, heavens," exclaims Orson La Prima. "You missed him by minutes. He was there! Rifling through her desk, for collectibles and mementos, he said."

Perla shakes her head in wonder. "Right about the time we were running back to the car to make sure the case was safe."

"The fates are looking out for us," Lockwood sighs. "But right now I need a place to collect my thoughts for a few hours."

"And we need a place to celebrate our treasures," says Orson.

"The Poodle Club!" he and Perla exclaim in unison.

Perla decides that the safest place for the briefcase while they all go to a bar is in Lockwood's hand. They leave the Saab parked near the Señora's condo to confuse Hollywood Hank, and the three of them crowd onto the truck's seat with Lockwood squeezed in the middle. "Off to Louie and Louella's Poodle Club," Orson sings.

Lockwood puts in a cassette of Mercè Casals in *Aida*.

Orson drums on the glove compartment with his hands. "I cry every time she's buried alive. I can hardly believe the Señora is dead, you know. What if she isn't?"

"What are you, *tonto?*" Perla says.

"Well, excuse me. I think of stuff like that. We can't help what we fantasize. During the visitation, I wanted to slip a cell phone under her hand."

"A weird thought," Lockwood says. "You didn't, right?"

"No time. Besides, the Rossinis wouldn't let me get too close while *en costume*. They thought I was being disrespectful."

Lockwood is intent on the singing, but with occasional furtive glances, he gets a good look at Orson for the first time. At forty-something, over six feet tall, with wide shoulders and strong hands, he is a sharp contrast to the prima donna he portrays in his lip-synch act.

"Now what?" Orson finally turns and meets Lockwood's gaze.

"Nothing."

"Yes, something. I know when I'm being checked out." He reaches across Lockwood to tap Perla on the shoulder. "Perla, tell him to stop ogling."

"I did not mean to stare." He adds gently, "Just can't help wondering about you."

"You're guessing I'm queer?"

"Not the point," he says. "I mean, Perla freelances deathbeds, I write for money. How do you manage to be a full-time opera queen?" He adds, "Maybe it's none of my business."

"Money is the last secret in American society." Orson laughs. "Nobody will ask you how much money you make or tell you how much they have stashed away. Why do you ask?"

"I'm a writer." Lockwood shrugs. "I ask questions."

"The truth," Orson says after a pause, "is that I'm not really La Prima but actually a very familiar old Santa Barbara name that you would recognize in a heartbeat, which makes me the beneficiary of a trust fund. I get a fat allowance as long as I abide by strict conditions. One, that I not bring embarrassment to my parents and siblings. Two, that I never show my face at certain family affairs like weddings and funerals, unless specifically invited by the host. Hasn't happened yet!" he adds cheerfully. "Three, that I not reveal my real name except under official government duress."

"Sounds terrible," Lockwood says.

"I'm used to it. The family jumped to conclusions when I was about twelve and started dressing up in Mother's party dresses. Now, *she* was a diva."

"Where are we going?" Lockwood asks Perla as they head beyond San Diego. "We missed the Hillcrest exit."

"Louie and Louella's is in one of those neighborhoods where nobody has heard of you, or Mercè Casals, or Hollywood Hank. One of those south-side neighborhoods. One of those neighborhoods where normal people live. Africans, Mexicans, Cambodians. White people, too."

They reach an intersection where a drugstore, a car wash, a hardware store, and the Poodle Club face each other as the final outposts of urban solidity before the neighborhood stretches into industrial wasteland. Even though it's early in the evening, the Poodle Club beckons with a pink neon dog wagging its tail.

"We'll have beers," says Orson. "You'll collect your thoughts. We'll get to know each other, the three of us."

A waitress with a pink poodle embroidered on her black apron shows them to the circular booth at the back of the dim lounge. "Excuse me, you two," says Orson, slipping in between Perla and Lockwood. "I'll be the chaperone."

"Right," says Perla. "We don't want Mark making vulgar displays of affection."

Lockwood is visibly irritated. Why can't he sit beside Perla? he wonders. It's bad enough that the briefcase keeps getting in the way. "I can't believe you are the protector of morality," he says.

"Oh, my," Orson says with a grin. "Am I getting a whiff of moral superiority from a two-timing husband?"

"Gracias, querido." Perla laughs, sliding toward Orson.

"Have a drink, Scribbler," Orson says. "You'll feel better."

Perla and Orson start out with white Russians in tall glasses with poodle swizzle sticks. Lockwood orders a beer. He's feeling shut out of the party. He reminds himself that being at the Poodle Club is a respite that will give him a chance to breathe without Hollywood Hank, in turn, breathing down his neck.

The rest of the lounge is mostly empty, with only a man and a woman arguing about the death penalty from one end of the bar to the other. The woman wants to fry rapists, child molesters, drug lords, pimps, and certain cops. Three strikes and you're gone. "Bye-bye. For-fucking-ever," she snarls. She's all bones and angles in green satin that creeps up to reveal sharp knees and pale thighs.

The man, a comfortably soft business type in a rumpled blue suit, is shaking his head like he can't believe he is having a conversation with someone he has never met and would normally not be speaking to, because he is a professional having a strong drink after working late at the office. But you can't shut up a guy with ideas: His thing is that he'd like to establish a penal colony in the Pacific. Just take all the criminals out to a balmy island with thatched-roof communal houses where the convicts will be free to marry and breed and plant pineapples and bananas for food. Let them build their own town and see how they like living among a bunch of delinquents.

Green Dress calls him a liberal and a softy. She's winning the argument by virtue of having the louder voice with much hatred inside her.

"Don't mind them," the waitress says with a nod in the direction of the bar. "They're part of the entertainment."

Lockwood holds the briefcase between his legs, and with his free hand points to the Miller sign on the wall. "I will have another."

"Not expected at home by the little woman?" says Orson.

"Right!"

"Not?"

"Yeah."

"Sorry. I pry sometimes." Orson takes a long swallow. "You have a right to be impatient with me. I mean, you were already hooked up with Perla, then I show up, and now there's some mysterious energy going on around this table, if you know what I mean."

Lockwood frowns. "Do I know what you mean?"

"I think you do. It's like we three are destined for an adventure."

"You think there's something cosmic about us sitting here in the middle of nowhere having a drink."

"You're being sarcastic, right?" says Orson.

"Right, the Poodle Club in east San Diego is not exactly the middle of nowhere," Perla says after consulting the address on the Poodle Club matchbook.

"That's not exactly my point," Lockwood says. "My point is that everyone is having a good time here. Except me."

"And whose fault is that, if I may ask?" says Orson.

At about that moment, two white poodles that have been dyed cotton-candy pink suddenly appear under the table, sniffing around the men's feet, tongues hanging out, eagerly nuzzling their knees, begging to be petted. Lockwood feels one of the dogs put its two front legs around his calf and pull itself up until its nose is nuzzling his knee while its rubbery penis insistently presses against his shin. He reaches down to push it away, and the dog responds with more jerky humps.

"Qué simpático perrito," Perla coos at the dog under the table.

Lockwood jerks his leg, sending the poodle sliding into the middle of the room. The yapping attracts the attention of the bartender, who rushes to gather the dog in his arms. "Did these old meanies hurt you?" His baby talk is edged with menace.

The woman who had been voicing the virtues of the death penalty swivels around on her barstool and scowls at Lockwood. "I would also fry people who kick innocent dogs," she says.

"There would be no dogs in the island prison," the man who has been arguing with her decides. "That would be part of the punishment. No cats, no dogs, no goldfish, no hamsters."

"Serve the evildoers right," the woman agrees with him for the first time.

The bartender cradles the poodle and carries it to Lockwood's booth, "This is Louie. He has as much right to be in the Poodle Club as anyone. Now, I don't know which of you three kicked him. But I think Louie is entitled to an apology. My grandparents, Louie and Louella, founded the Poodle Club forty-two years ago. When you kicked Louie, you kicked tradition in the teeth."

"I did not kick your dog," Lockwood says. "I pushed him away with my leg because he had fallen in love with it."

"You've hurt Louie's feelings. You could buy him a beef-jerky treat. One for Louella too."

"Sure, we were about to leave anyway." Lockwood takes a bill from his wallet, slaps it down on the table, and starts to slide out of the booth. But the bartender, still holding the poodle, blocks the way with his protruding midriff.

"What a good idea," the bartender says. "Now, before you leave, which one of you is going to apologize to Louie?"

"I can apologize for the group," Orson jumps in. "*Pardonnez-moi*, Louie," he says. "My friend Lockwood didn't mean to kick your sorry ass."

"Sorry ass," Lockwood echoes as if it's the funniest thing he's ever heard.

"You should lose the attitude." The bartender shakes his head sadly. "That attitude will not do at all."

There's a silence between them. Lockwood wraps his trembling hand around the beer mug. A calming influence spreads from the frosted glass up his arm to his brain. Perla and Orson lean back and watch with a bemused look.

"Dog kickers should die," screams the death-penalty woman from her barstool.

"What a cowardly thing to kick an innocent creature," the pudgy man says, shaking his head in disbelief.

Lockwood glances from the man and back to the woman and feels that streams of hatred that have been gathered from different sources are now being directed at him. Everywhere he looks he bumps into dark omens. He glances back at the poodle in the bartender's arms and wonders if it is not some devil in disguise, the traditional goat being too obvious, bats and rats too scary even if they're not the devil. The poodle, on the other hand, seems so fluffy and girly to be evil incarnate. Whatever satanic qualities he perceives in it are meant just for him. "There's my money for the drinks." Lockwood indicates the bill on the table. "And for the doggy treats." He moves away from the table.

Orson and Perla get up at the same time and hover around Lockwood. "Well, come on, man," Orson pulls him by the arm as Perla leads the way in a determined march. "This is the part where we walk away with our dignity intact."

Lockwood feels relieved that a potentially nasty scene has been avoided. "You saved my life, friends," he says when they reach the safety of Perla's truck. "It was getting ugly back there."

"Oh, we would have done okay in a bar fight." Orson shrugs off the gratitude. "We're in this together. Us, the Señora, the book."

"It's what she would have wanted," says Perla. She comes up to Lockwood and holds him in a warm embrace. A momentary spark of pleasure fades as he feels Orson's long arms squeezing him and Perla around the shoulders.

Good-bye to Pep Saval

The battle for Barcelona ended in a whimper. The bombing from low-flying Stukkas had deliberately spared architectural marvels, Gaudí's jeweled edifices, the hospital of Sant Pau, the monastery of Montserrat, the cathedral. The pilots targeted life itself. The Rambla, crowded with strolling couples, families, and children, was strafed. Trucks loaded with the wounded were blown up. The front walls of apartment buildings were peeled off to reveal a kind of spectral dollhouse, the rooms inhabited now only by heirlooms and family treasures, brass bedsteads and mahogany chests, sofas and chairs festooned with fringes and tassels, shelves with books still in place, a crucifix on a wall, a crystal vase standing at the center of a table intact, its flowers rotting in murky water.

I remember the day that Franco's Moroccan troops marched into the city. I was hiding in the basement of the *pensión* because we were told that young women were at risk. The cellar was used to hide crates of potatoes and hunks of salted ham and sacks of beans. Franco sent the Moorish battalions from Almería in the south. The war had lasted longer than anyone had expected, and they blamed Barcelona, the seat of the

Republic, for resistance. Around the basement, narrow air openings allowed a view of the pavement. All I could see through them were feet. Throughout '37 and '38, I used to sit in the safety of the basement and try to figure out what was happening by how people walked. They strolled under the sun. Ran from the rain. Toppled under the bombing. When I think of the war, I think of shoes. Men's shoes and women's shoes and children's shoes. Military boots goose-stepping to a sharp drumbeat. Glossy bourgeois ankle boots and wingtips in the English style. The shoes of dead feet and wounded feet and running feet.

A child's foot inside a yellow sock, twitching outside its shoe which had slipped off when she'd tripped and fallen.

A bloody clump amid shreds of brown leather after several bursts from a Thompson repeater sprayed the street. The other foot was still inside a glossy cordovan. That was how I knew the foot belonged to Señor Cantarra, the pharmacist. He was very careful about his appearance.

Hundreds of steel-tipped boots, marching in unison, making the ground shake with the impact of their heels muddy from the roads. They were the Moors from the nationalist regiments in Almería and Cádiz. Franco had sent them because, having no friends or relatives so far north, they would have no local loyalties and would be resentful of being dragged from the south to our bitter winter.

They started arriving early on a Tuesday morning in December. They kept coming all that day and most of the night and into the next morning. The ground shook with the stamping of boots and the rolling of trucks and tanks. It wasn't constant. They came in waves. Just when I thought it was over and would start to fall asleep, the shouts would begin again, echoing down the street and growing in volume as the soldiers approached, finally passing a few inches away from the vent grates.

For days I did not leave the basement. I slept and took my meals there, and tried to entertain myself reading by the faint light from the narrow windows. I was not political. But it was understood that it would be dangerous for me to be seen outside during those first few days of the occupation. I had sung for certain people. Men in the government. Other girls had fallen in love with Russian volunteers or taken care of the wounded or worked for the Republic. I had only sung, usually in return for a shank of salted ham or a bag of potatoes. But mainly I sang because I have only felt completely alive, fully awake to myself, while singing. When I'm not singing, I'm half asleep, only occasionally stirred by the taste of food or the quickening of my skin to another's touch.

The news filtered down. The nationalist troops and the rich young men, the sons of bankers and industrialists, were roaming in bands hunting out women they considered traitors. People saw these things happen. Girls' heads were shaved. Their clothes were torn off and burned. My friend María Garcés was attacked by toughs who decided she had been the lover of a communist journalist. These were boys who knew María and who had visited her family, whose sisters had gone to sewing classes or walked along the Rambla with her, who had studied French and music and grammar under the same nuns. The rumors about her were not true. The journalist was a cousin. He was able to escape to France, so they decided to turn their anger on her.

She was stripped and her body stretched on the roof of a car, secured by ropes from her wrists and ankles held by the hooligans inside. *"Puta Roja"* was scrawled in red paint on her stomach. They drove all through the town, honking and cheering and yelling curses. I heard them go by the basement windows, saw the wheels of the car turning slowly so that people could look down on María from their windows and rooftops, and I know it was they because their voices became louder, their shouts somehow directed toward me because they knew I was her friend.

In those days the whole city seemed under the grip of anarchy. Some of us had been relieved when the military had come to restore order. The streets, blocked by heaps of garbage, sandbags, and the occasional mule carcass used as a gun emplacement, were oddly quiet in the middle of the day under a cloudless sky. Legions of cats and dogs, suddenly orphaned, had a run of the streets. Rats picked through the rubble on the giant banquet of the dead. And from rooftops and apartment windows, white flags had replaced red ones. Soldiers in long black coats and boots gray with dust gathered at street corners, smoking and conversing in low voices, no longer vigilant, their aggression spent and replaced with boredom and uncertainty. Around them, shops were shuttered, kiosks were stripped bare, and the homes still standing were locked tight. The army owned the city but there was little for it to claim. It was all about waiting, for orders, for relief, for the trucks that would take the soldiers to the next battle zone. The lucky ones would be mustered out of the city before the fever spread.

It took weeks before the generals ordered the cleanup. They had not expected the extent of debris and flooding from burst pipes. City services had broken down as the sanitation workers, mostly good unionists, had joined the stream of refugees heading toward the French border. The streets were left to the ravages of an ill wind and an untimely rain that, rather than scrub the city, served to spread the muck.

The first crews were recruited from homeless shelters and the prison camps. Anyone deemed not too threatening was put to work. Old men shoveled garbage onto carts and the occasional truck spared by the military. Children shuffled along pushing brooms. Women scrubbed the bloodstained pavement with brushes and buckets of lye. These brigades of the indigent, the unemployed, and the solitary became the first victims of the typhoid epidemic.

I saw Pep Saval, for the first time since the bombing, standing at a makeshift parapet and using the edge of a shovel to break apart a mule carcass. Still trying, in the midst of his brutal task, to look dignified in his rumpled suit, black beret, and string tie. I had stepped out of the pensión for the first time in days. Running water had started flowing in the bath again and I felt clean and attractive for a change. I had taken some pesetas I had been saving and set out to scour the newly opened stores for a tin of sardines, fresh bread, and cheese. I had never been so hungry. The whole city looked gaunt and hopelessly sad.

I didn't remember anyone looking as sick as Pep Saval did. His face, thin and unshaven, was flushed from the exertion, yet he was shivering inside his woolen jacket. He dropped the shovel to the ground and opened his arms to embrace me, his face stinging hot against mine. *"Nena del meu cor!"* he rasped. Oh, child of my heart. I stiffened in his arms.

"I'm sorry." He let go suddenly. "I forget how I must smell."

I did not want to comment on his appearance, on the shocking stink of his breath when his face had been close. "Are you ill?"

"La tifoidea." He shrugged the word away as if it were some annoying insect. "Everybody has it. Try not to spend too much time on the street. It's in the air."

"Why are you doing this work?" I asked. "You are sick."

"Oh, I was not considered too weak for it." He laughed. "They decided I did not have anything better to do with my talents. There is not much opportunity for card players these days, with few sheep worth fleecing."

"Is there something I can do?" I somehow could not express the full gratitude that was due him after his looking out for me these past years.

"Gracias, nena," he said, coming close again. I braced for his embrace. Instead, he reached for my hand. "I could come to your *pensión,*" he said. "To take a bath. That would be nice."

I pulled my hand away at last, feeling a sudden urge to escape him. I didn't know if typhoid was contagious. I was frightened by the startled look in his eyes, the heat of his fever. "You know how strict the manager is," I said, "about men visiting."

"I'll come in the middle of the night." He smiled sadly. "When nobody is watching, and you can let me in and run the hot water and lend me a bar of soap. A good bath could save my life, you know."

"Of course, Pep," I said to his back as he turned to go back to work on the dead mule. "I will open the door for you, if you come by."

For several nights I expected his knock. When I realized he was not coming, I kept thinking back to our last meeting and wondering whether something in my tone or expression had discouraged him. Certainly I'd never told him not to come. I had offered, I reassured myself. But I didn't see him again. Months later I received a notification of his death, at the Hospital de Sant Pau. He had named me as his next of kin. His body would be cremated and the ashes would be available for a month, before being disposed of.

SHOW ME ONE FALSE LINE . . .

It's past midnight by the time Lockwood arrives home, leading the way down the interstate to Anaheim, then down a dark and silent Hyacinth Street, followed by Perla and Orson and his treasures on the truck—the chair, a carton of vinyl records, two picture albums. The neighborhood hums with the whirs of air conditioners and fans. It's only when Lockwood stops the car just shy of the garage door and turns off the engine that he senses the deep quiet of his own house. There's a rock-like stillness that makes the chipped stucco by the downstairs picture window, the weathered front door, the muddy bed of wilting begonias seem alien and forbidding.

"There's no one home," Lockwood murmurs as he turns the key in the front-door lock. His other hand holds on to the satchel. Perla and Orson hang back, waiting to be invited in. He pushes the door open and faces a folded note at his feet. Lockwood signals to the pair that it's okay to follow him into the house.

In Claire's rounded hand is a message: "I left everything clean," the note reads. "It'll be up to you, again, to make a mess of things. C."

"Está furiosa," Perla says over his shoulder.

"It doesn't say where she went," Lockwood says. "I could've been killed last night," he shakes his head, "and she'd be nowhere to be informed."

Perla peers at the rooms beyond the entrance foyer. "Nice house," she says, stepping around Lockwood. "I haven't ever lived in a house, do you know that? Always apartments, first in DF, then LA, now San Diego."

Orson waves his hand like a Realtor. "This is a truly gracious residence—the sunken living room so '70s, the central air so refreshing, the plush carpet so plush."

Perla adds, "I'd like to live in a house someday."

Moments later, Lockwood notices that Claire's frogs carved out of onyx, ivory, and ebony are gone. All twenty-two have been swept off the shelf. He rushes upstairs to find that his wife's drawers have been emptied, that half the towels and half the sheets and her favorite bedspread are gone. The bathroom counter has been wiped clean of her bottles and tubes and brushes. The plastic case with her diaphragm and a full tube of Gynol II are absent, too. She has systematically gone through the house and removed every intimate sign of her presence. There is something rancorous about her thoroughness.

Sadly, she has left him significant mementos of their shared past; untouched are the envelopes stuffed with photos, old letters and postcards collected during their various trips together. Their memories of Venice, Santa Fe, Aix en Provence, Bryce Canyon, Oaxaca, are all his to keep. He sits on the edge of the bed with the satchel at his side and buries his face in his hands. The enormity of the situation starts to dawn on him. *Claire, Claire*, he thinks. *Don't leave me now that I'm about to make money and find fulfillment. No small things these in the life of a writer.*

The smell of sautéed garlic and eggs frying in olive oil pulls him away from his musing. He bounds down the stairs into the kitchen and finds

Orson hunkered over the stove, a dishcloth apron hooked over his belt. "It's almost one A.M.," Orson says. "Not too early for breakfast."

He's in the process of folding a huge omelet in a cast-iron pan. Coffee brews and toast browns. Orson's penchant for the dramatic is manifest in the kitchen. The counters and stovetop are littered with eggshells, garlic skins, smears of cream cheese, and bread crumbs from the first slices of toast.

"You didn't know omelets were my métier, did you?" he calls out.

"I'm starved," says Perla, pouring herself a cup of coffee and taking a seat at the kitchen table.

"I gather you found everything all right," says Lockwood, unsure how he feels about the two suddenly making themselves at home in Claire's kitchen.

"Freshly ground pepper would be nice. Or did your wife take the pepper mill?" Orson asks.

"Middle cabinet above your right shoulder. Cost fifty bucks at Williams-Sonoma," he says.

"Can't spend too much on a good pepper mill, Lockwood. Those little grinding gears take a lot of abuse. Sprinkle some on the omelet before I give it another turn. Set it coarser," Orson directs. "You want to be able to bite into an occasional chunk."

Orson lifts the edges of the omelet, looking for the perfect balance between yielding firm and springy tender.

Lockwood pulls plates and mugs from the cabinet and sets them on the table. He remembers how Claire always uses place mats, and he chooses a set of Mexican ones with a yellow geometric motif on cobalt blue. He pulls strawberry and plum preserves from the refrigerator, wanting to believe that Claire left the Bonne Maman for him.

Perla holds out the plates as Orson divides a twelve-egg omelet. Scraping the bottom of the black pan, he places charred scrapings of sizzled garlic and the last of the oil on top of each serving. Lockwood watches with growing appetite.

"This the breakfast you had in mind?" Orson smiles. "You buy shitty coffee, by the way. Next time you're out, get us Lavazza espresso and Chiapas Altura Pluma. Mix them together and you've got the brew of the gods. Roman gods, Mayan gods, and us."

"Us?"

"Not good to talk business while eating," he says, taking a forkful of eggs into his mouth.

"You did say something about our becoming *socios*," Perla adds

"I did?"

"Yes, partners." She follows the eggs with a bite of toast and washes everything down with gulps of coffee. "That's all I'm saying at this point. Enjoy your breakfast." She points the fork at Lockwood's plate.

Orson takes in the exchange with interest. "You two," Orson says, "are very cute together." He glances from Lockwood to Perla.

"This is tasty," Lockwood replies.

The moment reminds him of a Sunday morning. He and Claire having a big, slow breakfast. Up early to savor the day, to enjoy the sunshine coming into their cheerful kitchen, to enjoy the fat newspaper with the book reviews, the analysis of scandals and political mayhem, and the latest natural disasters.

Instead of Claire's, he finds himself staring into a pair of bright dark eyes as hard as marbles. Lockwood lowers his head and eats in earnest. The tightness at the back of his throat eases.

After breakfast, the three park themselves around the living room. Orson sits back on the big couch and loosens his belt. Perla takes the Señora's chair. Their long, heavy sighs and muffled grunts of contentment echo each other in some atavistic preverbal language. Lockwood escapes to his bedroom. Somebody will clean up the kitchen, he thinks. Already he's slipping from Claire's sense of order.

Wherever his mind wanders during those first hours, Lockwood remembers something Claire always says, or the way she looks in a certain light. He finds himself glancing repeatedly at his watch and wondering what's keeping her, fearing she might have had an accident, expecting the phone to ring at any moment, not with her voice explaining her whereabouts but with the voices of the police or the hospital. He finds himself imagining that she's hurt in some strange town and that she will call and he will rush out to help her heal or that he will be too late and she will be dead.

But the phone does not ring. There are no calls from Claire's friends or her mother or the public library or Planned Parenthood, where she volunteers. The answering machine signals steady unblinking silence. Claire's disappearance is complete. It's only when he reads and rereads her note that the sound of her voice comes back and the memory of her personality fills the vacuum. From the moment he discovered the note lying on the floor in front of the front door, he has not dared to read the whole thing from beginning to end. Instead he has scanned through disconnected passages, absorbing the overall meaning from a few odd words and phrases.

I'm not taking this action lightly. . . .

Don't blame yourself. . . .

The post office will be forwarding my mail. . . .

If anything for me does come, send it on to my parents' address. . . . You'll be fine. . . .

It's a difficult decision. . . . Don't blame yourself. . . . These things happen in the life of a couple. . . . Nothing is meant to last forever. . . .

Don't blame yourself. . . . This has been a long time in the making. . . . Don't blame yourself. . . .

No, he won't blame himself. He's the innocent victim of circumstance. His peaceful existence as a contented husband and writer of handy and helpful booklets has been turned on its ear by a rogue muse. He will start by blaming Mercè Casals, for dying unexpectedly and bequeathing to him the one story he's wanted all his life. He blames the famous writer Alonzo Baylor for deciding to chase the same story, despite the fact that he is already rich and celebrated, and old. He blames Hollywood Hank because he's fulfilling all his paranoid fantasies. And he blames Perla.

Lockwood would like to sleep. He's been up all night and is punchy with exhaustion and emotionally sapped by Claire's note. He's vaguely aware of Perla and Orson left free to wander about his house, probably snooping in closets and bathroom cabinets, reading his mail. He's not able to fall asleep until he slides the satchel under his head and uses it as a pillow, even though it makes his face numb.

He awakes the next day after noon to the murky darkness of his bedroom all shuttered and curtained against the summer glare. His eyes open slowly, gradually focusing on the blurry figure of Perla sitting in a chair by the side of his bed, only a few inches from his face.

"You're one oblivious snoozer," she says. "I could've taken your car keys and been out of here hours ago. I could've stolen stuff."

"Why didn't you?"

"I thought we were going to talk business, for one."

"And for another?"

"We're friends, Lockwood. I told you."

Lockwood sits up on the bed. Perla has changed into a pair of his wife's khaki shorts and an old halter top she found in one of Claire's drawers.

"You look cute," he says.

"She seems to have taken the nice clothes with her." Perla shrugs. "Anyway, I wanted clean things to wear after my shower."

"Is our opera queen still here?"

"Yep, he's showering and picking through closets. He wants to go grocery shopping. There's nothing in the house, he says."

"He's helpful."

She nods. "He has already cleaned the mess from breakfast."

"I feel like a guest."

"So, relax, Lockwood, and do your job."

"I'm scared to sit down and actually write."

"What's so hard about writing?"

"Telling the truth," Lockwood says. "That's the main requirement. Be true. It's also the rule most often broken. Untruthful writers should be locked up without a computer or a pencil or even a nail they can use to scratch their lying shit on the walls."

"You're never phony, I gather."

"Never. Show me one false line I've written and I will eat the page."

"I saw the special shelf with all your books neatly lined up like trophies in chronological order. *Two Loaves of Bread* was the first one."

"That was some time ago."

"I gather that. It's in a different style from the rest."

"That's very astute of you."

"I actually started reading the one called *Talking to Your Teenager About Crime.*"

"Did you learn anything?" Lockwood asks.

"You seem to take the position that crime is an act of nature like rain or snow that we all have to learn to live with. So we take precautions, like carrying an umbrella or not talking to strangers."

Lockwood nods. "You can count on a little crime coming into your life like you can count on getting the flu every couple of years."

"That's really subversive, you know. Your publisher must not actually read that nihilistic crap you're laying on the young and impressionable. Kids have to be brought up to believe that law and justice will eventually prevail."

Lockwood smiles. "You weren't bored, were you?"

"No, I was amused." Perla shakes her head in mock amazement.

"I'm probably the first writer you've known."

"You and the guy who tried to bribe me at the wake. I get one writer that wants me to steal from another writer. I thought you guys stuck together."

Lockwood shakes his head sadly. "Not Alonzo Baylor."

"He's the famous one, right." Perla is impressed. "I see him on TV. Lots of curly chest hair creeping out from under his shirt collar. Arms like hams. Laughs like a horse."

"Every time he has a new book out."

"Yeah, but that's a guy with several contradictions from the waist down. I'm a good judge of character," Perla says. "Comes from seeing so many people in their last moment. That's when they are truly themselves. Alonzo crosses his legs like a little old lady and wears dainty Italian loafers. They don't go with his image."

"You can discern character by a man's shoes." Lockwood nods.

"That's the first writerly thing you've said so far. I'll keep an eye out for that sort of revealing detail from now on."

Lockwood gazes at her curiously. "Don't you have any place to go, a shift at the ICU?"

"What?" she asks. "Am I getting too close for comfort now? What if your wife should pop in? You'd like me to go away, wouldn't you? All that stuff about us going into this deal together, about you paying me more than my patients, about me helping you cash in the million-dollar stash locked up in that grubby bag of yours. It was all drunk talk at the Poodle Club."

Lockwood grasps at wispy threads of the night's conversation. "No, I meant everything, Perla." He gets up and heads for the bathroom. "If you don't believe that, you can walk out on me."

"No such luck, Lockwood. I like your house."

"Did I invite Orson, too?"

"You sure did. You said we would all work on the Mercè Casals memoir as a team."

Lockwood sighs and hopes that by the time he's fully awake, everything will have fallen into place. "Okay. Look, I'm going to shower now. Then let's have a conversation about all this. You know, call a meeting."

"So I'm your secretary now?"

"No. I'm asking this as a favor. You're the writer's trusted adviser, confidant, and comfort woman."

"I prefer secretary. Thanks."

Enter the Prince

The audience stretched back fifty rows in shadowy waves, then swept into the high reaches of the vaulted ceiling. Seen from the stage, the crowd took on a singular, monstrous consciousness, forgoing reasonable individuality to become a multiheaded, thousand-tongued beast.

But around the world, night after night, from one stage to another, I became aware of a man with a plump, bland face who was somehow both part of the monster and separate from it. He always sat in the same center seat in the second row, his head tilted up. His soft eyes clouded with tears during every one of my four appearances in *La Sonnambula*. He was there for my Norma, Violetta, Micaela, Aida. He followed me to Athens, Paris, New York, Barcelona, London. I grew to depend on his presence. When the leviathan lurked in the dark, I would seek out the man's eyes and find reassurance in their light. Even after the applause died down and the theater was left dark, I would remember his presence.

There had been obsessive fans in the past, cloying, oppressive personalities that claimed my attention, somehow demanding reciprocation. One young woman who had stalked the stage entrance at Covent Garden had told anyone who would listen that if she could not serve as La Señora's personal attendant, she preferred not to live. Her name was Dinorah Patrowski, and the story was in all the papers. The day before she died, she mailed a Polaroid she had taken by holding the camera in front of herself. I recognized the face in the photo as belonging to the woman who'd been found curled up inside a Dumpster, dead from barbiturates and Scotch. The envelope sat around my suite for days, seeming to shift on its own power from the coffee table to the top of the TV and finally to the bottom drawer of the dresser. I could not bring myself to throw it away.

In the '70s, six fellows who called themselves Casals' Cuties ran naked streaks across the stage whenever my current chief rival, Domenica Quatorze, was in the middle of an aria. The offended singer was usually forced to interrupt her performance until things calmed down. The group disbanded after a performance of *Aida* in Dallas when a disapproving supernumerary threw his spear at one of the streakers. After that I pleaded in an interview in *Opera News* that the different claques limit themselves to showing approval for a particular performer rather than sabotaging her sisters' work.

The fan who kept appearing in opera houses all over the world was in a class by himself. I was not surprised to learn that he was of royal descent, his highness the Crown Prince of Montefino, Liviu Gregoriu. He was discreet, at first. He disguised himself to avoid gossip. He had mustaches, beards, and hairpieces. He wore thick tortoiseshell glasses, or wraparounds with nearly black lenses, or others with mirror glazes. The glasses came off once the lights were dimmed, and I would recognize his questioning blue gaze.

Gifts arrived to celebrate opening night or the closing performance of a successful run. In Oslo, in the middle of February, it was six perfect peaches. In Tokyo, truffles. In Paris, persimmons. The gifts were accompanied by an unsigned card that expressed in florid handwriting an admiration bordering on worship. One example: "Oh glorious diva! A holy scent filled La Fenice from your first exhalation. May you taste sweetness upon the tongue every day of your life. Signed, An Admirer." This note was affixed to a small chest made of silver and filled with pine-nut confections, the rare *dulces de leche y piñón* from the legendary Dulcería de Celaya in Mexico City. By then, through deduction and gossip, I had figured out Prince Liviu's identity.

Ordinary people know nothing of royalty. Wealth has little to do with actual nobility. It's only a small attribute. Until we meet one of them close up, we like to think their birth is the work of holy destiny, fated accidents of parentage. The truth is that the difference between us and royalty is not in our heads but, more precisely, in theirs, which function on an entirely different wavelength. That is, we do not imagine that the royals are different from us so much as they know beyond the slightest uncertainty that their ancestry makes them a breed apart.

Take the Prince. His country had ceased to exist at the end of World War I. He'd been born in Scotland while his parents, King Sebastian and Queen Ulrica, in exile, were golfing at St. Andrews. He has never set foot in Montefino, not even as a tourist. He has a trust fund but no subjects, no castle, no royal guard, no royal tax collector. His crown is in a museum in Albania along with shelves and shelves of monarchic bric-a-brac. I suppose he could have claimed his family heirlooms in some court of law, but the successive governments of what was then Yugoslavia and is now Bosnia-Herzegovina have agreed on one fundamental point: that if any royals return to Montefino, they will star in a reenactment of the French Revolution.

What the Prince did have was a basic wardrobe for traveling in royal circles—jodhpurs for the hunt, a tuxedo for the casino, a smoking jacket for lounging, and a studded leather bomber jacket for speeding around on a Harley. He liked to travel light. He had no royal palace, but always a good hotel suite. The man could check into the Plaza, and within minutes suite 1295 would exude a royal air, as if the atmosphere had become charged by his very breath.

I saw bankers and maître d's and generals perform, when in his presence, the most absurdly self-effacing contortions. It was a nonverbal, nonrational language that acknowledged the man's lofty status. He knew what he was. And the world, without anyone having to cue it in, agreed.

Naturally, when the Prince courted me, I succumbed. Happily, I might say. Without a backward glance. Without a thought for dear Nolan. Without a moment's consideration for my contracts in Milan, New York, Mexico City. I canceled everything. Appearances, plane reservations, meetings with lawyers and agents, and even my daily lunch with Nolan. He realized then that I was drifting away; he took it hard. Day after day I would clear my whole agenda to be available for the Prince at a moment's notice. He was used to living by his own schedule, which was no schedule at all. He would give me an hour to get dressed, to do my hair and my makeup, and then a car would appear. Other times, I would sit around and mope for days, still refusing all invitations, locking Nolan out of my room, canceling performances. My calling was to rise in the world. I was lifted higher by the Prince's infatuation than I was ever lifted by a high C.

It's time to correct a myth that has been around for years: I did not trade my voice for a five-year fling with Prince Liviu. True, falling in love with the Prince meant living the life that the fast set of dethroned royalty demanded: late nights and smoky casinos, the chatter of endless parties, and the damp sea air of Mediterranean cruises.

I had been pushing my voice for years, and by thirty-three I had lost significant range and flexibility. The first time a wobble emerged in my *"Vissi d'arte"* it went unmentioned. The next time, Maestro Serafini dismissed it as a fluke due to the dry air inside La Scala. Another time during a rehearsal of *Madama Butterfly* at Covent Garden, there had been a slight hesitation, not quite a crack, which had forced me to retreat from those dangerous heights. Dust from set construction was blamed.

The list of threatening factors grew: pollen, air conditioning, exhaust fumes, French perfumes, certain months in certain cities. It was all a mystery. Occasional cast members were perceived as particularly threatening. For example, and to name only one, I could not do *Norma* with Flavia Gesualdo as Adalgisa. I quite admired Gesualdo, but for both of us to breathe the same air resulted in quavers, wobbles, and squeaks. Parts of *"Mira, o Norma"* have sounded like a pair of parrots in a cage.

I was eager to accept any excuse made for me. I was grateful for the excessive praise on the ever fewer occasions when a performance went flawlessly. And there was always Nolan Keefe to come home to. He knew what was happening; the unspoken truth was obvious in the way he would hold me through the fearful, sleepless night before an opening. When we performed together, however, he would look at me with a mixture of encouragement and terror that I found unnerving. After a while, I let it be known that singing opposite my husband was one factor that disrupted my singing. Nolan took the loss of bookings with good grace.

I canceled performances with a frequency that alarmed management and irritated my public. Singing the principal soprano role in an opera is a demanding physical and mental feat. Many things in the physiology affect pitch—menstruation, constipation, respiration. The pressure is compounded by the expectations of an audience that knows the role nearly as well as the singer does. Opera fans stand in line for hours, pay an extravagant ticket price, and might have been waiting years for a particular performer to sing a particular role. If I feared I might not live up to their expectations, I canceled.

Still, my reputation for unreliability is unearned. Taking my whole career into account, I may have called off no more than five percent of my performances, usually with plenty of notice. There are bureaucrats and bankers who don't have such a record. When I did appear, not many people knew of the stage fright that afflicted me. It was not uncommon, even as the orchestra was well into the overture, for a fabulously costumed and jeweled Violetta to rush into the nearest ladies' room and, one hand holding her wig and the other her bodice, vomit her lunch in one racking eruption.

On one occasion, while waiting in the wings to go on as Norma, I turned to my dear friend Giuseppi DiStefano for support. I hoped for a smile of encouragement, perhaps a firm push toward the stage when my cue came. But when he turned toward me, his face, too, was ashen from stage fright.

In the middle of this crisis, Prince Liviu came to the rescue. It happened during curtain calls after a *Tosca* for which I had been in good voice. I remembered thinking that maybe the earlier lapses of control were behind me. I was luxuriating in the applause and the cries of *Brava* and the red roses at my feet when there was a sudden hush as the audience became aware, even before I did, of the two giant peacocks that had been let loose on the stage.

The magnificent birds strutted in like awkward angels as I was rising from a languid curtsy. Following some hidden cue, they stopped and, with a sudden whir, fanned out their feathers. From the neck of one, a white envelope hung by a gold ribbon. An attendant rushed to the bird and removed a card. My arms still embraced a bouquet, so I signaled him to open it. "Read it for everyone to hear."

Years later I can still hear the contents of that card being read to the thousands packed to the highest reaches of La Scala. It was quite likely the most public declaration of love any woman had ever received. "*Querida* Mercè Casals, *Usted vive para el arte, mientras yo muero de amor por usted. Me rindo a sus pies*, Liviu Gregoriu . . . Príncipe de Monte-fino!" You live for art while I die of love for you. I fall at your feet. The crowd cheered.

Prince Liviu was known for his extravagances. He had an apartment in Monaco, a palazzetto in Venice, a suite at the Ritz. His parties could last three days, usually just him, a couple of pals from the fraternity of dispossessed royals, and the chorus line of the Moulin Rouge. He was reputed to have the appetite of a goat and the touch of an angel.

Meanwhile, there was the remainder of that night to be dealt with. The peacocks had no cage to hold them. As beautiful and dramatic as they were, Nolan decided, over my halfhearted protests, that we couldn't live with "Scarpia" and "Iago," as he named the birds. He made arrangements to donate them to the Livorno zoo.

But this was a Saturday night, and the zoo would not pick them up until Monday. Fortunately the bedroom was separate from the parlor, which was where we'd had the hotel staff lay down newspapers. Signor Scalfo, the night manager, was reluctant at first until I reminded him of La Tebaldi's cats and La Sills's matching poodles. Fair is fair: La Casals would have her peacocks. But there was no escaping their cries and squawks and tearing of newspapers and pecking of the upholstery and the wallpaper and the mirrored wall where they seemed dazzled by their own reflection. Their extended plumes vibrated menacingly in a giant fanning action that had some of the implied threat of a snake's rattle.

Once Scarpia and Iago recovered from the crazed cheers of the crowd, the cacophony of the traffic along Via Milano, a lurching luggage cart, and an erratic elevator to our nineteenth-floor suite, they quieted down. Considering the stresses of the day, their appetite was good, and the Ritz cuisine, especially the creamed corn and tossed salads, much to their liking. Whenever we came close, Scarpia and Iago responded with anxious shrieks, whirring plumes, and an occasional warning stab from their sharp black beaks. Of the two, Scarpia was the larger, meaner bird. He had a way of bearing his head high with a certain arrogant tilt so that the blue-and-turquoise plume punctuated every squawk with an imperious toss.

For a time the birds were busy with their dinner while Nolan and I, as was our custom after a performance, relaxed with a late supper of champagne, shirred eggs, and sliced tomatoes with fresh basil. Occasionally Scarpia or Iago would waddle over to peck a round of melba toast right from my fingers, and then, by way of thanks, retreat while shrieking obnoxiously.

Later the birds followed us, craning their necks just beyond the threshold of the bedroom, while we undressed and slipped into bed. Nolan, by now in pajamas, pushed them out of the room.

I could have taken a Nembutal with hot milk, I suppose, but I wanted to savor that evening to its fullest. After months of self-doubt, that night was a return to a finer time when the voice had unparalleled range and agility, when my roulades dove like a bullet without slurring a note, touching down and instantly soaring back into a wide-open sky, as exhilarating for the singer as for the listener.

I rested on my elbow and watched my husband feign sleep. Even as I knew that I would soon love another man, I could not help also loving the familiar details of Nolan's face—the russet glow of his cheeks, the wispy strands of reddish-blond hair that hung down his forehead, his fleshy earlobes tufted with hair, the slightly asymmetrical mouth, one side thinner than the other, which resulted in a crooked, vaguely mischievous smile.

"I should probably challenge Prince What's-His-Face to a duel," Nolan said finally.

"Don't be silly, darling." I found myself patting his hand consolingly. "It's all show with men like that."

"Is it all show with women like you as well?"

"Let's stop imagining things, shall we? It's as if I made a big thing out of every squeeze you gave your girlfriends in the chorus."

"Girls are like a candy bowl I dip into. Sweet for a moment, then gone."

"I'm not pursuing this conversation."

"With you, it will be different. There will be no place for me in your life with the Prince."

"You're confusing fantasy with reality," I said. "There isn't going to be a life with the Prince."

"Good. We should kiss to that." As our lips touched, a sudden hammering on the door startled us apart. It came in bursts as if someone were drilling a hole. A moment passed, and when I reached to the back of Nolan's head to pull him down again, the angry rapping resumed.

The hammering stopped only when our lips separated. I had the notion that the peacocks could somehow follow our every move through the door. Nolan slid his hand into the sheets and down my breasts and belly. He never pushed his hand between my legs; there was always a seductive progression to his caresses, starting slowly as if afraid to startle me. This time, as he grew more intimate, the birds threatened to pierce the door panels with their beaks.

Nolan reached beside the bed for a black wingtip and threw it against the door. Scarpia and Iago seemed to retreat in stunned silence. Taking advantage of the lull, we embraced and, tangled in a swirl of sheets, enjoyed a few rushed moments of lovemaking, too absorbed in the moment to notice the birds' resumed hammering.

"They'll stop if they think we've fallen asleep," Nolan whispered.

But they didn't stop. Around three in the morning, I decided to have a talk with Scarpia and Iago. Even if they were somehow defending the interests of Prince Liviu, the fact that he had given them to me meant that if I ordered them to stop banging on the door, they should. They were my birds.

I took a deep breath and pulled my shoulders back. I opened the door. Scarpia and Iago, standing one directly behind the other, craned their scrawny necks at an odd feisty angle, their beady eyes peering into the bedroom. When my icy glare didn't rattle them, I inhaled deeply and let loose in full voice a clear, if somewhat metallic, C-sharp "*Si . . . len . . . zio!*"

They hastily retreated a couple of steps as if the sound of my voice had borne with it a gale. I had managed to drive the birds into a humble retreat. They stood a few feet beyond the door with lowered heads and seemed to study the pattern on the carpet.

"*Brava!*" Nolan applauded from the bed. "What power. What temperament, *Signora!*"

But even with Scarpia and Iago somewhat tamed, it was to be a long night. Left to his own thoughts, Nolan couldn't help returning to his earlier fears: Prince Liviu would take me away. As a reminder, the bigger of the two peacocks, Scarpia, stood an inch from the threshold and stared inside. We awoke intermittently, always to face the bird's tail expanded, those improbable blue and green and gold feathers shimmering and menacingly whirring in the moonlight.

o—╫ IL MIO TESORO.

Nolan Keefe hardly speaks now. Ever since Lockwood and Perla dropped in for tea on Wednesday and he learned through their hesitations and evasions that Mercè has died, he has clung to glum silence. Management at Villa Age d'Or fears he might swing into one of his famous depressions. Attempts are made to lift his spirits. The entire staff from Millicent to Hansen has been instructed to be particularly cheerful, their voices burbling with the barely suppressed chuckle of the professional optimist. A new pill is added to his mix. He can't tell the difference but he does take advantage of the surrounding concern to cajole extra desserts and X-rated videos. His answer to inquiries regarding his well-being is always the same, a manic "Hunky-dory!" accompanied by dramatically raised eyebrows. He suspects the act may not be entirely convincing. The loss of Mercè grips his heart and will not soften its hold as he lives with the reality of her absence day after day.

Nolan looks at himself in the mirror and has to admit, gazing into his own large, bloodshot eyes, peering back above the rubbery folds of his gouged cheekbones, that he strikes an alarming figure. He sees a pathetic version of himself, treated like a child, the sadness making him shrink even more inside the rumpled corduroys and baggy Irish sweaters he favors on the days when no company is expected. So when the two visitors of the previous week call to invite him for a walk along the shore, to breathe fresh sea air, to enjoy ice cream, he seizes on the invitation like a lifeline.

On the day of the outing with his new friends, Nolan rises early and calls for Marisa to come to the Villa to shave him and trim his hair. He asks for her special lotion, then takes the bottle and splashes himself with handfuls of lavender and bergamot.

He puts on a pair of pleated linen shorts and a Tommy Bahama shirt with a motif of parrots and coconuts and a pair of Italian basket-weave sandals. A full hour before the appointed time he's ready and waiting, sitting primly in the parlor.

The couple, familiar from their previous visit, speak to him cautiously. "Are you ready to roll?" Lockwood asks.

Nolan waits happily while the writer buckles him up in the Saab's backseat. Then they head toward the pier at Pacifica Cove. Up front, Lockwood and Perla chatter like an old couple. They argue about the best way to go, about which turnoff to take, about where to park. Occasionally they turn to the backseat, to involve their passenger in the plans.

"Cool shirt!" says Lockwood.

"Mercè bought it for me when we were planning a Caribbean singing cruise."

"So how have you been, Mr. Keefe?" Perla asks.

"It will be strange not to see the old bat anymore."

"You two had a long history," she says kindly.

"A rich roller coaster of a history, isn't that right?" Lockwood prompts.

"So, you're asking what I felt like after Mercè dumped me for that phony prince?"

"It might be something you want to talk about," Lockwood says gently.

"Tell me something, writer. Why would an old man who has made his peace with the past dredge up the dark ages of his life? Mercè could have told you what I felt like. God knows she saw me suffering, heard every possible curse I could hurl at her. She even had me arrested once when I supposedly went after her with a butcher knife. But she wouldn't have told you any of that; she was a woman who knew how to respect the privacy of others."

"Actually," Lockwood smiles, "I do have all of that on tape, including the peacocks."

"I hated the peacocks. I went to the zoo and jumped inside the enclosure. That's when I was arrested. And in the confusion of things, the press said I had tried to attack Mercè. Pick your version."

"I'll include both. Readers like that stuff. You know, with knives and all."

"What version did Mercè give you?"

"That you wanted to kill her out of insane jealousy."

"Right. She never did get to sing Desdemona, you know."

"Well, that explains things."

"You're catching on, kiddo."

"Hey, that's the beach ahead," Perla exclaims, hoping to change the moment to a more cheerful tone.

She chats up Nolan about what flavor of malt he would like. Maybe strawberry, or chocolate, or something different like piña colada.

He avoids looking at them, glancing wildly from side to side, not focusing, not staying on either face for long, meeting eyes only in a flash, before choosing to gaze at the sea, at the tiny white sails just below the horizon, at the frothy whitecaps closer to shore.

They've parked near the pavilion and the ice-cream shop. Nolan Keefe is clearly overwhelmed by the sight of so many lovely people—all buttery limbs and golden hair and tiny bathing suits. Boys and girls playing volleyball or Rollerblading or jogging all bouncety-bounce along the beach. So many nearly naked people together. He seems to enjoy the freedom to walk along the water's edge, letting the cool waves lap at his toes, feeling his feet make deep prints on the sand.

"What flavor malt would you like, Mr. Keefe?"

"There's only one flavor," he chuckles, "you know that."

He nods happily when Perla says, "Chocolate." He says yes, thank you, but that first he needs to pee. Lockwood watches him go into the men's room and decides, for the sake of the old man's sense of dignity, not to follow.

Meanwhile Perla gets the malts, chocolate for Lockwood and Nolan and strawberry for herself. She gives one to Lockwood and waits with a cup in either hand for Nolan to return. "How long has he been in there?" she asks.

Lockwood shrugs. A moment later a skinny man nearly stumbles into them as he rushes out of the men's room. Perla thinks at first that it's Nolan because the man is wearing a green shirt with parrots. When she realizes he's not, she demands to know where he got that shirt.

"Why, lady, do you like it? I got it at Neiman Mark-ups." The man forces his mouth into a gold-toothed smile.

"An older gentleman wearing one just like it went into the men's room. Did you see him?"

"No, ma'am." The man turns away and runs off, sprinting across the parking lot, across Coast Road to a bus stopping at the corner. Perla shouts for the bus to wait, but the driver roars ahead, signaling that he doesn't pick up passengers holding drippy ice-cream treats. Lockwood drops his malt and rushes into the men's room. Quickly his eyes survey the bank of urinals at which four men stand with an air of patient concentration; Nolan is not one of them. He walks along the row of stalls, searching under the doors, seeing feet in sneakers, huaraches, Birkies, but none in Italian sandals. Past the line of sinks along the mirrored wall, he realizes there's another door that opens to the beach.

Outside, the beach teems with swimmers, sunbathers, runners, surfers, bikers. Lockwood takes several steps in one direction, then the other, his eyes searching the shore. He darts back through the men's room to exit at the pavilion where Perla waits.

"He's lost," Lockwood announces breathlessly. "Or rather, we lost him."

"The asshole took his clothes," she says. "Nolan is in his underwear, probably strolling along with the rest of the preening mob."

"Thousands of seminaked people. But only one of them eighty-something," he adds hopefully.

Perla nods. "The old fool." She places the cup on the ground in front of a shaggy dog that had been hovering around her, trying with its fat pink tongue to reach into the cup

They agree to comb the beach and meet back at the pavilion in an hour, hopefully with Nolan. "I'll let loose with my secret signal if I find him." Perla puts two pairs of fingers in her mouth and demonstrates a loud piercing whistle. "What's your signal?"

"I can yell really loud."

"You can't whistle?" she asks, her eyes wide with disbelief.

"Of course I can." He puckers his lips and produces a soft, quavering tone.

"Call out if you find him," she says.

They head in opposite directions. The possibility of losing the old

man makes Lockwood queasy. While not officially incapacitated or insti-
tutionalized, Nolan Keefe is a frail, dotty, naked wanderer. He has handed
over most of his money to Villa Age d'Or in return for their care for the
rest of his life plus a modest allowance for his small needs and occasional
pleasures. There are other things that brighten his days—an occasional
touch of fashion by way of a silk tie or a nice shirt, a $40 bottle of wine,
tickets to something or other. Nolan likes a night out—the circus, a play,
or a concert. But not opera; young talent leaves him with a bitter taste.

Lockwood walks down the beach calling, "Nolan, Nolan," like a man
who has lost his dog. Minutes later he hears Perla's whistle. He rushes
past the throng, a quarter mile beyond the pavilion, to a section of the
beach cordoned off for body builders, jugglers, and gymnasts. The crowd
is fragrant with sweet lotions and burning weed, the range of naked expression goes from the pinched-in chicken-breasted to the pendulous to
the round and buoyant, most tanning or swimming or surfing or volley-
balling. At the height of the day, under a beating sun, audiences gather
around interesting performers. Today: Illya Karamazov juggles anything
the audience throws at him—kitchen knives, baseball bats, bowling balls.
Next to him "Strong " Mahaffey walks around all pumped up, isolating,
on demand, a deltoid here, a carotid vein there, a glute that strains to rip
its spandex wrapper. Standing between these two, a small old man, in a
lime-green Speedo and a t-shirt with *Surf Bums* above a row of naked
butts, draws warm applause.

Nolan Keefe bows in all directions and waits for the crowd to become
silent. He shuts his eyes against the sun, tilts his head to a dreamy angle,
clutches his hands close to his heart, and begins to sing in a tremulous
tenor, *"Il mio tesoro."* A collective sigh rises from the impromptu audience. The sweet melody weaves its way against the rumor of the surf, the
still strong voice rising unaccompanied, so heartfelt that, even if hardly
anyone has any idea what the old man is singing about, tears well up.

Nolan acknowledges the applause with a couple of quick nods and then allows Lockwood and Perla to guide him by the elbows off the beach and to the pavilion. He appears vulnerable in his tiny bathing suit and loose t-shirt. Perla puts a souvenir visor on his head and a smear of orange zinc on his nose.

Lockwood gets him a fresh milkshake, and the three of them sit on a bench at the edge of the pavilion. They congratulate him on his impromptu performance; they ask if he's enjoying his malt, and then just how he happened to lose his clothes.

With a mischievous smile, Nolan turns first to Perla, then to Lockwood, and then back to Perla again. "I traded them," he says.

"You traded the $80 silk shirt?" Lockwood asks.

"Sure did," replies Nolan somewhat defiantly.

Perla insists, "What on earth for?"

"I liked the t-shirt. It seemed more appropriate for the beach." He sticks out his chest and concentrates on drawing the last of the malt through the straw, the final slurp marking a return to his earlier silence.

Nolan feels the sea breeze on every pore. He ogles the girls, his milky-blue, cataract-veiled eyes darting from one bright bikini to the next, the lime-lemon thong replacing the floral beach miniskirt which in turn had distracted him from the Day-Glo tube top straining under the weight of ripe breasts. He refuses to move until the sun goes down in a glorious blaze and the crowd has thinned out. On the walk across the parking lot there's a bounce to his walk, and once in the car he insists that Perla get in the backseat so he can sit up front, his elbow hanging out the open window, visor turned backward and the wind blowing in his face.

When they reach Villa Age d'Or, he refuses to get out of the car, clinging stiffly to the buckled seatbelt, facing straight ahead as if unaware that they've reached the place where he lives. He remains still even when Lockwood guns the engine impatiently and Perla holds the door open for him.

"We're home, Nolan," Perla sings.

There's no expression on the old man's face beyond a stubborn pursing of his thin lips.

"Nolan," she insists quietly.

"No," he answers. "I'm having too good a time here." The manager at the reception desk inside the Villa shakes his head sympathetically. "Mr. Keefe is free to come and go as he pleases," he explains. Villa Age d'Or has no particular hold on its residents; Mr. Keefe does require more attention, but this is not a facility where he's committed as a patient.

No, he explains, they do not have attendants on staff to lift this resident out of the car and carry him to his bed. Certainly the old man is their charge when he is inside the Villa, but their responsibility ends at the front door. They will not touch him, for, in fact, they could be liable to all manner of legal havoc if he so much as dislocated a shoulder or caught a cold en route from curb to threshold. The manager turns his attention back to the perusal of whatever papers he was able to dredge up from under the counter.

Lockwood leans back into the car and turns Nolan's head to face him. "Nolan," he pleads, "we're home. Perla and I will come to visit next Wednesday. We can go to the beach again, if you want. Watch the babes, stop at Dairy Queen. You name it. But for now, our little outing is over."

"He says *no*." Perla sighs.

"Actually, he's not saying anything," Lockwood points out.

"Don't get technical on me," Perla insists.

"She's correct, the smart one," Nolan interrupts. "I am saying no. Couldn't be clearer, don't you think?"

"We're not taking you home with us, if that's what you're angling for."

Lockwood and Perla step back from the car.

"We could take him home," she says. "He knows all kinds of stuff about Mercè Casals."

"Yes, he does. But he doesn't *say* anything about all that."

"He might warm up, once he hears her tapes." She has a vision of Nolan's expression brightening as the Señora's voice intrudes into his consciousness. "It would be as if he were waking up from a long sleep, a kind of therapy."

"Either that," Lockwood says, "or push him over the edge. I mean, the guy needs care. Look what he did today: He gave his clothes away to some stranger."

"He traded them," Perla says. "How many times does he have to explain that?"

In the end, Lockwood returns to the passenger side of the Saab. He carefully unbuckles Nolan's seatbelt, then gently pries the old man's fingers one by one from the strap. Nolan stubbornly does not speak. Lockwood slips his arms under Nolan's hips, neatly lifts him off the seat, and carries him across the Villa's threshold. He stands in front of the reception desk until Harley, the desk clerk acknowledges their presence. "I hope you're not planning to lay him on the counter."

"Where would you like him?" Lockwood asks. "Call it special delivery."

"Elevator to second floor, down B wing, into room 216." Peering down at Nolan, he adds, "Glad to have you back, Mr. Keefe. I certainly hope we enjoyed our little outing and that we are glad to be home. Are we not, Mr. Keefe?"

"I feel like a bride!" Nolan says.

Harley watches him for a moment, then shrugs. "We'll take that as *Yes, thank you.*"

The Princely Life

I was happy to be in Prince Liviu's company during our first year together. He showed me off in the best light. I was made to laugh so that
he could display my teeth, stroll down the lobby of the Plaza to reveal my
legs, and sing a little something as if to prove that he had snared a real
star, not some former headliner past her prime.

Eventually the singing became incidental. At first there were intimate
recitals for groups of twenty or so. I would sing one or two arias. But if I
went on for more than half an hour, Liviu would nod off, eliciting discreet titters from the guests. I went along, I was so much under the spell
of his wealth and lineage. After he gave up on songs he bragged to his
buddies—Henry Kissinger or Ferdinand Marcos or Prince Rainier—that
I could still hit E-flat as I had in that famous recording of *La Sonnambula*. I would smile graciously, relax my throat with a yawn, take a deep
breath, and let fly with that single note. I would go for almost a minute,
my highest note a few inches from someone's face, until I sensed that
fingers were twitching to keep from flying to the ears.

I felt like a performing pony. Yet I couldn't pull myself away from the parties, the intimate gatherings, the cruises on the Mediterranean. Singing for Ferdinand and Imelda, for whom quick getaways from Manila to Paris, Venice, Monte Carlo, had a seductive appeal.

The Marcoses were the world's handsomest couple, both dressed in white: lacy, pleated, crisp shirts for Ferdinand and layers of shantung and taffeta that gave Imelda a bridal, virginal quality. Their black hair was shiny and their nutty-brown skin so smooth it had the sheen of bronze. However, they had abominable taste in music. Imelda liked to hear me do the Habanera from *Carmen*, sometimes two or three times in the course of an evening. Ferdinand felt equally passionate about Julie Andrews. "The hills are alive with the sound of mucus," I sang. I didn't sound like the real Julie at all, but he seemed pleased enough.

As casually insulting as they were, I felt it a privilege to listen to their small jokes and their gossip and their whining about the nuisances of running a tiny, hot, undereducated, and fairly shabby country. Once I heard them chat with Princess Grace about trading Monaco for Manila for a year, just so Grace and Rainier would know what it was like having to deal with a democracy.

"Democracy?" They all laughed. Years later, when the photos of her shoe closet appeared, I recalled that Imelda's dainty feet had been encased in satin slippers richly beaded around the toe and sides.

After some parties, especially if the guests had been either terribly glamorous or rich or at least touched by a titillating scandal, Liviu and I would linger with a final glass of champagne and wallow in self-congratulation. We would chatter about one guest's dull conversation, another's body odor, how the countess was charming but the count a lout. At that time the Prince knew everything about everybody. He collected intimacies and confidences the way some people hoard postage stamps or demitasse spoons.

And he had his crushes; I could tell by how long he carried on about some woman's good taste in clothes and dismal taste in husbands. We had only been together for six months when I realized that Liviu knew everything there was to know about Madame Marcos. He knew more than her taste in trashy movies, her preferences in flowers, and her shoe collection. He'd learned from a shadowy accountant in Barcelona that Imelda controlled the top prostitution houses in Manila. This gave her a little money of her own, so she wouldn't have to go to Ferdinand every time she saw something she liked at Cartier or Ferragamo. The Prince couldn't get the idea of Imelda-as-national-madam out of his head. He fantasized visiting them in Manila and getting the keys to the presidential whorehouse.

He wanted to sleep with Imelda while I watched. He wanted me to sleep with Ferdinand while he watched. That was the start of my years as a worm.

Liviu was particular about my appearance. He said he adored my face, but was constantly suggesting improvements. The first time I met his family, an old aunt and uncle, twice removed, he arranged for Mister Enrico on 5th Avenue to redo my hair, face, and nails. At the end of three hours, the reflection I saw in the mirror belonged to a different person. My hair had been stripped of its natural auburn color and dyed a brassy blond. It sprang up from my head like a swirl of meringue.

The Prince also said he thought I might enjoy a massage in the mornings. A Valkyrie called Inga came in at seven every morning with her ropes and belts and boom box. Instead of a massage, I was put through a workout with rubber bands and weights and tapes of disco hits. At the end, Inga gave me a short, rough massage with sesame oil—to prevent lactic acid crystallization.

I was forty-one and had just resigned from the part of Amina in *La*

Sonnambula because I was fatter than Domenico Stenza, the bass who sang Rodolfo. Moreover, the chorus, which had its fair share of stout peasants, were rolling their eyes and nudging each other when Elvino, a skinny little tenor, sang his first aria to her, all about being smitten by the delicate young thing who reminded him of his elusive first love long ago.

The Prince and Inga put me on a scale and decided between them what I would eat that day. The Prince was efficient in his servings. Little half cups of steamed carrots, three tomato slices with lemon juice and pepper, and cubes of nearly raw meat were all I was allowed. For lunch I would fall like a starving orphan on a plate of steamed vegetables sprinkled with chives.

I learned that it is possible to exist on a thousand calories a day: Chew slowly, make it last, get your salivary glands going so that you extract the last hint of flavor from a bite of broccoli before swallowing and losing it forever. Twice a week Inga gave me an injection; the syringe was full to the brim with a soupy concoction that hurt going into my butt and stung like the devil coming out—B12, iron, potassium, and God knows what else.

Inga's injections turned me into a jittery, irritable insomniac. I was even hungry in my dreams, long, involved reveries of being back in Spain during the war, queuing for potatoes, a handful of grapes, an egg. Beyond the obnoxious strutting of the fascists, I had hated Franco for making me hungry. And I began to hate Prince Liviu for the same reason. The feeling started slowly at the pit of my stomach as a vague, nagging antipathy that eventually blossomed into full-fledged loathing.

The world knew La Casals was dieting. It must have been the management at the Met who saw value in my being in the news regularly even if I had disappeared from the stage. The gossip columns started running a weekly tally of how many pounds I'd lost. The information was surprisingly accurate. I became so self-conscious about my appearance that I turned into a hermit.

When Liviu and I dined out, I carried meager premeasured portions in a stacked-pot lunch carrier that I handed discreetly to the maître d', Luis at the Cote Basque or Serge at Twenty One. The kitchen would warm up my portion and arrange it nicely on their china. The Prince would order from the menu, his beloved tripe à la mode de Cannes or oysters Rockefeller, and eat to his lip-smacking satisfaction, while I nibbled one pea at a time.

The results were dramatic. Clothes spilled away from my body; I was able to sit and bend and twist completely unconstricted. I was free from the pains of binding seams and pinching buttons and zippers. My skin, for once, was not imprinted with the pink bas-relief of bands and straps. When I wasn't feeling like a starving prisoner, I felt weightless and springy and graceful.

Sometimes when I was alone and particularly courageous, I would strip down to nothing, stand in front of the mirror, and wonder whether this was the day that I would go out. But then I would notice a bulge below the navel or a sagging of my butt and decide that the work was not done, and I would continue in hiding. I would dissolve all my excess flesh, pare my body down to its essence of bone and hair and tissue. Even the little food I was eating began to make me feel guilty. I eliminated any spices that made my meals more palatable. I would sprinkle soil from the potted plants on half the plate to keep from finishing the measured portions. I weighed myself every day, sometimes morning and evening. Every gram that disappeared was a small triumph.

During that time, I sang only recitals and made a few recordings, mostly sacred music—I hoped that prayer in any form would keep me from dying and, at the same time, give me the resolve to stick with the diet. Throughout all this, Prince Liviu bore the brunt of my anxieties and obsessions. If at first I blamed him for trying to starve me, now I suspected him of trying to slim me down to make me helpless and fully dependent on his whims.

Then one morning the scale tipped at 119, a loss of over sixty pounds, and we both decided I was thin enough. And still beautiful, which was a miracle considering all the strain I had gone through. The morning of the climactic press conference, I had a breakfast of black coffee and grapefruit. My stomach churned. At the appropriate moment, when a reporter would ask how much Mercè Casals now weighed, a scale would be rolled in. I was to step on it.

It all went as planned. The crowd gasped and the flashbulbs popped all around me and the reporters' questions tumbled as each jostled to get the best quote. As soon as I was free of the press, I had six chocolate éclairs from La Patisserie de Lyon. They tasted so good I wept.

However, I had grown too weak to sing through a whole opera. I could do an aria or two, of course, and sound as lovely and youthful and delicate as I looked, but the idea of plowing through three hours of *Tosca*, for instance, seemed ridiculous. The fear crossed my mind that I had traded power and stamina for a waif-like body. I'd get winded just crossing the lobby of the Plaza.

Liviu had me photographed in a bikini, a cheesy glamour pose on a rock overlooking Acapulco Bay, one leg out, the other bent at the knee, one hand on my head, the other pointing at an imaginary ship on the horizon; copies were slipped to *People* and *Paris Match* and *Hola*. The headlines trumpeted the transformation that love inspired.

It never occurred to me to question why this pear-shaped, jelly-bellied, pale-eyed gnome had any right to expect physical perfection of *me*. When I asked him what he saw in me worth loving in the first place, he said it was my fame. Not my singing.

Soon enough, I started performing again: *Traviata. Norma. Butterfly. Aida. Tosca.* Everything. I expected to be a big success. Instead, there were murmurs that grew into a babble as the critics had their say. The Casals voice had lost stability. There was a persistent wobble. The breath fell short. The power was diminished.

I owed it all to the Prince.

Lockwood's senses sharpen at night; he hears things; he grows increasingly sensitive to moving shadows and changing light. Once the Señora's voice has been switched off and the house is still, he awakens to the glare of headlights sweeping through his bedroom, to the slow muffled throb of a car coasting down Hyacinth, to the creaking and sighing of hardwood floors and settling foundations. He's sure that there is menacing stuff out there in the night, in the streets, creeping across his lawn. It's keeping him awake.

Lockwood announces it's time to "hit the mattresses," a term he learned while planning a book on the mafia. Curtains are drawn, the front door and the kitchen door dead-bolted, all window sashes secured.

Perla organizes the recordings and the clippings file, sorts mail, and tries not to be treated like a wife in charge of general emotional support. Orson names himself the head chef, because if it's up to Lockwood, they will eat nothing but the messy chili he perfected in grad school, or fast food, which Orson swears will make them all constipated, fat, and pimply.

Since Lockwood called the others to come and help, it's understood that they will share in the financial rewards of the great publishing event in the making. But more significantly, they have gathered to protect the memory of Mercè Casals, as detailed in the hours of recorded interviews that only Mark Lockwood has a right to. He was, after all, the Señora's appointed Scribbler.

No other writer, no matter how famous—and Alonzo Baylor is about as well-known as a writer gets in modern-day America—is to be trusted to reveal the Señora's life in her very own words. There is much at stake here, including the secrets every fan has a right to know, but that have to be disclosed with a measure of discretion and sensitivity. Nolan Keefe's enduring love for the one woman in his life, for example, has to be placed at its proper mythical level: His love for La Señora set the standard for the love that the whole world had for her.

One also has to consider Nolan Keefe sitting alone waiting for afternoon tea at the Villa Age d'Or, Wednesday after Wednesday, pausing in the course of the conversation he and Mercè started when they met sixty years ago, and for which he has lived the remaining days sometimes in silence, or momentarily jovial, often sly and manipulative.

This is not the sort of place where the residents sit around like overripe fruit waiting to wrinkle and sag down to their elemental nothingness. For every client inside, there is a devoted daughter or a spouse who prefers not to be depressed during visits. Funds are set aside for makeup, hairstyling, massages, and dry cleaning. The precise combination of medications is found for every client, for no two minds agitate in the same direction. Fingers need to be kept from scratching imaginary sores. Tears must be replaced by smiles. Obnoxious, vulgar language (Nolan's favorites are "cretin," "scrotum face," "dyke dog," and "swine dick") results in banishment from the parlor, the game room, the cafeteria.

Anger and vituperation have been replaced by a calm commentary on such uplifting subjects as the weather, the fates of the San Diego Padres, or life before television. Patients are encouraged to share their wisdom. "Sweet talk is happy talk," reads the scrolling text on the hanging monitors that are used to post messages to the patients: *Nolan Keefe, you have an appointment for a trim and shave. Your visitor is due for tea in half an hour. Have a sweet talk!*

Lockwood desperately wondered what Nolan Keefe and Mercè Casals discussed once a week. La Señora never did say, and now Nolan talks only when he feels like it. From the first time that Lockwood and Perla visited him, there have been times when all they get out of him is a thin hum seemingly formless and undirected but which, occasionally, if someone is paying attention, will be heard to drift into a bit of melody from *Trovatore* or *Carmen*.

As Lockwood's house settles into a routine, beyond its doors signs of life become suspect. This is a neighborhood that empties in the daytime. Husbands and wives drive away to their offices; children are packed off to school. Lockwood has noticed that the expression on the faces of adults and kids is equally wan and harried, as if classrooms and cubicles were merely the cells where penance is to be exacted in compensation for the neat houses with their nice lawns and their rooms full of gadgets. The ecstasy of multichannel satellite TV, games of digital thump-'n'-shriek, cosmic roaming through the web of the wide world, all have a proper time. Staying home during the day is a sign of an embarrassing dysfunction—illness, unemployment, bipolarity, plain sloth.

The neighbors along Hyacinth and Germaine Streets wonder what

Lockwood is up to when they leave for work in the morning, when they return in the evening, when they sit out on their backyard decks and broil dinner. They grow curious about the lights burning in certain windows for most of the night, the curtains always drawn, Orson's unfamiliar Subaru wagon and Perla's red truck parked askew in the driveway, tires biting into the spongy, unnaturally green lawn.

When nights are calm and the wind blows a certain way and the children are quietly asleep, yells, shrieks, laughter can be heard rising and falling from Lockwood's shuttered, curtained house. In particular there is one voice, a woman's prattle, going on for hours, leaping from a spoken monologue into the anguished trills of a distressed lover.

None of this is natural, the neighbors comment. They could be filming pornography or growing dope or running telephone scams. The stuff of headlines always happens next door to somebody. But Lockwood's neighbors would not be particularly excited by the slow, grinding pace at which a particular book is being written. The project has become an unwieldy beast to be tamed and contained, all flesh and blubber, without head or tail, without a spine or limbs to help it stand or sit or even lie with a measure of grace. Instead, it bulges and spreads like nerveless ectoplasm quivering Jell-O-like across time and space.

Overwhelmed, Lockwood is caught in the minutiae of its folds and wrinkles. The contemplation of a comma can go on for minutes, a single word might be worth an hour, the particular turn of a sentence—the order of subject, verb, and predicate—can consume the better part of an afternoon. From lunch until tea he might be hunched over the keyboard gazing at the screen, watching the blinking cursor, bathing his face in its glow. It's all in the waiting, he knows. The answer to his unraveling will come to him, from the voice of the Señora or the pentagramic design of the sun shining through window slats on the rug.

■ ■ ■

Orson La Prima is Violetta today. Reclining on the edge of a couch in the living room, turquoise silk folds cascading from the gathered bodice and cinched waist down to the floor. His model is a newspaper picture of Mercè Casals wearing the same dress, taken on opening night of her first *Trav* at the Met in 1957. La Prima has the look down cold, the lush head of golden curls, the skin like porcelain, red lips in contrast to the pale features that already anticipate the physical undoing of the wayward party girl. He is as motionless as if he were sitting for a painting. Lockwood walks around him, lifts an errant strap onto the right shoulder, steps back to get a clearer view of the overall effect.

From a hidden speaker, Casals' voice pours out *"Sempre libera."* Standing to one side, Perla as Alfredo, in black pinstriped pants and waistcoat, looks on adoringly. The fog unleashed by frying onions for Lockwood's signature chili brings tears to La Prima. "I'm lodging a complaint here. That stuff is streaking my makeup."

"You're out of character again," says Lockwood.

"Excuse me. Violetta would feel the same away about your so-called cuisine. She wasn't a chili kind of gal."

"Caviar's more like it?" Lockwood tries to humor him.

"And champagne. And cocaine."

Lockwood: "Don't confuse your tastes with Violetta's."

"They had cocaine in Paris in the nineteenth century," Orson says. "Germont and the doctor show up with some just before Violetta dies. That's why she dies happy. Her very last word is 'joy' . . . *Oh, gioia!* What else could she say? She was high!"

Lockwood breaks in, "You are not Violetta right now. And you are not you. You are Orson La Prima as Mercè Casals as Violetta."

Orson turns to him in surprise. "So which of me do you see when you stare at me like you've been doing?"

"It depends. Right now I'm seeing Orson La Prima being an asshole."

"Wrong. I'm Mercè Casals being a diva. Divas don't take crap. And they don't eat chili."

Lockwood turns away unhappily. "Divas don't eat chili. Now, there's a chapter title. More than that. Divas don't eat. Divas don't defecate. Divas don't sweat. Divas don't fuck."

"Divas sing," Perla sighs.

"No," Lockwood says. "Divas *are*. You can look at them or worship them or imitate them. But you can't touch a diva or talk to a diva or write about a diva."

"Sounds like we have a problem." Orson La Prima rises from the couch and goes to Lockwood. He puts his arms around him. "Is our Scribbler being blinded by the light? Maybe if he gets a good hug direct from the diva he will get his act together again."

"Divas don't hug writers," says Lockwood.

"Oh, sure we do. Mercè Casals was known for coming to the aid of the stupid and the feeble. She married Nolan Keefe!"

"Nolan Keefe was a star in his own right," Lockwood protests.

"She needed him more than he needed her at that point," says Orson.

"Only in a manner of speaking. He needed to be needed in order to reclaim his own dignity. I mean, the man was slipping on the great banana peel of lost fame. By coming to the aid of Mercè Casals he redeemed himself in the eyes of those who thought he was a total failure. Anyone the diva would choose as her companion would be allowed to bask in the glow of her reflected light. The man actually got some gigs after they got back together."

Lockwood searches for a particular tape. He puts it in the player, cues it up, and lets it spin so that Mercè's voice takes over: "Stop picking at that scab. I've told you all there is to tell. Nolan and I simply took up where we had left off when the Prince came onto the scene. One moment he was in the picture, and the next he was out of it, and Nolan and I just kept on as before, hardly skipping a heartbeat."

"You two-timed him for five years," Lockwood countered calmly.

"He was not without his own slips."

"Mere distractions compared to your princely affair."

"You're stepping over a line here, Scribbler. I don't need your moralizing."

"Surely, we should be able to explore some moral issues in these conversations."

"I acted according to my understanding. I thought I was entitled to everything the world had to offer. The Prince was just one more reward."

"It had its consequences. You stopped singing."

"There was no connection between the two things. I was too busy to sing. We were always on the move, at a moment's whim. Paris, Venice, Buenos Aires. Sometimes the local music community would hasten to arrange an impromptu recital. Bellas Artes in three days, but I might be up and gone just as they were putting up the posters and printing the tickets. The Prince was like that, operating on impulse and random invitations from his friends around the world, all those members of the exiled royalty club. I thought he loved me for myself, not for my voice."

"And when you decided to sing again, you discovered that your voice was gone."

"You're exaggerating for effect, Scribbler."

"You did not in fact lose your voice?"

"No. It had matured."

"During your first rehearsal for a revival of *Aida*, the great vehicle for your comeback, you opened your mouth to sing, and you cracked."

"Yes, like glass."

"Is that when Nolan realized it was all over between you and the Prince?"

"I can see that our book will not be without humor."

"So there was a period of recrimination and doubt."

"Neither. I told you we just took up where we'd left off, as if barely a heartbeat had been skipped."

"So he did forgive you."

"That's the kind of man my Nolan is."

A Ladies' Lunch

The day before I left the Prince began as a radiant New York fall morning. All that week the view of Central Park from suite 1295 at the Plaza Hotel had revealed the gradual paling of the green foliage and its replacement by a golden hue. Starting with an occasional maple tucked into the city's forest and spreading like wildfire to the neighboring trees, the ocher tones mutated into orange and red until the whole of the park seemed to be exploding in scattered bursts of color and light.

I would take morning tea in the room so I could gaze out the window and marvel at the smartly dressed young men and women striding along the paths on their way to work, their clothes changing with the leaves and the new chill of the mornings; dresses and suits snapping from linen into tweed, blouses slipping into sweaters and jackets, finally into coats; jewel tones for the women, always gray or black for the men. With a pair of opera glasses, I followed my favorites, morning after morning, at the same time along the same route—women with slim briefcases in hand and streaked blond hair cut blunt to the shoulder, and men walking with long, even steps as if to a martial beat, drilling themselves that they were important and successful.

The morning of the day before I left the Prince, I was not aware that I was going to do so. Aside from the spectacular view in the Park, the day held little in store that would alter the routine of an idle life.

I had tea around seven-thirty. Half an hour later, a simple breakfast would arrive—melon balls in port wine, dry toast, unsweetened yogurt. I had been dieting so long that I had forgotten what it was like to have marmalade and butter on scones and to taste the wonders of sweetness and creaminess and saltiness with the whole of my mouth.

If I thought of eating at all, I felt like the only person on the planet who was not permitted to do so. Fully one-fourth of my body had been sacrificed to the whim of not quite a husband but no longer much of a lover, pounds of my flesh surrendered to him much as one might slice off a finger or an ear to placate a deity.

I had the room-service fellow place the roll-away table inside the sitting room. I signaled him to be quiet because I didn't want to wake the Prince, who slept in the bedroom adjacent to the parlor. The waiter's name was Carlos and he was from Havana. "I've been in Havana," I said. He nodded but did not take up the opportunity for conversation. *Perhaps he's shy*, I thought. I wore a blue silk robe over my nightgown. The robe was loosely belted. When I sat down I realized its lapels parted to reveal a breast, but I did nothing to conceal it.

The handsome boy kept his eyes on the pen with which I signed the bill. He refused to look at the breast that he surely realized was bared for him, and his refusal to look made me angry. I was not out to seduce him; I only wanted a wordless exchange on a purely physical level. All he had to do was look, hold his gaze on my breast for no more than moments— how awkward even seconds could be in such circumstances. And then, after having had a good look at what was still, for a woman of forty-six, a lovely breast, acknowledge the proffered gratuity and quickly leave me to my breakfast.

By then, I rarely sang in public. The rewards were sufficient for simply being La Casals without having to do terribly difficult things with my voice in front of thousands of people. And the less I sang, the harder it became to break my inertia. At first I tried to discourage offers by stipulating a particularly elusive accompanist, absolute control of the program including last-minute changes if I saw fit, my suite at the Plaza for three days before and two days after the concert, the sizable retainer, no-penalty cancellation for medical reasons. If the house accepted anyway, I would pray that my resolve would not weaken. Offered a recital at Covent Garden, I would arrive in London two days before the performance and cancel with the obligatory twenty-four hours before curtain on the pretext that my throat was irritated by the city's dense pollution. In Paris it was allergies. In Barcelona it was emotional upheaval. In Milano digestive unrest. In Mexico City the thin air of its high altitude.

On the morning of the day before I left the Prince, I was plotting an excuse to get out of my recital at Carnegie Hall the following evening. I had the rest of the day to cancel for reasons of health. As I sipped hot tea, I was aware of the beginnings of a scratch, the barely perceptible accumulation of mucus, the hint of pain that came with every swallow.

I knew what Pep Saval would have said. Or better still, what he would have done—set me to fasting on hot tea and grapes and then push me onstage with whatever voice I had. "Even the greatest athletes never feel like running," he had said. "Like a marathoner, you will never feel you can actually run forty kilometers. But once you start, you just put one note after another and soon the voice warms up and the music pours out and you are free to enjoy the very act you feared."

But Pep Saval was dead. In the other room was the Prince, who would be quite happy if I canceled. He wouldn't have to share me with my gushing fans and suffer my not paying any attention to him, even though he was the man who owned me. Sometimes I was sure that when my allergies struck or my head throbbed with a migraine, it was the Prince who, like a master poisoner, was sabotaging the part of my life that he had no claim over.

That morning the Prince hovered in my thoughts while I lolled in the big tub, sinking slowly into water as hot as I could stand it: first the feet, waiting for the tender soles, for the space between the toes to adjust to the heat, my hands gripping the sides of the tub while I dipped my seat one inch at a time, the heat feeling dangerous as it covered my thighs and belly. Stretching out my legs so that only the knees protruded above the surface, I felt like a heretic being boiled by the Inquisition.

I would remain resolutely silent. Even if I could save my life by singing, better to die with dignity than to turn into a trained seal. The hot water sent up plumes of steam, and I could hardly see the tiled walls, the quaint bidet, a commode ample as a throne. I felt my skin flush. Beads of perspiration collected on my forehead, tumbled down my cheeks like tears, settled on my upper lip, and rolled saltily onto the tip of my tongue. I opened my jaws in a big, slow yawn and allowed the steam to penetrate the tissues of my throat. I slouched into the tub until the water reached my chin and sang a relaxed vocalize.

Later in the day when I decided to leave the Prince, I went shopping. At Bergdorf's I sat on a comfy chair while my favorite clerk, Clarissa Chandler, a lovely young woman with a degree from Wellesley, brought out silk blouses in white and cream and ivory. It would boost my confidence, I thought, to wear something new and special for the recital. And I knew that I would recognize the perfect blouse as soon as I saw it. It should have fabric-covered spherical buttons. Flat bone buttons would be nice enough, if they were of good quality. Or they might be concealed by a pleat. Or they could be in the back. At $800 for just two ounces of silk and six buttons, I had to consider all the options.

In this hushed redoubt of Bergdorf's, within these muted cream walls, in this space scented by classic number 9, I settled into a state of peace and contentment. The air was barely disturbed by the beeps and trills of phones and cash registers, the whispers and murmurs of credit-card scanning, the faint meandering string renditions of vaguely familiar pop ballads. Clarissa brought out half-a-dozen blouses and paired them with various black skirts and pants. She laid them on the pearly carpeting so that La Casals could survey them from her chair.

Eventually a decision was made. Or rather two decisions. The first was marked by a signal for Clarissa to wrap up the middle blouse on the far row, cream—concealed buttons, cuffed pirate-style sleeves, $975. Clarissa carried it away in both arms like a baby.

Once alone, I made my other choice. This time the simpler round-collared, natural-sleeved, back-buttoned number by Givenchy, which remained undisturbed at my feet. The whole maneuver took no more than seconds. I had only to reach down from my low chair and scoop the blouse into my handbag.

Clarissa returned with a package done up in fine tissue, sealed with foil, nestled in a BG shopping bag. I took the parcel, signed the charge slip and returned it to Clarissa's waiting hand. I held the younger woman's eyes, keeping her too flustered to focus on anything except my kind, caring look. Then, linking arms, I allowed her to guide me outside to the waiting car.

Back at the Plaza, I was flushed with the thrill of my small crime. I had made a decision: In the event that I did go through with my performance, I would wear the second blouse, the more discreet one, a steal at $699. Awaiting in the room was a message from a Miss Chandler. I'd been caught! I called her right back. "Come to the Plaza, dear," I told her. "Of course, right now. We will have a nice ladies' lunch in the Oak Room."

I told the Prince that I would stay in all day. I said my throat was starting to tingle. I was also developing a bad case of jitters at the thought of singing with less-than-perfect health. He chuckled and said it sounded to him like I was getting ready to cancel. I thanked him for his understanding and insisted I would have lunch alone. I did not tell him that the thought of having to face him over lunch was enough to make me gag. I did not say anything like this because I had come to realize that this was *the day before* I would inform him I was leaving him.

Ladies' lunch in the Oak Room was mostly men. Women preferred the Garden Room, where they could have tea and thin sandwiches and watch everyone. The secluded table in a dark corner of the Oak Room offered privacy for the small confrontation at hand.

The salesclerk across the table announced simply that $699 for a lost blouse was more than her paycheck could stand. I decided that I liked Clarissa Chandler very much indeed. She was a young woman of poise and self-confidence, much as I had been. But this young woman carried herself quite well on the status of a sales clerk, while at her age La Casals had been burning through every regional concert hall and opera house in

Europe. It was easy to be poised when you were a success, a harder trick to pull off when scrambling to save your job.

"Will you be okay if I write you a check right now?"

"Of course," Clarissa said. "We often take items to a customer's domicile for private consideration. On the other hand, I could also take the blouse back and report that it did not, after all, please you very much."

I wrote out a check to Bergdorf Goodman in my careful, ornate hand.

"I feel like keeping it to have your autograph."

"I'll sign whatever you want, just don't go around trumpeting that the famous diva Mercè Casals is a kleptomaniac."

"No, I wouldn't 'trumpet' it."

"But you might tell someone special?"

"It does make a good story."

"So you won't sit here and swear on the Oak Room menu that you will keep this secret forever."

The young woman shrugged in mock helplessness. "I don't see how I could, Señora."

"Let's eat, dear." I perused the menu. "A lunch of liver and onions or bloody rare steak and potatoes. Sometimes a singer needs to eat like a stevedore."

"The chicken looks good."

"Why chicken when you can have duck? If you're going to eat a bird, make it a wild one."

"All right, then. Duck."

"Duck for me, too. We'll have wine. And baby clams as an appetizer. And then one of their spectacular desserts."

"I thought you were always on a diet."

"You don't imagine that Muhammed Ali has watercress salad and crustless cucumber sandwiches the day before a fight."

"I suppose not."

"You suppose accurately, my dear." I turned toward the waiter who stood by the table and started to ask for two glasses of wine. But then I changed my mind and ordered a whole bottle of the hearty Priorat. "Besides, the person that I'm supposed to be thin for is not a very important person to me anymore." Even as the words were leaving my mouth I heard them as if someone else were speaking them. "Gosh, I hardly know what I'm saying."

"You should look wonderful for yourself, Señora."

"But it's the men in our lives that we want to look slim for, with our clothes off."

"I want to be touched, Señora, not looked at." My young friend blushed and took a long sip from her glass.

"Well put." I marveled at the unexpected insight. "Men's eyeballs can be downright offensive."

After I had eaten my fill and drunk most of the wine, I leaned back on the heavy leather chair and let out a sigh of satisfaction. "Clarissa, my dear friend," I looked at the young woman through the raised glass, "you have helped me enjoy the best meal I've had in years. Thank you."

"Thank *you*, Señora Casals. This has been an adventure."

"Well, here we are, two chums ducking out on our obligations. You're here, instead of at Bergdorf's, and I'm here as well, instead of being charming for the Prince. I daresay we're both enjoying the brisk air of momentary freedom."

"It gets so stuffy in the store it's hard to breathe sometimes."

"Same thing with me and the Prince."

"Some customers treat me like a servant."

"As does the Prince me."

"At least he is attractive."

"With most of his clothes on."

"At Bergdorf's," Clarissa added, already giddy from the wine, "the clothes are nice, and employees get a third off."

"We have so much in common. You get high fashion at a discount and I get cut-rate royalty. You can tell your sister that you had lunch with Mercè Casals on the day she decided to drop the world's most eligible bachelor."

"I'll miss those pictures in *People*, the two of you sailing, dancing, smooching even."

"A picture is worth a thousand words, usually contradictory."

"I'll think of that when Robert and I shake our last coins from the cookie jar for dinner together."

"Oh, my sweet Clarissa. All over the world couples are coupling. The only one who has any idea at all of where we're headed is the Conductor of the big orchestra. The rest of us are just piccolos and oboes and tubas and violins going *tweet tweet* and *oompah oompah* and *squeak squeak* with no idea how the whole score is supposed to sound."

"Perhaps, but some of us get to sing, while the rest of us mark time."

"You don't know how frightening a thing it is to sing an aria."

"Is that why you keep canceling?"

"I didn't know you followed opera."

"There's usually a picture of you waving good-bye through a limo's rear window."

"Ah, yes. And the story beyond the edges of the photograph is that my fans, who've been in line for hours, are booing me. All the time I smile and delicately wave my white-gloved hand as if I were going for a drive in the country instead of making my getaway to the airport."

"Escaping," Clarissa said quietly.

"Like a thief in the night." I nodded.

"Because you're indisposed?"

"Cognac with our espressos might be nice, don't you think?" I said after a long pause. "It's all part of a ladies' lunch. Isn't it?."

"Are you going to leave the Prince before or after you sing tomorrow night?"

"'Leaving' is only an expression, Clarissa. I'll be staying put and sending *him* away."

"You need to do what's best for you."

"He expects me to cancel. Wants me to cancel, in fact. He actually enjoys the spectacle of the disappointed audience and the flash-popping photographers milling about. He likes the sense of danger. The crowd forms a gauntlet and, with the police keeping everyone in line, I'm supposed to march calmly through them. I feel naked. I suspect it's an image he quite happily entertains."

"I've never heard you sing. Tomorrow's concert has been sold out for months."

"There will be one ticket for you at the box office, seventh row center. It will be the Prince's ticket, so claim it early in the rare event that he should want to attend."

"I'll be there," the younger woman said. "It will be such an honor."

"If I do sing, you'll know that I'm a free woman."

A star can't go on disappointing audiences indefinitely. One minute people will forgive anything, and the next they will forgive nothing. It happens without warning. After three years absent from any major stage, and a half-dozen cancellations around the world, hardly anyone thought I would make it.

But I did.

I was petrified. When the Prince knocked on my door to make plans for supper, I could hardly open my mouth to speak, much less contemplate singing. I told him, faking a hoarse rasp, that I would be sipping hot onion broth and nibbling on dry toast, that I wanted to avoid the night air, cigarette smoke, loud talk. The Prince stared as if he could read on my face the thoughts I was hiding from him. He looked quite dashing, with an ivory holder for his cigarette, which after a moment he stubbed out. He was wearing one of those belted velvet jackets he had seen on Hugh Hefner. He envied the fact that Hefner spent all day in pajamas sorting photos of women on his big circular bed. The Prince liked to think of himself as a more refined version of Heffner.

He wanted to know what I'd been doing all day. I told him I'd stayed in to rest my throat, studying the music I would perform and watching soap operas. I did not tell him about my shoplifting or getting drunk over lunch and deciding I was fed up with his company. He looked from my face to the sheet music scattered about the room and asked if I was definitely going ahead with the next day's recital, because then he would have to make arrangements to entertain himself elsewhere. By then it had become obvious that he had an ear of stone and the attention span of a goldfish.

"Let's have a late supper," I volunteered.

"We'll see. I can't promise anything."

"Make a point of it," I insisted. "You know how keyed up I am after a performance."

"I'll send a car for you. I'll find us someplace for a quiet evening."

He left and I went back to my music. I was anxious to prove myself. I worked on the Bell Song from *Lakmé*, a dangerous aria. It is sung with sparse accompaniment, parts of it a capella, and it demands isolating notes from A to E and down to C like swinging on a trapeze. Howard, the accompanist, paled when I handed him the music. "Relax," I told him. "I will do it as an encore, but only if things go very well." It was like the old days; I loved singing without a net.

After the concert, the applause and cheers still quickening my heart, I was driven down 57th Street from Carnegie Hall, then up 5th Avenue to the bar of the Pierre Hotel. The maître d' guided me to a secluded booth. The Prince arrived a couple of minutes later as if he'd been paged, muttering vague explanations about being delayed. He sidled in beside me, though I wished he wouldn't sit so close. I knew he had not showered at the Plaza because he didn't smell of the English lime lotion that he splashed on by the bucketful and the French brilliantine that he always daubed on his hair. He smelled of hotel-issue soap; his face looked rosy and freshly scrubbed and his hair was damp. I held his superficial kiss longer than I might have ordinarily. He quickly moved his mouth away. But by then I had caught a scent of the tropics: ripe mangos and coffee beans and limp seaweed. He loved his little Puerto Ricans, Dominicans, Haitians.

"So, how did it go?" he asked, quick to cut off any accusation.

I shrugged in mock resignation. "In the *Lakmé* I sounded like a parrot instead of a bell."

"Surely you did better than that."

"I'm actually surprised to have gotten through it. Almost as surprised as the audience. Just the fact that I showed up drove them wild. They were still applauding and calling out bravas when I scurried out the stage door." I could not quite make out his expression in the dimly lit room. It occurred to me that in only three years, the Prince and I had gone from visible adoration and public courting to hiding in the secluded booth of a hotel bar.

"I want us to have a serious talk," he began tentatively. This surprised me. I wanted to interrupt and say right then and there that he was wrong. That it was my talk we were going to have. But I thought it would be interesting to hear what he wanted to say first, to put him in the position of having to explain himself. I could listen for a few minutes. And then I would say to Prince Liviu in my best American style, *Go jump in a lake.* Just like that, so that the words, which I had never before said to anyone, would burn a path into his ear canal, straight to the center of his brain. That's the beauty of rough language, its surprise, like pulling out a pistol. But when he started talking, I never really thought to say anything.

A dark veil came over Liviu's eyes. "It's time for you to stop singing," he said. His lips quivered as he tried to control a coy smile that kept threatening to burst out in a full-blown, bare-toothed grin.

"What?" Just when I was ready to shock him, he had turned the tables.

He was sitting back, legs crossed primly, one slip-on dangling from his toes, the skin of his calf above the sock line surprisingly white and hairless. The Prince's legs were a source of embarrassment to him. He avoided beaches and saunas and picnics. On cruises he preferred linen trousers to shorts. He had sex in pitch darkness until he trusted his partner.

"Don't look so alarmed, dear," he said. "You can either retire as a legend or die by inches. In either case your voice is gone."

"You don't know anything about voice."

"I know what I hear," he said with unbearable smugness.

"You haven't heard me in years." I insisted on winning a stupid argument.

"It's not your singing that I hear; it's the comments from others who have heard you. The top notes are escaping you, Mercè. They say you're leaving holes in the aria."

Pep Saval had said that high notes were like heartbeats; one is allotted a finite number. And the idea of dying, note after note, over the course of a lifetime, had appealed to me. After three years of fearing the stage, I decided early on that I would make an art form of dying. I would bleed slowly and surely. I would commit musical hara-kiri, gutting myself with *La Sonnambula* and *Lakmé* and *Norma*. And all the time audiences would jeer and heckle and hiss, so that my final days would be spent in a vipers' nest.

Years after that decision came our ludicrous world tour. We'd been close friends, Nolan Keefe, Harold Penrod, and I. And I didn't think our going downhill would matter because even though we had all slept together, even Harold and Nolan with each other at least once in the '60s, we had for each other the love that friends have, where you don't hold the other person's failings against them. But here we were, the three of us checking in and out of hotels, climbing in and out of taxis and planes and trains, finding our way in and out of strange theaters and recital halls and even a basketball court. It was pathetic. Harold had to stop and pee all the time. A prostate condition, you see. Nolan and I used to tease him that he had a secret ambition to baptize all the public restrooms of all the world's airports and train stations and bus terminals. We accused him of leaving little bronze plaques that read, "Harold Penrod, Accompanist to the Gods, Urinated Here."

We had fun. But there were some uncomfortable moments, too. I mean, what could we do when eighty-year-old Harold felt a sudden passion for the cowboy-bellman at the Dallas Hilton? His nameplate read Lamar. So Harold started making jokes around the boy's name: "Did you know that *'la mar'* means the sea in Spanish?" He says, "I bet you're a stormy fellow. Your undertow must be dangerous, strong enough to suck a man right on down to the bottom." Lamar just smiled and said, "Thank you very much, sir." And he didn't blink when Harold handed him a twenty-dollar bill for bringing up his luggage.

From the other side of the connecting door, Nolan and I could hear Harold calling down to the front desk at all hours of the night: *The drapes are stuck. Help me hang up my garment bag. I can't get any hot water. The TV is coming in fuzzy*. The kid must've gotten the idea. Harold showed up at breakfast the next morning with a small, pink-cheeked smile and his quick blue eyes beaming. I was relieved. After a certain age men have been known to die in the act. But Harold had actually played, probably with unaccustomed vigor, that night.

What was not fun in the least was Nolan's sudden spell of souvenir collecting. It began when he started lamenting that at our age we would likely never again sing in this or that city and asserted that we should begin grabbing mementos.

One city was Acapulco, of all the insalubrious tropical paradises. From the moment we got there I had a strong desire to sing my part and be gone, never to return. I didn't like the row of hotels and condos that ringed the beautiful bay. Our hotel was shaped like a pyramid, which I thought was disrespectful. Building such a thing was like making a hotel in the shape of St. Mark's cathedral and sticking it in some vulgar little beach town like Sorrento. Almost like the real thing, you know, but with a bar and disco right where the main altar should be.

Unfortunately, Nolan loved Acapulco. We were booked for a performance during an international pathologists' convention. I didn't want to accept the job, but Nolan insisted. We were going to be in Mexico anyway doing the capital plus Guanajuato and Morelia, lovely cities, and he thought a weekend by the sea, at the midpoint of the tour, would do us all good.

But there is nothing very lovely about Acapulco beyond the young seminaked women lounging at poolside and wriggling on the dance floor. He was all fired up by the mariachi music, the guitars and the trumpets and the yells, and he even stood up to sing with them. They did "Granada," the one by Agustín Lara. Lovely piece really, and Nolan was in good voice. This, however, prompted a few rounds of margaritas. Which in turn gave him the courage to ask a tall Mexican woman to dance. She was Amalia Camino, also known as the Wildcat, a famous Mexican actress known for her portrayals of evil, sensual women. Now, I've played a few femmes fatales in my time, so it wasn't something I would hold against her. Although judging from her elaborate makeup, the eyes drawn out like peacock feathers and the lips practically dripping blood and the hair piled on her head like Medusa's snakes, she didn't seem to know where art gives way to tart. "Ta-ta," said Nolan. "I'm going souvenir hunting."

What makes a desirable souvenir? Most people want a demitasse spoon or a mug or perhaps a nice shell from the beach. But for Nolan it was something with personal resonance, preferably stolen—a spoon from Lutece, a tube of lipstick filched out of Maria Callas's purse after their performance at La Scala, the hood ornament from the Mercedes that drove him to his debut at the Met. In Acapulco, I thought he would be happy with an autographed photo of his new friend and dance part-ner Amalia Camino. Do I sound jealous? Irked? I mean, here he was, dancing all night with some living sexual archetype while we were sup-posed to be enjoying the waning passion of our twilight years.

They were dancing. Amalia Camino was quite a bit taller than Nolan, and it wasn't just her big hair towering over him. He was trying to dance close to her, and his chin was resting on her squeezed-up bosom overflowing the top of her dress. I kept my eyes on them. I thought that as long as I was watching, they wouldn't dare do anything besides dance. And so I stayed behind sipping a margarita. I had a good view from a table by the dance floor. But when I glanced back, Nolan and his prize Wildcat had vanished into the crowd.

I hate being alone. I have no capacity whatsoever for solitude. The sound of my own thoughts rattling inside my head is enough to drive me crazy. And to be alone while surrounded by people is even worse. That night I felt that every eye was upon me, that I had become this pathetic creature sitting by herself in a crowded disco with a melting drink in her hand and a befuddled smile on her face. I was furious with Nolan. I decided then and there to break it off with him. If it meant canceling the rest of the tour in order to punish him further, then I would. After all, he was no longer the tenor he used to be and was in fact using me to resurrect his career.

I tried to sit with some dignity while I considered my course of action. The longer I sat, the more pathetic I looked. But still there was a chance Nolan would return. At least I wouldn't have to leave the place unescorted. I was growing anxious, so I stood up to see if I could spot him and his dance partner. Then I decided I would return to my room and be done with all this nonsense. As I was walking away, a waiter, quick as a ferret, scurried toward me with the check.

Nolan was the one in charge of the money. I didn't have a cent on me. I tried to wave the waiter away and sat down on the stupid little stool again. He started to clear the glasses, and only by wrestling with the man was I able to hang on to my nearly consumed and now tepid margarita. By god, if I couldn't leave, I could still make believe I was enjoying myself.

One can do that, you know. Bury the anxieties, anesthetize the pain, generally not give a damn. It's all a matter of surrender. Once I stopped fighting this miserable moment, I was free to experience it to the hilt. That's the key to living in the moment, facing the inevitable with grace, pain with equanimity, joy with detachment, confusion with balance. And sometimes, when I think I'm being put to a wicked test by some capricious being up there, I muster all these hidden spiritual resources and feel that I am totally enlightened.

The worst was still to come.

But I never lost my composure. It was all like a dream when at some level, even in your sleep, you know you are dreaming, that it's not you falling down the well or being eaten by lions.

Nolan waved at me from across the dance floor. "Yoo-hoo," he seemed to say. "Here I am! Did you miss me?" There is very little correlation between a privileged voice and the intellect. He was just another fool with his vocal cords coated with honey. For a time he had been able to make glorious music.

He was alone, weaving and bobbing his way around the dancing couples. I didn't see Amalia Camino anywhere, but I figured if Nolan was back, she wouldn't be far behind. I wanted to read her face. Well, no need for that. When Nolan reached our table and bent down to kiss me, as if nothing had happened, I smelled the whole story on his mustache.

I told him he was disgusting. He told me he had his souvenir. I told him he should rinse his mouth out. We were talking louder and louder and people were starting to look at us. But Nolan was not aware of anything. He had both his hands behind his back and was asking me to pick a hand so I could see his souvenir. Just to shut him up, I pointed at his left. Wrong! he sang out and raised his right hand. I thought he was waving a kerchief until I realized he was holding a huge pair of purple lace panties.

I don't think there was any doubt in anyone's mind whose they were.

The guys at Amalia's table were scowling and muttering unintelligible stuff. The waiter was handing Nolan's charge card back to him because his excesses had been rejected by a suspicious credit-card company.

One thing about Mexican policemen is that they dress sharp. I knew right away that the two men suddenly standing in front of our table were officers because of the sunglasses—inscrutable reflecting things that must've made the dimly lit club as dark as night. But there was more—narrow little Italian loafers, the kind with sandal weave on top. And shiny polyester jackets—bright blue on one and mustard on the other. And knit shirts that allowed just a glimpse of the gold chains around their brown necks. Right away I was wondering which of the two would prove to be the good cop and which the bad. I'm afraid that reveals how much of my education in the ways of the world has come from watching American television.

They took us away in a large black car. They were not friendly. Neither of them. When Nolan took out his wallet, just before they pushed his head down to guide him into the car's backseat, the one in blue took it from his hand. The other gave his cheek a sharp, stinging slap that made Nolan's eyes water.

The officers sat up front. They didn't seem very worried that we might jump out the door and escape. They were supremely confident of their power over us. I asked to call the American consulate. I knew it was the middle of the night on a weekend, but I wanted to convey to them that they were flirting with the possibility of an international incident. I asked them if they knew who we were. Now, I didn't mean anything arrogant by that. But as soon as I asked the question, I realized that I was uttering the ultimate cliché of the rich and famous when they think they are being treated disrespectfully. "Do you know who we are?" I asked. And the two policemen looked at each other and broke out in huge grins.

"'No, Señora,'" they said. "Who are you?"

I didn't see their eyes until we reached the police station. And when I did, I saw that they didn't look at us with hatred or contempt or righteousness. They looked at us with greed. "Are you the famous opera singers?" they asked, and dollar signs glinted in their dark eyes.

But first there was paperwork to do. We had to be formally charged. We were accused of attempting to leave the nightclub without paying the bill—a common form of theft, it was explained to me. Things could be worked out right then and there. The bill came to $2,174—dollars, not pesos—not including tip. It did include cover charge, songs at tableside by the mariachi group, a selection of hors d'oeuvres that I didn't remember eating, three bottles of tequila, and twenty-eight cocktails of different stripes, which I realized were all the ones that I had thought people were buying for each other and for us after Nolan had sung "Granada" with the mariachis. A minor misunderstanding.

Nolan Keefe was charged with sexual assault and the theft of a Belgian lace undergarment. The officer handed the Wildcat's panties to the clerk behind the counter, who folded them lovingly into a triangle, smoothed out the wrinkles, and placed them inside a plain brown envelope as evidence. I glanced at Nolan and guessed that his main worry was that the valuable souvenir was slipping out of his hands.

Well, I offered to pay the bill right then, but when the officer handed Nolan's wallet to me, it was empty, except for his driver's license and a photo of me when I was thirty that I had no idea he carried around with him. "Where's the money?" I asked. Nobody knew. If only I could locate Harold at the hotel, he would bring the required funds to pay the bill, the fine, a gratuity for the gendarmes. When I asked where there was a phone we could use, nobody knew that either. But they knew what all our crimes had been.

We were told to sit quietly and wait. Was I worried? No. As soon as I could, I would call our agent in Mexico City and have him send lawyers, money, clean clothes, and someone to do my hair. Meanwhile, I had to sit on a stiff wooden bench next to my pervert, who was on the verge of tears because the bad publicity would ruin the last of his professional reputation. As a frequent guest soloist with the St. Patrick's Cathedral choir, he said, he was practically a man of the cloth with a reputation to protect. I hadn't realized he thought so highly of himself.

The holding pen of the police station smelled of smoke and urine. The floor was tile, its natural red color barely visible under a patina of mop streaks. The room was quite bare. There were only these benches and a big clock on the wall and oil cans full of sand that served as ashtrays and brass cuspidors at each corner. I thought they were a nice touch, the shiny sort-of-art-deco spittoons. The green paint on the walls was peeling and underneath was gray paint, which in places was also flaking so that you could see a third layer of light blue and finally, underneath all the colors, patches of plaster.

There were about a dozen people in the room, all of them sitting on benches, some of the men either drunk or sleeping. Two fellows attached to each other by handcuffs had bloody noses and swollen eyes and cut lips. They seemed to be getting along well by then, whispering comments to each other, occasionally breaking into snickers. I wondered what their problem had been. Rivals for the same woman? I hoped it was that, the chivalric confrontation of two masculine forces with a woman as the prize. Nobody ever thinks of the woman in these situations. It's assumed that she will be flattered and gladly go with the winner. There was no duel when the Prince seduced me away from Nolan.

We were freed around six in the morning. The judge turned out to be one of my admirers. He berated the two cops for showing us such disrespect. In gratitude, Nolan and I sang *"Un di felice eterea,"* such a fine Alfredo he was even then. It was beautiful. There we were in this utterly depressing room, filling the place with our voices. The drunks woke up. The two beat-up guys were in tears. The judge was in heaven. *Gracias, gracias!* He kept bowing to us. We were out of there before the paparazzi even heard we'd been arrested.

Nolan's Death Impulse

One of the problems with Nolan—perhaps the principal problem of his whole problematic life—is that he developed a suicide obsession.

He liked to talk about the beauty of a fully conscious death leaping from a tall building. He imagined the flight earthward, the rush of the wind in his ears, the blur of the passing facade, the quickening focus of the approaching pavement, perhaps the glitter of a parked automobile or the pearly luminescence of a tree's dewy foliage, and finally, inevitably, the instantaneous letting go of one's hold on life, which he thought must bring forth a kind of peace and release of the world so that, if for only a moment, one can, while still alive, enjoy the peace that passeth understanding.

Nolan required that death be gradual but painless, deliberate and therefore fearless and sober. Only suicide offered a guarantee of these conditions. And so he proceeded to study, to consider, to plan for his passing. It became a hobby. When not haunting the observation deck of the Empire State Building or the Eiffel Tower, he read books, studied physiology, perused medicine labels. He could argue the merits of oleander versus foxglove, fifty tablets of Darvon versus seventy of Demerol, the drama of leaping into the tiger cage at the zoo versus diving off the Coronado bridge or crawling partway into an old-fashioned gas oven. He found comfort and stimulation in the poetry of Sylvia Plath and Anne Sexton.

I told him he was not funny. Not even remotely interesting. People who kill themselves on purpose are inconsiderate and therefore properly damned to hell for all time, certainly according to the Catholic Church, that most sensible of all churches when it comes to arranging sins in their proper order. What can I say about the man except that he thought he was living an opera? His life would have to end in a glorious death scene, the virtuous hero and heroine would walk to their death by fire, by precipice, by self-immolation.

I've often been accused of living a fabricated life, when the real dreamer is this squat little Irishman with a penchant for good whiskey, fine shoes, and women other than his wife. And yet we had our history. We went on remarkable adventures, were together at exciting times, forgave each other a multitude of sins. There's no point in leaving the person after so much because you keep on dragging the life you've led wherever you go.

After the years of separation, Nolan and I had approached each other with caution. I was emerging from my anxious time with the Prince. And he was trying to find a way to extricate himself from his latest fling, second fiddle in some upstate New York pickup orchestra for a touring production of *Forza*. I called her the Dragon Lady. She became his Yoko Ono. That same stubborn possessiveness—and the temper as well—got him into trouble with the Met, La Scala, Covent Garden. She talked him into *Nolan Keefe Sings Broadway; Marvelous Nolan at Midnight; Nolan Keefe's Classics for Christmas, Hanukkah, and the Solstice*, records that brought what was once the world's finest tenor voice to the masses. They sold like hotcakes. The Dragon Lady supervised the arrangements and kept a chunk of the money.

Meanwhile, knowledgeable opera lovers abandoned Nolan. And when the public realized he was no longer a major opera star, sales of his popular recordings fell. The two strands were tied into an interdependent downward spiral—loss of standing hurt his popular recordings, and the more he did to make up for lower sales, the further his standing fell.

Our Grand Tour was supposed to revive both of our careers. My voice was quickly slipping and wavering into the mezzo range; his had become a cliché. But abroad we still had credibility as living and breathing legends—for the first time in years, in the flesh, close enough to touch in Tokyo, Warsaw, Brussels, Buenos Aires, Mexico City. It was in Mexico City that Nolan nearly died on me.

We had been married for thirty years. And we had become lovers again out of desperation. Perhaps we could be to one another what we had once been. I was able to see past the tired eyes, the flaccid jowls, the belly. He could remember me at twenty-three as Norma and himself as Pollione; he had been so in awe of me during rehearsals back then that he could hardly meet my gaze. He sang to my breasts. Zeffirelli was directing. "Look Señora Casals in the eyes, Signor Keefe. You cannot let Norma push you around more than the script calls for. She is the woman who loves you!"

Now, thirty years later, on the balcony of the Gran Hotel de la Ciudad overlooking Mexico City's historic plaza, I was moved to tears. We were no longer the same people, but I had expected that we could be kind to each other. Kindness was no small thing; it could keep us going that endless year. That and love from the audiences. I had thought there was enough love remaining for us that Nolan and I could simply assemble a program of forty or fifty minutes of actual singing, and that the evening would go to an hour and a half with drawn-out curtain calls.

We were determined not to tire ourselves out too soon. We were like marathon runners who needed to pace themselves in order to last for twenty-six cities. Dangerous, stifling cities, some of them, full of smog and traffic, dangerous food and unsanitary hotels. I longed for one night at the Plaza with tea in the Palm Court.

Much has been made of that night at the Gran Hotel de la Ciudad. Some call it the final unraveling of Mercè Casals' life, the brutal end of a ridiculous love affair. The truth is that Nolan and I were beginning to show the strain of months on tour. The Amalia Camino episode in Acapulco was the first sign that the stress was growing intolerable. I had always managed to rise above Nolan's ludicrous flirtations. The arrest and the night spent pleading our case before a judge had left me exhausted. And I realized that the less I saw of Nolan, the happier I would be. But when I tried to exchange our suite at the Gran Hotel for two rooms, I was informed that the hotel was booked.

Barely speaking, I anticipated a long night in one king-sized bed and a love seat too small for either of us to sleep on, followed by a strained recital the following evening. We set out to be civil about the whole thing. I vocalized, took a long bath, and ordered hot onion broth. Nolan went for a walk through the historic downtown and came back with a bottle of Scotch, which he proceeded to drink neat from the bathroom glass.

As the afternoon grew dark, the shapes about the room—the bed, the chair, the love seat—softened into shadows. Nolan napped, supine and spread-eagled in the middle of the bed, while I curled up to one side. Twice he woke with a sudden shudder, as if a dream had scared him in his sleep. Each time he bolted off the bed and lurched into the sitting room, glass in hand, toward the bottle on the bureau.

Nolan was not ordinarily a heavy drinker. These bouts of overindulgence showed he was unhappy with himself. He didn't like his singing, but he refused to work on the repertoire. He didn't like being soft, but he kept on eating. He didn't like it that his shoes were too tight or the sleeves of his shirt too long. If he was rude to Howard or snapped at a waiter, they were all sins to him, lapses in Christian charity. Naturally he felt guilty. He also felt guilty about not being in good voice. And he felt particularly guilty that the crowds cheered him on nonetheless. He thought of them as know-nothings; whether in Buenos Aires or Warsaw, there was precious little comfort in their adulation.

But mostly, Nolan was bothered about us being together. We were not in it for the thrills but for comfort and companionship. If we had a moment of passion, it was purely out of the kindness that our old friend-ship required. The fact that my fee was double his did not help. But I'd been earning more than Nolan for twenty years. I was the reason tickets sold out, at $85 apiece.

I worried about him. I wanted to be helpful, but I hadn't counted on the misery he was feeling after the long week of misplaced notes, insuffi-cient breath, and sham emoting. "You're on a masochistic binge," I tried to tell him that night after the performance. "Self-destruction is not at all interesting."

Then, seemingly out of nowhere, he said, "You want to see self-destruction? Watch this." He opened the glass door that gave onto the balcony and stepped to the edge. "*Hola*, Mexico!" he called out above the street, which even after midnight was still busy with the stream of traffic circling the square. "*Hola*, Mexico!" he shouted louder. "Are you ready to catch a falling star?"

By then he was sitting astride the balcony railing. From inside the room he looked like a horseman about to ride off into empty space, his long, thin hair waving in the breeze, one hand clutching the ironwork, the other up in a jaunty wave.

In a foreign country, whom does one call in the case of a suicide in progress? The fire department, as when you have a cat up a tree? Those gallant young men from the Mexican police? The man's wife? How about a close friend to talk things over with? I was proving sadly inadequate. "Forgive me, my darling," I said to Nolan, "but if you don't stop this foolishness, I'm going to call for help."

"I don't care what you do. I will do what I need to."

"If you wouldn't be so overdramatic, we could talk this over quietly."

"There's nothing left to say," he insisted. "Here," he said, reaching into his hip pocket, "you can have my money, and anything else you find in the wallet. There's enough cash for you and Howard to have drinks on me."

"What a wonderful idea." I tried to sound cheerful.

Nolan gazed at me suspiciously. He fidgeted. He was growing uncomfortable mounted on the railing. His mood had become serious. He no longer acted as if he were riding a horse. When I turned away from him, Nolan demanded to know where I was going.

"To call room service, of course. They make a nice club sandwich. That and a bottle of Bohemia beer might prove comforting."

"I'm trying to say good-bye, Mercè, not plan dinner."

I slowly inched back into the parlor. "Well, all this excitement has given *me* an appetite. You know how I am with stress, dear. Give me a crisis, give me a sandwich."

The phone rang as I spoke. Nolan seemed startled, his look accusatory, as if I had somehow provoked a phone call through sheer will. I let the phone ring. Simply by looking at Nolan, I was retaining him in the land of the living; should I direct my attention elsewhere, I feared he would take advantage of the distraction to leap. As if to make sure I understood the seriousness of his intent, Nolan raised his left leg over the railing. He was now standing outside it, his heels on the narrow overhang, arms hooked into the top iron bar. The phone kept clanging in the otherwise silent room.

"I think I should pick up," I ventured. "They'll think something's wrong. And barge in."

"Go ahead, answer it," he said.

"You won't jump yet, will you?" I still felt my gaze was the one thing holding him back.

"Why shouldn't I?"

"Well, we're not done yet. We won't have another opportunity to talk once you do this thing."

"Answer the blasted phone, Mercè. It's driving me crazy."

"*Bueno,*" I said softly into the mouthpiece. In that moment, as soon as I picked up the phone, the room became quiet again. "*Con quién quiere hablar?*" I asked into the silence.

"Mr. Keefe, *por favor*," said a highly agitated voice. "This is Alberto, the concierge."

"Hello, Alberto." I tried to sound cheerful.

"Señora, do you know where the *señor* is?"

"Yes, of course," I said, glancing quickly at Nolan. "But it is not convenient for him to come to the phone at this time." I made it sound as if he were in the shower or taking a nap. "May I take a message?"

"Who is it?" Nolan called out suddenly.

"It's Alberto, the night concierge," I answered. "He asked if I knew where you were."

"What does he want?"

"I think he would like to speak with you personally."

"Tell him I'm busy."

"Señor Nolan wants to know if there is a message."

"*Sí*, Señora. Tell him there are many people, at least a hundred people, gathered in the street in front of the hotel looking up at him. They, and all of us, too, his friends here in the Gran Hotel, want to know what he is doing up there."

"Alberto, that is a hard question to answer at this time."

"I think I understand, Señora." He sounded as if he were about to break into tears.

Nolan shouted, "Tell everybody to move back. I don't want anyone getting hurt."

"Alberto, please send those people away. They are only encouraging him."

"It's too late for that, Señora. The journalists want to know for what reason the tenor Nolan Keefe is about to walk off the fourteenth floor. They want to interview him. They want to take a picture when he comes down."

From the street I could hear a cacophony of auto horns as the traffic tried to maneuver through the jam created by the crowd and a TV remote truck. "The press wants shots of you landing on the pavement," I called out. "Do they have your permission?"

"Tell them to go away." Nolan was making wide arm gestures signaling for people to move back.

"We're past that option, Nolan. They smell blood." But of course they already had some of what they wanted. Nobody is more ridiculous than the indecisive suicide. He'll jump. He won't jump. Heads he jumps, tails he doesn't. From the street below, one of the TV trucks had aimed a spotlight at the balcony, so that Nolan in his loose shirttails and flying hair cast a dancing shadow on the parlor walls and ceiling. Nolan Keefe, the world-renowned tenor, the man who had always conducted himself with the dignity befitting a great artist, was about to have a silly, messy, unphotogenic fall, not just from life but also from style and grace.

"Alberto," I felt myself swell with indignation, "I'm afraid there has been a misinterpretation of the actions of Señor Keefe."

"*Sí*, Señora," the clerk said, eager to hear whatever line of reasoning I might be able to concoct on such short notice. "What shall I tell the press is the correct interpretation of the situation that concerns us?"

"Only that Nolan Keefe loves Mexico City. That on this the last night of his triumphant tour, he wanted to look out on the bright lights of this jewel among cities, Mexico City, La Capital, the Paris of the Americas."

"*Sí*, Señora. I shall tell them this." And then after a moment, he added shyly, "It is for this reason that Mr. Keefe wants to die here?"

"Nonsense, Alberto. This is not about dying, it's about celebrating. You tell the press and the people out there and the traffic to be quiet, that Nolan Keefe has a surprise for them."

"*Ay*, Señora. This surprise is what they are afraid of."

"There's nothing to fear. Just be patient."

I stepped out on the balcony, trying to move gently, avoiding any abrupt movements that might push Nolan over the edge. The murmur from the crowd and the traffic seemed to have quieted down. The layer of smog that normally obscured the stars had thinned out. A rare cool light washed over the ornate facade of the Gran Hotel, its glow highlighting the figure of Nolan on the edge of the balcony. He reminded me of the Acapulco cliff divers who stand on a single jutting rock and pause for a moment, perfectly balanced above the breaking waves and the rocks. They wait for the wind and the surf and their spirit to be in harmony before leaping into those few breathtaking seconds of pure poetic flight.

There the similarity ended. Nolan seemed anything but heroic, his shoulders fleshy and hunched over, his pants flapping around his skinny legs, the crown of his head showing pink scalp under the strands of blowing hair. He was about to fall in defeat rather than fly in victory. I would not let it happen.

"Nolan, darling?" I called softly.

"Leave me alone." From the catch in his throat I guessed that he was about to break into a sob.

"It's too late for solitude, my dear," I reminded him. "You are totally surrounded. There are a thousand people staring up, and the press has their telephotos and their microphones aimed at you. And I am behind you every step of the way. There hasn't been a time in your life when you've been better accompanied."

"Gawkers and paparazzi are not company."

"Well, you'd better look again. These people surrounding you, and I include myself in this group, expect more of you tonight than a cowardly escape from the plight of living. We all know that life is a mystery. We expect our artists to illuminate that situation rather than fall into darkness. If you jump to your death tonight, you will have betrayed not just the hundreds who are gathered here but millions around the world who also contemplate the occasional horrors of existence and depend on the likes of us to make the passage from one crisis to another somehow bearable. For every genius who kills himself, the following night a thousand ordinary people commit suicide. You will cause a thousand deaths. That is a luxury, and a horror, you have no right to indulge in."

I knew Nolan was not going to jump. That's not to say that he wasn't capable of falling by accident, given his propensity to slip and trip—and then there was the Scotch. The greater challenge was to help him extricate himself from the present situation with his dignity intact. Slowly he turned, maintaining at least one hand firmly gripping the bar.

I must have held my breath for a full minute, just watching him precariously raise one leg over the railing, then straddle the thing before finally swinging the other leg over and landing with both feet safely on the balcony. Light applause rose from the street through the quiet night and into our suite.

"They love you, Nolan."

"And I haven't even sung," he said, wiping the tears.

"They deserve something for their concern, don't you think?"

He stayed at the edge of the balcony and lifted his arms in a wide greeting. The crowd's cheering wafted up softly. Then, as if the idea had that moment come to him, he began the *"Una furtiva lagrima."* His voice was tentative at first. When he realized the crowd had hushed and was listening, his singing grew stronger. It had been years since he had been able to tackle anything so challenging, even in the intimacy of a recital hall. Here he was, fourteen stories above the street, performing as if he'd planned and rehearsed for weeks. The farthest reaches of the night seemed to resonate with the purity of those notes, somehow rescued to rise in celebration one more time.

Now, years later, the performance exists only in memories, in Nolan's, mine, and that of the people who were there in the street. One can't help thinking that with all the cameras and microphones pointed at him, there may somewhere exist to this day a precious recording of those moments, perhaps treasured by one of the reporters covering what had started out to be the suicide of the tenor Nolan Keefe. If anyone reading these pages knows of such a recording, please contact the publisher. A reliving of that miracle would bring rare joy to an old man.

o—H THIS BOOK IS NOT ABOUT YOU, NOLAN.

The following Wednesday, when Lockwood shows up at the Villa promptly at four o'clock for tea with Nolan, he learns that the singer has been gone since early that morning. Harley Friendly, the desk clerk, has to be coaxed to reveal that earlier in the day two men stopped by to pick Nolan up.

"Just taking him to lunch," they announced cheerfully as they left in a Porsche 944. Mr. Keefe seemed fascinated with the automobile and when the driver folded back the top, he immediately claimed the front seat. The driver was an old Hollywood type, with the shades and the ponytail and the gold chains. The other fellow looked like a retired boxer with a bullneck and rubbery ears and a nose like a potato. "They were both terribly nice, and very generous," Harley adds.

"I would like you to call me when Mr. Keefe returns." Lockwood slides a tightly folded $20 bill and his Mark My Words, Inc. business card across the counter.

"You're paying me to betray the confidence of a resident?" Harley squints.

"Actually, it's only to pay for the phone call."

Harley Friendly's smile congeals. A distinct shadow veils his eyes. "And I'll tell you what: You can leave right now," he says tersely. "Because you are stalking one of our residents."

For the next few days, the group at Lockwood's takes turns calling the Villa Age d'Or and asking for Nolan Keefe. He's not there. No, the management is not aware of his whereabouts; Mr. Keefe is free to come and go as he wishes because his rent is paid up forever. "The other thing covered by his rent," a voice on the other end of the line adds pointedly, "is a measure of privacy. Mr. Keefe will not have calls put through if he chooses not to talk to anyone. The management will not reveal whether he's in his room or not. He will receive only those visitors he chooses to see, for tea in the lounge at his reserved tea time."

No, Mr. Keefe has not had guests this past Wednesday; his table in the lounge is vacant. But it's still his table at his hour on his day, whenever he does choose to receive for tea. Certainly, he will get the message that Mr. Lockwood has been inquiring about him.

"He's been with them a week," Lockwood mutters.

"My guess is that they've set him up in a nice hotel, with round-the-clock room service, a pool, and an occasional drive to the beach. They're going out of their minds babysitting a spoiled old man," Perla says.

Orson suggests that Nolan Keefe should come live with them on Hyacinth Street, and that way they could all reminisce with him and add to the Señora's legend.

"Yes," Lockwood says, suddenly animated.

"The idea is totally impractical," Perla insists. "For two reasons. One, Nolan would be a very demanding houseguest. The other is that we don't know where he is."

Lockwood shakes his head unhappily. "He's being bribed by Holly-wood Hank and Alonzo Baylor. He's probably talking his head off in return for milkshakes, massages, dirty movies."

"Or hookers," adds Orson. "These guys know what works."

"These are all things we could provide." Lockwood sighs again. "Plus we would give him the one thing Hollywood Hank and his hack do not have."

"And that would be?" Orson pipes in right on cue.

"Friendship," declares Lockwood. "This would be evidenced by our intimate conversation, our generosity with ice cream and drives to the beach."

"And a slow hand job," says Perla cheerfully.

"Perla, I'm awed by your generosity," says Lockwood, his face reddening.

"You're talking to a night nurse. I've had my share of terminal acts. There's a secret sense of fulfillment in eliciting a faint moan of pleasure from a patient who knows he is near death."

Meanwhile Lockwood keeps bad news to himself. He has heard from three different agents that his *The Wonder Singer: My Story*, by Mercè Casals as told to Mark Lockwood, is of little interest. "Who needs more than one book about a former opera singer who has not been heard in the twenty years prior to her death?" they ask.

According to *Publishers Weekly* Alonzo Baylor has already received a six-figure advance from none other than Top Jane at Viking. Word in the hallways and elevators of the big Manhattan houses is that Baylor is milking a variety of revealing sources, from a mumbo-jumbo analysis of the singer's actual DNA to exclusive firsthand revelations from her former husband and mentor, Nolan Keefe.

The word at Diva, Inc. is no word at all. Lockwood doesn't dare break up his happy team with the news that the project may be as good as dead. Sure, a couple of publishers will consider the manuscript once it's finished; they're not fully slamming the door. And if he can finish it before Alonzo Baylor turns in his, it would be delicious to beat the more celebrated author to the punch while capitalizing on his prepublication buzz. It's a long shot; Lockwood has no choice but to take it.

In the stifling LA evening, in the upper reaches of Mulholland Drive, the breeze that wafts from the east feels like fever and smells faintly of dust and smoke. Far from the Villa Age d'Or, Nolan Keefe sits by the pool on a terrace overlooking the city shimmering in the valley and the ribbons of freeways snaking in constant streams of light, merging white and red, finally fading to inky blackness where the ocean meets the land. The house, which clearly belongs to the taller of the two showbiz types—not the bullnecked thug but the spindly one with the poofy hair—opens behind sliding glass doors into a living room carpeted in soft mauves and plums, furnished in cushy white leather, made cozy by a fireplace with molded cement logs. To one side there's a buffet permanently stocked with wines, cigars, and interesting little pizzas from Spago.

Wrapped in a paisley silk robe, Nolan is puzzling things out beside the lit turquoise pool. He is a hostage of sorts. He has deduced that the pushy hospitality has little to do with him; all the two men want is what he knows about Mercè Casals. He is used to that, of course. The reporters', the fans', the world's attention has always been on Mercè, as if he had not been her equal in talent and temperament, if not in gossip value and premature self-destruction. If people still remember and listen to her 1958 Norma, they are also drawn to the recordings he made in his own prime, especially the 1959 Alfredo and the 1962 Nadir. But as long as these two yokels keep asking only about her, he will continue to keep his lips pursed and teeth clamped in obstinate silence.

They insist on bribing him, which makes it all the more amusing to stay quiet. Once he spills whatever they're after, it will be the end of the star treatment, no more ice cream, no more foot massages, no more sushi, no more Johnny Wadd and Dementia Darling videos. The idea of going back to the Villa, to a life of Wednesday teas and mah-jongg, is a definite step back to the zombie time of the past twelve years, ever since Mercè got the bright idea of putting him away. He hadn't had much of a choice; she'd told him he was old and broke.

He can't explain her sudden rejection. It had been up to Mercè to make sure their comforts were paid for: the park-view apartment, the Belgian chocolates, the Ungaros, Valentinos, Diors that were her public vices and the vintage Château Margaux and Tío Pepe sherry that were his occasional pleasures. He hadn't seriously objected to handing most, but not all, of his money to her. Watching for the arrival of the postman became something of a game; she tried to open his mail and grab his checks before he had a chance to cash them into rolls of $100 bills which he secreted inside the pages of forgotten books. These were the lovely green notes that made him the life of the cafés and the darling of aspiring songbirds getting by as salesclerks and waitresses.

From somewhere deep inside the LA basin, Nolan hears the soft strains of an orchestra, rising and turning with the wind so that he can catch isolated groups of notes, something that sounds like Beethoven, a moment later Mozart, then Schubert. Definitely Schubert, he thinks, a piano concerto, because a flash of brilliant staccato riff breaks out of the fabric woven by the strings and woodwinds. He guesses that in this cooling summer night the music is coming from the Hollywood Bowl. He is in thrall to the music, both familiar and full of secrets, intimating a direction, then changing, then echoing and rhyming and finally delivering the inevitable, yet surprising, resolution.

Sometimes Hollywood Hank and Alonzo Baylor play Good Cop– Bad Cop. The famous writer wears a black turtleneck; his sweaty head emerges from the collar in the shape and size of a small planet. Hollywood Hank wears white linen slacks and loafers without socks. A gold chain glitters from within a forest of chest hair and an open black shirt.

Nolan Keefe stretches out on a pool recliner. With his eyes concealed by wraparound sunglasses, shaded further by the wide brim of a straw hat with stenciling around the crown spelling *The Cabo Is Cool,* he convincingly feigns sleep. When Nolan Keefe is not faking a nap he is actually taking one. In truth, he has managed to be in a deep snooze whenever Hollywood Hank and Alonzo Baylor have wanted to talk to him. Napping is the natural state of cats and old men. Whether the sleep is real or not, Nolan can be slow to awaken. And then he continues to be mostly silent, conducting his end of any attempted conversation with intermittent head scratches, shrugs, and winks.

"Up and at 'em, sleeping beauty," Hollywood Hank sings out softly, his lips close behind Nolan's head, moist breath tickling his ear.

"Rise and shine," his burly friend chimes in as he shakes the side of Nolan's lounge chair.

Nolan pretends he's in a coma. He figures his act is so convincing, the bubble of saliva at the corner of his mouth so pitiful, that for a moment they might think he's dead. After practically abducting him from the Villa, it would serve them right having to explain a famous body to the cops.

"He looks dead," says Alonzo Baylor.

"That's what eighty-something looks like when it's taking a nap." Hollywood Hank chuckles. "You should see yourself when you're asleep."

"I'm not eighty."

"And nobody would mistake you for dead, either."

"What's eating you?" the famous author grumbles. "You've been a pain in the ass lately."

"Well, excuse me. I've only gotten us a huge advance on a book that is showing no visible signs of progress."

"I've been lacking crucial material. You know that. And this Irish tenor manages to occasionally talk about everything except what I need out of him."

"I got a call from our hack ghostwriter," Hollywood Hank finally reveals with a sigh. "Mark Lockwood is willing to make a switch: a pizza carton full of cassettes in return for Nolan Keefe."

"Which cassettes? I need early career stuff."

"He will gather a bunch at random," he explains. "He's doing it only to protect the old man, whom he thinks we're torturing."

"Tell the guy we insist on getting all the tapes."

"Sure, I can do that," the agent explains with methodical patience. "But since we don't know how many tapes there are, he can agree to our conditions and then give us whatever he wants anyway."

"This old man knows stuff," the writer says. "There's got be a way to get it out of him."

"We're being taken for a ride, Alonzo. How many more trips do you want to make to Venice Beach with Nolan?" He adds with an air of reluctant resignation, "I think he's forgotten whatever he knew about Mercè Casals in the first place."

Nolan Keefe lets out a groan and opens his eyes, blinking his heavy lids as if to get his vision into focus. He seems about to say something, and the two men turn their attention to him.

"There's stuff I know that neither of you two hacks will get at on your own. Things that Mercè would never speak of."

"Fine. We'll do what you want. Take them Nolan Keefe. Get their tapes. I'll start making stuff up."

"You don't have enough imagination to do Mercè Casals' life justice," Nolan sneers at the writer.

"Shut up, old man," Baylor says. "Or I'll pick you up and throw you over the side of the cliff."

"Oh, my, are we getting sensitive?" says Hollywood Hank.

Nolan Keefe is not surprised at the change of plans. For the past few days his hosts have grown impatient with him. Well, no problem; he's a free spirit, willing to go wherever they take him. He rides in the front seat of Hollywood Hank's Porsche while Alonzo Baylor has to curl himself up in the back. Nolan is traveling light; he can keep his growing collection of t-shirts (Venice, Baja, Knott's, SexWorld), but they reclaimed the silk robe.

On the way to their meeting point in front of the La Brea Tar Pits, Nolan makes them stop at a gas station. Hollywood Hank is worried that the old man might simply walk away and leave them with nothing to trade for the Señora's tapes. By the time they make the stop, the writer and his agent are so obviously eager to get rid of him it hurts the old man's feelings. In retaliation, he locks himself inside the men's room and refuses to come out until they apologize for various alleged insults.

"But we haven't said anything," Hollywood Hank pleads through the locked door.

"It's the looks," Nolan replies. "I've seen eyes rolling and lips smirking. After all I've done for you guys."

"Just for the record, Mr. Keefe," says Alonzo Baylor, joining Hollywood Hank outside the restroom, "what have you done for me?"

"I've opened up my whole memory bank to help you out. Without me you wouldn't have access to all sorts of important things. Like, for example, how I used sexual rewards to get Mercè Casals to do her drills."

"You wait until now to bring this stuff up?" the writer exclaims.

"The subject is not new. We chatted about our intimate relationship before. But there was more to our life than sex. I taught her how to speak English, for starters. She was fresh off the boat in 1939. The only English she knew was what she had memorized from *The Messiah*. I made her an American. I taught her to love baseball and hot dogs and the fox-trot. I taught her how to keep Mirella Freni from upstaging her in the 1947 *Aida*."

"This book is not about you, Nolan." Hollywood Hank hisses through the crack in the bathroom door. "You want to see yourself in print? Write your own damn memoir."

Hollywood Hank stands outside the men's room of a Texaco station and has to contend with the people who want to use it. "I'm waiting for my dad," he explains whether anyone asks or not. "It takes a while for his bladder to drain."

Nolan emerges with new determination: He will make whoever wants to milk him about Mercè Casals pay for the privilege. Even after her death, he is not happy playing second fiddle to her greater hold on the public's imagination, to her greater instinct for self-promotion, her greater need for self-aggrandizement. During their life together he had never felt as diminished as when she'd persuaded him to move to the Villa Age d'Or and he'd had to content himself with the charity of her visits for Wednesday tea.

He realizes for the first time that he'd envied her strength, her energy, and her independence while he'd slowly sunk into idleness filled with TV reruns of *Laugh-In* and *The Smothers Brothers*. He had spent long afternoons gazing before him as if the wallpaper pattern held the key to life's deeper mysteries. And all the time, he'd known that she was alive and fully in the world while he had been shut inside; there was no reason at all why she should be happy and he not.

Unlike a physical condition where the offending organ can be carved out, the death of Mercè Casals did not alleviate Nolan's dissatisfaction. It did, however, add color and nuance to his pain; resentment is now edged with bereavement. His envy is flecked with guilt. His occasional silence is now countered by the absolute silence caused by her death.

Hollywood Hank and his pal the World-Famous Writer do not understand this. They think Nolan Keefe is holding out on a rich vein of information that he will mine for his own ends. Everybody wants to be a star, they conclude. So they pack the old man off to his friends and let them deal with his fuzzy mind, capricious bladder, and unpredictable cravings. "Good-bye, Nolan!" they call as the old man weaves his way across the Wiltshire Boulevard traffic to the safety of the La Brea Tar Pits. There, standing at the railing and staring into the torpid bubbling of the greenish-black pool, Nolan Keefe senses Perla and Lockwood close by.

"Oh, it's you two," he says.

"It will be like old times," the nurse whispers in his ear.

"You are among friends now, Nolan," murmurs Lockwood in his other ear.

"I am so unhappy." Nolan finally breaks down in a series of hard sobs. "Mercè is dead, and we'll never be able to resolve all these things between us."

"What things?" Lockwood tries to coax from him.

"I don't want to talk about them."

"What do you want? Do you want tea?" Perla asks.

"Yes."

"Perla says it will be like old times," Lockwood reassures him. "We can have tea, then go to the beach and have ourselves some fun."

"Fine. But I won't feel like talking. The other guys wanted to talk. I didn't say much to them."

"Conversation is good for the soul," Perla points out.

"Okay, take me home with you," he says cheerfully.

Nolan in Exile

On Nolan's eightieth birthday, I persuaded him to change out of the terry-cloth robe he'd been wearing for the past week into something more suitable for a celebration. He used to be such a fastidious dresser, and now the best I could do was coax him into a pair of baggy gray trousers, a blue blazer, and a wide floral necktie. I had to talk him into shaving and trimming his nose hair. "You have to get spiffed up for the next big phase of your life," I said.

Nolan pleaded that he did not want a party, and that if guests were invited he would lock himself in the bedroom. It wasn't until I invoked my dead mother and my vanished father and swore that the celebration would be for the two of us alone that he consented to put on clothes.

"You need a haircut, too," I added. "I'll call Marisa to make an appointment."

He was standing in front of the bathroom mirror, still dripping, a thick white towel wrapped around his waist, frowning at his reflection. He pulled his shoulders back and thrust out his chest and drew his weak stomach muscles in. He ran his fingers through his thinning hair, parting the strands to reveal a latticework of pink scalp. "Well, as long as you think I need one," he said. "Nobody gives a haircut like Marisa."

But when I called Marisa, she explained that Nolan was no longer welcome at the salon. She could put up with his flirting, his propositions that she run away to Tijuana with him, a hand occasionally wandering from under the sheet to brush her thigh. She'd almost clipped his ear once, she was so startled. But then he'd started annoying the other stylists with leers and comments. They could see he was aroused, too. Marisa offered to come to our building and give Nolan his cut as long as I kept an eye on him.

I could hardly contain my shock. "Nolan, you've been banned from Marisa's Salon. How ridiculous is that?"

He pleaded innocence, of course. Said that his reputation preceded him, and that young women were too quick to misinterpret the harmless flirtations of an old man. In any case, he accused me of not keeping up with him, especially in light of his new little blue heart pills that made him feel as vigorous as a stallion. I did not want to spend the rest of my golden years with the same Don Juan who had caused me such grief throughout my life. I could either flush his new pills down the toilet and risk his heart failing, or arrange for separate residences and enjoy a little peace.

It was only when we were halfway through the fine dinner of co-quilles St. Jacques, brought in by that nice young man from La Valencia, meals on wheels for the affluent, that I broached the subject that had been preying on my mind. For a moment I thought I was not going to muster the resolve, but I did search for the kindest words. I knew that no matter what I said or when I said it, the effect would be the same.

"Nolan, I feel like a tired old woman," I began. "And I've long looked like one, too." I paused to let the weight of the words find a place in his awareness. Nolan was prone to distraction even then.

"Darling, we're like a couple of ghosts drifting around these four rooms. I see us standing in front of the refrigerator trying to remember why we opened it, searching through the shelves, questioning our stomach for signs of hunger, our mouth for signs of thirst. I worry about getting in and out of the tub, falling asleep in the water. The world is dangerous for people our age. We choke on steak, fall on wet tile, lose our pills. We forget to turn things off: water, lights, gas. We can't take care of each other; we need taking care of." I paused to steady my voice. "I have an idea you will like."

"You're a lying hag," he said.

I realized that the direction of my thinking had dawned on him. "My poor darling."

He gazed back at me with such disbelief.

"It would be better if we lived apart. You will be happier at the perfect place I've found," I insisted. "The Villa Age d'Or has lovely food, pretty nurses, and a spectacular ocean view. It's more like a luxury resort."

"More than what?"

"Than a residential community or a hotel or an apartment building."

"Or a mausoleum," he said at last.

I was not going to be drawn into an argument. "You've never been there," I said. "We can go take a look. It's in Del Mar. You love Del Mar. We'll go for a Sunday drive and have lunch at the Villa; if you don't think it's a great place, we'll think of something else."

"A solution to this problem," he said.

"Yes." I added, "One that we can afford with our dwindling finances. I can create a fund that will cover your expenses at the Villa for the rest of your life. We must be practical. It's a practical solution."

"A final solution."

"Stop it, Nolan. Your morbid attitude makes me think you do need professional care."

I awoke the next morning intent on finishing the conversation. It was too late to take back my words now; I would proceed with unwavering certitude. I set a nice table for breakfast. I brewed the Darjeeling tea that Nolan liked with hot milk. I diced up a lovely red papaya. I buttered his whole-wheat toast more generously than he would dare. He sat at the table, his expression bemused at the attention that I was lavishing upon him. He smiled at his serving of papaya and methodically stabbed the scallops of fruit arranged like a bright mosaic, deep red on the blue of his plate. I followed the tentative nibbling of the toast, the careful sips from the steaming cup. I noticed the appreciation with which he observed the careful placing of flowers on the table, fruit in a bowl, the crystal dishes that made the strawberry jam look like rubies and the orange marmalade like gold. I waited for him to express some appreciation for the nice breakfast, or, more typical of Nolan, to wonder aloud what was up.

"Is the tea okay?" I asked. "Not too strong?" He reached for the mug in front of him—the Pablo Picasso peace-dove mug we had bought together at the airport in Barcelona—and blew on it, sending a puff of steam in my direction. He took a sip, then stared at the cup as if the answer to my question demanded long and careful meditation. Apparently satisfied that the question had been disposed of on its own, he went on with his breakfast.

In the time it took to reach for my own slice of crisp toast and gingerly spoon a dollop of the strawberry jam onto it, I decided there was no turning back. I took a noisy bite to mask whatever telltale expression might have brushed across my face.

At that particular moment, I had no idea where Nolan Keefe should be. Another building, another city, another country. The farther the better: Alaska. I pictured him in an igloo, his short, pudgy body wrapped in bear fur, three days' growth of beard sprouting on his cheeks, his frostbitten fingers clutching the photo album he'd been poring over for the past weeks. It held a collection of snapshots of picnics with forgotten friends, indeterminate celebrations, happy curtain calls, distant nephews and nieces.

"What on earth do you see in those pictures, Nolan?" I had asked.

"It's amusing." He smiled. "I don't know what the hell is going on in half of them. It's as if the pictures had been taken of people who looked like us, but were not us. All rather interesting in its own way."

Two days later I had Nolan packed and ready to spend a trial week at the Villa Age d'Or. I had laid his open suitcase on the bed. When I went back in the room to check a half hour later, the case was empty except for the photo album. He sulked like a boy being sent to summer camp.

"They have a music room with a piano, Nolan. And a billiards table. You used to enjoy a game of pool now and then. They serve high tea in the parlor every afternoon. You can have tea with visitors or other guests. They have interesting people staying there, Nolan. Quality people from the arts and business and even the film world. I understand Beth Lavalle was a resident at the Villa. You used to be crazy about Beth Lavalle."

"She died in 1988."

"Whether she's still living there is not at all the point. The fact is that people of her stature, and ours, have lived at the Villa. This obtuseness of yours is making it very hard for us to communicate."

I stood in front of him and combed his hair away from his forehead, straightened his tie, and tugged at the lapels of his blue blazer, inexplicably two sizes too large. He took short, reluctant steps as I guided him by the arm, out the door, into the elevator, and past the building's main entrance to the waiting taxi. Preston nodded affably from behind his desk. "Good morning, Mr. Keefe, Señora Casals. Out for a drive on this fair day?"

"She's throwing me out of the house, Preston," Nolan said, even as I was gently pulling him by the arm. "Out like a dog."

The guard chuckled as if delighted to be let in on a joke by his famous residents. "You must've misbehaved, Mr. Keefe."

"Oh, yes, I made the mistake of being too sexy for La Señora." He punctuated the word *"señora"* with a grand gesture of his free arm. "Not willing to be as *dignified* as she would like. Now I'm paying for it."

I felt myself blushing angrily. "Say good-bye to Preston, Nolan. Tell him you'll be back in a week."

Once inside the car with the door shut and the windows rolled up, I scolded the old man. He had been childish and inconsiderate and rude. He recoiled as if he feared I might strike him. I turned away from him and forced myself to look out the window, and as the steep ocean cliffs dropped off suddenly from the edges of the narrow road, I made up my mind to accept that I would never again live with him. With my husband.

As we approached the winding road that led to the Villa, I rummaged in my purse for a tissue to blot my tears. I expected Nolan would put his hand on my shoulder, that he would indicate with such a gesture that he understood. And I knew that if he did I would not be able to go through with my decision. I would take a deep breath, and place my own hand on his, and ask the driver to return home. That was all it would have taken, a reach of maybe eight inches, no words or explanation necessary. I waited for the familiar touch of his fingers, warm through the sheer fabric of my blouse.

By the time we reached the front gate of the Villa, my tears had stopped, and heartache had given way to emptiness.

Claire calls one morning and begins to leave a message on the machine saying that she needs to have a talk with Lockwood, that she wants to pick up some last things so she can get out of his life forever. It won't take a second, she assures him. Orson answers finally, then passes the phone to Perla, who hands it to Lockwood.

"Who are all those people?" Claire asks when he finally picks up the phone.

"It's the team," he explains. "I'm on this deadline push to get the Mercè Casals book out before Alonzo Baylor and Hollywood Hank finish theirs. It's a race to the finish. The team keeps distractions to a minimum."

"I suppose this team is made up of editors or research assistants?" she asks.

"No. It's a nurse and a very specialized consultant."

"The nurse I already know about." Her sigh proclaims patience and forbearance. Having decided to divorce him, she can be magnanimous.

"You don't know anything, Claire," he says defensively. "Perla organizes my pages, checks my facts, takes my blood pressure."

"What does the other do?"

"Orson cooks. Soup, pasta, stew. I eat whenever I get hungry."

"He's a jerk on the phone."

"It's part of his job. Orson is in charge of security. He screens phone calls, blocks solicitors, petitioners, Mormons. The door to the study is kept locked. Nobody can get at me while I'm writing this book." Even as he speaks, the words tumbling frantically on top of each other, Lockwood can feel his voice climbing to a higher, more excited pitch.

"You're on drugs, Mark," she interrupts at the first moment's pause.

"I'm high on creative energy, Claire. I haven't been this productive in twenty years, working twelve hours a day. I'm living on Orson's stews and Diet Pepsi. That's the edge you're hearing, the Pepsi."

"I'm coming over, Mark."

"Sure, after eight," he says, proud of how reasonable he sounds. "Orson will let you in."

"No, right now. I want to see that you're all right."

"Not possible, dear. Against the rules. The book has to get written."

In the end, Claire repeats to Lockwood that he sounds very stupid on the phone, and that if she can't see him, she'll call the cops and report that he's been kidnapped and held in his own home.

"I've got to run, honey. Eight more pages to go today." Even as Claire is talking, Lockwood turns up the sound on the stereo so that the Señora booms from every speaker in the house. First her voice, then Lockwood's asking a question, finally hers droning on about the horrors of singing Norma opposite Leticia Guilmain's Adalgisa, and how difficult it was to perform that celebration of friendship with someone she couldn't stand.

"Are you listening to me, Mark?"

"I'm not here, honey. I'm in Barcelona, 1935, war everywhere. Good-bye, *adios, ciao . . .* "

"Who else are you talking to?"

"Ghosts, ghosts." He disconnects abruptly. The computer's blank screen pulsates with expectation. He imagines it saying, *Feed me, feed me.* He starts to type; anything will do to regain the flow.

Lockwood forgets that Claire is coming until, through the continuous murmur of the Señora's voice, he hears the front door close. A moment later, the lock to his study clicks open and his wife stands at the entrance.

"Claire," he says dumbly, looking up from his screen.

"You look surprised," she says.

"No, of course not, I knew you were coming," he stammers. "I hadn't thought about *when* you'd actually be here, but I knew you were coming."

"I told you I was on my way. When did you expect me?"

"Well, later, I guess. Not right now."

"Which is not a good moment, I gather." She looks around the room as if surveying the damage a hurricane has wrought on the previously es-tablished domestic order. Forgotten mugs with remnants of scummy tea or cloudy coffee sit on the desk and on the windowsill. A couple of dic-tionaries serve as paperweights to hold down the manuscript stacks on the floor.

"It's a fine moment. Nothing wrong with your timing, except that I'm working." He keeps glancing from Claire to the glowing screen.

"I can certainly see that." She makes an effort to speak calmly. Then, glancing in the direction of Mercè Casals' voice, "Don't you want to stop the tape while we talk?"

"Not really." He shrugs. "I've grown accustomed to her going on and on."

"Even when you're writing?"

"And all through the night as well. We lower the volume to a murmur. It's actually soothing once you get used to her, a kind of white noise. Usually it's interviews, but there is also her singing. After she died, I took her bootleg tapes. She collected every recording of herself that she could find. There are tapes of her rehearsing with Tullio Serafin and Bernstein and performing at the Prince's parties, once, actually leading a crowd in 'Happy Birthday,' and in roles she only did once, like Semiramide and Micaela. She hated *Carmen*, thought that Micaela was a doormat and vowed never to sing it again after that first and only time, even though she did it beautifully. Mostly she goes on like this, talking, talking, talking. Those tapes are her whole life, Claire. Sometimes, it's very stimulating to hear her. Every once in a while she'll hit some topic, and bingo, I've got a chapter."

Outside the room, the murmur of hurried, whispered conversation betrays the presence of Perla and Orson. "Tell your team to leave us alone, Mark," Claire says. "We're entitled to a conjugal visit." She waits until the door is firmly closed behind her. "Just for a few minutes, could you turn off that damn woman's voice?"

Lockwood walks reluctantly across the room and turns off the cassette player. The whir of his computer, the hum of the air conditioning, and the ticking of a Budweiser wall clock fill the vacuum.

"That's better," Claire says in the perky false tone he recognizes. "Thank you." She sits on the edge of the rumpled daybed. He turns his desk chair to face her. Even though they're close enough that their knees nearly touch, she looks so aggressively corporate it takes an effort to keep from rolling his chair back. Her hair hangs crisply along the sides of her face; precisely cut bangs lie across her forehead. She looks unnaturally pale, her lips wet with a slather of very red lipstick. He realizes he doesn't remember the last time he has seen her wearing such heavy makeup. Or a new dress, a flowing liquid silk in a pattern of gold rings, the size of wedding bands, he thinks, against a color like eggplant. It's the sort of thing she wears to client meetings. Her expression makes him think of life insurance, mutual funds, time-share vacation condos. He braces himself.

"Bert Foster has been trying to reach you for a week." She sighs deeply and shakes her head as if revealing some absolutely incomprehensible fact.

Lockwood stares back at her blankly. "Who's he?"

"You know Bert." She gazes at him in disbelief.

In the back of his mind, the answer to his question takes the form of a needle-nosed man with incisive eyes staring at him through thick lenses.

"Martha Foster's husband, the lawyer," she finally reveals.

"Of course." Lockwood nods, hitting his forehead with the heel of his hand.

"You refused to speak with him."

"I'm having my calls held. If he'd left a message I would have called him back eventually."

"He's left tons of messages."

"Tons?"

"At least six." She breathes out a sigh of exasperation.

Lockwood shrugs modestly. "A lot of people have been trying to get hold of me lately, Claire. It's a new thing for me. I'm not sure how to handle it. Remember how days would go by without my phone ringing? Not a measly assignment in days. I used to sit right here in this chair and stare at it as if by the sheer force of my will I could make it ring. In '92 Hollywood Hank went a whole year without turning up a single project. When I called him, I had to remind him who I was, that we had done a half-dozen *How to Talk to Your Teen* books together. Now I hear him in my sleep. I hadn't realized what an emotional range the guy has—he threatens, he pleads, he cajoles, he begs, he nags, he insults. He calls me babe, friend, buddy, asshole, jerk, sweetheart. He's called me so many different things I'm considering an identity crisis. He has sent all kinds of goons after me, at least three lawyers, one hit man, I think, two editors, a professional burglar, a famous writer, and now the loyal true wife."

"I'm here on my own, Mark. I discussed this whole situation with Bert, and he thinks I should share in this project as part of our divorce settlement. In fact, he thinks we could both make more money by stopping now and *not* writing the book."

"Claire, Claire, Claire." Lockwood shakes his head in mock despair.

"Don't 'Claire-Claire' me, okay?"

"Mercè Casals entrusted me with her *voice*. I'm meant to tell her story."

As he leans toward his wife, he sees the Señora's face emerge slowly from her features. A cotton-candy cloud of carrot hair crowns Claire's forehead; pendulous earlobes strain under the weight of the diva's favorite diamond-cluster earrings; the eyes blinking under the weight of thick mascara and liner make Claire look like a surprised owl.

"Why are you staring?" she says.

"Sorry," he mumbles and shuts his eyes tightly. Even with the Señora's tape switched off, she insists on being present, on taking over every bit of space around him, so that he can't hear anyone's voice but hers.

"You're not hearing me," Claire says.

"Sorry." He tries to concentrate on the real-life moment. Meanwhile, the Señora's voice comes from the farthest reaches of his imagination, accusing him of not listening to her, not paying the attention required of him as the custodian of her true story.

"You're actually in luck," she says. "You sell all the tapes to Hollywood Hank. We have a very profitable parting of ways."

He thinks for several seconds, about luck and such. "Do you remember the first time I saw you, Claire?"

She stares at him blankly.

"I bet you don't. Not the way I do. Because you had your head bent over a book, and I was sitting across from you at a café table, and you were trying to ignore me while I was laying my head down as if I were trying to rest it on my forearm to read the book sideways, but what I was really trying to do was position myself to look up into your face and see what color your eyes were, which was hard to do because you had bangs. Finally, I saw that your eyes were green and I told myself that, even if I never saw you again because you proved to be a visiting scholar from Peoria, I would remember your eyes for as long as I lived."

"Mark, what are you talking about?"

"Luck," he answers confidently. "You said I was lucky. I agreed."

"I meant it's lucky that you're sitting on maybe fifty thousand dollars."

"And I meant that your eyes are green, and I'm fortunate to gaze upon them even now, twenty-some years after the first time I saw them."

Twenty-four years, to be precise; it's one of those moments that calls for precision. Because once things are set on the path of their undoing, those that are being undone can hardly focus on one another, such is the rush of the events that lead to dissolution. From concreteness to vagueness. Rooms spin, walls close in, lights dim, objects dance, faces blur. A quiet, small death creeps over the body inch by inch, a pinch of flesh and a splinter of bone and a few cells (half a dozen out of a billion available) at a time. The hard stuff of reality recedes into the realm of shadows and echoes of former selves. The years mush together into primordial plasma. Lockwood leans back on his chair. In the simple backward motion, as smooth as a fall, as unexpected as a faint, the features of his wife, the finer details of mouth corners and nose ridges and eyebrows, reestablish themselves.

"How about tea?" he offers.

"I know where it is," she says. "I used to live here."

A few minutes later at the kitchen table he asks, "How many times have we had tea like this?"

"You don't have to make this harder than it is, Mark."

"It was only a question. Something to make conversation. An ice-breaker."

"Is there ice here? I wasn't aware of any ice."

"We have probably had tea, like this, ten thousand times," he ventures, his forehead wrinkling as if under the strain of serious calculations. "You could look at the bottom of the pot and analyze the sediment of those ten thousand brewings and see our life divided into chapters. The Earl Gray phase and the era of the cheap Indian gunpowder and the year of green tea and the days of English Breakfast. Remember those green-tea times? We got up at five A.M. for Zen during seven months. I had a beard and you had a Buddhist-nun haircut. We were so earnest. We went for the whole thing—the wok, the brown rice, macrobiotics, less yin more yang. Then, on our way to visit your parents in Sacramento, we broke down and had hot-fudge sundaes at a DQ in some little town off the freeway. We held them like trophies, big gooey things, with the fudge running down the sides onto our fingers, the whole peak of creaminess studded with peanut chunks and crowned by a perfect cherry. By the time we finished jamming all that wonderful sugar into our bloodstreams we were back to being normal Americans."

"It's weird the way you start talking like a writer."

"As opposed to talking like a plumber?"

"You know what I mean. Like you don't really care whether anyone is listening or thinking that you're making sense, as long as the words resonate in your own head." Claire sets her cup back on the table and stands up suddenly, brushing away invisible crumbs. "Thanks for tea," she says.

Her getting up to leave reminds him that she has been, in fact, gone for over a month. "You just got here."

"I think we're done talking."

"Actually, no." He stands and takes the soft fabric of her sleeve to guide her back into the chair. "I want to talk about our first trip to Venice."

"Why on earth?"

"It has to do with what I'm writing. Help me here, okay? There we were, newly in love, on our big bed at the Danieli."

"We didn't stay at the Danieli. We stayed at a *pensione* called L'Academia."

"We decided the whole of Venice smelled of musty tapestries and incense and the salt spray of the sea. Altogether it made for very stimulating air. Remember, Claire?"

"I don't know what you're talking about, Mark. The smell was of sewers and dead fish and fresh garbage and gasoline from the *vaporettos*. I couldn't wait to get the hell out of Venice. We were lost everywhere we went. We couldn't find the Bridge of Sighs or the church of San Giuliano or the Campo dei Frari. We'd walk for hours and then couldn't find our *pensione*."

"We couldn't stop making love, Claire. Remember?"

"We hardly touched each other in Venice, Mark."

"Oh, but of course we did. We were like teenagers."

"I don't know what you are talking about," she repeats. She tries to hide the trembling in her hands by straightening the place mat so that it's perfectly aligned with the corners of the table, rolling the napkin tightly inside its ring, and finally interlocking her fingers around the blue cup. Her eyes remain downcast even as he reaches out with the teapot and fills her cup again. She ignores the pitcher of milk he pushes in her direction. She's had enough tea; it's not a question of staying and drinking more tea. Or even of continuing the thread of this mystifying conversation. The familiar, precise details of these rituals are so deeply ingrained they anchor her to the chair. She can only sit and listen.

"We celebrated over a bottle of Château Margaux at Café Florian. The pigeons erupted from the burning Piazza de San Marco with a tumult of flapping wings and a rush of flickering shadows into the blue sky of an afternoon in May that will remain forever etched in our memories. How we loved each other then, Claire. Tears streamed down our cheeks. You reached out to wipe them away, but I held back your hand. 'Let them flow,' I said. 'They are cleansing our souls.' Through the blur, I could make out the great bell towers of San Marco and the bronze horses, their legs frozen in the perfect curve of their dancing hooves, their heads tossing as if impatient to charge ahead. Even the waiter at the café, a starched old man who had been there forever and who exuded little more than contempt for the tourists at his tables, was moved by our sudden purging of emotions. Two kids, a brother and sister not quite ten, pointed at us with the rude confidence of children and then, when we smiled through our tears, ran squealing to their parents' side. We walked back to the Danieli feeling lighter than our clothes, blood as thin as air, bones of smoke, our bodies as free from gravity as ghosts. We felt we could walk through walls, float up stairs. But of course we didn't. We allowed doors to be opened for us, we were swept along ancient hallways. Once in our room, we soaked in hot water until our skin was pink, our toes and fingers wrinkled to rubber. And then when we saw that we hadn't become entirely disembodied, that there was still some sensation, we fell laughing on that nearly endless bed with its shimmering sheets and the fringed canopy sheltering and enclosing and crowning us. We pushed aside the things we had bought, the masks and hats, the parcels wrapped in crepe and the boxes tied with gold string, things thumping and clattering and falling all around us, and then, embracing, we rolled from one side of the bed to the other, not knowing whether to laugh or cry we were that happy. We stayed in the room for three days and got fat on *salmone fumiccato* and chocolate and champagne. We were like teenagers. We couldn't stop fucking."

"That's not the way I remember it, Mark. You've been listening to that diva of yours too long," Claire says. "You're starting to sound like her."

He laughs. "It's very shrewd of you to sense that."

"You need help."

"Yes, we could all work together—Perla and Orson *and* you—all of us working on the book. Because hers is an amazing story, Claire. "

"I meant *help* help."

"Nonsense. This woman, Mercè Casals, was not just the greatest soprano that ever sang, but a huge personality, a diva. You have no idea what a privilege it is to tell her story."

"I guess not," she says with a shake of her head. "I'll have to wait for the book." Claire nudges her chair back.

"Oh, you don't want to leave on that note." Lockwood holds her back by simply touching her arm; her shoulders slump in temporary surrender.

"Why not, Lockwood?"

"You think I'm nuts, don't you? This is a delicate time, Claire. Rumors of my going obsessive might reach Hollywood Hank and Alonzo Baylor. They would use this information to screw up my auction with Warner and Morrow and Random House and any other houses that might be interested in publishing *The Wonder Singer: My Story.*"

"Tell me you are not as crazy as you sound," she pleads.

"As the CEO of Diva, Inc., I'd say I'm as sane as any great entrepreneur can be. Think of Steven Jobs or Ray Krok or T. Boone Pickens.

Men of vision. This is more than just about writing a book, Claire. It's about a vision: Diva, Inc. will reissue the Señora's old recordings. We will manage the fan club and the website and the videos. We will license mugs (Say Laaaaaaaa!) and Mercè dolls (Barbie of Barcelona), t-shirts (Divas do it higher), and 1-800-now-sing. There will be the *Fat Lady's Cookbook* and Lyrical Lingerie and Diva's Divine Delights, a line of mail-order gourmet goodies. In the movie—*The Wonder Singer*—we will make millions and Mercè Casals will be bigger than Elvis. Only one thing is missing. Two things, actually," he adds reluctantly.

He waits for Claire to ask what they are. But she has decided not to pretend that she finds his fantasies plausible. With a sigh, he withdraws his hand from her arm, and she's able to push back the chair and stand up.

YOU TWO HAVE A THING GOING?

Self-imposed deadlines loom. The race tightens, and Lockwood is working sixteen hours a day. Quantity is important. He needs at the very minimum eight hundred pages to stay competitive with Hollywood Hank and Alonzo Baylor. This book will be heavy enough to prop open doors, sprain wrists, sell for $29. He listens to tapes and types what he hears. Frequently, there is a gap in the sequence, allusions that he doesn't quite understand. Conversations spin on without any recollection of his having had them. If it were not for his voice breaking in now and then with a question or a murmur of assent, he would swear he hadn't been there when a particular topic had been discussed or an important revelation made.

He is under house arrest, cut off from his wife and friends and former business associates. He's a forced-labor drudge slogging away in the twilight darkness of the curtained study with only a small oval of light illuminating his hands at the keyboard. No radio. No TV. The only music he's allowed is opera, as much as he wants as long as Mercè Casals is in the cast. The three Ts give him chills—*Traviata, Turandot, Tosca*.

He hears Mercè with his throat, as if her voice, disembodied and amplified, were coming from him. He opens his mouth as wide as it will go to allow the rising, unstoppable notes, the cries of pain and exultation to emerge unfettered from the cave of his larynx with its palpitating walls of cartilage and muscle, his vocal cords enveloped in folds of mucous membrane, resonating like some hermaphroditic organ that can utter the ecstatic high D of a tragic heroine flirting with insanity.

To focus his memory he tries to recall the arrangement of Mercè's living room, the waning light of evening, the position of the tea service on the marble-topped table, Perla's presence, watching and listening from a discreet position behind him. Knowing she was there, her mysterious but imperfectly concealed body breathing and stirring inside her nurse's crisp white pants and tunic, her imagined pedicured red toes wriggling nervously inside clunky white shoes, distracted him from his task to the point that now, weeks later, he doesn't remember anything. He shakes his head, trying to focus again on the drifting sense of La Señora's musings. He tries the door and finds it locked. Perla and Orson La Prima and Nolan Keefe are lounging on the big leather couch in his living room watching his TV and drinking his wine. It's for his own good, Perla said when he agreed to spend a full twelve hours a day in his study without distractions. He lives for her regular visits to take his blood pressure, the pressing of her fingertips against his wrist, the inflating snugness around his biceps.

Orson toughens up security and keeps a lookout through Lockwood's living room window. He screens visitors and takes messages for Lockwood to deal with when he comes out for air. At the drop of a hat, he lip-synchs the Señora's signature arias. Perla decides what and when Lockwood eats. She keeps the meals light and high-energy to maintain wakefulness and concentration on the task at hand—baked acorn squash stuffed with herbed basmati rice, spinach sandwiches, pasta with a *sughetto* of eggplant and garlic. No meat, no cheese, no eggs. He will live like a monk and eat like a dancer. This is big business now. The queen and the nurse are out to protect their cut of the deal—an even twenty percent each for the Señora's two number-one fans.

Over the course of several days, signs of malaise appear like green mold on white bread. Lockwood is seized with a desire to sleep. Leaning back on the chair that cost him a thousand dollars because it was guaranteed to be ergonomically miraculous, the perfect support for back, buttock, and upper thigh that only a professional writer would fully appreciate, now seems to suck him into lethargy instead of propelling him into the authorial attack mode that has produced a million published words.

If he remains at his desk instead of moving to the couch, he will settle for less comfort and his nap will be short. No harm will be done by shutting his eyes briefly, no one will jump into the study and shake him by his shirt collar. He doesn't fear Perla's aloofness or Orson's sarcasm. In any case, the brain will be awake even if the lids are at rest. At the first glimmer of an idea, as soon as the next word in the sentence takes shape, his eyes will snap open and his fingers resume pushing one word after another.

His legs slip off the desk and crash to the floor; he awakens hungry. According to all the clocks that surround him, from the one mounted on the wall next to the study door to the numbers in the right-hand corner of his computer screen to his father's pocket watch hanging from a hook on the wall, it's only ten in the morning. It's not breakfast or elevenses or lunch or tea or dinner or bedtime-snack time. This is the dry rot of the idle mind asking to be fed. He wants jumbo-sized Doritos, milky lakes of Technicolor Lippy Loops cereal, shovelfuls of bite-sized peanutty Butter Nutters. He craves sugar and salt in equal quantities, caffeine and carbonation, citric acid and reconstituted cocoa powder. Manna for the torpid soul.

He charges into the kitchen and edges his way past Perla and Orson, who, deep into domesticity, are making the week's shopping lists. Even as they debate adding rice cakes and more fresh fruit to the diet, Lockwood rummages for comfort victuals.

Perla has accused him of gaining weight from his compulsive snacking in the middle of work and has purposefully reduced temptation. She offers him prunes. He stares at her in disbelief. Sometimes, he explains, in the middle of writing a certain word, the rhythm of a phrase or the whiff of a forgotten flavor—garlic, basil, cumin—will set off a firing of dormant brain cells.

"There's nothing to eat around here," he complains.

"You want to add something to the grocery list?" Orson holds his pencil above the notepad.

"Sure, I've got lots of requests. But is there nothing to eat in this whole house *right now?*" He glares at Perla.

She gazes back calmly. "Try crunchy julienned carrots. We also have sugar-free, salt-free, whole-grain shredded wheat. Plus yogurt, raisins, sunflower seeds, two apples, and one nicely ripened banana."

Lockwood holds the soft banana, its peel mostly blackened. "This thing is beyond ripe, it's mummified."

"It's going into the banana bread, thank you very much," Orson says, snatching it away.

Lockwood makes a halfhearted attempt to recapture the banana.

"I'm the chef here," Orson snaps. "If I say it goes into the banana bread, that's where you'll find it. The day after tomorrow, to be exact."

"You may be the chef, but I'm the chief. I pay for the groceries. I pay the bills. And I'm trying to write us up a six-figure advance."

"I wish you two would stop squabbling," Perla pleads. "If writing this book is going to be a team effort, we'd better start acting like a team."

"Fine. But I'm still hungry."

"We'll get you treats, Lockwood," she promises. "Meanwhile, make yourself a peanut-butter sandwich. With salty, crunchy, sugary Jif."

"We've even got Wonder Bread," Orson adds generously. "For the wonder boy."

"Fine. I want to mash the banana into it."

"That's disgusting," says Perla.

"Worked for Elvis," says Lockwood.

"That's the role model we're looking for!"

"Give him the banana, Orson," Perla says with an air of resignation.

"Whatever you say, honey." He tosses the limp banana to Lockwood.

"Honey," says Lockwood glumly.

"Honey what?" asks Perla.

"He called you 'honey.'" His eyes shift from one to the other.

"It's a Southern thing." Orson shrugs. "A term of endearment meant to mask irritability at the slow pace of events."

Lockwood nods skeptically. "It's more than that. You two have a thing going."

Orson goes to Perla and puts his arm around her shoulders. "Sweet, isn't it? Our writer is jealous."

Lockwood waits for her to move away from Orson's reach. She doesn't. "Damn right," he says.

"You're being stupid," she says, slowly shrugging off Orson's embrace.

"You keep dangling yourself in front of me as a future reward," Lockwood says. "I'm supposed to put all my energy into work while you two play."

"It's okay," Orson says. "I'm just an old opera queen."

"No, you're a sneak." Lockwood gathers the Jif, Wonder Bread, and Chiquita in his arms and retreats to his study. He mushes peanut butter and banana on one slice of bread, then presses down with the other until the filling starts to squeeze out the sides. The imprint of his fingers is visible on the top slice. He eats and sulks and waits for the creative juices to resume their flow.

Orson is the first to notice that a week after his arrival, Nolan Keefe appears thinner, smaller, shorter. "I keep piling on his breakfast, lunch, dinner, snacks," he observes. "He stirs the food on his plate until it gets cold and all mooshed together, and then he says he's lost his appetite. No wonder."

"Ask him what he would like," suggests Perla.

"I have. He says ice cream."

"So let him eat as much as he wants." Lockwood raises his hands at the obvious solution.

"We have five flavors of Ben & Jerry's in the freezer," Orson says, "and dishes of melted ice cream in the bathroom, the basement, the downstairs hall closet, everywhere."

"What was he doing in the closet?" Lockwood asks.

"Besides melting his Cherry Garcia?" Orson raises his shoulders in an exasperated shrug. "Getting away from us is my guess."

The truth, as Lockwood figures out eventually, is that Nolan Keefe is trying to escape the droning recordings of Mercè Casals. His expression, a sudden wan softening of his mouth, a welling of tears in his eyes, provides the clue that the Señora's voice is making him unhappy. He answers some questions with non sequiturs and evasions.

"Did you and Mercè ever think about having kids?"

"Ha! Imagine Mercè as a mother!"

"I take it you never discussed it?"

"Wouldn't want to bring a child into the '50s."

"How did you learn that Mercè Casals wanted to come back to you after her years with the Prince?"

"It's complicated, don't you know."

"Complicated how?"

"It makes me tired just thinking about it. That's how complicated."

"How about tea, Nolan? Want Perla to brew you a pot?"

"Fine woman, that Perla!"

"She likes you, too, Nolan. But I have the feeling you're toying with me again."

"I don't care about all this crap you're asking."

"Maybe we can all go for a drive later. Spark some thoughts."

"Maybe you'll get Mercè's darkest secret?"

"I'm always listening, Nolan." But the old man has clammed up again.

Nolan shakes his head and rolls his eyes in mock bafflement whenever he spots Orson La Prima *en costume*. Tonight Orson stands in the middle of the living room, Violetta waiting for her Alfredo, looking as terminally tubercular and poetically distraught as makeup and vintage costumes—from the 1962 Dallas Opera production—will allow. Violetta gazes skyward, eyes fluttering and rolling into her head in a barely controlled swoon. She twists her mouth around the stubborn Italian syllables and breaks into a sweat as Orson mimics the struggle for breath control on the way to the final triumphant *Gioia!* With the actual voices of the young Mercè Casals and Nolan Keefe ringing out from every corner of the house, Lockwood hopes that the performance with its innocence, its endearing clumsiness and unabashed adoration of its subject, will amuse Nolan. Instead, it makes him cranky; the ghosts in the room are unwelcome visitors.

He turns toward Lockwood, shaking his head at the sound of his own voice. "I can still hit high C without getting red in the face."

Lockwood holds his breath: Nolan is finally talking. "I don't know, Nolan. It sounds like you're reaching a little in that recording."

"I had the flu that night."

"You remember the performance?" Lockwood asks incredulously.

"April 18, 1969. Covent Garden."

"How can you be so certain?"

"I'm hearing myself sing with my throat in a vise. I never went on if I had a cold. I always considered it more professional to cancel than apologize for squawking."

"Why did you go on sick that day?"

"I wanted to see Mercè. She had moved out days before to be with Prince What's-His-Name."

"What did you say to her?" Lockwood asks.

"Not much. If you can sing a duet from *Traviata* there's nothing else to say."

"You just sang? You didn't talk?"

"I apologized to her, actually."

"You apologized because she was leaving you?"

"No. I told her I was sorry that I was not in good voice."

"You're making me crazy, Nolan."

"Thank you." He is always polite. He leans back in the sofa and crosses his legs, primly allowing one high-top sneaker to dangle over the other. His eyes, though tired, gaze at Lockwood with a glint of malice. "Welcome to the club, Writer. I've suspected for years that everyone was out to drive *me* crazy."

"Some would claim that the effort was successful," Lockwood mumbles.

Nolan looks at him sideways.

Lockwood raises his hand apologetically. "A small joke I couldn't resist."

"The joke could be totally on you." The threat colors Nolan's absent tone. "If your main source turns to be a nutcase, you'll be chasing Mercè down more blind alleys than Barcelona's Gothic quarter."

"Can we start over again?" Lockwood pleads. "We can talk about whatever you want."

"There are confidences I must not betray."

"Please have no concerns on that account. In my brief friendship with the Señora, I developed great respect and affection for her. This will be a very positive book."

"Unlike Alonzo Baylor's."

"Well, yes, if the truth be told."

"If the truth be known," Nolan said softly. "Be it known that it ain't all pretty."

Life Without Nolan

I could finally breathe. For years Nolan had taken up most of the available oxygen. Now, with him gone, the entire apartment was filled with clean, fresh air. Every ugly thing that Nolan might have known about me was safely shut away. The luxury of total privacy was almost too much to bear. I could prance around nude from one room to the other, play my music as loudly as I wanted, talk on the phone without having to watch him straining to overhear and guess at the other side of the conversation.

He was nosy that way. Never could refrain from checking my mail, trying to guess its contents even before I opened it. If I'd gone out for lunch with a friend he would quiz me on the details of our chat. He loved gossip for its own sake, even if he didn't know the principals in a story. Actually, he followed the marital travails of some of my acquaintances so closely that even if he hadn't met them, he built whole personalities around their names: Carl was a lecherous smoothie with a penchant for prepubescent boys; Harriet was his long-suffering wife who had become shrill and brittle from so many years of deception; Barney was an oaf who had grown bleary-eyed and sponge-brained from too much beer; Felicia was his patient wife who had no recourse but to find solace in the arms of a tennis instructor. It's interesting that, whatever the details, Nolan's sympathy was always with the woman. It was one of the qualities that made him such an irresistible seducer. He could sniff out a wounded heart or a blistered ego or a body aching from lack of touch with the relentless accuracy of a bloodhound. Here was a man, women intuited, who knew the pain a female goes through. He too had been abandoned for a greater prize, his devotion spurned, his pain made public by a betrayer's notoriety.

It worked with me as well. Nolan was the purer spirit. Whenever I complained about his escapades, he would reach out to me with such tenderness that I would forget that the comforter and the instigator of my suffering were one and the same. I envied his capacity for nursing the hurts of love. When I came back to him after five years with the Prince, I saw how old Nolan had become, his face lined from the constant confrontation with my betrayal: I cruised the Mediterranean, I skied the Alps, I stumbled out of nightclubs at dawn. It was all fodder for the paparazzi, the gossip columnists, the TV psychologists. There was no place where Nolan could hide from my adventures.

I was at a loss as to how to help him heal. If I just acted as if things were now back to normal, we might simply go on as before. But it was easier to make believe that the previous five years hadn't happened than to confront the damage I'd done. Everything seemed to be as I had left it: the photos on the mantel, the pending correspondence in my secretaire, the half-read books on my bedside table.

I questioned Nolan about whether he had found other women to be with. He'd been well-accompanied, he admitted, not without vanity. But he claimed he hadn't brought any of them home with him. This was my space, he told me, and my presence had been everywhere, even after I had packed up and gone.

. . .

I remember returning to the apartment after leaving Nolan at the Villa. I opened the door of the flat, and the silence was so profound. Nolan was gone. We'd never had cats or children, so any noise we heard was reassurance that the other was home. His clothes in the closet and drawers were like the lifeless remnants of a visitor who had overstayed his welcome. It took me only about an hour to sweep through our rooms and dump everything of his into old suitcases. I was a force of nature intent on erasing any evidence of poor Nolan Keefe's presence. I gathered ties and suits and sweaters and squeezed them into the overflowing baggage. I took his books, all those histories and biographies and thrillers, and packed them for storage. I stuffed old letters into envelopes, threw out his collection of *National Geographic*s, sent his exercise cycle to the Salvation Army.

I'll admit there were things of his that I was attached to. You don't live with a man for fifty years without also falling a little in love with some of the objects that were an indispensable part of his personality: his calfskin gloves, a white silk scarf, a cracked belt grown too small for his burgeoning tummy but kept in a drawer nevertheless, close to the orphan cufflink and the tie clip no longer fashionable. There was a tortoiseshell letter opener, the handle worn smooth from countless afternoons of opening correspondence.

Nolan took great pleasure in his mail, even when it didn't contain checks or fan letters, even when there was nothing personal or important for him. If it was addressed to him, whether an *Opera News* subscription reminder or an invitation to apply for the latest American Express Diamond-Studded-Platinum plastic, he enjoyed the ritual of slipping the point of the letter opener under the flap and, with a flick of his wrist, neatly slitting the envelope open. I can't look at his desk without seeing him there, toying with the letter opener, gauging the sharpness of its shell blade with his thumb.

After about an hour, I was drenched and out of breath; my clothes were rumpled, my hair in chaos. I must have looked like a half-crazed harridan, the kind that spanks babies, bites dogs, throws out husbands with the trash. But the truth is that I felt rather triumphant. I celebrated by eating plums, ripe purple ones that I twisted apart into halves to reveal the golden flesh tinted with pink close to the pit, and half a bottle of Veuve Clicquot. I thought that rather appropriate because I felt as liberated as any widow, much like Madame Clicquot must have felt when she'd eradicated any memory of her poor husband to become the doyenne of the province of Champagne. Whatever the shabbiness of her motives, she would live and die and be remembered as simply Veuve, the widow, a plucky Frenchwoman who prospered.

Long live the widows, I say. Even if by nomenclature they are incomplete beings.

I feel a bond with women who are set free in their later years, free to run their lives without the drag of tired, sickly, depressed men. Old men are so pathetic if the truth be acknowledged. Their heads still fevered with their little lusts and fantasies, but reduced in the end to asking for a little stroking, a little squeezing, a little milking.

⊶━╂ I DON'T THINK YOU WOULD BE MUCH FUN IN BED.

All week Lockwood has been four pages short of finishing *The Wonder Singer*. No matter how long he makes himself sit at his desk, after eight or ten hours he remains four pages from the end. He writes three pages and then realizes he still has four to go. Completes two more; still four pages left. When he lights up the screen the following morning, the reachable goal begins perpetually to recede; four pages to go. He is Sisyphus rolling words uphill. He is a greyhound chasing a mechanical rabbit.

If he once aspired to writing a big, wonderful book, his goal is now reduced to a few hundred pages from his printer in a stack five inches thick, weighing something over four pounds and stuffed into an 8"x11"x5" cardboard box. His money and his resolve are running out; the one interested publisher is sending dark signals that there will be no second-place finisher in his race with Alonzo Baylor. There will be one book on La Casals, and at this point, it does not appear that it will be Lockwood's; he is not the one with the track record, the marketable name, the knack for turning out biographies that read like tabloid exposés.

Lockwood blames his lack of progress on deteriorating conditions at 579 Hyacinth, once the headquarters for Diva, Inc., where everyone came together to be with La Señora. He had planned for there to be quiet conversations and earnest discussions about the moments in her life. They would all keep him pumped up so that he could write the impossible book in record time. He had estimated three months. The world would be put on hold while he cranked the pages out as fast as he could, letting the facts dangle and fall where they might. Niceties would be sacrificed for the rush of immediacy and personal vision. He would sail and churn and whirl his way through the Señora's life story. There would be no coming up for air. He would grab at the pieces of her life, follow the trail of a chance word. He would speak with her voice.

The book's raw energy would emanate from the page like the smell of fresh ink and travel along the reader's lacy network of veins and capillaries to rush to the brain and dance along the synaptic gaps, tickle the neurons and make breath short and pulse fast.

"Leaves you breathless!" Kakutani would say in the *Times*. "A high-concept bio-epic in the tradition of Norman Mailer."

Lockwood had once trusted the collective energy of the Señora's three admirers. Now he feels weighed down by his contentious "team." He emerges from his study one morning after half the night at the keyboard; he draws curtains open and raises blinds. Under the morning light, a staleness seems to have been rubbed into the drapes, carpeting, and furniture. The things he sees fill him with unease: a scattering of cigarette butts in three ashtrays, dirty dishes on the table. Orson La Prima's pink silk pumps lie before the couch like dead birds. Dirty dishes have piled up, and a pot holding the remnants of the latest stew congeals on the cold stove. The bathroom sink is full of hairs, fine chestnut ones from Perla's once adored head, tracings from Orson's razor, strange ones from God knows whom. The unflushed toilet gleams Mountain Dew yellow. And everywhere he is followed by the murmur of heavy breathing, snores, the occasional moan. He falls on the couch with a sigh.

Down the hall a door opens with a creak; Lockwood waits for Perla to emerge from her room. Even just out of bed, her hair bent and matted by the pillow's work, she causes in him a rush of tenderness. She wears one of the Señora's velvet dressing gowns, the belt snug around her waist. Wandering barefoot like a child in her mother's clothes, she seems small and vulnerable within the lush folds.

"You look very nice in royal purple," Lockwood declares.

"You caught me." Perla shrugs. "We were not supposed to take anything of hers, but she wouldn't mind." She holds the robe close to her body and bends her head to rub her cheek against the collar. "Many of the world's ills can be withstood if one has something really soft to wear."

"It's something the Señora would say."

"Well, she didn't say it." Perla sits on the couch. "I did." She pushes the full ashtray on the coffee table away from her and puts her bare feet up. "Put it in the book, if you like."

After staring for a long moment, Lockwood looks away from her small golden feet with the bright red toenails. "The place is a mess," he says softly as he sits at the opposite end of the couch. "Who's been smoking, anyway? I thought you'd quit."

"Orson La Prima had a relapse."

"You should've tried to talk to him."

"I did. I counseled him not to continue to smoke. I said the damn things would kill him. He said he was going through an emotional crisis. I said he should tell me his troubles."

"You slept with him." He finally realizes.

"I'm a nurse. I take care of people."

"You never really wanted to sleep with me, did you?"

"I don't think you would be much fun in bed. You miss your wife."

Lockwood shakes his head. He doesn't know what he needs, short of finishing the book.

"Are we going to stare at each other all day?"

"I'm not staring at you. I'm staring at your feet."

"I can't wait to know what you're thinking."

"I'm a spontaneous kind of guy, Perla. Different thoughts cross my mind at different times. Right now, I want to suck your toes."

"You're just bored," she says. "In any case, having my toes sucked is not a priority for me. I was about to get coffee." She starts to rise from the couch, but he pulls her hand.

"I could go down on your feet while it brews." He slides closer to her on the couch.

"I'm half asleep, Lockwood."

"How awake do you have to be to have your toes sucked?"

She bursts out laughing. "Now I get it, Lockwood. This is not really a seduction, or even a conversation. You're writing something."

He nods reluctantly. "I have reason to believe that the Prince had a thing for the Señora's feet. I wanted a woman's perspective."

"And I thought it was all about me," says Perla. "In any case, the real attraction would be in having one's toes sucked by a prince. Not at seven in the morning by some writer who hasn't even brushed his teeth."

"Thanks."

"Call your wife, Lockwood. Tell *her* you want to suck her toes."

"She'd tell me to go away." Then he adds, as if the realization had suddenly occurred to him out of a vacuum, "*You're* telling me to go away. Is everyone telling me to fuck off?"

"You're not going anywhere, Lockwood," she says. "I am."

"You're bailing on me?" he asks in disbelief.

"It's what needs to happen now, Mark. You'll be all right."

A moment later he emerges from the kitchen with two mugs of coffee. He's undaunted by the fact that when he returns to the living room Perla is sitting in the same place on the sofa, but with her hair combed, her face washed, and her feet in a pair of his socks.

By noon the house is silent. Perla and Orson packed quickly and left in her truck. Lockwood had expected more than a firm handshake, but things had been rapidly cooling among them. They promised to call to keep tabs on his progress. Meanwhile Perla had to get back to her terminals at Scripps. Orson had tickets to the Met season.

Perla and Orson have taken their romance with them. Lockwood and Nolan Keefe inhabit the empty rooms like lost ghosts. The sounds of hissing oil and clattering pots have faded from the now idle kitchen. The Señora's recordings have been turned to a barely audible murmur seeping out of the shuttered study:

"You seem surprised to see me this morning, Scribbler."

"Not at all, Señora. It's a day like any other day. I would be surprised if you had stood me up."

"Would you be surprised if I had died?"

"Unhappily, yes."

"Why? I'm ancient. I could have a stroke and die in my sleep, you know? There would be nothing surprising about that."

"You are so full of energy. I would not expect you to lie down and die."

"Some mornings I'm surprised to see myself. I stand in front of the mirror before resurrecting my face with makeup, and I'm shocked that this fat, wrinkled beast still breathes."

"You do much more than breathe, Señora. You think, you feel, you joke, you scold. All well-known vital signs."

"Perla would not be shocked to find me dead one morning when she shows up with my coffee. She's a nurse, after all. She knows about the unpredictability of the body."

"She would be as surprised as I would be."

"I don't intend to die suddenly. In fact, no matter what ultimately happens to me, I've been dying for months. I have visions that are like dreams, only I'm awake and my eyes are wide open. I see things. I see Pep Saval and he absolutely shines with kindness. A switch for him. But his face is beautiful and he extends a hand to me. Of course I don't take it. I'm not ready to put up with Pep Saval again. I see faces I don't recognize. I see a road that goes on and on beyond the horizon, and a well so deep I can't see bottom, and a bright silver sky. I've told Perla about these things. She says she has heard of others, patients of hers, seeing similar things as they approach the end."

"Too many meds. There's nothing mystical about brain chemistry."

"You don't know anything. Ask her."

"It's not the sort of topic I'm apt to discuss with Perla."

"You Americans are too squeamish when facing the subject of death. You won't even say 'dying.' It's passing, leaving, going away, joining the Lord."

"I don't think there's much that Perla is squeamish about."

"Yes. She's quite the angel, isn't she?"

"There must be different kinds of angels."

"She's of the darker sort."

Even after Lockwood stops the tape, the house is not entirely silent. From one end there is the on-and-off percussion of his fingers on the keyboard; from the other, Nolan Keefe rummages around the kitchen; he boils water for tea, warms muffins in the microwave, makes anxious phone calls for pizza. Sometimes, when they cross paths to piss in the middle of the night, they seem equally surprised by the encounter.

Lockwood wants to ask, *Are you still here?*

Not actually speaking, they exchange nods, monosyllabic greetings, shake their heads as if there were no point in asking questions that will eventually answer themselves.

One morning, Lockwood thinks he sees Perla padding down the hall but realizes it's only Nolan, wearing the purple robe. He wants to run to the old man and pull it off him. He's about to tell Nolan that if he wants to look like an apparition he would do well to look like himself and not disturb the still restless memories of Mercè at the end of her days, possibly looking just as she did heading for that final bath.

Lockwood himself appears absent these days, wandering about his own house with the look of someone who has lost his way but won't admit it. Nolan looks at Lockwood with an expression of familiarity. The two of them are sinking together into a murky state of half consciousness, not fully awake even after coffee, not fully conscious even while chewing a slice of cold pizza. Nolan seems to recognize that, as the manic with the most experience, it's up to him to pull the younger man out of his state.

"You need a bath," he mutters one morning as he nearly bumps into Lockwood coming from the bathroom. "You didn't take a shower in there, did you? I mean, you don't look like you did."

"Are you still here?" Lockwood squints in the early-morning gloom.

"Ha, that's a good one." Nolan forces out a laugh.

"A good what?" Lockwood looks puzzled.

"Joke. It has to have been a joke. I mean, you brought me here. The only way I wouldn't be here is if you had taken me someplace else."

"Why are you being antagonistic all of a sudden?"

"I've been antagonistic since the day we met."

"You know something, Nolan? I'm under the impression that you're actually itching to have a conversation with me."

"Really, Lockwood?"

"You don't have to take that supercilious tone. We're getting along, aren't we? You were enjoying your stay here. Orson's cooking, Perla's charms. Our theatrical hijinks. We had our fun, right?"

"Living with a snoop is not my idea of fun."

"You're afraid that if you start talking, you'll spill all kinds of beans about you and Mercè."

"There are no beans to spill."

"I'm betting there's stuff just crowding your brain, eager to be vented, to provide relief from the pressure you must be feeling ever since she died."

"Manure."

"Talk to me Nolan. It'll do us both good."

"Why should I talk to you when I didn't talk to Alonzo Baylor?"

"Because I'm someone you can trust. Mercè Casals trusted me. And you can trust me, too."

"You're recording this, aren't you?"

"It helps me remember."

"Turn it off."

"Will you talk to me if I do?"

"There are things about Mercè and myself that I won't discuss."

"Understood."

"So what are we going to talk about? Once you turn off your recorder, of course."

"You tell me. Whatever you have to say will be valuable, will help me finish a book that Mercè would have been proud of."

"What makes you think I care what kind of book Mercè would have liked? She's dead, her opinion doesn't count in this matter. You want to do a book that will make you some money. I want you to do a book that won't embarrass me."

"I want to do a book we can all love, Nolan."

"That would take a minor miracle."

"I've thought so all along, ever since I started this thing."

"I gather you and she were doing quite well as a literary team." Nolan gives a strained smile. "I suppose her dying has made things more difficult."

"Harder in one way, easier in others."

"Why easier?"

"Well, I can make stuff up, for one thing. To cover anything she didn't want to talk about."

"You would do that? I thought you were writing her memoir, not a novel."

"I wouldn't put anything in that I didn't think was highly likely."

"Be careful. There will be those of us who will speak up to set the record straight."

"You'll call a press conference to deny that you used to beat Mercè with a riding crop?"

"That's a ridiculous claim."

"Just making a point."

"I'm being blackmailed."

"Let's just chat and see where the conversation goes."

"What about?"

"I told you. Whatever comes to your mind. Anything about you and Mercè together is good material."

"I thought you were almost done."

"I can always add touches."

"Like what?"

"Favorite Restaurants. Memorable Performances. Stolen Moments. Secret Places. It's the sort of thing people want to know about. The ordinary details that colored your life together."

"Sounds trivial."

"So tell me something that isn't."

"Even after talking to Mercè for months, there is stuff about us you will never understand, Lockwood. Unless I choose to enlighten you."

"So talk."

"Fine. Turn off that thing."

"Okay. No problem."

"Is it off?"

"See the red light on top? It goes off when I switch it off."

"You're not recording?"

"Nope."

"Did Mercè ever say anything about me as a man? Not as a singer, but in the way I was with her?"

"In bed."

"Yes."

"Only that she was very much in love with you."

"Back in Spain, during the war, in New York when we married. She tell you about those times?"

"Yes."

"How about in later years?"

"Well, I gather you had your troubles. You ran around, she ran off, she came back."

"And then she ran *me* off."

"She thought you would be comfortable at the Villa."

"She hated the sight of me, Writer. She couldn't stand to be with me one more day."

"She never said anything like that to me."

"That's because she was not aware of it. For over fifty years she couldn't stand me to touch her. And I didn't want to touch her. She had flesh like a sponge. We had to make love in the dark, our bodies covered in lotion. Once we had enough grease on us, we could slip in and out of each other like snails. Have you ever watched snails mate? The little fat things go at it with a kind of cosmic passion. They are so alike in their blubbery shapelessness, slipping and sliding. You can't tell where one ends and the other begins."

"Okay. I get the picture."

"Lots of lubrication: Take my word for it—it's the way for old couples to perform."

"Marriages get tired, Nolan. Fifty years is forever."

"You are not listening, Lockwood. This is about truth. Not about being reasonable and explaining everything away with platitudes."

Lockwood nods as if coming to a belated agreement. "Well, I need to get back to work."

"It's not the writing that keeps you going, is it?" Nolan says. "It's more like love, like obsession, like clinging."

"And you know a thing or two about being clingy."

Nolan adds cheerfully, "Take a shower, friend. Shave. Put on clothes."

"I'm trying to write a book, old man."

"Well, nobody cares much about that. Your agent is gone; your friends are gone; your wife is gone."

"Even my subject is gone."

"Okay." Nolan raises his hand in truce. "Let's not dwell on the negative."

"So what's positive?"

"You need a break. Get cleaned up. This girl I know, Marisa, gives a very sensual haircut. I was banned for being too excitable, but maybe she'll take me back if we go in there together. Get shampooed, manicured, generally prettied up."

"I don't have time for that."

"Yes, you do. She'll touch you. She has great hands. She will lay a steaming herbal towel over your face, and your pores will open up like tiny flowers, and then she'll rub a soothing balm on you. When was the last time you were touched?" Nolan stands very close to Lockwood, blocking his path in the narrow corridor that leads from the bathroom to his studio.

"Why are you so concerned, now?"

"Can't stand to see someone in worse shape than me." He laughs. "Too depressing."

Lockwood has been leaning against the wall, trying to put a safe distance between himself and Nolan. He feels his legs grow weak and buckle under him as his back slides down along the wall and his butt finally rests on the floor. He hasn't realized until that moment how very tired he is. He buries his face in his hands as if to contain the groan that emerges from his throat.

"Now, now," Nolan says, sitting down next to him.

"I feel really stupid," Lockwood says.

"Take a shower, shave, change clothes."

"What gives you all this energy so suddenly?"

"I like you, Writer. You remind me of me," Nolan says. "Two of us running around in a funk is way more than the universe can take."

Two guys out on the town, Lockwood and Nolan emerge from Marisa's alchemy with their hair poofed up and a glow on their cheeks. They share a bottle of expensive cabernet in Del Mar at a bar with a terrace jutting out over the ocean. A gentle glow from the wine and the magic of Marisa's fingers and the warm radiance of the afternoon sun spreads from the center of Lockwood's stomach up to his chest and down to his groin. He doesn't stop his chase but keeps asking Nolan about the years during the war in Spain when he was in the United States and Mercè Casals was still in Barcelona.

"You already know about that."

"There's a certain time I'd like to get to." Lockwood tries to sound brisk and business-like even though, after wine, he feels his tongue numbing. "When you were still in love."

"Why?"

"I'm trying to understand something here, Nolan. I think there is something about you and the Señora that sheds light on the nature of love."

"Don't look at my life for answers," Nolan finally says, shaking his head impatiently. "Look at your own."

"I don't have a love life."

"You have a wife, don't you?"

"That would be stretching the truth." Lockwood finishes off the last of his wine and pours another glass. "Claire and I seem to have lost touch."

"We're getting somewhere." Nolan winks.

"We're getting drunk," Lockwood says.

"This is to the good. All-American guys can't talk about personal things unless they're drunk. And you, my young friend, have an urgent, nearly vital need to talk about your personal life."

"I didn't know that."

"Scary, ain't it?" Nolan Keefe smiles.

"Ask me anything."

"Okay, let me get the right words." Nolan takes a breath as if preparing to take aim.

"Anything at all," Lockwood challenges.

"Why did your wife leave you?"

"Anything but that."

"Want another drink?"

"Yes." Lockwood takes a gulp of wine as if to give himself courage. "I think she left me because I am no longer interesting."

"She left you for another man?"

"I liked being married more than she did. She left me for another life."

"What kind of life? A glamorous life?"

Lockwood shrugs. "There's nothing glamorous about buildings and vacant lots."

"Beats spending time with a self-absorbed egotist."

"Is chasing the Señora's life about my ego?" Lockwood asks. "It's not my life I'm writing about."

"Is your wife enjoying herself these days?"

"How would I know?"

"Do you writers get a lot of sex?"

"I've been with three women other than my wife. I wasn't very good at screwing around." Lockwood signals a skinny waiter with lime-green hair for another bottle of wine. "I need to be married to a woman in order to have enjoyable sex with her."

Lockwood waits for the waiter to end his struggle with the cork, pour a taste, then fill the glasses, his hand shaking. "Somehow sixty-dollar wine doesn't taste right when it's served by a kid with Kool-Aid hair," Lockwood says as he sips thoughtfully. He makes a mental note to start *How to Talk to Your Teenager About Wine* as soon as he's done with the Casals project.

Nolan insists, "My guess is that real estate can be glamorous."

"You're a pain in the ass when you're trying to be helpful."

"I bet you'd like to know who she's sleeping with." Nolan leans over toward Lockwood and gives him a small punch on the shoulder. "Tell the truth, now."

"It doesn't matter. We're finished."

"These things are never finished, Mark. People leave each other, get divorced, become widowed. The thing is never finished. There's a lifetime of resentment and regrets that linger. Like scar tissue."

"I'm not about to ask her who she's sleeping with," Lockwood insists.

"You don't find out by asking. You stalk. It's an art."

Lockwood and Nolan Keefe drive to the blue glass office tower where Claire works. The building is part of a complex of five identical structures arranged in a pentagon with space for parking in the middle. An artistic arrangement of towering palms and thick shrubbery and a trickling fountain makes the lot look like a piece of transplanted rain forest. After driving in circles around the five identical buildings Lockwood finally spots Claire's new black Mazda.

"Great. Pull in right next to her."

"She's going to know I'm nearby," Lockwood says nervously. "There are not many old yellow Saabs in the world. Not even in Sweden."

"We *want* her to know you're close," Nolan explains. "You're hovering, not spying."

Nolan coaxes Lockwood into the lobby of one of the buildings. They sit on matching kidney-shaped sofas with a clear view of the two cars. After about an hour, close to eight o'clock, Claire appears among a crowd of late workers exiting the elevator. She seems to be alone. Nolan and Lockwood slouch into the couch and hold copies of the *Wall Street Journal* in front of their faces. She walks briskly out of the building and doesn't slow down until she notices the Saab. She's halfway to the parking area. She looks around suspiciously, then, without giving Lockwood's car another glance, gets in her car and speeds out of the parking area, gravel flying in her wake.

"Ah, we made an impression," Nolan says.

"She hardly gave my car a second look."

"She knows you're on to her."

"What's there to be on to? This is where she works, that's all," Lockwood argues.

"She doesn't know what you know," Nolan tries to explain. "She will think you've been following her for days."

"I really don't know what the point of all this is."

"To show her you care, dummy. She needs to know that you haven't given up on her. It will make it harder for her to leave you."

"I *have* given up on her. She *has* left me."

"That's exactly the kind of stupid passivity that will make you bitter and resentful in your old age. You will hate her for leaving you, when in fact all that anger and recrimination is actually turned against yourself."

"What next?"

"Make your presence felt here and there. Crawl into her mind and stay there. Mystery hang-ups on her answering machine. Glimpses of your ugly yellow car on her street. Accidental meetings in her new hang-outs—you'll loiter in the bookstore, the coffee place, the grocery store."

"Can't do that. I'm on deadline."

"Like writing a book is more important than saving your life. What a dunce."

"Aren't you overdramatizing?"

"Love is war, dummy. When Mercè left with Prince Smarming, I basically curled up and let her go. She never forgave me for seeing her leave without so much as a whimper of protest. I never forgave myself. Not even after she came back. Once a hole is dug out of your life, it can't be filled again."

The Passing Moment

Wednesday. Promptly at four in the afternoon, Nolan would be ready for my tea visit. He'd be waiting in the secluded alcove, adjusting the position of the pot with his long, graceful fingers, handle to the right, perpendicular to the edge of the low table between the two purple chairs. A cozy kept hot a brew of gold-tipped Darjeeling. The two settings of cups and saucers and small starched napkins and silver spoons faced each other. To one side, a plate of sugar cookies awaited my sweet tooth. He'd glance at his watch and note that I was already ten minutes late. I might have encountered heavy traffic on the I-5. I had been on time for our four o'clock date ever since he'd moved into the Villa Age d'Or. It was only in the past several weeks—after I'd begun work on my memoirs, he was quick to notice—that I had grown less punctual.

The truth is I couldn't visit him without remembering the day I'd taken him there. Or rather, the evening of the first day. The night and the sea blended into an absence of light and movement. Thunderclouds gathered like invading armies only to be worn down before they reached the glowing towns and villages that dotted the coast. In the quiet of the room where I nursed the last of the champagne, I could make out the faint murmur of the surf breaking on the rocky shore, of the tide coming in, of the more distant rumbling of faraway storms.

Twice I had reached for the phone, only to change my mind before the connection was completed. After an hour it had grown too dark in the room to read the numbers. Calling Nolan was necessarily postponed.

For now I felt too spent to get up and turn lights on. This was unlike me. I liked plenty of light around me, all the lamps in the apartment glowing, every light a small sun competing with every other light, bathing the mauves and pinks and rich crimsons of my cherished rugs and furniture with contrasting values: the softness of warmth behind a shade, the crystal-hard drops of frozen light from the chandelier, the smoky topaz yellow from the sconces causing the wall fabrics to shimmer like beaded silks.

On this first day of our separation, a few hours really, there was not much that I could say to Nolan or that I wanted to hear from him. Still, we were in the habit of talking every night. When the phone rang, I knew it was him.

"I am not going to like it here," he finally said, after I had said hello three times into a dead silence.

"Nolan," I tried to sound positive, "it's temporary. Try it out for a couple of weeks."

"You want me to live here, don't you?"

"I want you to be where you will be cared for . . ."

"Room service here is limited to 911 calls," he broke in.

". . . where you will meet interesting people. Where you will be comfortable."

"They do have a nice parlor with velvet chairs and love seats that are much nicer than what we have in our place—it's all a front, you see. One could meet interesting people here, *if* there were any around."

"You've only been there seven hours."

"How long do you have to be in Death Valley to know you're in a desert?"

"Stop it. You're making me feel guilty."

"That's okay. I can suffer in silence, too."

"Good, because I'm about to hang up."

"When are you coming to see me?"

"Whenever you'd like."

"Come for tea. They serve tea in the parlor. Come Wednesday at four, Mercè." He added, "Check first to see if I'm still here."

"I'll see you next Wednesday, Nolan."

"You can call me before that, can't you?" he asked, the anger in his voice softened. "This thing will be easier if we can talk."

"That's a change. Now you want to talk?"

"You're saying we can't?"

"Of course we can talk, Nolan."

"When?"

The abruptness of his question threw me off for a moment. "Anytime. We are talking right now, aren't we?"

"It would help if I could picture you. What are you doing this very moment, Mercè? Where are you?"

"I'm in the red chair, my feet on the ottoman."

"Is anyone sitting in my spot?"

I dutifully squinted and thought that even if someone were sitting on Nolan's favorite place on the purple sofa, I wouldn't be able to make him out in the dark. "No one, silly. How can you ask such a thing?"

"You have your feet up, on the ottoman?"

"Yes, Nolan. I'm sitting like I always sit. Except that the lights are all off. I'm sitting in the dark. Just a little light from the moon is shining through the window. The clouds have broken to reveal a big fat full moon, and there is only enough light from it to make out the faint outlines of the furniture nearest me."

"If you're sitting in the dark, how can you tell you're alone?"

"I just know."

"But if I told you that you were not alone, that there was someone in the chair opposite you, you wouldn't be able to see through the dark to tell whether it was true or not."

"I'd hear him."

"He's not saying anything. He's not moving, Mercè."

"He wouldn't stop breathing, would he?"

"He's hardly breathing, Mercè."

"I told you," I insisted. "There is no one here."

"How can you be so certain?"

"Nolan, you're scaring me."

"Would you know if someone was in the room with you?"

"Yes, I'd be able to smell him."

"A ghost, Mercè. Would you be able to smell a ghost? I could be there in the blink of an eye if I were dead."

"I wouldn't take notice, Nolan. I don't believe in ghosts."

"You'd believe in them if you were able to smell them, wouldn't you?"

I said good-bye, promised to call the next day or at the latest Tuesday before my visit for tea, but for now I said he sounded cranky and tired, and what we both needed was a good night's rest. He started to protest, but my finger was resting lightly on the Off button, and before the next word was out of his lips, I pressed it firmly.

I silenced the ringer because I did not want to talk to him again. Did not in fact want to worry about him calling me back, or not calling me as the case might have been. Then I turned on all the lights in the parlor because sitting in the dark made me feel too alone. I also left on a night light in the bathroom and a small lamp in the entrance foyer. After I closed the door to the bedroom, light seeped in, under, and around the edges of the door frame.

I instinctively hugged the right side of the king-sized bed, leaving empty the larger space where Nolan liked to fall spread-eagled. Time, I expected, would help erase what was left of Nolan's presence after all his things had been packed and taken away. There would be other ways to ease him out: I could repaint walls, change linens, reupholster, move furniture. Meanwhile, even without a sound, without the murmur of his breath, of his occasional snoring, his frequent mumbling in sleep, the last tendrils of Nolan's presence clung to my consciousness. I was kept awake by smells. Nolan's physical presence was everywhere, the intangible vapors of aftershave and hair oil and toothpaste, even shoe polish, which lingered at the bottom of his closet hours after all of his shoes had been packed away.

More persistently, from the opposite side of the bed, there was the memory of his skin, often glistening if the night was warm or the covers too close around him. I could recognize the smell anywhere, reminiscent of brandy and lavender. Sometimes, when ugly dreams assailed Nolan's slumber, his body would be drenched in perspiration and his breathing would grow short and scared. Then I would reach across the bed and place my palm on his chest, directly over his heart. Sometimes he would wake up, confused at first as to where he was, then relieved that whatever was haunting his sleep had been so easily thwarted.

"Sing to me, Mercè," he would murmur.

And I would hum. A thin, improvised line that coiled unstructured from my throat and then, not finding release through my open mouth, resonated in my head, in the bones of my face. We would lie on our backs, bodies touching, and the purity of my hum would connect us at some level more intimate than touch. The melody emerged with such innocence that I would not know where it would lead. I would take a deep breath and follow a sinuous, teasing line until I was out of breath, and then I would breathe again and go on. If I wandered into *"Casta diva"* or *"Un bel di,"* for instance, or a bit out of *Lakmé*, I would juggle the notes and drift from the familiar thread. Sometimes, when I started to fall asleep and the song vanished, Nolan would give me a firm nudge with his elbow, and I would awaken to continue the song that made his sleep peaceful.

On this first night of Nolan's banishment, as he later put it, I gazed open-eyed and alert into the darkness, the whole of my body awake, knotted with tension. Ordinarily, I would be afraid to disturb him. Now I could wander around like Amina from *La Sonnambula*, watch TV, eat spoonfuls of plain whipped cream, turn on lights, open curtains. The freedom was bewildering; I was not yet at ease with it. It was the first night in my life—after living with Father, with Pep Saval, with Nolan Keefe, then briefly with Prince Liviu, and back to Nolan—that I belonged to no one but myself. A few minutes past two I thought that perhaps a hot bath would ease me into drowsiness.

Water rushed into the sunken tub. I stood before the mirror that covered the whole of the wall behind the sink and vanity counter. From the clusters of pinpoint bulbs set into the ceiling, a fine rain of light cascaded over and all around me. I saw my reflection softened by the gentle glow so that even after I dropped the shoulder straps of my nightgown, and its lacy neckline slid down my arms, past my collarbone and chest, below my breasts, I was in my own eyes a soft, rose-hued figure, rounded along the shoulders, belly, hips, in lush abundance. I was free to be large, and soft, and even a little fuzzy in my thinking; the surrounding dimness reflected the shadows in my mind, memories of cities without streets, faces without names, voices without words.

I palmed the underside of a breast so that the lights from the ceiling shone on the nubby aureole. I marveled at how insubstantial the breast felt, its firmness seeming to have migrated to flab under my arms, to a sort of pouch under my belly, to the flesh that swelled my thighs. In the soft light I could not see the lines that I knew creased my breasts, neck, collarbone.

Water awakened dormant feelings. Behind me the green marble tub filled to nearly overflowing, Jacuzzi nozzles glinted below the surface. I drew the bath so hot that stepping into it was painful and, I dared to suppose, dangerous. It was a kind of self-inflicted torture that allowed me to feel I had overcome pain and turned the steaming bath into a balm. My skin reddened, the line of what was tolerable, not yet quite pleasurable, rose along my calves and knees and thighs until, finally supporting myself on the edge of the tub, I slowly lowered myself and let the water lap my body with heat so intense it acted like cold and raised goose bumps even as sweat beaded on my face. After all these years since the war days in Barcelona, the times of rationing and scavenging, a hot bath is a reassuring luxury.

At last, unable to hold out any longer, I sank into the water and breathed in the rising steam, allowed the Jacuzzi jets to strum my flesh and bubble up all around me. From the speakers installed in the four corners of the bathroom I listened to *Un Ballo in Maschera*, with Nolan as Riccardo at the Vienna Opera back in '73.

That season the young and talented and insufferable Ada Bastille was Amelia, and she sounded so girlish and light you could hardly envision the sumo wrestler she eventually became. Then again, Mercè Casals was not one to talk; in later years my weight had ballooned again. Still, it was not the same thing to waddle onstage like a water buffalo as to soak in your own soup, in the privacy of your home, in the secret hours before dawn.

I tried to ignore the jealousy that uncoiled as I heard Nolan and silly Ada carry on. The very night of that performance I had searched for him in the theater; it was to be a surprise visit to reassure him that he would be wonderful in a part that he had never sung. When I didn't find him in his dressing room, I walked out the stage door and turned into the alley behind the theater, and there, partially concealed by shadows and a fire escape and some discarded crates of rubbish, were Nolan and Ada.

Now, all these years later, I couldn't help seeing them again in my mind's eye, stealing a few moments out of rehearsal, like a pair of vagrants rutting on their feet against a wall in the alley outside the theater. He was standing on a brick to gain leverage and make up for his shorter stature. Ada had hastily stepped out of one leg of her panties, which were trapped under her other foot. She was holding her skirt up with both hands. Her head was pressed to his chest, face turned to the side. But it was the younger woman's eyes, wide open as if in fright or surprise, and her lips, which had grown puffy and moist, that I remembered.

I was lulled into a doze by the hot bath and the relentless massaging of the Jacuzzi jets. It was only after the water had begun to cool that I felt restless. I turned off the whirlpool and the electric hum ceased. The voices of Ada and Nolan rang with greater clarity. I opened the drain and allowed the water gradually to undrape my body.

A chill in the air caused me to sit forward. My limbs rested heavy and still, as if their vitality had been drained as well. I didn't have the strength to climb out of the tub. I managed to push myself up to a kneeling position before the dolphin spigot and turned the water back on. I adjusted the faucet handles until there was no difference in temperature between my skin and the water that gushed from the bronze fish, its eyes blank and unfocused, snout pointing skyward, mouth in a grin. There was such power in the dolphin's leap from the green stillness behind it. I turned the water on full strength, splashing first against the bottom and sides of the empty tub, then, cupping the dolphin's head with my palm wrapped around the fish's mouth, I directed the stream against the tops of my breasts, the hard spray bringing a blush again, stinging my nipples, then in a burst of inspiration, I directed the water in a thin, hard stream at the awakening center between my thighs. I turned it hotter, then suddenly cold.

Perhaps two minutes passed. I reeled with images of Nolan Keefe and Ada Bastille, of the smell of the alley behind the theater, of the moist feel of his grunting, Ada's delicate even teeth on his lips. The younger woman bit Nolan so I would see and understand and not want to kiss him. Not while his lip was swollen and caked with dried blood, and his gaze humbled and avoiding mine.

My desire grew; I wanted to be someone besides who I was. If only for a few moments, I would have been the younger woman in the alley. Would have wanted to taste the blood from Nolan's mouth, oblivious to the smells of summer garbage and the hard brick wall digging into her back, the rub of a zipper and the gouge of fingers. The effect was sudden. The moment passed.

Lockwood finishes *The Wonder Singer,* types the final period, hits the return key three times, and centers the words "The End" on the page. He then clicks Print, and paper starts cascading out from the printer to his desk and onto the floor. He gathers the warm sheets, eight hundred pages of typescript, inside a cardboard box and runs to his car. Once on the freeway he drives impatiently, darting around slower traffic, breaking out of the pack with a heavy foot on the accelerator, switching lanes with a snap of the wrist. He plays a tape of La Casals' 1949 Covent Garden *Rigoletto*, her famous *"Caro nome"* soaring all about him.

He presses his palm on the manuscript, and a glow travels up his arm to the center of his chest. He wants to prolong the moment; this warm sense of accomplishment will be replaced by a new anxiety as soon as he slides the box across the FedEx counter. He exits to the coastal highway; through the open windows gusts from the sea carry the faint spice of salt and rotting sea weed. A beachside café called the Queen of Hearts makes him think of Mercè Casals when she was dressed all in red and wearing one of her regal hats.

He stands at the bar and orders champagne, which comes in a pint plastic bottle with foil capping a screwtop. He wants to remember these moments forever.

"I just finished a book," he announces to the waitress behind the counter. "*Writing* one," he adds when her expression shows little interest.

"Good for you," she says with a firm nod. She goes back to wiping circles into the worn linoleum counter.

"There's nothing quite like the feeling of getting to *The End*," he adds. "You feel deliciously empty and light inside, as if you had taken a long psychic piss, and all the ghosts and tensions of the past months had been siphoned from your system in a rush." The words sound rehearsed, as if he had stopped to write down a proper pronouncement to the end of his opus.

The woman looks at him kindly. "I can identify. I always feel good when my shift is over."

It's his first attempt at a celebration, and while the champagne is cold and sparkly, he feels a lack. He wants people around him who will slap his back and light his cigar and give him high fives. He wants his wife to forgive him. He has always rushed to tell Claire whenever he's finished one of his projects. It's a time of such relief and quiet triumph that he realizes there's no one else he wants to share the news with. He takes his glass of champagne to a table and opens his cell phone.

"Can you turn down the music?" he calls out to the waitress.

"Depends," she smirks. "Who you gonna call?"

"My wife!" His own enthusiasm surprises him.

The waitress shrugs. "I have that effect on guys."

Lockwood punches in Claire's new number. "It's me," Lockwood ventures.

"Just the man I've been wanting to talk to."

"Don't hang up on me, okay?"

"Don't worry. Your actually saying something is an improvement on the usual heavy breathing."

Now that he has her attention, he wants to confess that he is in pain, that he loves her and doesn't want to be apart from her any longer. He also knows that he should apologize. For the egotism that has turned the fine emotion of love into a creaking, painful exercise of will.

"If this is to be a conversation, Mark, you have to talk when your turn comes. Otherwise I'm hanging up."

He grips the phone tightly to keep it from shaking against his lips. "Claire, no matter what has happened to us, you've got to know I love you," he blurts, as if rushing to stanch a wound. He senses the waitress hovering near him. He turns his head and sees her leaning on the bar, smiling maternally. He turns again and lowers his head and holds the phone against his collarbone.

There's silence so empty he's sure she has disconnected. Finally, coolly changing the subject, she asks, "How's the book coming?"

"It's finished!" he almost shouts. "An hour ago."

"Happy day," she says.

"I'm not calling to talk about the book. It's time to turn the page on the book. I want us to get together. That's what I want to talk about."

"Not while you're out there being obsessive."

"I'm obsessive about loving you. Is that bad? I didn't want to let you go without trying to win you back."

"Stalking me is courtship?"

"I didn't just follow you around. I also sent you flowers, Claire. Amaryllis and lilacs and roses. They're your favorites."

"You sent them by taxi, at two in the morning, without a card."

"You knew they were from me."

"You've been acting crazy."

"That's how a man in love acts."

"I could call the cops, you know. I have lots of reasons."

"I would go to jail for you, Claire." He has gradually raised his voice until he remembers the waitress listening behind him. "Just talk to me," he rasps.

"We're talking. What else do you want?"

"Come home. You'll see how fast I get back to normal."

"I'm not going back to that circus." She doesn't want to see a transvestite, a morbid nurse, and an aging tenor eating from her dishes, standing barefoot in her bath, sleeping on every available bed and couch.

"Everyone has left Dodge, Claire. The last one to go, Nolan Keefe, is in a taxi right now, heading back to his asylum."

"I'll think about it."

"We'll think together," he insists. "We'll have an end-of-book ceremony, like we used to. I have the manuscript with me, all eight hundred pages of wonderful stuff. I want Mercè Casals to see it."

"You're going to show the book to your dead diva?"

"Symbolically."

He begs Claire to meet him at Seaview Memorial Park, where Mercè Casals' remains have been placed in a marble crypt.

"You can't miss it," he says. "Turn up the drive to the Avenue of the Angels and you'll hit something that looks like it's right out of *Aida* on a double bill with *Giulio Cesare*."

"Why the cemetery?" Claire asks. "What's wrong with Starbucks?"

"It's something we have to do, Claire. Talk. I see it as a formality, letting go of the dead, embracing life. I've got a camera."

"You're going to take pictures?"

"To mark the moment. You'll understand once you get there."

"I doubt it."

"Just consider it. I'll meet you in an hour. Six o'clock, at the entrance. Seaview Memorial Park in Del Paseo."

He wants to believe there is some ambiguity in her silence.

Lockwood reaches the cemetery a few minutes before six. He stops the yellow Saab in the middle of the deserted parking area, where it sits on the black asphalt, lonely and fragile like an egg yolk. He rolls down the window, leans back, and waits for Claire. On the passenger seat is an old Polaroid camera and the box containing the manuscript. The package is securely bound with strapping tape and addressed with bold marker strokes to Marvella Bloms of Causa-Perduta Author Representation, the lone New York agent who showed interest.

After a few minutes he punches Claire's number. There is no answer after a dozen rings. He wants to believe that she's not sitting by while her phone rings, but on her way, maybe delayed in traffic, perhaps late because of a lingering indecision.

With the waning afternoon light, the realization that she will not show becomes inescapable. The hours since he emerged from his study, tired and rumpled from his final hours with the book, have brought with them a sharper perspective. Over their sixteen years of marriage, Lockwood and Claire developed a rich language. Sitting across from her at breakfast, he had been free to pronounce judgment on the day's evils. In their conjugal shorthand, a gesture, a look, a phrase, or a groan was enough to deal with war and famine and financial collapse. The well-timed shrug, the eloquent snicker, the dramatic sigh were the rhetoric of domesticity, as much as the way she held a cup of coffee to warm her hands (a blue mug she favored over a dozen others in the cupboard) or the way she spread butter on hot toast, from the center out, taking the glistening pat under her knife to the very edges.

He hits redial. Still no answer. He gets out of the car and finds himself walking with a quick step. Awakening that morning to an empty house, greeting a computer screen finally blank, feeling the solid weight (six pounds, four ounces!) of the manuscript box under his arm, and the present, eloquent message of his wife's absence, all seem to free him for new, unexplored vistas. He feels the light sensation of nakedness. He will explore.

At the entrance of the cemetery Lockwood peers through an iron grille of lilies and vines and angel wings at the shady road that leads into a landscape of small mesas and rounded hillocks. The gate swings noiselessly on its hinge. The scent from the row of stately eucalyptus is lively; a golden light seeps uncertainly through their leaves. There is, however, no view of the sea at Seaview Memorial Park, only a gray band of condensation rising to meet the blue horizon. Considering its captive audience, this betrayal of language strikes him as cowardly; the Señora will miss her view.

He wanders off the road that leads to the section reserved for celebrities and soon finds himself disoriented, pacing aimlessly up and down paths through the miniature city of bones and memories. He feels like an accidental Gulliver, directionless, noisy and awkward among the toy-like Notre Dames, cakey Taj Mahals, truncated Versailles, their turrets and cupolas and spires reaching no higher than his eyes.

Putting the dead to rest is a complex undertaking. Throughout the graveyard, the sensitive visitor will perceive on carved granite and wrought iron frequent assurances of love, rare signs of forgiveness, or the nagging worms of guilt. The dead are more present in the awareness of those left behind than when they were alive: the final revelations of the cheat and the scoundrel, the inheritances of lies, resentments, and punishments, the last word in an argument, the lingering word of regret, the final word of the condemned, the gasp and sigh and rattle of those that in life were a nuisance and in death are a reminder of the path that all must tread. Stone walls, iron gates, brass plates sustain the presence of Gandalf Martinau, of Brenda Harvey, of Felix and Serena Castillo, a Beloved Brother here and a Cherished Wife there, a Darling Baby and a Tender Rascal. Good wishes to all that dwelled here: *Rise to Heaven, Remembered with Love, Eternal Life Among the Angels.*

Lockwood nearly stumbles over Mercè Casals' grave. Her memorial is set apart from its neighbors in a small clearing where two paths intersect. One moment he'd been following a winding trail through the silent city; the next, as if he had somehow intuited her presence, he is facing her name on the bronze plaque at the front of a tiered monument. Before him rise three steps leading to a vaguely Hellenic temple lined with Doric columns, appointed with angels, crowned with an unlikely Egyptian Horus bird god. He can sense Mercè's hand through the jumbled mythology, proof that among the mute and the closed now dwells La Señora. She who had once been heard around the world is now ground into ashes, rough and gray as gravel, locked in a steel box, sealed in a niche at the center of her temple. Lockwood sits on his heels to be eye-level with the plaque, *Mercè Casals, 1921–1999.* The strip of grass that fronts the granite structure shows signs of foot traffic, scuffed patches of muddy ground, a trampled flower border, a cigarette butt, a foil gum wrapper, a single rose floating in a wineglass.

There are many signs of visitors: letters inside sealed envelopes addressed respectfully to Señora Mercè Casals or to the Greatest Diva or to the Purest Voice. The yellowed leaves from an old Metropolitan Opera program for *Turandot* rest under a rock. A lipstick tube, China Red, her color. A sprinkling of glitter. A lock of hair inside a glass box. Careful not to disturb anything, Lockwood runs his fingers lightly on the steps leading to the actual tomb.

The third step, which also serves as the base of the memorial, has been turned into a message board. Brief, cryptic notes have been posted by those who've traveled from distant places—Boston, Bombay, Bilbao. Some are attempts to reconnect with long-lost friends:

"To Stella, who once lived in Minneapolis: Call G."

"Tuesday, 4:30. To certain missing members of the Verdi Viragos from Dallas: Where are you? Signed, Your Tour Guide."

"To whomever: I want to touch and be touched while listening to La Casals singing *'Vissi d'arte.'*" There's a number with a 612 area code. "Leave message if I'm not in. This is not a joke. This is a serious request. I'm attractive. But desperate. Either a man or a woman will be considered." It is signed, "True Fan."

Under it someone has written, "Dear True Fan, Will a vampire do?" Signed, "Neither Man Nor Woman."

Lockwood takes in the flurry of offerings, the chatter of unheard voices. He feels he's in a more privileged category. Nobody has seen into her depths as he has. He has touched her in the faint shadows of her memory, has perceived the silence behind her voice. He can't wait to put it all to rest. He pulls out the Polaroid camera and composes a picture of the manuscript package resting vertically against the column, under the bronze *Mercè Casals* plaque.

He would like to include himself in the picture. He stands and looks around the neighboring gravesites for some fellow mourner, perhaps a groundskeeper. There's nobody. He places beside the manuscript the red rose in the wineglass. Overall, a pleasing shot. He clicks, pulls out the developing picture, waves it to dry the chemicals. Even as the image rises to the surface, he accepts the hole in the air beside his manuscript, the space occupied by the ghostwriter.

The photo makes an adequate offering. He takes a pen from his shirt pocket, pauses a moment, and finally scribbles on the front of the picture. He wedges it firmly into a crack between the base of a column and the top granite step. The words read, *I was saved by her voice. Her voice became my voice—Lockwood.* It gives him great satisfaction to know this.

By early afternoon, Lockwood is looking forward to a silent house, a blank computer screen, an empty mind. He will open the last good bottle of cabernet, defrost some leftovers, and wallow in the elegant geometry of a baseball game. It's been nearly a year since he's had the luxury to splurge three hours in front of the TV. The hard ache at the center of his chest caused by Claire's rejection will soften in favor of the quiet celebration of work completed, its fortunes left to the fates and the FedEx guy. With the Señora's voice no longer murmuring, arguing, singing throughout the house, he already feels her presence grows fainter, finding silent refuge in the shadowy rooms of memory. He climbs the stairs to his study but stops abruptly; light glows through the crack around the door, possibly left on that morning in his haste to rush out with the manuscript. He pushes the door open and sees Nolan hunched over his desk, his face only inches from the glowing page on the screen.

"You're still here? I left you dressed and packed up. You had cab fare in your pocket."

The old man turns with a start. "How *are* you, Mark? Book get off all right?"

"The book is on its way. How come you're not?"

"The taxi never showed. I got tired of waiting."

"You could've called to remind them."

"There is a reason why I had to stick around."

Lockwood reaches in front of Nolan and turns off the computer. "You've taken up spying?"

"A better reason. You will owe me big time."

He gently pulls Nolan up from his desk chair and points him to the couch across the room. "Are you about to share this reason with me?"

"Not yet."

"Meanwhile, here we are." He sits next to Nolan on the couch.

"It's fated."

"There's no fate about it. Why are you in my study? Nobody is allowed in the temple of the high priest."

"There was nothing on TV. I happened to walk by. The door was open. The computer was on."

"You were reading the book."

"It was right there on the screen, the story of my wife, and my life. I couldn't stop scrolling."

"You were snooping."

"What have *you* been doing for the past year?"

"That story is over, Nolan. I'm putting you in a cab."

"Can't we talk first?"

"I feel all talked out."

"There's stuff still left. About Mercè and me. Stuff in your book that I can set the record straight on. Stuff that only I know, because I was there."

"I'm ready to let Mercè Casals rest."

"It's not only about Mercè. I'm talking about you and me. I thought we were hitting it off. You need a buddy, an older brother, to give you good advice, to help you with the things that count."

"What things would those be?"

"Your marriage, for one."

"You advised me to stalk my wife. And you see where that has taken me."

"Where has it taken you?"

"She's so pissed she didn't meet me at the cemetery for a little celebration."

"I know."

"You know?"

"Yes she called. She was going to leave you a message. But she got me instead of the machine."

"You talked to Claire? Better still, she talked to you?"

"I told her I was your best friend," Nolan says. "I could have told her I was your only friend, but I didn't want to embarrass you."

"You talked . . ."

"For over an hour." The old man nods. "About things like life and marriage and love. I'm an expert on all those, you know? And about you."

"What about me?"

"I told her you're not as deranged as you appear. I'm a very persuasive guy with women, as you know."

"And she believed you?"

"I don't know." He does a deep, cartoonish shrug. "I turned on the charm. She has a lovely laugh. I bet it's been years since you've heard her laugh."

"What gives you the right to meddle?"

"I'm your friend. I'd like to see you happy," he says. "You wouldn't have been happy with Perla. You wouldn't be happy by yourself. But you would be happy with Claire. And with me."

"With you."

"Yeah, like a *menage*." Nolan pauses as if to muster the courage to continue. "Besides, you wouldn't want to be the second person to banish me to that hellhole of a mausoleum."

"I am *not* any happier with you here."

"Maybe not now, but we've got work to do."

"I finished the book, Nolan."

"I mean the housework. Scrub bathrooms. Vacuum carpets. Mop kitchen."

"Since when are you any kind of help to anybody?"

"Since I invited your wife to dinner."

"Claire is coming to dinner?"

"She might. She didn't promise."

"You're a lunatic."

"Can I stay if she shows?" Nolan gets up from the sofa and marches to the kitchen, with Lockwood trailing behind. "We've got a couple of hours to cook something edible, Scribbler. It's the least you can do for the love of your life."

Lockwood stands in the middle of the kitchen, suddenly frozen in a state of confusion, facing the sink full of dirty dishes, the grimy floor, an ancient soup pot on the stove. All unite to overwhelm him.

"Don't just stand there, man. You don't want your wife walking out as soon as she gets here."

Yes, Lockwood decides. Claire will not be seduced by apologies or promises. Instead he will honor her with the power of his pure heart. He will rub out grime, vanquish errant hairs, dissolve soap scum, all in her name. A calm blue pond at the center of pristine porcelain will be a refuge of freshness. Shiny chrome, gleaming glasses, fragrant linens, squeaky dishes. These will be his humble offerings. The proof of his renewal.

An hour later, Lockwood begins to gather the papers, cassettes, and notes that are strewn about the study floor. He opens his satchel and gently places everything in it. The case swells with the detritus from the past months' wrestling with the story of the Señora's life. He picks off the yellow notes stuck all around the computer screen, gathers up envelopes fat with newspaper clippings, photos, and letters. Soon the room begins to revert to a calm emptiness, its chaos reduced to the elemental components of desk, chair, couch, bookshelves. Finally he buckles the burgeoning satchel. It feels heavier than he remembers. And suddenly he is relieved that he no longer needs to carry it wherever he goes. He pushes the bag into the depths of the closet. Then he turns to the center of the room.

As he faces the open studio door, Mark Lockwood's entire body is suffused with lightness.

ACKNOWLEDGMENTS

In the time that I worked on this novel, I grew in my understanding of the curious gift of the operatic singer, a combination of extravagant natural phenomena and personal will. A key resource offering delight and instruction is *The Queen's Throat* by Wayne Koestenbaum.

Don Hoiness (d. 2005) was a gifted teacher who allowed me to observe his voice lessons. I'm particularly grateful to him and his students for their generosity in displaying the torturous path toward taming the gift of voice.

Chris Arneson gave the final draft an exacting reading. Any remaining slips are due to my own neglect in following his advice.

I was raised with my parents' stories about their experiences during the Spanish Civil War, 1937–1939. For documentation and insight into its horrors, I'm indebted to Bruce Lincoln for enlightening conversation and his book *Discourse and the Construction of Society*.

It took years for the disparate ingredients of this paella of a novel to coalesce into its current balance of flavors and textures. I'm grateful to friends and colleagues who read early drafts and provided thoughtful advice, not always immediately heeded:

J. Z. Grover read the first version and, to her credit, did not talk me out of continuing the project. Bart Schneider critiqued two drafts years apart and provided encouragement along the way. Greg Hewett proved to be a companionable opera enthusiast and consultant. Toni Dorca reviewed the intricacies of Catalan orthography. Andrew Proctor provided much-needed demolition just when I thought I was done with my masterpiece. Jim Cihlar continues to be an astute reader of my fiction and a trusted adviser. Fred Ramey wields his publisher's baton with grace and generosity. And over the course of our life together, Juanita Garciagodoy has been my reader, my believer. She knows my stories as well as I do.